I0843005

United States Space Force
Project Jupiter

Screenplay

By

Paul D. Escudero

This publication contains the opinions and ideas of its author. It is intended to provide helpful and informative material on the subjects addressed in the publication. The author and publisher specifically disclaim all responsibility for any liability, loss or risk, personal or otherwise, which is incurred as a consequence, directly or indirectly, of the use and application of any of the contents of this book.

WORKBOOK PRESS LLC
187 E Warm Springs Rd,
Suite B285 Las Vegas NV 89119 USA

Website: https://workbookpress.com/
Hotline: 1-888-818-4856
Email: admin@workbookpress.com

Ordering Information:

Quantity sales. Special discounts are available on quantity purchases by corporations, associations, and others. For details, contact the publisher at the address above.

Library of Congress Control Number:

ISBN-13:   978-1-963718-54-6   Paperback Version
                978-1-963718-55-3   Digital Version

REV. DATE: 05/07/2024

THE UNITED STATES SPACE FORCE STANDS UP

EXT. DAY KENNEDY SPACE CENTER SPACE SHUTTLE LAUNCHING

VOICE OVER
(DURING LAUNCHES)

The United States Space Force or what is commonly called USSF came into existence when the recently elected President made one of the most astute judgements of any chief executive made since President Roosevelt issued the Lend Lease Proclamation at the beginning of World War II.

The United States Space Force started the week the new President was sworn in. A U.S. law states all the intelligence agencies must brief a newly elected President to explain what they are doing, how they are spending the intelligence money, and what issues existed that could additionally end up as an embarrassment to the administration.

EXT. NIGHT KENNEDY SPACE CENTER SPACE-X HEAVY LIFT LAUNCHING NASA'S SPACEX CRS-27 MISSION LAUNCH TO THE SPACE STATION.

VOICE OVER
(DURING LAUNCHES)

The spy agencies are required to reveal to the incoming president any clandestine activity that could blow up in our faces such as what occurred during Reagan's Iran-Contra scandal and John F. Kennedy's Bay of Pigs fiasco.

If the President gets re-elected, the intelligence agencies must brief the President again. And since he is their boss and is cleared as commander in chief and the head of all intelligence agencies, they must answer any questions that come up during the briefing. In some cases, the answers to the questions are not readily available and the previous president was still waiting on some answers as he was leaving office. One of which he suggested to the new President, Look into aliens and UFOs, and particularly Area 51.

EXT. NIGHT VANDENBERG U.S. NATIONAL RECONNAISSANCE UNITED LAUNCH ALLIANCE DELTA 4 HEAVY ROCKET NROL-91 SPY SATELLITE

VOICE OVER (DURING LAUNCHES)

The new President was far more sophisticated than his political enemies would ever imagine or believe. He knew he needed to heed the previous President's advice, especially since as the former President was leaving office, he had a sudden grasp of the importance of the turnover for his legacy. Being an astute Harvard graduate, the outgoing President knew vividly what the historians would start doing in about fifty years, so if he sandbagged the new President, it would eventually destroy his reputation, possibly even while he was still alive.

The first few months during the new administration are a wild ride. The new President and his transition team must nominate quite a few people to fill positions and vacancies from the prior administration, many of which must have the concurrence and confirmation by congress.

Therefore, it was going to be extremely difficult to leave town and avoid any exposure to the public. If word got out the President visited Area 51, the media would go crazy and foreign governments would suddenly take a keen interest and focus their attention there. Area 51 already had significant undue interest merely because of its secrecy, but also the way information was controlled.

Some of the INTEL agencies required to brief the President were involved in Area 51, S-4 operations. Being that this new President was very sophisticated, he knew how to garner cooperation and discovery into the business that went on there. The other groups that a former president miss-trusted were far more open and truthful than these Area 51, S-4 people who were allegedly under heavy influence of a secret government group code name Majestic 12.

EXT. NIGHT KENNEDY SPACE CENTER USSF SPACEX FALCON HEAVY LAUNCHES BOEING X-37B OTV-7 (USSF-52)

>VOICE OVER (DURING LAUNCHES)
>
>Even though it appeared Majestic 12 was slowly fading because of people involved who began involvement in the 1947 UFO crash at Roswell, New Mexico and a year later at Aztec, New Mexico, had mostly died off. Also, because there had been very few UFO crashes in seventy years, their relevancy slowly diminished and the few remaining members and new appointees were no longer active having either passed away or achieved their ultimate mandate, to keep UFOs and aliens out of the newspapers and out of the public's persona.

EXT. THE FIRST UNITED LAUNCH ALLIANCE (ULA) VULCAN ROCKET LAUNCH PAD 41 AT THE CAPE CANAVERAL SPACE FORCE STATION. 30 SECONDS

>VOICE OVER (DURING VIDEO)
>
>Nevertheless, there were rising stars within the Air Force who were propelled by the previous President, were in fact truthful arbiters and worried the strict secrecy was in fact placing the United States at risk since only black projects ever dealt with aliens, and due to the lack of disclosure there could never be the priority on funding to do the kinds of things to mitigate scenarios that ostensibly put the planet at risk.

EXT. SPACE. MOON. VULCAN'S MAIDEN FLIGHT COMMERCIALLY BUILT ROBOTIC LANDER TOUCHDOWN ON THE SURFACE OF THE MOON, LANDING 30 SECONDS

>VOICE OVER (DURING VIDEO)
>
>These Air Force Officers used that special relationship with their benefactor, the previous President, and as conscientious Americans and Patriots, gave special input to the previous President during their brief periods of privacy with him.
>
>Unfortunately, the previous President discovered there was a huge amount of information withheld from him as well as previous Presidents because Majestic 12, the CIA, and powerful figures within the administration felt it best to hide all the UFO business from the President to shield him and give him plausible deniability should

those operations create embarrassment or possible social evil that many felt disclosure might create.

INT. DAY WHITE HOUSE OVAL OFFICE

During that Area-51 (S-4) Air Force Presidential INTEL briefing, General John Harris entered the oval office to meet and brief the incoming President.

General John Harris is the briefer who had tipped off the previous President and now disclosed to the new President some items he might not want to hear, but as a concerned patriot, General Harris, thought he had to hear.

Nobody was allowed in the briefing room alone with the President except for three people, which included the Vice President, Director of CIA, and the Secretary of the Treasury. The Vice President was in the room during the S-4 briefing. The only reason why the General was allowed in the room with the President is because a third party was also present. The President does not have to allow the Vice President to hear intel briefings, and many did not, especially was the case with FDR. but this President who had negotiated a modus operandi with the Vice President had him present. General Harris might have been apprehensive had the President not explained the working arrangement at the beginning of the briefing.

General Harris felt he was carrying an undue burden on his chest knowing the implications of the CIA, General Whitman, and Kevin O'Toole who wanted the President to know as little about their Area-51 (S-4) operation as possible. It was more than compartmentalized. Aside from being worried about the former Soviet Bloc, Chinese, and the EU discovering what they were up too, they were also profoundly aware of the skullduggery that corporations would undertake to obtain technology from the reverse engineering programs derived from crashed alien space craft they discovered over the years.

General Harris knew he would be interrogated by General Whitman, and Kevin O'Toole the minute he returned. Furthermore, he knew that if the Vice President revealed the plan to anyone in a short period of time that information would be presented to General Whitman, and Kevin O'Toole and his time at S-4 and in the United States Air Force would be short lived since he crossed over the imaginary line that Air Force officers are not to cross in dealing with politicians. In addition to getting a rung up under the previous president now his new potential patronage developing with the new President could put him in double jeopardy.

The President was sophisticated enough to realize the position he put General Harris in and unlike the public who really had no real idea of the inner personal workings of the White House and relationships of complicated men such as the President and Vice President, would be quite surprised to see how much of a team the President and Vice President really were. The Vice President was not going to risk losing the confidence of the President by exposing those inner personal working relationships which mutually beneficial each of them.

PRESIDENT

General Harris, I know you might be a little nervous communicating to me since the Vice President is here. I want you to know whatever you tell us will not be shared with others. I want the Vice President briefed with me in the event I have a sudden departure, as you realize I have plenty of enemies out there.

GENERAL HARIS
Understand sir.

PRESIDENT

General Harris, remember you work for the American people, so it's best you confide in me and the Vice President. Nobody in your chain of command will support you any better than the two of us.

GENERAL HARIS
Thank you, sir.

Regrettably, General Harris only had about five minutes of privacy to convey the information in a manner without tipping off others that would attempt preventing such disclosure to take place. The Secret Service would soon come back into the room in five minutes when his allotted time was up. Therefore, he simply got right to the issue immediately at the start of the briefing.

The first disclosure to the president was mildly unsettling.

PRESIDENT
You got to be kidding me.

GENERAL HARRIS

No, Mr. President, there are several people who do not want me to brief you on that information and would do anything in their power to stop me.

PRESIDENT
I realize we probably need to keep this under wraps, and you certainly don't act like an Air Force General that is about to run to the press.

GENERAL HARRIS
Nor would I.

PRESIDENT
There are probably a lot of questions I might want to ask.

GENERAL HARRIS
If we go over the five minutes allotted to me by the Secret Service, they will be in here and any conversations we were having would be curtailed. I need more than five minutes to describe some of the issues and situations like the lack of infrastructure we now have there.

PRESIDENT
After spending $50 million on that new building in S-4, how could you possibly have a lack of infrastructure?

GENERAL HARRIS
Some of the aliens we have there do not get along. They need to be separated and we need new buildings to keep them away from each other.

PRESIDENT
General Harris, how about this: I know we need to keep this conversation confidential between us as I do understand there are powerful forces at play here. I have an idea.

GENERAL HARRIS
Such as, Mr. President?

PRESIDENT
General Harris, I'm going to pay you a visit in about two months. I should have a lot of my pressing matters here taken care of by then. I'll fly there in one of the executive jets they give me for special trips like this so that nobody will know where I'm going.

GENERAL HARRIS
We'll be looking forward to your visit, Mr. President.

PRESIDENT

General Harris, it will be best for you and me if we do not discuss my plan to visit you out at Area 51 until the day before. I don't want any leaks or people standing in our way as I know you have a lot of things you wish to explain to me.

GENERAL HARRIS
Understand, Mr. President.

PRESIDENT

Get your information together and all the facts and figures and even possible impromptu dog and pony show. Here's my business card with my private number on it. Let's plan for about two months from now. Call me the day before you want that meeting, that way I can get there without tipping off people that don't want me to know what really goes on out there.

GENERAL HARRIS

Yes, Mr. President, I understand fully. Are you aware of President Eisenhower's threat?

PRESIDENT
No, what did President Eisenhower do?

GENERAL HARRIS

He sent out a couple CIA guys to tour the facility and report back exactly what goes on out there. The General in charge at the time refused them access. President Eisenhower sent them back out the following day with the message that if they were not allowed an unobstructed visit, he would have the Army Division then stationed in Colorado to surround the base the following day and arrest everyone there.

PRESIDENT

Did that get them all the proper information President Eisenhower requested?

GENERAL HARRIS

Yes, it did, and later President Eisenhower went on one of his numerous golf games and just happened to land

Air Force One tail number 26000 at Groom Lake and was given an exclusive tour.

PRESIDENT

Okay, General, I think our time is up, my handlers will be coming through that door in about a minute to escort you out of here. I'll be looking forward to your phone call in about two months when you are ready for my surprise visit.

GENERAL HARRIS

Thank you, Mr. President. You will soon learn why I believe we should have a Space Force.

PRESIDENT

You don't have to sell me on the Space Force, General Harris, but my surprise visit to S-4 will obviously help me get it pushed through.

GENERAL HARRIS
How will that help?

PRESIDENT

Either they give me a Space Force, or I'll do full disclosure.

GENERAL HARRIS

Some say that's what got Kennedy killed, I would be careful.

PRESIDENT

It's all about how you negotiate it. Don't ever bet against me!

GENERAL HARRIS

I will support you to my utmost ability, Mr. President.

PRESIDENT

I know you will, General Harris. And thank you for the short briefing.

GENERAL HARRIS
You are welcome, Mr. President.

The two men stood up, the President led the General to the door of the oval office and opened it and as expected waiting outside were twenty other people waiting for their turn and a couple Secret Service members to escort General Harris out to the south lawn where a helicopter would be touching down in closely choreographed waves that would quickly ferry General Harris out to Andrews Air Force Base where his Gulf Stream 250 waited to fly him back to Groom Lake.

General Harris flight back to Groom Lake was not comfortable. He knew that people there were gunning for him because he was one of those patronage officers with the previous president and the way the game is played, there were probably people of the other political persuasion already planning on moving him out of there.

General Harris wasn't even sure he had two months left where he could call the President. One thing is certain, he would not reveal to General Sandy Whitman or Kevin O'Toole anything regarding the President's plan to visit S-4. Especially if it appeared he might have instigated it.

General Harris might have been black and born and raised in Mississippi, but he excelled at the Air Force Academy and later had some very impressive experiences in Kosovo and later the War in Iraq. It did not hurt him that he was stereotyped as probably a Democrat since he was black. Even a Democrat President got it wrong. Although General Harris registered as an Independent, he always voted Republican and never discussed politics as his mentor at the Air Force Academy advised him.

> GENERAL HARRIS MENTOR (FLASHBACK)
> Avoid any political or religious conversations because
> they can negatively impact your career and you have
> enough headwinds as it is already.

True to the cause, General Harris always avoided those conversations and was so neutral everyone thought he was on their side. When the previous President reached out and promoted him, he did so with the stereotype and misjudgment that erroneously promoted someone who was actually a political enemy.

The Air Force has their system just like the Army and the Navy, and when rising stars move up quicker than classmates above them, due to perceived political influence, they end up with some of the worst jobs on the planet. Area 51, S-4 was a nightmare assignment to any officer who wanted a future promotion.

To climb up the next ring of the ladder, General Harris needed to be in Washington, D.C. Groom Lake was a dead-end job for him which meant he likely would be asked to leave the military when this assignment there was completed.

The President being a brilliant strategist and political operative played coy about the briefing he received including the standard cover story they fed to all the Presidents except for Eisenhower who called their bluff. Since it was never mentioned again like

90 percent of the briefings, the White House staff which was penetrated by the CIA and NSA as well as Joint Chief's operatives, had no reason to believe the President was focused on aliens, Area 51, or anything else that would concern them.

VOICE OVER

> In recent years it has been getting harder for the government to cover up UFO incidents. The recent revelation of U.S. Navy fighter jets chasing a UFO off San Diego including gun camera video, was released to the press by insiders which furthermore signaled the Pentagon may no longer be able to keep the lid on all the UFO activity.
>
> Someone must have had strong convictions to risk prison time leaking that video. That and many other incidents set off General Harris thinking. *The earth is ill prepared to deal with advanced aliens now showing up.*

General Harris and soon the President after his staff briefed him on international agreements to not weaponize space, both understood there would be some serious implications if this country went forward on a Space Force. But the San Diego UFO chase conveyed the notion the aliens craft was so much more sophisticated and capable than our own, we were at a very huge disadvantage. We have already waited too long. Is it too late?

General Whitman and Kevin O'Toole SES (Senior Executive Service) were still fully embroiled in the old Majestic 12 philosophy. Just like cold warriors are diehards, the Majestic 12 crowd would continue until the last dying member was gone. Majestic 12 was so well concealed, even President Reagan didn't know they existed. President Bush on the other hand knew quite well.

<u>EXT. DAY. AREA-51 AIR FORCE'S GULFSTREAM LANDS AT AREA 51 HOMEY AIRPORT.</u>

After the six-hour flight, the Air Force's Gulfstream 250 landed on 17R then headed for building 27, the hangar it would go into for storage out of direct sunlight and maintenance. The plane would be turned around and ready to fly in hours just in case it was needed, which was often the case.

<u>EXT. DAY. AREA-51 AIR FORCE'S GULFSTREAM 250 PULLS UP TO HANGER.</u>

The plane stopped in front of the hangar doors, a limo pulled up and as soon as the General stepped off the airplane, a man with shirt sleeves, and tie wearing pilots' sunglasses, walked up and approached General Harris.

AREA-51 (S4) REPRESENATATIVE
Welcome back, General, your ride is here, to take you
over to S-4 for a meeting.

GENERAL HARRIS
Thank you.

If it were not for 95-degree heat the man would have been wearing a suit jacket. Personal attire was given far more flexibility due to the desert weather, plus no uninvited strangers were ever allowed in, therefore dress codes could be relaxed a little. If a VIP was coming in for a visit the suits would be back on.

EXT. DAY. SUV TRANSPORTING GENERAL HARRIS LEAVES BUILING 140.

The car left the runway and onto a paved access road that swung in a counterclockwise direction around a hilltop south of the runways. That road eventually led up to a new tall black high-rise building. With all the secrecy of Area 51, including building 27, the fact they would build this large multi-level structure out in the open at S-4 was almost considered reckless disregard for security arrangements. However, in recent years practicality has crept into decisions.

Radiation from nearby nuclear test sites was seeping out of the ground making it more dangerous for people to be stationed at Area-51 (S-4), and by having a large building with atmosphere controls the residents would be far safer and comfortable.

EXT. DAY. SUV PULLS INTO THE CAR ACCESS OF BUILING 140.

 Due to the desire to hide the identity of some of the VIP visitors, this new building 140 had several special entrances inside what appeared to be a sophisticated garage. The vehicles with tinted windows would pull in, the garage doors would shut, and the occupants immediately went into an elevator that went up to the floor they stayed in with a security escort.

Very few people had ever seen who some of these VIPs were. In one case it was people such as Vladimir Putin who wanted to meet the Ponarian. To this day, only three Russians knew the Russian Leader had been to Area 51 (S-4).

The only reason why they were taking General Harris to building 140 stemmed from the ultra-secure SCIF that was located there, checked for bugs hourly.

The limo pulled into the parking garage. Once the garage door shut a security man opened the car door and General Harris got out and followed his escort to the nearby elevator. After they got inside a button was pressed and instead of going up into the tower they went underground. The elevator stopped approximately one-half-mile underground. The door opened and they walked out into the hallway that had several armed guards. They were soon led over to the conference room.

Cell phone holders were located outside the room. No personnel electronics were allowed inside, including watches. After several intrusions, they finally figured the resourceful Russian FSB employed a front company to use Swiss watchmakers to insert electronic surveillance sensors in watches.

As expected, General Whitman and Kevin O'Toole were there waiting for him. This would be an inquisition of course and if he didn't perform well, in due time he would be hooked up to a polygraph and they would get the truth out of him.

KEVIN O'TOOLE
How did your meeting with the President go?

GENERAL HARRIS
As good as can be expected, they gave me five minutes
alone with the President.

KEVIN O'TOOLE
What were you able to cover?

GENERAL HARRIS
In five minutes, you can't cover a lot. I noticed the
President seemed fatigued. He probably had several
briefings before I got there and is more than likely
overwhelmed with all the tantalizing INTEL thrown
at him today.

KEVIN O'TOOLE
Was he anything like the previous president? Did he
ask any poignant questions?

GENERAL HARRIS
I think the only thing he was interested in was how
much money we wasted out here.

KEVIN O'TOOLE
Why did he say that?

GENERAL HARRIS
He wanted to know why the hell we blew $50 million
on a building out in the middle of the desert.

KEVIN O'TOOLE
What was your response?

GENERAL HARRIS
I said it simplifies a lot of our housing issues out here
in the desert and to get into more details I would need a
lot more than the five minutes allotted for the briefing.

KEVIN O'TOOLE
How did he respond to that?

GENERAL HARRIS
He said his time schedule was very tight and didn't
have the luxury of getting into the details at this time.

KEVIN O'TOOLE
What did you plan on telling him if he pressed you for
information and gave you additional time?

GENERAL HARRIS
I would have stated that with radiation leaking from
the former nuclear test sites, this building is designed
to keep people safe so they can live near the base and
be able to support operations here.

KEVIN O'TOOLE
Well, that is true and a serious issue.

GENERAL HARRIS
I'd say it's the most important feature of the building
with its fancy air filtration system.

KEVIN O'TOOLE
We need to worry more about aliens than we do the
radiation.

GENERAL HARRIS
Yes, I suppose you are right about that.

CANCEL THE AIR FORCE

General Harris had to be careful how he collected information that he would show the
President up on his arrival. He also had to be keenly aware of all ongoing operations
for the time slot the President was planning visiting.

Some of the most important and spectacular operations take place on Sunday mornings. It was all because of Satellite coverage and other factors. If there were any snags it meant more daylight time to recover. Plus, the public would never believe the government did most of its super-secret operations early Sunday morning while people were having breakfast and getting ready to go to church or Sunday school.

To support the most sensitive missions, engineers and technicians were flown up from Las Vegas to Area-51 on EG&G's private Janet Airlines Saturday afternoon. Around midnight all the extensive preflight checkouts were done inside hangar building 27. Right around 07:00 while temperatures were still mild even in the summer months, the air frames were towed out of building 27 with flight test pilots aboard. Engines were started, final checkouts completed,

The experimental aircraft like a TR-4 would head for Runway 17L or 17R depending on what type of mission they were doing. These runways were not near runway 31 which is considered the main runway for Area 51 Homey Airport. Runway 17L or 17R are also camouflaged from Satellite or aerial photography.

Some of the craft being tested took off from the ultra-long 17R and ultimately flew out into space. An astronomer got lucky and filmed one of them sitting in a crater on the moon. To date that photo has been called a fake and photo etched. The guy who took the photo claims otherwise. Only people at Area 51 know the truth. It was actually a TR-4.

General Harris knew in his heart the tour he planned for the President would most likely result in his dismissal from the Air Force. He was lucky to have more than enough time to retire. General Harris was a modern-day version of Billy Mitchell who was drummed out of the military by the old battleship admirals who refused to acknowledge vast technological changes suddenly made battleships obsolete in their primary role.

Because General Harris lived a frugal lifestyle, staying single all these years even though he was an up-and-coming officer with plenty of opportunities, his financial assets were in order so if he had to leave today, he wasn't concerned. And each passing day his major motive in life was to see the United States Space Force get its legs, which he had done some great thinking about how it should be conceived.

A lot of ingredients to form a United States Space Force already existed. It would be nothing more than reorganization, which the military is always good at.

General Harris would be considered a traitor in the eyes of the Air Force as he felt over half of the Air Force assets, including all of its space assets, belonged to a newly formed Space Force. By the time the Pentagon gutted space out of the Air Force and transferred all space related assets to Space Command, about all that would be left would be direct ground support and the land attack fighter bomber roles.

The Air Force would also continue with air logistics support with C17 and C5 big jets and the smaller C-130s especially those backfit with the anti-gravity machine to make them considerably lighter and require much shorter runways.

Looking to the future when spacecraft deployed fighter bombers from space that could fly in space or in the atmosphere like a modern-day Navy Aircraft Carrier, should those aircraft be part of the Air Force or the Space Force?

The Navy already had muddied the waters back in the 1920s when it began developing its first aircraft carriers. As it turned out the Navy ended up with more than half of all the American military jet fighters.

John Harris figured it out. He knew the history and he would be treated as a traitor if it ever manifested like he would recommend, and the Air Force brass found out.

Cancel the Air Force was the ultimate solution. After gutting space out of the Air Force, it should once again become the Army Air Corps.

The Air Force Academy in Colorado Springs would be converted to Army Air Corp training. West Point would continue graduating students. But just like we learned in WW2, West Point didn't have the capacity to turn out the number of pilots required. Colorado Springs would fill that gap, but it would be Army Air Corp pilots. The added benefit to the new organization is Air Force Academy graduates could also fly helicopters and new VTOL fixed wing transports and VTOL fighter-bombers like the F35B. f35b - Search Images (bing.com)

The new Space Force needed to be near launch pads. That meant Florida and Vandenburg California. Based on what General Harris experienced, he knew the number of space force officers would grow to an extreme amount especially as soon as the galactic situation became known.

The United States Space Force would have to also train Europeans, Russians, and Chinese as risk to the planet became more understood.

With distributed learning and the fact during World War II, America had basic pilot training and OCS spread across the country in civilian schools. Therefore, having two campuses didn't pose an issue and would allow more people to train closer to home. General Harris read a lot of World War Two history, the process that Hap Arnold did to train vast numbers of pilots was quite extraordinary. Not only did America build 267,000 aircraft in World War Two, but America also trained a pilot for each one of them. The goal was 10,000 pilots a month. And within a year after the start of the war, Hap Arnold achieved this goal.

<u>EXT. NIGHT TR-3B VIDEO</u>

VOICE OVER
(DURING VIDEO)
The game changer of course would be a carrier in space. Luckily, we already had the space capable fighter bomber to deploy, the TR-3B.

With future possible space wars, needing 10,000 pilots a month might be a distinct possibility. The lethality of weapons now made pilots far more vulnerable than ever before as the technology seemed to double every year. And General Harris knew most of the aliens visiting this planet out classed Earth by at least several thousand years if not more.

<u>EXT. DAY AT-SEA TRIDENT II UGM 133A BALLISTIC MISSILE LAUNCH FROM A SUBMARINE</u>

VOICE OVER (DURING VIDEO)
The big decision to come would be what constitutes a Space Force. General Harris figured out a simple way to make the determination is that if it touched space, it belonged in the Space Force. That meant ICBM's, Trident Missiles, and other systems currently owned by rival services.

There would be some bitter fighting ahead. But just like when the Air Force split from the Army, there were perceived drivers to that decision, right or wrong the prevailing wisdom made the determination and it happened with a former Army officer then the President in the White House.

General Harris could not collect many samples of information without tipping his hand. He realized that he and the President both needed the element of surprise and get him to AREA-51 and briefed before the skullduggery could work out their offensive to prevent the legal authority and oversight to see what the people at this base were really doing now and how they are spending the public's money and not on some boondoggle.

General Harris presidential briefing materials would be sparse because they could only be printed at the eleventh hour and with all the Information Assurance operatives canvasing all print media in the complex, it would have to get done almost serendipitously.

Area-51's reverse engineering program only led to one meaningful development at this time, the TR-3B. The most exotic spy plane ever built. But just like the SR-71 and A-12 in the 1960s was suggested as the base platform for ultra-fast interceptor planes to shoot down Russian Bombers before they got to their cruise missile launch baskets, that role never materialized as the DOD suddenly had other priorities of the Vietnam War. Kelly Johnson did however prove the SR-71 interceptor concept and some observers felt the decision not to implement them as anti-air assets was short sighted. Would they be willing to build a space carrier and use TR-3B's as fighter-bombers?

TR-3B was not well adopted by the Air Force because the CIA sponsors did not want to release the technology to the Air Force for fear a technology transfer might happen without their concurrence.

THE PRESIDENT VISITS AREA 51

<u>INT. DAY. AREA 51 GENERAL HARRIS BOQ ROOM</u>

Time passed and when General Harris believed he had done all he could without creating a spectacle he was up to something, he was in his BOQ room at S-4 and called the number on the President's business card. After two rings it was answered and since it had caller I.D. the President quickly answered the phone.

PRESIDENT
Hello General Harris, is it that time now?

GENERAL HARRIS
Yes, it is, Mr. President.

Within five minutes, General Whitman was notified by security, they had intercepted a phone call from the base calling the White House.

DUTY SECURITY OFFICER
Someone in your command is calling the President
and apparently has his personal phone number.

GENERAL WHITMAN
Find out who the caller is and report back immediately.

After another five minutes security called again to inform General Whitman,

> DUTY SECURITY OFFICER
> We have identified the caller.

> GENERAL WHITMAN
> Who is it?

> DUTY SECURITY OFFICER
> General Harris.

> GENERAL WHITMAN
> God dammit!

> DUTY SECURITY OFFICER
> I'm sorry, sir, for the discovery. That's all the information that I have currently.

> GENERAL WHITMAN
> Thanks for the heads-up, I'll handle it.

Within moments General Whitman called General Harris.

> GENERAL HARRIS
> Hello.

> GENERAL WHITMAN
> John, this is Sandy.

John Harris instantly knew the voice and the tone indicated it was going to be something unpleasant.

> GENERAL HARRIS
> Yes, Sandy, what can I do for you?

> GENERAL WHITMAN
> John, can you tell me what the hell you are doing calling the White House before I charge you with insubordination?

> GENERAL HARRIS
> I called to confirm the President's visit tomorrow.

> GENERAL WHITMAN
> What the hell are you talking about?

GENERAL HARRIS
I'm sure the Secret Service will be contacting you shortly to make all the arrangements.

GENERAL WHITMAN
If this is something you arranged, I'm going to arrange to have your ass tossed out of the Air Force.

GENERAL HARRIS
This is from the President, I'm just the messenger.

GENERAL WHITMAN
Can you tell me why this guy wants to come here? Did you divulge something to him you are not authorized to reveal to anyone?

GENERAL HARRIS
No, he'll find out what he's looking for when he gets here.

GENERAL WHITMAN
This really puts me in a very difficult position. As soon as Kevin O'Toole is made aware of this, we are going to get a lot of uninvited visitors. I would suspect your hell will commence around midnight since you are the chief security officer.

GENERAL HARRIS
I imagine so.

GENERAL WHITMAN
Is there any other thing you want to tell me about or are there some more surprises you have for me?

GENERAL HARRIS
None that I know of Sandy.

GENERAL WHITMAN
We'll probably have a meeting two hours from now. I need to call Kevin O'Toole. Meet me at the SCIF at 14:00. By then I might know more about why he's coming here and what he expects to see.

GENERAL HARRIS
Roger that.

General Whitman hung up and there was just a dial tone.

Shortly after the President received General Harris' phone call, he contacted the Vice President.

<u>INT. DAY WHITE HOUSE OVAL OFFICE</u>

> PRESIDENT
> I'm flying out to Area 51. I'm signing a delegation of authority letter for you starting tomorrow at 8:00 A.M. my intended time of departure.

> VICE PRESIDENT
> You don't want me to go with you?

> PRESIDENT
> No. I want you here in case something happens to me out there, so that we have a continuity of government. I'll fill you in when I get back and can arrange for you to go out there later to look for yourself.

> VICE PRESIDENT
> Don't you feel like you are stepping on some big toes?

> PRESIDENT
> Yes, of course I do, but if we are ever to have a Space Force we need to start now. We don't necessarily need to expose it to the public, but it will be easier to convince the military to reorganize after they know we know the truth about all these UFOs.

> VICE PRESIDENT
> Okay, if you think that's how we should approach it, I suppose you are right.

> PRESIDENT
> It's the only way, it's going to be a tough nut to crack.

<u>INT. DAY AREA 51 DEEP UNDERGROUND SCIF</u>

Kevin O'Toole started his career as a new mechanical engineer working on Navy ultra-secret black projects that were highly successful. The CIA was the actual sponsor for some of those programs and their oversight people had a lot of exposure to Mr. O'Toole. At some point in time the reverse engineering program suddenly had some serious focus because of the TR-3B and the possibility of applying artificial gravity making it far faster and more maneuverable.

Thanks to a captured Alien's information and indoctrination, top scientists in the program that flew those EG&G Janet Airline jets up to Homey Airport at Groom Lake, Area 51 every day, discovered they could create the inverse gravity waves thus canceling the normal gravity felt on a body near this planet.

No device, including the Alien spacecraft systems had ever perfected the process to the point of 100-percent gravity elimination. However, suddenly with the help of an obscure Extraterrestrial Alien marooned on this planet for five years wanting to be allowed to return to his civilization traded the information for his ticket home. All Area 51 scientists had to do was give him his communicator and he could call home for rescue which he ultimately was allowed to do, but not until his usefulness was fully expended.

During those years Kevin O'Toole climbed the ladder of success in the CIA rising to the Area 51, S-4 Technical Director position. Even though military personnel such as Generals John Harris and Sandy Whitman were there and administered a great deal of the leadership including control of all the Air Force pilots assigned to Area 51 doing numerous test flights, Kevin O'Toole wielded the ultimate authority.

One might assume the military were the top authority at Area-51, but since it was a giant science experiment, the Area 51, S-4 Technical Director was virtually running the show with concurrence from the military brass. It did not take very much time for a newly arrived Air Force General to discover, that civilian administration called all the shots and the folks back in Washington, D.C., gave AREA-51's Technical Director the power over all military components assigned to the base.

Over a sixty-year period with a lot of intense designs and implementations, natural modus of operandi was developed. The military knew their role and so did the Technical Director who had to be ruthless at times with several scientists who either had loose lips or were on the verge of sabotaging the mission because their political, moral, and ethical values were diabolically opposed to the culture that permeated in Area 51.

Scientists in general wanted disclosure and felt the ultra-secrecy created a nucleus of gestapo like agents who infiltrated their daily lives and observed every action they took. To head off any undue disclosure some of the more liberal scientists wished to do, some brutality manifested secretly.

There were reported cases of essential scientists who wanted to exit the program were threatened and blackmailed into staying. As one scientist said, Area 51 is like the Eagles song "Hotel California," where you can never leave. He had no idea how close to the truth he was.

<u>INT. DAY. AREA 51 UNDERGROUND FACILITY SCIF.</u>

Kevin O'Toole, having spent quite a bit of time in Crystal City on projects, was fully immersed in the beltway bandit world. Career expectancy could be cut very short for simple trivial matters. After General Whitman informed Kevin O'Toole about the phone call to the White House, and the implications, an observer would see he rapidly seemed more animated than General Whitman. He arrived at the SCIF for the meeting a mere five minutes before the two Generals arrived.

As the Technical Director, Kevin O'Toole took his place at the head of the table. Out of tradition, just like the captain's chair in the wardroom, this seat was reserved exclusively for him, and if some neophyte sat down there before a meeting started, one of the room-monitors and security men would calmly and politely confront the person and ask the person to move to another seat already set aside to seat people that made similar mistakes.

Kevin O'Toole had not thought much about the President, or the briefing General Harris gave him a couple months back, since it all seemed rather innocuous at the time. But now that the President was coming out to Area 51 with an array of Secret Service agents in tow, there was suddenly a new reality and the more he thought about it the more likely the President's briefing General Harris attended probably resulted in the President deciding to come to Area 51 (S-4).

Normally a government agency enjoys the President of the United States visiting. It adds prestige to their reputation. For Area 51 that wasn't necessarily the case. President Eisenhower's visit and later his remarks about the military industrial complex and UFO business he turned over to President Kennedy caused them a lot of grief back then and almost wrecked an alien exchange program.

Kevin O'Toole wasn't around back in those days many years before his time, but lessons learned from it still applied today and further intensified the security around the project.

Different managers had different management styles. Kevin O'Toole wasn't a screamer, but he was a schemer. General Whitman might have been considered a screamer, but military brass didn't like the word management. The military operated off leadership. This mixed civilian-military organization offered the witches brew of management spiced with leadership provided by the generals to senior ranking enlisted men who often were the respondents to their leadership.

Whereas the military stationed at Area 51 thought of it as a dead end to their careers, civilians like Kevin O'Toole viewed it as another ring in the step ladder to success in that it opened the door to executive positions at Langley Virginia or the NRO near Washington Dulles Airport.

Since Kevin O'Toole was already a GS-16 SES, he would not get any pay raise with the promotion but being in an important project could lead the way to a political appointee position within the administration, which was the steppingstone to an ultimate cabinet position.

Like many individuals, Kevin O'Toole wasn't all that keen on the new President and had similar feelings that one would hear in the media from interviews with politicians' rank and. As far as Kevin was concerned there could be no good coming from the President's visit and the mere thought of him revealing Area 51's innermost secrets was a chilling thought.

Security at Area-51 already had to deal with every nut job in the world trying to break into Area 51 to see what was going on there. Kevin O'Toole thought, just after one disclosure, there might be one many more trying to break in to see the *alleged aliens* that were supposedly here.

Kevin O'Toole knew he could not outright order General Harris' removal. That was General Whitman's call. However, the way it worked in a mixed bag organization where over 50 percent of the organization wore a uniform, the Technical Director could make suggestions. Since Kevin O'Toole's evaluation of General Whitman to the Joint Chiefs might have a major bearing on his future assignments, he had leverage.

Generals assigned to Area 51 usually recognized which side their toast was buttered and often went along with any requests or demands the Technical Director made. The ace up Kevin O'Toole's sleeve was he could outright ask General Whitman to remove General Harris from Area 51.

But before Kevin O'Toole did that he had to first ascertain exactly what General Harris' role was in scheduling the President's visit. What exactly did General Harris say to the President in that Washington INTEL briefing?

Kevin O'Toole knew General Harris would not be allowed alone with the President, so either a Secret Service agent had to be present or one of the three key individuals allowed to be alone with the President.

Once Kevin O'Toole found out who that person was, he could then inquire exactly what transpired during the meeting and whether the meeting was recorded. Hopefully he would not have to go to those extremes if he could get General Harris to offer up the details. Reflecting back when General Harris returned from that Washington DC meeting it was now apparent to Kevin O'Toole that General Harris had been rather coy when first confronted when he arrived back at Area 51 after briefing the President.

One of the administrative aides who worked for Kevin O'Toole, and often pampered him approached Kevin at the briefing table.

ADMINISTRATIVE AIDE
Would you like a cup of coffee or a soda or chilled
bottled water before the meeting starts?

KEVIN O'TOOLE
Yes. A diet Dr Pepper would be nice.

Adjacent to the SCIF conference room was a pantry that had drinks, coffee, snacks, and other items that allowed them to stretch meetings sometimes late into the evening when critical issues had to be reconciled such as deciding to terminate a test flight scheduled because of some last-minute SNAFU.

The cute blonde administrative aide, an Air Force female, Sargent Baker, handed Kevin O'Toole his can of Dr Pepper just as Generals Whitman and Harris walked into the room. They were sitting themselves down as Kevin O'Toole opened the can of soda and quickly took a drink before they all got started.

This was a very private meeting, there were not any notetakers present and the conversation did not get started until Sargent Baker left the room.

KEVIN O'TOOLE
General Harris, thanks for coming. I wanted to
discuss with you the President's visit.

General Harris nodded and continued listening knowing some poignant questions would soon be coming and figured this would end in a heated argument, possibly resulting in his dismissal as chief of security and subsequent transfer.

The big problem for Kevin O'Toole is he couldn't do that today without some justification, especially with the President's slated arrival in the morning. It would not look good for Kevin O'Toole if he removed the head of security just hours prior to the President's arrival.

The dirty deed would most likely be carried out shortly after the President departed. And if there was any mention of any *disclosure* during the visit, Kevin O'Toole would have General Harris' ass, big time. The Secretary of the Air Force would be asking for General Harris' resignation the following day if all went as Kevin O'Toole expected.

KEVIN O'TOOLE
Are all the arrangements being made?

GENERAL HARRIS
Yes, sir, the first contingent of Secret Service personnel
has arrived and are briefing our security managers

and watch officers of what their plans are and giving them instructions on security measures they must accommodate.

KEVIN O'TOOLE
We have some test flights scheduled for tomorrow and the schedule is very tight, what about them?

GENERAL HARRIS
After consultations with the Secret Service, those flight tests have been delayed a day, people in Las Vegas were notified and the technicians and scientists will not be flying in today.

KEVIN O'TOOLE
Why wasn't I informed before those test flights were canceled?

GENERAL HARRIS
You were emailed on the high side one hour and forty-five minutes ago. In that email I said I had to terminate the flights and needed to inform Las Vegas to avoid putting those people on the flights up here.

Kevin O'Toole had a poker face now knowing this was a big screwup on his part. General Harris gave him plenty of warning.

GENERAL HARRIS
I didn't get a response from you, so I called, you were not in your office, so fifteen minutes ago I canceled the test flights and sent you another email on the high side informing you in accordance with standard protocol.

General Harris had Kevin O'Toole by-the-balls. Had he not been on the golf course during working hours he would have read his emails and not been embarrassed by his inattentiveness. He also knew he wasn't the only one on distribution of those emails, General Whitman and his chief of operations was most likely included. As chief of security, General Harris had the legal right to cancel any test flight immediately without prior notification.

General Whitman set there all smug knowing he was in the catbird's seat and didn't have to do anything but observe these two powerful men spar. When the meeting first started, he felt Kevin O'Toole had General Harris by the balls and would soon start squeezing, but it wasn't starting out like it all seemed it would.

Kevin O'Toole talked with strict respectful tone in the most serious manner as if he was getting ready to dish out the medicine.

KEVIN O'TOOLE
Okay, General Harris, tell me when you first knew the
President's intentions to visit surfaced.

GENERAL HARRIS
Mr. O'Toole, I didn't know until I called the White
House today as the President requested, that was his
intentions.

General Harris fudged the truth slightly and if Kevin O'Toole thought for one moment, he should strap on a polygraph to find out for sure, he was in for a rude awakening. General Harris was not in the mood for a Polygraph and would refuse and let the Secretary of the Air Force weigh in on what would be seen as retribution for exposing Kevin O'Toole's inattentiveness and playing golf during working hours.

Just like the brilliant President planned in this surprise visit, it got scheduled so quickly that the establishment could not stop it or affect it in any manner. General Harris knew that if Kevin O'Toole didn't think for a minute the President would be asking for his presence when he arrived, then he was a fool.

Therefore, to attempt to hang General Harris out to dry now might backfire on Kevin O'Toole.

General Harris knew this was one sharp President and if Kevin O'Toole took adverse actions towards him this close to the President's arrival, the President wouldn't be happy with General Whitman and Kevin O'Toole. Even though the President couldn't shut down the operation he could clearly shuffle people around including directing the secretaries of the CIA and the Air Force to reassign people. That would be the end of Kevin O'Toole's career, because SES people removed always retired immediately.

KEVIN O'TOOLE
Did any of this visit surface during your meeting with
the President?

GENERAL HARRIS
No.

KEVIN O'TOOLE
Then why did you call the President?

GENERAL HARRIS
He asked me to call him.

KEVIN O'TOOLE
When did he do that?

GENERAL HARRIS
Two months ago.

KEVIN O'TOOLE
He asked you to call him in two months, just like that.

GENERAL HARRIS
That's correct.

KEVIN O'TOOLE
You got to be shitting me, you expect me to believe
that crap?

GENERAL HARRIS
Why don't you ask him that tomorrow when he gets
here?

Kevin O'Toole knew General Harris would not be a General and stationed at Area 51 in charge of security if he didn't have some smarts.

This man was cool and calm under pressure, and unlike many of the military "screamers" Kevin O'Toole saw in his days, the leadership style of General Harris was unusually calm and agile. His testosterone simply did not ascend to the surface like a lot of *leaders*.

General Harris was never negligent and paid close attention to detail. He simply figured out as a junior officer how to get the most out of men and women without yelling at them. And because of the way he treated and interacted with the enlisted military, they respected him. They knew he was a hard worker and expected the best out of them, and he went about it in a way to get their buy in and appropriate responses to the challenges bestowed upon some of the toughest assignments in all the Air Force.

General Harris security force at Area 51 had the same lethal permissions of someone guarding nukes. And they were authorized deadly force and were given the paramount instructions they were to prevent any disclosure, and if some journalist or entrepreneur got lucky and photographed an alien, that device would be destroyed. Nobody could complain since the warnings were all posted on the perimeter of the base stating all cameras and recording devices would be confiscated.

Cell phones created an added challenge. Area 51 had no choice but to jam cell phone signals. They could not permit some guy in his cell phone to photograph and quickly text or email high quality video to the world. There had been some spillage in the past and the NSA boys had to go into people's private accounts and wipe them out to get rid of the evidence before that information made it to the world wide web.

Thanks to NSA's operation PRISM, anyone working at Area 51's cell phones were constantly monitored, and Artificial Intelligence (AI) sifted through pictures, text messages, and all files looking for anything associated with Area 51. If key phrases such as TR-3B or SU-57 they were test flying stolen out of Russia by a defector was found on any cell phones or mentioned in a telephone call, AI would swing into motion and make appropriate reports. That person's cell phone could be confiscated unexpectedly as they were attempting to leave the base.

Kevin O'Toole could ramrod just about any military person other than General Harris. Because of the unique scenario that was now unfolding, because of the sophistication and complexities of the President, Kevin O'Toole was seemingly powerless to immediately censor General Harris. Now it started to appear the best he could do is damage control after the fact.

The phone lines between Kevin O'Toole and Langley tonight with their special scrambler would be ablaze. The DCI would be perturbed, of course, but he would know the fall guy Harris was responsible for all the upheaval soon to be coming their way. Kevin O'Toole assumed that within 48 hours the Secretary of the Air Force would be asking General Harris for his resignation.

General Whitman had his own issues going through his head now, but the fact the President apparently had some discrete deal going on with General Harris, he knew better than to have a confrontation until it was revealed what the President's real motive happened to be.

The meeting was soon adjourned as each of them had a myriad of things to get accomplished in preparation for the President's visit. General Harris would be the busiest of the three as he would have numerous interactions with the Secret Service later that evening.

What General Harris thought was rather interesting is in some of the preparations and discussions the Secret Service insisted on only discussing it on their plane which was currently sitting inside building 27's hangar. Because of aliens present at S-4, unprecedented precautions were administered. And just like Vladimir Putin, the new President wanted to see the Ponarian. How did he know about that? General Harris certainly did not disclose him.

Finally, by 02:00 A.M. all the plans were finally complete. General Harris took a quick shower and lay down to try to catch a few hours' sleep before it all unfolded in the morning. This would be an extraordinary day for an unordinary President and the establishment was just now starting to recoil. All their extravagant attempts to marginalize and diminish a President they couldn't control were failing. The new president is a maverick set out on his own course with his own agenda and the world would soon be aghast at his various initiatives.

The President often did the unexpected such as flying in on an unmarked air force jet to hide the fact the President was aboard. This event was just one of many sophisticated actions the President took knowing it would reduce or eliminate a lot of public pressure that such a visit would manifest.

The President had jet fighter escort the entire trip. The Air Force was a little dismayed when he demanded they take off an hour earlier than planned. Being commander in chief they *could not tell him no*. It would not come as a surprise to someone like General Harris when air controllers at Nellis who were informed by NORAD, the VIP was going to be in their airspace a lot earlier than they planned.

<u>INT. EARLY MORNING. AREA 51 GENERAL HARRIS BOQ ROOM. (BOQ ~ BACHELOR OFFICER QUARTERS)</u>

General Harris was hoping he could sleep until 6:00 A.M. and get four solid hours when his phone rang, and the Command Duty Officer was calling him.

Command Duty Officer
General Harris, air traffic control estimates the President's plane will be arriving in an hour.

General Harris
Thanks for the heads-up, Captain, make sure the welcoming party is present and standing by to welcome the President no later than 5:45 A.M.

Command Duty Officer
They will be ready, sir.

General Harris
Thank you.

Command Duty Officer
You are welcome, General.

General Harris skipped breakfast, had his dress uniform on and was pulling up on the side of building 27 in VIP parking at 5:30 A.M. As soon as he got out of his unmarked Air Force Sedan, with government plates on them, he immediately witnessed the hustle bustle of the welcoming party.

They were throwing out the red carpet for the President. But soon they would all be disappointed as the Secret Service directed them to take the President's plane all the way inside building 27 and shut the large access doors prior to the President's contingency departing the aircraft. It appeared he didn't want anyone to know he was at Area 51.

<u>EXT. EARLY MORNING AREA 51 PRESIDENT'S GS-450 BUSINESS JET AIR FORCE 29001, LANDING AT HOMEY AIRPORT</u>

The welcoming committee observed the President's jet taxi over to building 27 aircraft hangar. As soon as the two jet engines shut down, the jet was towed into the hangar and doors shut.

The sudden up-posture of the base, usually only done with certain flight tests of advanced HAVE-PURPLE designs or TR-3B, meant the welcoming party was quite small and only included Generals and Colonels. So, it was only fitting the welcoming was in the hangar. Per the Secret Service direction, the unmarked limo carrying the President that day was also parked inside the large hangar. The Gulf Stream 450 had only three passengers on board which included the President.

The President walked down the ladder to meet the welcoming party which included General Harris, Kevin O'Toole of course was out in front. This was the first and probably the last time Kevin O'Toole would meet the President. Kevin O'Toole poured on the charm.

KEVIN O'TOOLE

Welcome to Area 51, Mr. President. I'm Kevin O'Toole, Technical Director of the research here.

PRESIDENT

Pleasure to meet you, Mr. O'Toole.

The President smiled and his handshake was solid.

On the flight over, the President read Kevin O'Toole and General Whitman's dossiers. The President had previously investigated General Harris and knew a lot about him. People can say all they want about this President, but one thing he was adamant about, he wanted to know about the people he had dealings with. In doing so he figured out their character flaws and what angles they would approach him, which enabled him to avoid many mine fields the establishment laid out for him.

The amazing President stayed three chess moves ahead of the establishment in his sophisticated chess match he was winning every day. His clandestine visit to Area 51 was another one of his fantastic moves his political enemies could not predict.

KEVIN O'TOOLE
Let me introduce you to General Whitman,
commanding officer of Area 51.

PRESIDENT
It's a pleasure to meet you, General.

The President held out his hand and grabbed the general Whitman's hand, then with his other hand squeezed his upper left arm in a warm embrace.

General Whitman was taken back slightly. He wasn't a big fan of the President; in fact, he voted against him in spite of the fact he knew the President's opponent violated a lot of security rules and regulations and had not been treated with exceptional consideration and given a pass by political support apparatus and the establishment, would not have been in the campaign. Like a lot of supporters for that candidate, they picked the wrong horse, and any thought of patronage was eliminated when their candidate lost.

Like General Harris, General Whitman was no fool and never voiced his political ideology and hid his disdain for the current President. Even with General Whitman's negative emotions, he felt a sense of electricity flowing through him by the way the President was touching him during the handshake.

It's one thing to see a person on TV, it's another to be face to face with them undergoing an extraordinary glimpse into the apparatus he now appeared to have taken a bold move towards.

But soon, when the President's plan was announced, General Whitman would be far more perplexed and realized he like many had underestimated this leader as the shocking revelation manifested one of the largest structural changes the military experienced since the Civil War.

The President then released General Whitman's hand, then looked directly at General Harris, and approached him and before Kevin O'Toole could begin an introduction, spontaneously stated,

PRESIDENT
General Harris, good to see you again.

GENERAL HARRIS
Thank you, Mr. President.

PRESIDENT
General Harris, would you mind showing me around
your base and areas you think I should, see?

GENERAL HARRIS
I would be most proud to do so, Mr. President.

PRESIDENT
Good, I want you to ride with me in my limo so we can
talk about the base as we drive around to the various
sites.

GENNERAL HARRIS
As you wish, Mr. President, I'm at your disposal.

About that time the Secret Service Agent standing next to the President spoke.

SECRET SERVICE AGENT
Mr. President, your limo is right here.

As requested, one of the presidential limos and a couple black SUVs without any markings had been flown out on a C17 Air Force Jet with the President's fleet of support aircraft. When the President goes somewhere remote like Area 51, even though the Vice President has all the legal authority of the President with the temporary delegation of authority [has the football], a communications and support plane was with them in the event a nuclear war started and the President would soon be airborne in a craft that had a lot of self-defense ability and refueling capabilities to stay aloft more than a week if necessary.

A Secret Service Agent was the driver. Another Secret Service Agent was riding shotgun in the front with the driver, packed with some very capable weapons to defend the President, and since General Harris would not be permitted alone in the Limo rear area with the President, a third Secret Service man was there as well. The Limo door closest to the Airplane was open and the President was led there to get him inside and protected as quickly as possible.

To Kevin O'Toole's chagrin, General Harris was led around to the other side of the Limo and led into the car after a gentle pat down to make sure he had no weapons on him. The former Marine Major in the President's Secret Service detachment apologized.

SECRET SERVICE AGENT
I'm sorry for the inconvenience, General.

GENERAL HARRIS
Understand, as head of security for Area 51 I can
appreciate you wanting to protect the President.

SECRET SERVICE AGEINT
Thank you for your understanding, General.

GENERAL HARRIS.
You are welcome, sir.

General Harris climbed into the limo and the Secret Service agent shut the door and said something into his microphone the occupants could not hear, but the driver and his deputy heard the statement.

SECRET SERVICE AGEINT
As soon as the hangar doors open, you are ready to depart.

About that time the huge hangar doors started opening. Nobody on the outside saw the President get off the plane and nobody knew he was at Area 51. This visit was TOP-SECRET NOFORN with instructions and no dissemination of information or details without Secret Service approval, which was not likely to occur.

When the hangar doors were open sufficiently to allow safe egress, a couple SUVs on the other side of the aircraft headed out first, then the presidential unmarked limousine followed. After the three vehicles were clear of the hangar, the doors slid shut under remote control. Suddenly the floor of the hangar started moving downwards. The remaining Secret Service men knew this was going to happen as it was planned. The elevator went down one level, where an electric powered tug hooked onto the aircraft and pushed it back into its parking area.

These Secret Service personnel were not permitted to leave the vicinity of the aircraft. Nobody without special Air Force One maintenance crew certification and two-man rule were allowed near the aircraft. A Secret Service agent was required to always remain onboard the aircraft while it was deployed.

Because of the expected departure in a couple hours, the pilot and copilot, air force officers were to remain on the plane, and they went through their checklists. The Gulfstream 450 was not allowed to have any faults at takeoff. In one of the C17s that landed at Area 51 with the President's fleet included tech reps and spare parts to handle any possible issue with jet engines, electronics, or any item that could possibly put the President in danger.

The cleaning crew was now brought onto the plane under strict supervision. This President was a stickler for cleanliness. You didn't want him doing a white glove inspection. But at the end of the day, the crew didn't feel bad about him because he treated them with respect and curtesy if they conducted themselves in a professional manner that he expected out of anyone around him.

As an autocrat and former Corporate CEO, the President did not tolerate incompetents very long. He also believed in rewarding his people for doing their best and achieving results. During the previous administrations due to the culture surrounding these Presidents, the White House staff and Air Force One crews were not used to being ready for white glove inspections.

In just the short period after the transition to the new administration, there were broad shakeups and new ways of doing business. Some were shown the door and new blood was brought in.

Despite what many would think, it wasn't whites replacing blacks and Hispanics. It sometimes was the other way around as the best people were brought in. Even though the appearance might have suggested a patronage situation, the President had a cadre of troops he already knew could get the job done and, in some cases, he brought in his own former private plane employees to train the Air Force One crews on how best to interact with this President. The transformation was astonishing.

The folks standing by to support Area 51 observing this crew go into and clean the airplane and prepare it for its return flight were astonished at the amount of detail. It was not uncommon that pilots helped clean the President's private Boeing 757 prior to the election. The pilot was all smiles, and cleaning didn't bother him since he was paid twice as much as most private pilots flying large corporate jets.

Prior to this visit, the Secret Service had no idea building 27 had an elevator. And if they had traveled down to the 4th deck and saw some of the astonishing aircraft in there such as the TR-3B and the latest Have Purple Project, they would understand why security here was just as tight as what surrounds the President. They were all mostly Air Force or U.S. Marines observing each other in full awe of the other group as it all unfolded.

The limo followed the counterclockwise route around the hills south of the runways as they headed to their first destination: building 140.

THE PRESIDENT MEETS THE PONARIAN

<u>EXT DAY BLACK HIGH RISE BUILDING 140 AREA 51 ANNEX</u>

General Harris thought it would bolster the President's cause for the formation of the United States Space Force if he met the individual whom Vladimir Putin was allowed to meet just a few months prior, the *Ponarian*.

The President looked out the tinted glass window observing the tall black building out in the middle of the desert that oddly looked out of place with very few surrounding buildings or facilities and oddly no trees or landscaping.

PRESIDENT
So that's where we blew $50 million?

GENERAL HARRIS
In all honesty, Mr. President, it was actually $500 million.

PRESIDENT
The official record is $50 million.

GENERAL HARRIS
The rest of the funds came out of secret black funds.

PRESIDENT
I could have built a dozen skyscrapers in New York with that kind of money.

GENERAL HARRIS
Mr. President, what we haven't told you is most of the office space is actually underground.

PRESIDENT
Please explain.

GENERAL HARRIS
We have a very large underground facility under that building. One of the reasons for that large building is to disguise the facility, making parties interested in finding out what's going on out here think most of the action is in that building when it's mostly underground.

PRESIDENT
So, most of the work is being done in below surface facilities and that tall building is nothing more than a prop to keep people guessing.

GENERAL HARRIS
That's partly true, but the tall black building provides living quarters for people and Alien Diplomats that must live here.

PRESIDENT
Such as the Ponarian?

GENERAL HARRIS
That's correct.

The limo and the SUVs easily fit in the parking structure together before the garage door shut so anyone outside could not see who arrived in the vehicles. Immediately both rear doors were opened and Secret Service men stood by as the President and General Harris got out of the limo and were escorted to the elevator.

General Whitman and Kevin O'Toole got out of one of the SUVs and approached the group with a look on their face wondering why General Harris brought the President here, which is one of the few places they didn't want the President getting near. Unfortunately, while in the proximity of the President they could not confront General Harris nor stop him from what he was now doing.

Kevin O'Toole was slowly starting to figure out General Harris out maneuvered him, and he was powerless to stop what now unfolded.

Within an hour the CIA and NSA would be in hyper-intensive reactions to all these unfolding events. Phone calls to Langley would start in earnest in a brief period. The new President in a short amount of time had surpassed anything Eisenhower had done in the 1950s when the first revelation to S-4 operations was first exposed and Majestic 12 went into damage control.

The elevator said the capacity was twenty-one people. With all the steel and lead some of them were carrying, they had the weight of twenty-five people when they were all in and moving up to the 15th floor for the first stop.

The elevator stopped and the door opened. They walked into what appeared to be a small lobby with a security-guard behind bullet proof glass in a cubical right next to an access door with a combination lock and handprint mechanism.

General Harris walked over, keyed in a code, put his palm on the reader the placed his face up to the retina recognizing device and about ten seconds later they could all hear what appeared to be some type of chime and an automatic door lock solenoid click and the door started to open by itself as it was a fully automated door.

The security guard had a Secret Service man with him for this visit and knew all those in the party were fully credentialed. Immediately inside this room they immediately detected what appeared to be an increase in humidity which this whole floor of this building was tightly controlled to give the Ponarian the comfort he needed to survive.

<u>INT. DAY. AREA 51, BUILDING 140, 15<u>TH</u> FLOOR. THE PONARIAN'S LIVING</u>

<u>ACCOMODATIONS.</u>

In the background they could hear music, it was rather pleasant. The Ponarian enjoyed earth music and had been fully exposed to many types of music since he was first brought to Area 51 in 1947. Stravinsky, "The Firebird" was playing in the background, not too loud to be annoying, but loud enough to hear the articulation of the music and some of its finer components.

The Ponarian was not an engineer or scientist, so he was not really of much help in the reverse engineering program. But where his importance existed, was in describing his galaxy and some of the various indigenous beings that lived at various solar systems and the situations they experienced including galactic strife.

The Ponarian was marooned on Earth with no means of ever getting back to his civilization. Even though Ponarians lived to about two hundred fifty Earth years. The Ponarian was already three quarters into his lifespan. Even though the Ponarian would outlive everyone in the room, he would not outlive some of them by many years. He was on his downslide now.

Wasting away seventy-one years stuck on Earth did not please the Ponarian. The Ponarian was also semi-bitter towards his American military captors and their early treatment where under laboratory conditions he experienced brutality and the most inhumane treatment any civilized society could impose on a sentient being.

Inside one of the large rooms provided for him, the Ponarian was doing oil paintings. The Ponarian's only salvation was to be allowed to do whatever was possible within the security apparatus of Area 51. The Ponarian was humanoid and would pass for the typical European. His appearance now was that of a man who might have been around their 60s. He was showing his age though he aged slower than humans.

The Ponarian had a good memory and after extensive painting lessons, gradually figured out how to paint his prior life on canvas. The Ponarian brought to life his memories in the most spectacular paintings. Even though it was almost impossible that any Earth people would ever meet any being from the Andromeda Galaxy and from interviews with the Ponarian, no new expedition would occur probably for centuries if ever. Therefore, even though the information had no real value, it did at least convey to researchers in Area 51 projects the level of sophistication and intelligence of some of the beings from the Andromeda Galaxy.

This of course presented a chilling reminder to these researchers and the joint chiefs, that within our own galaxy we very well likely might soon meet up with entities that are a lot closer and posed a clear and compelling concern for our total disregard and preparedness to deal with such an eventuality.

Many concerns were deep in the back of the President's mind. The President who was an avid reader his entire life, did not limit the diversity to what he explored and studied. Space, science fiction, popular mechanics, aerospace magazines, and numerous publications slowly molded his persona. He was the first President since

Eisenhower to deal with the notion we are not alone in the Universe. President Truman created Majestic 12 when he created the initial Majestic Group after the Roswell crash in 1947. But President Truman was never informed about the Ponarian.

President Eisenhower became fully aware of the Ponarian and the Gray Aliens. President Kennedy got even more involved, and it's rumored his assassination was triggered by Majestic 12 over his executive order to disclose our alien involvement after the Cuban Missile Crisis to reduce tensions with the Soviets.

America's exposure to aliens and subsequent discussions about them to the Soviets had been few and far between. There simply was never any cooperation in this area, partly because reverse engineering had huge implications to the arms race.

When the Russian military invaded Crimea, the previous President worried a direct confrontation could lead to a nuclear war and sent a message to Putin the reason why we needed to cooperate and be less confrontational was due to compelling reasons and asked Putin to take a trip to meet him at Area 51 and he had some eye candy to show him.

Putin, who had just pissed off the United States and in specific the Joint Chiefs, was rather surprised at such an invitation. At first, he thought it might simply be the President showing off some new aircraft like the new Have Purple design which the Russians already knew about with their spies, but nevertheless agreed to the secret meeting simply to discover what the previous President was up too. Plus, Putin was even more surprised the President wasn't confrontational at all.

Putin flew into Area 51 on a new Russian Jet that looked very much like an Airbus design, but it was truly a Russian design, though it used Pratt and Whitney Jet Engines mainly to help convince international corporations to buy it since the supply chain of spare parts would be international.

Just like the current dog and pony show that was going on, Putin was brought to building 140 and met the Ponarian. Putin was suddenly a changed man, and quickly displayed a different persona as he reflected on this disclosure.

The previous president's calculations were in fact impeccable. This arrangement completely altered Putin's modus operandi and now Russian-American relations were being totally redesigned. Neither party knew exactly how to reengineer the relationship, and the sticky point of the war in Ukraine caused a lot of delay in implementing a new pathway towards a new relationship they had to form, because the Ponarian and his description of some of the Space Combat that existed in the Andromeda Galaxy should be a wakeup call for Earth Defenses.

The Ponarian had full access to TV, radio, and the internet, though his internet experiences were heavily censored, plus who would believe him anyway if he claimed to be an alien? The Ponarian had observed this President on TV many times during the campaign. The Ponarian was somewhat of a news and weather freak.

In persona the President looked and acted just like the man on TV. But seeing the person up close and live, creates quite a different psychology.

The Ponarian got perturbed now and then as he felt the Americans used him as a freak show. He also felt it was inhumane of them to leave him locked up in this high-tech prison, though conditions were a hell of a lot better than what they were in the 1940s and 1950s.

The Americans got a lot less cooperation out of the Ponarian than they might have otherwise had they treated him better. The Ponarian knew of threats to Earth he never divulged because he held a long-lasting grudge. Just like Nero played the fiddle while Rome burned, the Ponarian would be whistling or singing if he thought America was burning.

The President was not like a lot of the others who came in for the dog and pony shows. He was far calmer and more retrospective than most everyone including Vladimir Putin and his recent visit.

The Ponarian refused to give his name. He would only tell them Ponarian, so eventually that name stuck and the alien was always referred to as the Ponarian.

The Ponarian continued painting ignoring the crowd that had just walked into the room. On the canvas before him was a recollection of his home in the Ponarian World. At first sight one might assume it was an infantile painting until one stopped to think for a minute that alien worlds may not have the same building techniques experienced on Earth. If one had the ability to visit the Ponarian world and look at the real buildings and compare with what the Ponarian had on the canvas, they would realize his depictions were quite accurate.

The President had a short briefing about the Ponarian, including how long he had been detained and the circumstances he existed.

PRESIDENT
Sir, it's a pleasure to meet you.

The President looking at the artwork the Ponarian was putting on the canvas. For some strange reason the President's voice short circuited some of the Ponarians' thought processes and he suddenly turned and faced the President.

There was a strange feeling as the two men looked into each other's eyes. The Ponarian knew that based on the weapons this President had at his disposal he was no doubt the most powerful leader in the world. Only one other President had ever met the Ponarian, General Eisenhower almost sixty-two years prior. So, it was unexpected that such a sudden visit would occur.

Then the President said something that utterly shocked the Ponarian, and all those in the room with them.

PRESIDENT
Is there any reason why we must keep the Ponarian locked up? Can't we make some accommodation so that he can be introduced to our society and allowed to experience humanity?

Kevin O'Toole quickly spoke giving the party line.

KEVIN O'TOOLE
If the Ponarian were allowed to walk around free and the public knew he came from outer space, he might be assassinated right away as religious zealots probably would not want such information contaminating the minds of the masses.

PRESIDENT
There must be a way to grant him freedom and protect him.

KEVIN O'TOOLE
He's here for his own protection, Mr. President.

Kevin O'Toole fully carried the torch for Majestic 12's policy of none-disclosure and would do everything in his power to prevent such a disclosure even if they had to arrange another Kennedy event.

PONARIAN
You would free me and allow me intercourse with the public?

PRESIDENT
I believe it would be best for you and everyone on this planet.

KEVIN O'TOOLE
Mr. President, we have numerus studies done by think tanks such as Rand Corporation that suggests that

disclosure of the Ponarian would cause great public calamity.

PRESIDENT

I disagree. The public is far more sophisticated these days, plus I think well over half the planet believes life exists on other planets.

KEVIN O'TOOLE

Mr. President, before we implemented any such deviation from our current protocols, I think it should be thoroughly studied and the brightest minds possible meet with you and explain what all these studies suggest.

PRESIDENT

I'll agree to study it some more, but it's my intention to see the Ponarian walk out of here and experience freedom.

The Ponarian was in a state of shock and moved by what he heard.

C.U. PONARIAN

The President could see the tears forming on the Ponaria's eyes and knew the alien was entering an emotional state.

PRESIDENT

I would like to come back sometime soon and sit down with you and have a discussion. I also promise I will work hard for your release. I think you have been held far too long and most Americans would agree with me we have not treated you very well in your stay here.

PONARIAN

Thank you, sir, I would be glad to sit down with you and talk.

PRESIDENT

I'm going to be busy over the next couple of months, after that I'll free some time on my calendar to make another trip out here.

PONARIAN

I'll be waiting.

The President held out his hand and to the astonishment of everyone present, the Ponarian grabbed his hand having observed the tradition on TV numerous times and shook the President's hand. He had never done that before. Analysts watching the video who always had the Ponarian under observation were quite animated as they observed this unprecedented act by the alien.

PRESIDENT
Okay, General Harris, show me some more of what
you think I should see.

The President then turned and looked directly at Kevin O'Toole and could see his body language betray him. The President thought, *I need to keep an eye on you snake and send the message hands off General Harris.*

GENERAL HARRIS
Let's go back to the elevator, Mr. President.

As they all piled back into the elevator, the President positioned himself between Kevin O'Toole and General Harris and because of the President's large figure, Kevin O'Toole couldn't give General Harris eye commands or direction such as *don't take the President there.*

The elevator began its drop a half-mile down and Kevin O'Toole's biggest fear now unfolded. General Harris had just done the big no-no and took a politician down to the secret headquarters and nerve center of Area 51.

What Kevin O'Toole and General Whitman were unaware of, General Harris had just given instructions to his staff member Major Jones to send an email to everyone at the headquarters staff the President's visit and presence was Top-Secret SCI NOFORN. They were thus covered by rules and regulations on disclosure of the visit, and they all knew the brutal reality if they ever got caught leaking.

The elevator stopped and they got out, and after they got past the armed guards and walked past staff members down a hallway, the shock on staff members' faces was evident. Nobody knew the President was coming, and General Harris and the security department along with the Secret Service had kept the visit completely off the radar.

<u>INT. DAY. DEEP UNDERGROUND COMPLEX AREA 51</u>

General Harris led the President into the SCIF conference room where they all set down around a long table which had a big screen at one end and as soon as everyone was asked to take a seat and sat down.

GENERAL HARRIS
Mr. President, I've prepared a PowerPoint presentation
to show you what all we have here so that you can pick

what you want to see. You obviously do not have time
to see it all, so I recommend you pick three of these
and we can go look.

On the first slide it listed 15 different activities which quickly prompted Kevin O'Toole
to make a statement.

KEVIN O'TOOLE
General Harris, you can't show these things to the
President.

The President turned towards Kevin O'Toole.

PRESIDENT
Mr. O'Toole, just so you know, you work for me, and
I'm cleared for anything in Area 51. I will see anything
on that list I wish to see and if you in any way interfere,
you will be flying back to Washington with me later
today on a one-way trip.

Kevin O'Toole just received the message loud and clear. His career was dangerously
close to the limits. As much as he wanted to keep all politicians away from their
business, he knew the President had some awesome legal control over all of him
whether he liked it or not. He also knew public law stated the President was cleared at
all levels and it was up to the President to decide if he had the need to know.

Surprisingly the President only picked three things on the list he wanted to see, TR-3B,
the reverse engineering facility, and the nuclear radiation mitigation experiment site
because he was concerned about the welfare of the workers and if their attempts were
unsuccessful, they might have to eventually abandon the site after sinking $50 billion
into it since 1954.

Short videos were shown on the three areas the President was interested in hopes
that would curtail an actual physical visit. But true to his form, this was a hands-on
President who learned a long time ago, to go place his personal eyes on something to
make a better judgement.

PRESIDENT
The first thing I want to look at is the TR-3B.

<u>EXT./INT. AREA 51 HOMEY AIRPORT BUILDING 27 HANGAR</u>

The group soon drove back to building 27. As they were pulling up to the hangar the
President had to ask the question:

PRESIDENT
Why are we coming back here?

GENERAL HARRIS
This is where the TR-3B is stored.

Just like before the limo pulled into the hangar and the hangar doors shut behind it and the SUVs that came into the hangar with them. As soon as they were in the building with the hangar doors shut General Harris announced to the president.,

GENERAL HARRIS
Let's get out of the vehicle and have a look.

After the President and the others were out of the limo and SUVs General Harris looked at the President.

GENERAL HARRIS
The TR-3B is on the 4th floor. We are inside an elevator, and it will now take us down to the fourth floor.

General Harris then and turned and nodded to an aide. who then talked to the building manager on his cell phone.

GENERAL HARRIS
Gary, this is General Harris, our group is back in building 27. I want you to take us down to the 4th floor so the President can take a look at the TR-3B.

BUILDING MANAGER (a.k.a. GARY)
General Harris, repositioning to floor number four. Standby for elevator operations.

Shortly the whole room seemed to move, and the floor slowly started to sink. As they slowly went down to the 4th floor, they passed the floor where the Gulfstream 450 they flew in on was parked. As soon as the elevator stopped on the fourth floor, they walked over to one of the TR-3Bs.

The President looked at the ultra-streamlined craft in awe.

PRESIDENT
The TR-3B could help start of our Space Force.

GENERAL HARRIS
It is kind of unique in that it can take off from a runway and fly in the atmosphere as well out into space.

PRESIDENT

All we need now is a space carrier to carry several dozens of these TR-3B's so that we can project power to alien forces if necessary.

GENERAL HARRIS

The only way we could have a carrier that large would be to build it in space.

PRESIDENT

How could we build something in space now with the Space Shuttle no longer flying?

GENERAL HARRIS

The space shuttle program was canceled when it should have continued. There were numerous lessons learned in the program and by the time we canceled it, most of the bugs had been worked out. The final two shuttles were far more reliable than the previous ones that had disasters.

PRESIDENT

General Harris are you suggesting we could dust off the shuttles, put them back into operation and use them for the heavy lift to get the piece parts out into space to start construction of a Space Carrier to haul those TR-3Bs to various destinations as needed for planetary defense?

GENERAL HARRIS

Mr. President, those decommissioned shuttles repurposed could help out in the early phases of the program, but if we are going to build a fleet, we would need a Super Shuttle.

PRESIDENT

What do you mean by a Super Shuttle?

GENERAL HARRIS

The new shuttles would appear like a shuttle, but it would be stretched to at least four times as long as the existing shuttles.

PRESIDENT
Why would we need a shuttle four times as long?

GENERAL HARRIS
We could deliver steel and aluminum components that are four times as long, which would greatly improve the design and improve the Space Carrier to sustain some damage from enemy alien ships and still be able to function."

PRESIDENT
Give me an example of what you are thinking.

GENERAL HARRIS
Well, for starters we could build redundancy. We could have two power plants on each end of the space vessel and multiple catapult systems and multiple landing pads allowing us to retrieve TR-3Bs if one side of the ship is damaged."

PRESIDENT
That makes sense.

GENERAL HARRIS
Redundancy is necessary because some of these aliens we may have to engage have some very dangerous weapon systems and if we get into a slug fest, no doubt they will inflict some wounds.

PRESIDENT
Well, General, I think I'm going to have to allow you to come up with the name of the first ship since this is your brainchild.

GENERAL HARRIS
That's easy.

PRESIDENT
And what would that be?

GENERAL HARRIS
CSS Alabama, which is named after the famous confederate ship of the Civil War that put the fear into Yankee shipping more than any other ship afloat.

PRESIDENT
What does 'CSS' stand for?

GENERAL HARRIS
Carrier Space Service.

PRESIDENT
When is the next time one of these TR-3Bs is going to fly?

GENERAL HARRIS
We had one scheduled for a few hours from now, in anticipation of a time slot after your fleet of craft departed.

PRESIDENT
I think I may just wait and watch one of these take off.

GENERAL HARRIS
Mr. President, we cannot launch this plane while your support aircraft are here, we need to up posture the base. All those people flying the cargo planes hauling your limo and spare parts do not have security clearance to see the TR-3B.

PRESIDENT
General Harris, I'll have them all leave in advance, and we'll leave right after the TR-3B takes off.

GENERAL HARRIS
I'll arrange that, Mr. President, give me a few minutes. I need to make a few phone calls.

PRESIDENT
What about the reverse engineering tour?

GENERAL HARRIS
We can go there now.

PRESIDENT
Okay, us go there now.

GENERAL HARRIS
We are already here.

PRESIDENT
The reverse engineering is here.

GENERAL HARRIS
Yes, we only must go over to the elevator.

General Harris led the group to the elevator, large enough to carry some good size equipment. It was only one-tenth the size of the elevator they just stood on the fourth floor, but compared to any freight elevator in any major commercial building it was huge.

The group entered the elevator. General Harris keyed in a number on the keypad area and momentarily, they could feel the elevator drop and it went a good distance before it slowed and stopped, the door opened, and they exited into a vast underground complex.

<u>INT. AREA 51 UNDERGROUND COMPLEX REVERSE ENGINEERING FACILITY</u>

PRESIDENT
Holy smokes.

The President stated as he looked out into the complex that surpassed his wildest imagination.

They walked down a large open bay hallway that almost had a factory appearance with dividers every forty to fifty feet. And in each cubicle was some junk looking machinery of which some had a weathered appearance. A few of the devices even had barnacles.

PRESIDENT
Is this something you pulled up from the ocean?

GENERAL HARRIS
Yes, it crashed into the ocean maybe fifty thousand years ago.

PRESIDENT
It appears to have a lot of marine growth all over it except in a few places.

GENERAL HARRIS
Those are the areas we are systematically cleaning off so as to not damage the surface so we can restore it to the best we can as we figure it out.

There were some major scents but above each piece of equipment were ventilators sucking the air up to prevent the room accumulating a lot of the smell. Fresh air was obviously dumped somewhere.

As they walked a while, they came upon what appeared to clearly be a UFO that wasn't in too bad of condition.

PRESIDENT
This one appears like it's in reasonable shape.

GENERAL HARRIS
Yes, this is a spacecraft an alien made an emergency landing in.

PRESIDENT
Did he have some sort of mechanical failure?

GENERAL HARRIS
No, it was shot down.

PRESIDENT
By one of our jets?

GENERAL HARRIS
No, by another alien.

PRESIDENT
We had aliens fighting on this planet?

GENERAL HARRIS
Yes, this skirmish happened near Aztec, New Mexico, back in 1948.

PRESIDENT
Did we get any useful information out of this craft?

GENERAL HARRIS
In terms of metallurgy and some insights into alien electronics, yes. But the alien did not know much about how the propulsion system worked.

PRESIDENT
How do you know he wasn't simply withholding the information?

GENERAL HARRIS
This was before my time, so I don't condone the treatment they gave the alien, but from what I understand they tortured him to the point of driving him insane. They got a lot of information out of him, but in the end, they concluded he was being truthful, he didn't know much about how the propulsion system worked, nor did he care.

The President was fascinated as he took it all in and was compiling a list of ideas in his head on how this all related to the need to build a space force.

PRESIDENT
Based on what I'm seeing here, I'm convinced more than ever we need to create a Space Force. I think we have been lucky up to now, that some aggressive alien race hasn't come along and knocked us off.

GENERAL HARRIS
I agree, Mr. President, we are living on borrowed time.

By the time the President had seen all he wanted, he recalled seeing at least nine wrecked alien aircraft. This facility was cleared at the Q level required for nuclear weapon code access. There were not many workers in the facility. It was obvious that it was extremely difficult to recruit enough people that could be cleared at such levels. That also posed a problem for the future space force. At what levels would people be cleared? The chances of alien encounters were high. Therefore, it would have to be a high security operation. Clearable people are not always the brightest or the most efficient. Security concerns would hamper the Space Force.

PRESIDENT
Okay, I think I've seen enough. I'm ready to depart and go back to Washington.

The President stated and nodded at his chief Secret Service coordinator who shortly started the wheels in motion to get the President extracted from the facility and on his way back to Washington.

TR-3B FLIGHT DEMONSTRATION

The group walked back to the elevator which General Harris controlled and stopped it at the level the President's plane was parked.

GENERAL HARRIS
My suggestion is to have your pilot taxi down to the end of the runway where you can watch the TR-3B

take off and after your plane is airborne, we'll have the TR-3B do some fly-bys so you can see it in the air."

PRESIDENT

Thank you, I appreciate that.

In a short while the group stood near the ladder to the President's plane, still parked underground in the hangar. The President shook everyone's hand.

PRESIDENT

General Harris, thank you for showing me around. In the days ahead, I will be giving you a phone call because I have some questions for you after I talk to the secretary of the Air Force and the Vice President about everything we discussed today.

GENERAL HARRIS

You are most welcome Mr. President. I'll be waiting to hear your call. You will be seeing the TR-3B fly real soon. You can see your support aircraft are taking off now so we will be clear to fly the TR-3B shortly.

PRESIDENT

I appreciate the chance to observe TR-3B fly, General Harris.

The President smiled at General Harris then turned around, walked over then climbed up into the GS-450 aircraft. Shortly the door to the President's Gulfstream 450 was shut. The electric-powered tug towed the aircraft out of the parking stall onto the elevator which they all followed.

The elevator then rose to the ground floor. The large doors of the hangar, building 27 opened and the electric tug then pulled the aircraft out of the hangar and pulled it 90 degrees away from the hangar so that when it started up its jet engines the blast would not hit what appeared to be an empty hangar.

<u>EXT. DAY AREA 51 OUTSIDE BUILDING 27 HANGAR.</u>

The pilot started both jet engines on the President's GS-450 aircraft and after approximately fifteen minutes the President's plane pulled away heading towards the end of the runway and halted.

Meanwhile the doors to building 27 had been shut and momentarily later opened again. Suddenly a TR-3B was observed at a distance from the President's GS-450 aircraft and it was also towed out of the hangar and the electric tug uncoupled and drove back into the hangar. The pilot with call sign Woodpecker called Air Traffic control requesting permission to take off and do its planned mission that morphed into including a presidential side show.

WOODPECKER
Homey Air Traffic Control this is Woodpecker request permission to execute plan DELTA.

A Homey ATC tower REA 51 ATC
Woodpecker, this is Homey Air Traffic Control. You have permission to execute plan DELTA.

WOODPECKER
Homey Air Traffic Control, this is Woodpecker, understand, commencing plan DELTA.

The TR-3B made no noise. Its fuselage was the nearest thing to a UFO anyone could ever imagine. The pilot who had the call sign, WOODPECKER manipulated the TR-3B flight controls, and just like an F35B doing a VTOL takeoff, went vertical silently to one hundred feet. The control tower instructed by General Harris informed the pilot of the President's GS-450 Jet aircraft to ask the President to look out a starboard window towards the hangar. The TR-3B flew at one hundred feet towards the runway and soon exhibited four bright balls on the bottom of the craft. The triangular shaped craft had a bright ball on each corner and one large one in the midsection. The President suddenly received a text message on his personal cell phone.

C.U. PRESIDENT'S I-PHONE TEXT MESSAGES

GENERAL HARRIS TEXT MESSAGE
Mr. President, Here's the TR-3B. When you get a chance, Google TR-3B.

PRESIDENT TEXT MESSAGE
General Harris, I'm looking at Google now.

To the President's astonishment, there were numerous Google pictures of the TR-3B that had been leaked to the internet. *I wonder if they leaked those pictures on purpose.*

PRESIDENT TEXT MESSAGE
General Harris, WOW!

<u>EXT. CGI. DAY AREA 51, PRESIDENT'S GS-450 TAIL NUMBER AIR FORCE 29001 AT THE END OF THE RUNWAY READY TO TAKE OFF.</u>

Just like the images of what he saw on Google images, here was this fantastic space and aircraft slowly approaching and it went onto the runway and suddenly stopped in midair and hovered at 100 feet for several minutes slowly turning clockwise full 360 degrees with very low sound levels remarkably different than the F35. With 89% antigravity the propulsion thrust required was minimal to allow hover accurately at 100 feet above the runway.

Then the TR-3Bslowly lowered down onto the runway where it did a full 360-degree turn in a very limited space. It then went back into the air about fifty feet and then started traveling slowly down the runway. After it was a mile away approximately, the glowing globe like appearance in the middle of the craft got increasingly brighter almost dwarfing the entire craft and the plane shot up into the air quicker than anything the President or anyone on board had ever witnessed.

A Secret Service Agent then walked around the cabin with a stack of papers and handed one out to each person, then walked up to the cockpit and handed the pilot and copilot copies.

SECRET SERVICE AGENT

These are pre-filled out non-disclosure forms for the
TR-3B demonstrations Please sign your name on the
form at the bottom where I placed the yellow sticker,
in the space right below you printed name.

PRESIDENT

This document says we are forbidden from discussing
the TR-3B demonstration we witnessed for the rest of
their lives.

The Ponarian visit had already been handled by administrative processes. The TR-3B demonstration was an unplanned event.

SECRET SERVICE AGENT

That's correct, Mr. President. The document they
are signing is because the TR-3B is TOP-SECRET
NOFORN and clearly states it relates to a special
access program (SAP).

This would not be the first or the last time the President's party signed non-disclosure forms. The President was exempt from signing it, but on his final debriefing he was to receive upon leaving office, he was informed he would no longer be protected from security violations as a former President, he could be prosecuted and if he had any questions about any possible classified information, before he discussed it, he could go through his Secret Service protection to vet any circumstance before he discussed the matter for his own protection.

Homey ATC tower informed the President's plane:

HOMEY ATC TOWER
Air Force 29001, this is Homey ATC tower. You have
permission to take off in accordance with (IAW) flight
plan.

AIR FORCE 29001 PILOT
Homey ATC tower, Air Force 29001 understand
cleared for takeoff.

Air Force 29001 air space was now controlled by the Secret Service supervising the FAA.

The President's jet took off and since it had a light load, it got airborne in a very short run down the runway. The jet then headed up to forty thousand feet where it was soon joined by two F22 Raptor Jets flying escort in an offset wing. With one F22 jet above Air Force 29001 and the other below, each 1000 meters away from the President's plane.

Air Force 29001 pilot and the two F22 pilots were informed the flight demonstration plane would be coming in at a distance on their port side, knowing that's the side of the airplane the President was sitting.

The TR-3B suddenly arrived out of nowhere. It was almost as if it was invisible and suddenly appeared and again it had the four glowing globe shaped bright areas. The TR-3B came up about five hundred yards away from the President's plane, then slowly pulled ahead and when it was at about 45 degrees off the port side (315 degrees relative) it began a high-speed acceleration and within five seconds flew at such a huge velocity, it was no longer in sight.

WASHINGTON, D.C., USSF DEVELOPMENT

The President's plane had a special SATCOM device the President could hook his cell phone in and call anywhere in the world in flight or receive calls that he wanted. He then text-messaged General Harris.

PRESIDENT TEXT MESSAGE.
General Harris, I need you in Washington, D.C., a
week from today for consultations. I'll be contacting
the Secretary of Defense and the Air Force Secretary
to let them know to issue you a set of orders.

The President then sent text message to dual recipients the Secretary of Defense and to the Air Force Secretary.

PRESIDENT TEXT MESSAGE.
Secretary of Defense and to the Air Force Secretary, I've asked General Harris out at Area 51 to come to Washington next week for consultations. I want him relieved at Area 51 and reassigned to the White House staff for a period so that I can work with him on a new project I have in mind. Make these orders immediately.

General Harris had just been called into a meeting in the SCIF with Kevin O'Toole and General Sandy Whitman. The fireworks immediately started.

KEVIN O'TOOLE
General Harris, you were way out of line in what you did with the President.

General Harris had read the President's text message a while ago and no longer had any concern about Kevin O'Toole and General Whitman. They were in for a big surprise.

Kevin O'Toole and General Whitman had just had a private discussion and they were going to make movements to remove General Harris for insubordination. General Whitman was just about to begin a conference call with the Secretary of the Air Force to make this unprecedented move. But before he could call the Secretary, he received a call from her.

General Whitman saw on the caller I.D. was the Air Force Secretary Margarette Mackworth.

GENERAL WHITMAN
Hello, Madam Secretary, what can I do for you?

AIR FORCE SECRETARY
(Margarette Mackworth)
I need to talk with you and General Harris on a conference call.

GENERAL WHITMAN
He's right here, we are in SCIF with Kevin O'Toole.

AIR FORCE SECRETARY
(Margarette Mackworth)
Okay, good, put on speaker phone so I can talk to all of you together since it will affect everyone in the room.

General Whitman selected speakerphone so everyone could hear the conversation or chime in if needed.

AIR FORCE SECRETARY
(Margarette Mackworth)
Gentlemen, it's good that I found you all together as this will simplify what I must do.

GENERAL WHITMAN
What is it you wish to discuss, Madam Secretary?

AIR FORCE SECRETARY
(Margarette Mackworth)
Sorry to drop it on you this way, but I have my orders. General Harris, you are being transferred immediately to Washington, D.C. You are hereby relieved as Chief of Security for Area 51. General Whitman, you are now appointed Chief of Security for Area 51 with dual hat as commander until we can get General Harris replacement in.

Kevin O'Toole, you will be hearing from Langley soon, the President was very pleased with his visit there, job well done.

General John Harris sat there smiling because some of his friends had tipped him off about the skullduggery General Whitman and Kevin O'Toole were planning. However, General Harris knew it would be important to get some advanced idea of where he would be assigned in Washington and suddenly spoke up.

GENERAL HARRIS
Madam Secretary, this is John Harris, would it be possible for you to tell me what organization I'm being detailed to?

AIR FORCE SECRETARY
(Margarette Mackworth)
General Harris, your orders are now being processed and you should receive a message transmitted within a few hours. Your detailer will be contacting you to confirm all the information in advance of the transmission of your orders. Because of the necessity of quickly moving you to Washington in a brief period of time, your duties there at Area 51 are now curtailed and you are only to immediately turn over to General Whitman.

GENERAL HARRIS
Madam Secretary, I have household goods and items
to take care of before I leave.

AIR FORCE SECRETARY
(Margarette Mackworth)
General Harris, we have a contractor associated
with EG&G there APGC (All Purpose Government
Contractor) who will arrange shipment of all your
household goods and personal effects. That process
will begin in the morning. I've been instructed the
President wants you in Washington by a week from
now, and you will be given an office in the White
House with the military attaché and apparently the
Joint Chiefs are setting you up with office space over
at the Pentagon where you can work on your project.

GENERAL HARRIS
Madam Secretary, can you tell me what the project is
about?

The Air Force Secretary laughed slightly.

AIR FORCE SECRETARY
(Margarette Mackworth)
General, I think you know what it's about. However,
you have a meeting scheduled with the Joint Chiefs a
week from now, that's why you need to be back here
as soon as possible.

General Harris was stunned. He could only think this had something to do with the
Space Force.

The poker faces that Kevin O'Toole and General Whitman now had almost added an
element of serendipity to this whole matter.

It's kind of funny how the worm turns. Just a few minutes ago Kevin O'Toole and
Whitman were just about ready to tell him he was being fired and removed for
insubordination, and now he was more or less taken out of their legal jurisdiction, and
if they tried to pull a stunt now, the Air Force Secretary would be calling Whitman back
with orders for him he wouldn't like, such as the radar station up on the Northwest
Coast of Greenland. Based on the comment about Langley, Kevin O'Toole's days might
be numbered as well. He would find out soon enough the DCI was informed directly
from the President that Kevin O'Toole did a great job of pissing him off at Area 51.

AIR FORCE SECRETARY
(Margarette Mackworth)
That's all I have for now.

The Air Force Secretary then hung up.

The President was a far smoother planner than his enemies could understand. Everyone has their price, and he was an expert at figuring out how to obtain the correct price so that he didn't have to overpay, but at the same time he did not like to underpay for loyalty.

Just before the President's trip out to Area 51, the President personally invited the Margarette Mackworth the Air Force Secretary whom he appointed, to the oval office where he, the Vice President, and Margarette Mackworth discussed the fate of the Air Force.

The Air Force Secretary was a tough woman and had survived the Beltway and flourished in the swamp despite her revulsion towards the moral and ethical decline she observed on a daily basis, even though she had an element of her own vices.

Defense Contractor Lobbyists, a.k.a. *beltway bandits*, were in everyone's back pockets. They dished out the necessary inducements in some of the most ingenious manners. It could be anything from obtaining a loan with a super low interest payment, to magically obtaining a full ride scholarship to one of their dependents even though the student was only able to maintain at best a B average and an SAT score that only gave them about a 15-percent chance of getting into the bottom 50 percent of the good colleges.

In some cases, the *beltway bandits* offered a free ride on a private jet down to *Orgy Island* in the Caribbeans that offered amenities that might easily be misconstrued as human trafficking with recent shocking headlines of who was all involved including Royals, former president, and billionaires. Similar incentives to senior Naval Officers acting as contracting officers in forward deployed ship repairs were provided in Singapore by Fat Lenard.

The President had calculated the Air Force Secretary's price and knew what it would take. Normally she would resist any notion of a separate Space Force because it would cut deeply into Air Force funding if they suddenly lost all the money associated with NRO and other technology-based applications rooted in space operations.

What the President had to offer to get Margarette Mackworth the Air Force Secretary's loyalty as well as her buy-in was that future nomination of being the first Space Force Secretary. After that Margarette Mackworth didn't mind pulling out her meat carver and gut almost half of the Air Force. Even the Navy would lose a lot of funding and programs to a United States Space Force. The Navy would get their buy in too. Someone would have to operate the *SPACE-BASED AIRCRAFT CARRIERS*. These future monsters would be just like the Nimitz Class Carriers except instead of floating on water, they would operate in space and carry TR-3B instead of Northrup Grumman and Boeing (former McDonnel Douglas) jets and aircraft.

Also, there would not be a city of five thousand people like a normal carrier. There would be far more automation and the needs for the types of maintenance needed on a ship that experiences weather would not exist in space. Therefore, instead of a crew of five thousand they would probably not exceed a crew of more than five hundred which includes the Air Wing.

John Harris discovered after a couple days he had a Westinghouse Engineer as a personal secretary. He also had a few Rand Corporation people who had staff artists starting to work on artist conceptions. The eye-candy the joint chiefs would soon start observing, included a program flow chart of getting the space shuttle back into operation. They the follow-on super stretch shuttles would be designed and built, leveraging off lessons learned of the original space shuttle fleet.

Politically, the analysts would state the extended space shuttle was required to assure our ability to access our portion of the international space station. Then as the Space Force started socializing international space station modifications including larger sections, they would need to develop the stretch shuttles that would end up four times as long and instead of just two solid rocket boosters, they would have up to eight enabling them to haul heavy steel beams or aluminum sheets up. The first space carrier would have double hull construction with conformal slots making up independent hangar bays with air seals the TR-3Bs would arrive or exit out of. There would be lots of sensors and scientific instrumentation to allow them to detect alien spacecraft or space-based weapons to avoid.

To get Army buy in, they would reintegrate the existing Air Force back into the Army Air Corp like it was during World War Two.

To get Navy buy in, the Navy would crew up the first Space Carrier and submarine sailors were given every opportunity to convert to the Space Force since they had proven psychologically, they were best prepared to exist in long duration in isolated tight quarters and follow rigid instructions and operating guidelines.

As the President expected, General Harris was ready to show the joint chiefs artist conceptions of the new shuttle engineering as well as an artist concept of a Space Carrier. Rand Corporation artists could easily moonlight at Disney pictures, they were that talented.

Back at Area 51, Kevin O'Toole and General Whitman were stunned as it was now crystal clear why the President visited. And the problem is the President had been exposed to their operation and if anyone got in the President's way of a Space Force, they feared the disclosure that might occur after bloody infighting.

The administration lobbied Congress to reestablish the Space Shuttle Program and refurbish the last two Space Shuttles flown. It was going to be very expensive since the skin of the craft needed ripped off and changed as well as the internal electronics and cabling.

The current space program that was building a four-seat space craft to continue man space flight benefitted the new shuttle program computers, displays, and flight controls could all receive a tech refresh using the same hardware that was going into this new space capsule.

The same display technology used in the Boeing 787 Dreamliner and IBM's G6 processors were the heart of the *new glass* used for flight controls. Even though the technology was considered slightly obsolete, it was radiation hardened for space operations. And even though it didn't run any faster than home computers, NASA scientists and engineers were well versed on programming these devices using fault tolerant coding.

Mission packages flown had plugins that allowed more advanced processors. But the flight controls and basic ship's operation and control were running on the IBM G6 processors for proven reliability and radiation hardening allowing space operations without fear of damage by cosmic rays.

The whole Space Force program relied on the President's popularity. If the opposing political party took back the White House, no doubt the United States Space Force would become a farce and canceled. Most of the Air Force and parts of the Navy were strongly opposed. The Navy was dissatisfied that anything that touches space including Trident Missiles would belong to the USSF.

NASA and the military who would utilize stretch shuttles to take satellites up into orbit and train crews that would be necessary to fly the stretch shuttles as they were now secretly under construction with a black project.

<u>EXT. CGI. DAY VANDENBERG SPACE CENTER STRETCH SHUTTLE LAUNCH</u>

VOICE OVER
DURING STRETCH SHUTTLE LAUNCH
The very first stretch shuttle would be launched from Vandenburg overlooking the Pacific Ocean because the base was so huge, it was far simpler to compartmentalize it at that location.

The new stretch shuttles were almost four hundred feet tall standing erect weighing almost nine million pounds with the attached fuel tank full.

The thrust of the standard solid rocket boosters was estimated at 2.8 million lbf. Under maximum load with eight boosters during an expected steel and aluminum shipment would put out 22.4 million pounds of thrust. Upgraded engines that burned the liquid fuel supplied by the large, attached fuel tanks provided five million lbf.

Ten legacy shuttle flights occurred before a stretch shuttle launched. The materials delivered in space on the initial legacy flights provided framing material and the foundation for a Space Dock.

It was imperative the first space carrier built in space was built in an enclosure to prevent potential adversaries to copy or steal the design. The first stretch shuttles brought up habitat and Space Dock materials. The most spectacular aspect of this activity was all the spacewalks required to put together all the prefabricated pieces.

EXT. CGI. DARKNESS SPACE DOCK CONTSTRUCTION

VOICE OVER
DURING ELAPSED TIME SPACE DOCK CONSTRUCTION
Welding could be done in space but drilling, cutting, and activity that created debris could not be allowed. Once the Space Dock was completed and the hull of the space carrier keel was laid, some drilling and cutting could occur in special designed habitat, but every effort was made to prefabricate everything on earth and simply bolt it together in space. All parts had to be pre-painted and finished. Dynamic sealing was obtained by the materials inserted on surfaces that mated.

A 3D mockup was built at Area 51 and Kevin O'Toole once again was able to let his presence be felt.

The President managed to move the Space Force forward slowly evolved even though bitter infighting occurred especially with interested parties in the Navy's SSBN community, ICBMs, NRO, and satellites in general.

World politics also evolved and as the Space Dock slowly neared completion, relations with the EU, Russia, and China were at an all-time low. Too many leaks occurred and had the USA not been a member of the UN Security Council to veto attempts to internationalize the Space Dock, the first Space Carrier would never have been built.

Propulsion for the Space Carrier was one of the most acute issues confronted. Eventually a nuclear reactor to superheat Hydrogen became part of the prime mover. Electrical generation was provided by a modularized nuclear reactor that having a stretch shuttle made possible to implement. These highly specialized metal cooled reactors had to be replaced every few years. Likewise, the prime mover received damage from shock waves and had to be replaced almost as often. Having a Space Dock made those exchanges quite simpler.

Space fighting would be different than on Earth inside an atmosphere. Since there was no atmosphere to slow down objects, kinetic weapons were very capable of destroying enemy ships. A COIL laser was also being tested with thoughts that eventually the main battery would be several banks of these lasers that would focus their beams onto one aiming spot thereby increasing the intensity of the laser shot by the summation of multiple lasers. Having a long baseline would allow some very intense projections. The only disadvantage is the space carrier would have to maneuver to put the target on the beam to inflict such an intense salvo. But thanks to modal beamforming the multiple lasers would slice through reflective surfaces.

Finally, the main purpose of the space carrier was to take TR-3B's long distance to other planetary systems that confronted the Earth with hostile intentions. Since the TR-3Bs were designed for terrestrial or outer space operations, the space carrier would never have to enter the atmosphere of a planet to deploy its offensive weaponry.

The space carriers were designed to operate outside of a planet's atmosphere and did not have the heat shield required for planetary atmospheric penetration. And by some miracle if it survived such an entry, there would be absolutely no means of launching it back out into space.

In the early years the only way to travel to the space carrier was via one of the TR-3Bs or a space shuttle. A shuttle would fly up next to the space carrier and positioned by micro rockets to a mating maneuver and when in the correct position a mating tube deployed from the space carrier down onto the top of the space shuttle where a pressurized hatch mechanism provided a personnel transfer airtight chamber. Special couplers and grippers held the shuttle in perfect alignment utilizing guide pins, so hatch seating was always perfect.

TR-3Bs on the other hand were held in place onto a conformal slot in multiple locations around the space carrier. Similar personnel transfer tubes allowed pilots and crew members to egress to and from the space carrier in individual hangar bays for each TR-3B.

Even though workers on the space carrier worked in a gravity free environment, the Space Dock was designed to be pressurized allowing workers to have simpler clothing and bolt the space carrier together. Welding was allowed in environmental chambers that had special air filtration devices. The steel and aluminum hull pieces were delivered in specially designed containers with RFID chips installed.

One Super-stretch Shuttle flight brought enough material up to provide a substantial amount of material that was all contained within the container. After the first container was delivered the shuttle returned to Earth. On subsequent trips it exchanged empty containers with supply shipments. The empty containers were full of trash and debris. All the waste products were placed in plastic containers and stacked in the containers. Since the waste product was replacing steel and aluminum, there was no concern of overloading the shuttle for the return flight. When the containers were weighed upon return, it was found that they never exceeded one half the weight of the original shipment.

Containers were delivered to the Space Dock in a rather fantastic manner. The designers were conscientious about loss of air since they had to ship up air in cylinders aboard shuttle flights. The Space Dock had a container receiver with a hatch on each end of the dock. The new container would be hoisted on a hydraulic skid above the roof level with cargo doors on the shuttle fully open. This hydraulic skid had two racetracks along each side with plunger like devices used to shove the container into the special receiver in the dock. Each container was less than one third the length of the space dock.

Starting on the third delivery, after depositing the new container on the one end, the shuttle would undock from the Space Dock and maneuver to the other end of the Space Dock and re-orientate 180 degrees using its built-in thrusters. The hatch on the other end of the container receiver and the empty or partially empty container containing trash and waste would then be pulled by the plunger device onto the racetrack where it would later be shifted into the hull of the Super Shuttle for the return flight. Once the Cargo doors were shut and a fifteen-pound air test conducted satisfactory, workers would use special tie downs to hold the container in place so it would not bounce around in turbulence during shuttle reentry and landing.

Once the container exchange was completed and the container receiver hatches shut and airtight the receiver area was re-pressurized to fifteen pounds and equalized with the rest of the Space Dock. Once all this activity was complete the tops in sections of the receiver were lifted by hydraulic actuators and subsequently the special container tops also swiveled up allowing workers to access the contents for building supplies and consumables and in some cases, supplies needed to sustain life such as oxygen, air, and other cylinders along with CO2 removal materials were delivered in these shipments.

The United States Space Force readily used John Harris as a consultant after he retired around this time. The unexpected, good news permeating out of the incensed media after the Vice President managed to win a squeaker contest for President. What John Harris knew based on the numerous private meetings he had with the former President and his at the time Vice President who had just been elected, there would not be a huge policy shift and cancelation of the United States Space Force.

The secretary of the USSF was likely to be reappointed. The new President now going through turnover and his classified briefings could be alone with John Harris in the room when he was Vice President and thus helped craft much of the bureaucracy in establishing the USSF. Picking a female and the Secretary of the Air Force went far to disarm their political opponents. The USSF Secretary Margarette Mackworth astute in politics knew all about divide and conquer. She first went after the Navy because they were the low hanging fruit.

The Space Force Secretary knew if she offered up some tantalizing crumbs, she could garner support out of the admirals who up to then were fighting her tooth and nail. What most Americans do not know is a lot of the tactical satellites were put up by the Navy to support their nuclear submarine fleet as well as carrier battle groups and Tomahawk missile deployment. Those being classified as payloads were never in the press. The only information the public relations officers gave to the press was simply that they were classified missions and that was the end of the discussion.

Some of the early space shuttle missions before the program was initially canceled during one of the previous administrations to divert funds to social programs were those classified missions putting up Navy satellites.

The USSF signed a MOA with the Navy that stated the Navy would continue in leadership roles in developing future satellites even though the launch vehicles were USSF assets and the USSF had the final signatures on all launches or design approval.

Another carrot given to the Navy was the submarines, carriers, and ships that launched weapons and devices that went into space would be manned and maintained in the Navy's chain of command. The missiles and space weapons would however belong to the USSF including all logistics.

The Navy at this point was still fighting the USSF with brass knuckles. No inter-service rivalry ever existed to this extent. Even during WW2 when President Roosevelt could only have the Navy or the Army alone during his weekly briefings, saw the rancor this bad. As part of FDR's policy, Navy Intel would brief him for one week, and the Army

Intel the following week and never were the two entities were to be together in the room during the briefing while FDR was present.

The USSF Secretary Margarette Mackworth was terribly underestimated. She thought things through seven chess matches in advance before she made her move. She knew one way to reduce the friction between her and the old guard from the Navy was to pit them against the Air Force in one of the most highly charged political decisions she would have to make. And that was how to man the USSF fleet.

While the CSS Alabama would be the only operating space carrier for a while, the need was only a few hundred men appointed to the crew. Being an astute commander, USSF Secretary Margarette Mackworth realized that when the alien threat manifested and Russian and Chinese military commanders understood the severe risk to the planet, besides supporting the USSF, they would financially and materially contribute vast amounts as long as the United States operated the ships in a NATO like posture with foreign crew members aboard.

To create that diversion the USSF Secretary Margarette Mackworth informed the Navy brass, that only Navy Sailors would man the first space carrier CSS Alabama. If Air Force personnel wanted to participate, they would have to transfer to the Navy and be appointed by the Navy as a member of the USN in order to partake in Space Force Space Carrier operations.

That decision heavily embittered the Air Force Generals who viewed their former Air Force Secretary as a Traitor. But as she told one of her aids: The Air Force is so mad at me now, there is not much more they can try.

USSF Secretary Margarette Mackworth guesswork worked out handsomely. She effectively split the Navy and the Air Force opposition, and the Navy was soon conquered on terms they lavished because it meant an Admiral and not a General would be at the top of the org chart. In fact, the only Air Force names on the chart were liaison positions.

The Air Force was fully humiliated, but the damage was soon to be far worse than they could ever imagine when a former Air Force Officer, General John Harris convinced the newly elected President to give the Air Force to the Army which reduced the branches of service back to the original numbers, though ostensibly the Marine Corp fell under the Navy's command.

The Army never imagined they would ever send divisions into space. The thought never crossed their planner's minds. And long before they figured it out, at John Harris suggestion, the Navy and the Marine Corp were given orders to conduct a TOP-SECRET program that would entail building several Space Carriers as Gator Freighters. Just like Amphibious Operations on Earth, they were tasked to come up with planning to support Space Operations. By the time the Army discovered this program, thanks to their spooks imbedded in the NSA at Fort Meade that could read Navy and Marine Corp Top Secret messages and emails, the organizations were too far into development to change course.

The USSF Secretary Margarette Mackworth, being an astute history buff, cooled the Army off by telling them that just like in the Pacific Battles of WW2, after the Marines cleared the beaches, Army divisions would then be sent in to do the heavy land fighting. But initially groups such as the 82nd Airborne and the 101st Airborne would be the premier Space Army sent in with a task force if the time ever came to it.

The Army, being the most conservative of the forces, realized ultimately this would be the best approach as it meant the Navy and Marine Corp would incur the most risk and force protection for Army assets would be better arranged. Hence the Army slowly recoiled its rage and stood down its ad hominem attacks. When Army top brass discovered the former USAF would be inserted in its overall org chart, they were grinning like Cheshire cats. Furthermore, the USSF Secretary Margarette Mackworth could now impose upon the Army that wanted their fair share of the *loot* to force Air Force Brass now in their org chart to stand down.

Probably the most humiliating event in modern Air Force History was when Army Brass directed their Air Force Generals to adopt to army uniforms. On top of the former Air Force Secretary a Traitor in their opinion, she had just effectively killed the Air Force. Their resistance thus quickly dissipated as the new larger organization suddenly had synergism like they never imagined because of the new organization.

The U.S. Army had the largest air force in the world and the greatest number of pilots because of their vast number of helicopter squadrons. Airborne divisions were re-engineered by General Kinnard who, during the Vietnam War, pioneered the airmobile concept of sending troops into battle using helicopters. Along with the 82nd Airborne and other airborne troops helicopter ferried, so did regular army units. Hence the number of pilots' verses combat troops for the Army was substantially higher than any other service.

Training a combat helicopter pilot to fly an airplane is considerably easier than teaching a fighter pilot or cargo plane pilot to fly combat helicopters. As such Army planners realized flight schools could be combined and initial pilot training achieved for all.

Just like Hap Arnold's bold approach to pilot training at the beginning of World War II where he knew he had to train up to ten thousand pilots a month, this new organization was poised to pump out more pilots quicker, but also cross rate them in fixed wing or rotary craft and make them more versatile. There were actually a lot of Air Force pilots who didn't mind the extra training which made them more versatile. However, a jet fighter pilot is a unique breed and would never be satisfied flying a less than Mach 1.5 airframe.

Kevin O'Toole and General Sandy Whitman eventually fell on their swords because of their long period of attempted sabotaging John Harris. Once the new President was sworn-in they both retired. Their ages were now at the point they should leave and allow some new blood in. Unlike the dastardly deed they would have done to John Harris, they were given the dignity to leave with full honors.

John Harris arrived at another meeting with the Joint Chief with the Space Force Secretary Margarette Mackworth.

JOHN HARRIS
The Navy has benefitted greatly by being given the responsibility to crew the Space Carriers. For the CSA Alabama, since only way to get there was via the Navy.

MARGARETTE MACKWORTH
The handwriting on the wall was: If you wanted to be part of the Alabama Class Space Carriers, you had to be part of the Navy.

COMMANDER OF NAVAL OPERATIONS
I never believed I would be saying this, but I am an honest man. This recruiting inducement achieved far better results than any other mechanism the Navy ever attempted.

MARGARETTE MACKWORTH
I think part of it is because anyone who desired to be part of the Engineering Division aboard an Alabama Class Space Carrier has to go through the Navy's Nuclear Power Program to be qualified just like on a nuclear submarine or nuclear carrier. After all that they are screened for space duty, which adds a complete layer to the onion.

COMMANDER OF NAVAL OPERATIONS
Psychological Testing revealed submarine sailors were the most ideal candidates since they are routinely isolated and subject to long missions in tight quarters.

JOHN HARRIS
Nuclear Carrier sailors didn't pan out quite as well since they had never experienced tight quarters since a Carrier is basically a floating city with numerous amenities submarine sailors are not entitled. A nuclear

Carrier sailor can see daylight every day they wish. Submarine Sailors sometimes went ninety-plus days between views of sunlight and no contact with the outside world.

MARGARETTE MACKWORTH
But now the question became: Can submarine sailors withstand two years in space?

JOHN HARRIS
What if we must send a wrecking crew a distance that took ten years, round trip?

JOHN HARRIS
Space warfare dwarfs all previous conventions of war. One big concern is that if the enemy has good surveillance systems: They can see our space carrier coming a long way away, so the element of surprise is lost.

COMMANDER OF NAVAL OPERATIONS
Let's now get to the reason why I called this meeting. The CSS Alabama has one requirement never experienced by the Navy. The commanding officer chosen will be an Admiral.

We have no choice. The commanding officer will have a dual role as task force commander as well as ship's captain.

JOHN HARRIS
Astute Navy planners want to ensure no misunderstanding of the chain of command, especially if it takes the Alabama two years to get to their destination.

COMMANDER OF NAVAL OPERATIONS
The first few years of operation were traveling around near Earth to exercise the propulsion system and work out all the bugs.

JOHN HARRIS
Because of the preliminary nature of this first Space Carrier, the USSF must avoid the start on the second

hull because we need the Space Dock available for CSS Alabama just in case some issues arose that required extensive maintenance.

COMMANDER OF NAVAL OPERATIONS
Naval Reactors NAVSEA-08 wants to replace the nuclear generators before the 2nd hull is started to make sure there would be no conceivable requirement for the Space Dock until Alabama is outfitted, certified and ready to assume long distance space operations with new and reliable power and propulsion systems.

MARGARETTE MACKWORTH
(USSF SERETARY)
Consultants have requested the two huge nuclear rocket engines also be replaced and returned to earth for extensive analysis to determine how much damage the shock waves caused.

JOHN HARRIS
Not since the 1950s had nuclear rocket engines received such intensive investigation with Project Pluto.

MARGARETTE MACKWORTH
The consultants have stated the hot hydrogen jets that were discharged out of the nuclear rocket engines shot out in an explosive release of energy above light speed could cause micro cracks like experienced in Project Pluto. I have some images on this PowerPoint I wanted to discuss.

John Harris
Let's take a look at the PowerPoint presentation.

<u>INT. CGI. PENTAGON USSF POWER POINT</u>

C.U. POWERPOINT PRESENTATION

VOICE OVER
(PowerPoint displays during voiceover)
A surreal image shown with imbedded video in the PowerPoint.

PowerPoint narrative during the recorded imbedded video:

This is video recorded by the high-speed chase rocket showing the wake of the recent fusion nuclear rocket engine test.

As you can see, it took some time for the super energized hydrogen particles to slow down below light speed as the wake diffused thanks to the sun's gravity and the very small friction in space. The acceleration achieved was more than anyone had witnessed in their lifetimes.

The differential speed between the chase rocket and the fusion nuclear powered test rocket was far less than light speed so good imagery was obtained by the chase rocket.

Now we are observing images taken from satellites and observatories had bizarre modulating results.

One might conclude the images from all these other recording platforms except for the chase rocket gave the same effect as filming a propeller driven aircraft where the propeller appears to not be moving due to the sample rate.

If sustained acceleration is to be done, we believe everyone may have to wear pressure suits and lie down in their launch baskets or remain strapped in. The alternative was preferred, which also used a lot less fuel, a slow and gradual acceleration that could take weeks. But that may not be permissible in combat situations.

The calculations we could not fly above light speed was proven invalid with this experimentation.

What we have discovered is that in a true vacuum away from a solar system in deep space where there might only be one hydrogen atom per twenty cubic yards and away from gravity fields, we can travel much faster than presently assumed by Einstein equations.

Hence, when there is no appreciable friction and there was no resistance to acceleration the body may travel faster than the speed of light.

In essence there was no speed limit. The limiting factor was how much fuel you had on board for acceleration and later slowing down.

This rocket moving outside of gravity fields in deep space demonstrates the space craft has no relative velocity.

$$E = MC^{(\sqrt{-1})} \qquad \textbf{also written as} \qquad E = MC^{(i)}$$

Therefore E-MC² does not apply because C² is relatively nulled out in the vacuum of space away from gravity fields. Which means the result is E=MC² transforms to the number:

The possible top speed estimates of CSS Alabama is classified TOP-SECRET NOFORN Q, J, X, W, L which were special additional codes required to see the information. Plus, top speed can only be estimated since no actual flights occurred to prove what top velocity could be obtained.

The Relative Velocity Formulae E-MC⁽ⁱ⁾ will revolutionize science and create a whole new branch of study. Thanks to the results of the chase rocket approached by the test rocket while it flew more than one half-light speed that was already on course and vector when the test rocket came flying by with a relative velocity below light speed, we now have new science to ponder.

Incredible insights were discovered as we filmed a craft flying much faster than the speed of light because the relative speed and the calculated Doppler manifested a dataset that would give a lot of mathematicians and theoretical scientists much to think about and try to come to grips of how this all worked out. In some cases, scientists would claim it was a form of warp drive.

Director and staff please review these web sources:

Are Warp Drives Possible? (feat Dr. Miguel Alcubierre) (youtube.com)

Warp drive - Wikipedia

Miguel Alcubierre - Wikipedia

Zefram Cochrane - Wikipedia

Artificial Gravity (youtube.com)

Even measuring stars to calculate position in space will be nearly impossible since the space time distortion from excessive velocities creates what appears to be a curving of space time as a result. The best one could figure out would be how many revolutions a large planet like Jupiter made around the sun during the transit.

CSS ALABAMA COMMANDING OFFICER SELECTION

One of the issues in picking an Admiral to command CSS Alabama centered around the person's age. Due to the rigors of space, the typical fifty-year-old fleet admiral was his health. John Harris was called to a meeting with the New President just sworn in and USSF Secretary Margarette Mackworth.

JOHN HARRIS
Mr. President, I just reviewed the list of all the CSS Alabama Commanding officer candidates. USSF Secretary Margarette Mackworth.

USSF SECRETARY MARGARETTE MACKWORTH.
Their biographies are attached to each of these reports the FBI did on each one of them. Unfortunately, every one of them was over fifty years old.

PRESIDENT
What do you think?

JOHN HARRIS

Mr. President, I think what Secretary Mackworth is getting at is all of these admirals are too old for the assignment.

PRESIDENT

The Navy says these are their best leaders.

JOHN HARRIS

They may be great leaders, but it doesn't do us much good if he croaks a year from now halfway to the assigned battle space.

PRESIDENT

What do you suggest?

JOHN HARRIS

Contact the Navy, tell them we are also looking for a good executive officer and we want a list of fifty names of volunteers at the age of forty to forty-five whom they consider the finest officers in this age group. Then we select the guy from that group, and you immediately promote him to admiral, and we make him the CSS Alabama's Commanding Officer.

PRESIDENT

The Navy will counter that with their typical political BS.

JOHN HARRIS

You need to remind the Navy that in 1942 they had to relieve twenty-four commanding officers on their submarines who were ineffective and replace them with much younger commanders. The old guard isn't physically poised to be on special craft like a submarine or a Space Carrier in time of war.

PRESIDENT

John, what I like about you is you know your history well.

JOHN HARRIS

If you do not know the history, you might do the same follies.

PRESIDENT
What if we appoint a female?"

USSF SECRETARY MARGARETTE MACKWORTH
Ultimately as we build a fleet, we will no doubt have female commanding officers, but for the first ship, I strongly recommend we select a male because if we select a female and must go heavy handed on her, there will be an outcry that we are not being fair. If we pick a guy and must take adverse actions against him for some random reason, there would not be the political sex aspect of it.

PRESIDENT
You think there could be a time where we may have to use punitive renditions against our Admiral?

USSF SECRETARY MARGARETTE MACKWORTH
Yes, what if Earth's survival depends on sending the space carrier to another planet to annihilate it killing billions of aliens and the admiral has some ethical or moral objection?

PRESIDENT
I see your point there.

JOHN HARRIS
I support the Madam Secretary in her viewpoint. We need a person we know we can confidently depend on who will do as we direct him. Remember all the Generals Abe Lincoln had to fire until he selected General Grant?

The process evolved and, in a few weeks, a handsome and distinguished-looking man was ushered into Space Force Secretary's office where John Harris and a couple Admirals sat at a long table. The Admirals were not happy, they fought this selection process to the bitter end because they didn't like the outcome picking a young whipper snapper Captain Tom Gilbert.

Tom Gilbert, a nuclear physics trained sailor with his Master's degree from MIT, rose swiftly in the submarine force, obtaining the promotion to commanding officer of a new type of submarine that was replacing the Virginia Class. This capable vessel was designed to sustain 150 miles per hour submerged speed.

Even though the cold war was over, and USA and Russia no longer had visceral opposition towards each other, the explosion of drug trafficking by the cartel using conventional submarines secretly purchased from North Korea, Cuba, and a few other places made it almost impossible to find them and stop them.

Advanced rocket propelled heavyweight torpedo's shot from the new *San Diego Class SSNs* was starting to slowly take down the drug cartel that had achieved addicting 33 percent of all high school students in America to sophisticated synthetic drugs. The torpedo's traveling at speeds more than 200 knots could be fired 100 miles away from the target.

Tom Gilbert rose fast through the ranks as he mastered and helped design the guidelines of finding and sinking cartel submarines, sometimes operating along the coast of Central and South America. They were also sunk off China with large quantities of Heroin shipped out of Myanmar (formerly known as Burma).

These two gruffly Admirals were extremely agitated by this officer who had a reputation as a drunk and womanizer made the selection board, and worse yet, upset that John Harris looked so favorably upon him. But John Harris informed the New President in a private meeting between him and the USSF Secretary Margarette Mackworth his concerns about age and combat experience.

JOHN HARRIS

If we calculate the types of exigencies the CSS Alabama may soon be facing and appointing a clean-cut Boy Scout with no real combat experience on a major naval vessel is too risky.

PRESIDENT

John, that's what these admirals are advocating.

JOHN HARRIS

Mr. President, we need proven leadership. Captain Gilbert sank over a dozen drug cartel submarines. No skipper since World War Two has such a distinguished combat record. Plus, he's only forty-three years old and in great physical condition.

PRESIDENT

The report says he's a boozer and a lady's man.

JOHN HARRIS

The report minimizes some of the tangibles, he works out in the gym every day and runs ten miles three times a week at speeds a professional athlete can go. His medical record indicates his physical condition is significantly better than people his age.

PRESIDENT
What about his reputation as a womanizer?

JOHN HARRIS
He's unmarried, women are attracted to him, he's good-looking and suave.

PRESIDENT
No doubt he's a sophisticated charming man whom worldly travels and experiences created a debonair that breaks a lot of hearts, but in all his professional positions he's maintained a strict polished appearance.

USSF SECRETARY MARGARETTE MACKWORTH
Captain Gilbert is poised and dignified, and his submarine reenlisted far more crew members than any other in the fleet. According to the small print, Captain Gilbert has demonstrated he can motivate his troops. He has the strong leadership we need when sending the Alabama out on what might be considered impossible odds.

On that fateful day when Tom Gilbert sat at the table with the Four-Star Admirals, John Harris, USSF Secretary Margarette Mackworth, and the newly elected President, he realized the enormity of what he was now facing.

Captain Tom Gilbert initially emailed his interest in the XO position for CSA Alabama. Then after a few committee meetings in the selection boards, he was ushered into a room with John Harris and the Space Force Secretary for a meeting where he was duly informed what really was going on.

JOHN HARRIS
Captain Gilbert, we are going to inform you that you are in the final group for selection and will go before one more panel before your selection if you are chosen for the CSS Alabama. Now that you have come this far and this is near the end, we are now going to confide in you the real nature of your assignment.

CAPTAIN GILBERT
Are you going to tell me this has nothing to do with space?

At this point in time the President and the Space Force Secretary were on pins and needles because this was such an enormous challenge. They were letting John Harris be the master of ceremonies because they knew he would always steer the right as he has always shown in the past.

JOHN HARRIS
Captain Gilbert, this is for assignment to the first crew we are organizing, just like we have advertised, but there is a matter we now will divulge to you that we have kept silent about due to serious political reasons and the nature of what we are doing to obtain the best people possible, so now we will disclose to you, aspects of the job you have not been privy too.

CAPTAIN GILBERT
I understand the XO is the chief administrator of a vessel and does the day-to-day operations and the CO has all the authority.

JOHN HARRIS
Captain let us be frank.

John Harris then nodded towards the Space Force Secretary Mackworth.

USSF SECRETARY MARGARETTE MACKWORTH
We could not announce the real position description because we wanted to avoid dirty politics and be forced to select a person, we felt was too old for the job.

CAPTAIN GILBERT
I see.

USSF SECRETARY MARGARETTE MACKWORTH
Captain, you are not interviewing for the XO selection. You are in fact interviewing for the Commanding Officer's position.

Tom Gilbert sat stunned for a while. He knew the fact he was sitting in front of the United States Space Force Secretary meant his chances were probably good. Chills went down his spine as he suddenly realized the consequences to what was now unfolding.

CAPTAIN GILBERT
I'm not sure I'm worthy of such an assignment.

JOHN HARRIS

Captain, we have studied you in detail. We apologize for having to go through the process this way, but you as a seasoned Naval Officer know the pecking order and dirty politics often involved in the selection processes in the Navy.

CAPTAIN GILBERT
Yeah, it's difficult.

JOHN HARRIS

We view the rigors of this assignment are too great for a fifty-year old and thus have decided a man of your age is far better physically ready to do the job.

Tom Gilbert looked gravely into John Harris' face analyzing every word he said. The emotions were intensified. The shock was enormous, and the perplexities now created a charged atmosphere that had almost the same intensity as he remembered when he stood in his San Diego class SSN shooting that heavyweight torpedo at a former Chinese submarine loaded with Heroin destined to destroy the lives of a lot of American children.

Tom daydreamed for a minute, remembering his experience through a temporal flashback.

FLASHBACK

<u>EXT. CGI EVENING ROMEO CLASS SUBMARINE ON THE SURFACE TRANSITING</u>

VOICE OVER

Tom Guilbert's San Diego class SSN position was in very close distance to Chinese submarines and surface ships. If they somehow got the notion, he was shooting at them, there would be a real battle. So, his option was to sink the Romeo class submarine (known as Soviet Project 633) and get the hell away from Hainan Island as soon as possible.

In just the past few hours, the American submarine had reconnoitered Sanya Hainan port area through photonics mast making sure the few Chinese Naval assets in the area were still moored in port and would not be a threat to them as he waited for the old Romeo class submarine to come by so they could ambush it.

Part of mission planning required the San Diego Class submarine shoot in a southerly direction in case there was a torpedo malfunction, they didn't want to give the Chinese a working model of their newest fleet heavyweight torpedo that was the first major torpedo design since the MK-48 ADCAP.

Based on Intel reports the Romeo class diesel submarine would most likely be transiting on the surface at night coming by in less than an hour as Commander Gilbert positioned the submarine for the attack.

The Romeo had a former Chinese sonar operator and acoustic homing torpedoes so it could fight back, but on the surface transiting at 15 knots near its max speed, it had so much flow noise and mechanical propulsion noise, the Romeo's Passive sonar was severely degraded.

There would be virtually no possibility of the Romeo detecting the San Diego Class SSGN. Sonar soon reported a sonar contact S69 (Sierra 69) and based on tri-range from the towed array estimated it was one hundred and five thousand yards away and closing.

Sonar technicians manning the automated AN/BQQ-49 sonar system estimated the Romeo's speed 15 knots due to statistics on the noise created by the Romeo class submarine six bladed propellers. That speed estimate was soon checked with the chart as the BYG-33 Fire Control system gave a speed estimate of 15 knots and a course of 095 degrees.

One hundred and five thousand yards thousand yards was beyond the horizon, so periscope confirmation was not possible for a while. But the cool and calm Tom Gilbert patiently waited as he roamed around the control room asking poignant questions of the fire control operators and the sonar techs.

The ultra-high speed San Diego Class SSN remained at periscope depth so that visual and electronic surveillance could be maintained. The spooks on board were monitoring communications intercepts to make sure nobody had detected their San Diego Class SSN. All was quiet as the resort area of Hainan Island was going about its business in the late hours where the only activity was late night clubs and dancing.

At the present course and speed the Romeo Class Submarine would pass around thirty-five thousand yards south of Hainan Island meaning it would be beyond the horizon of anyone observing the attack from land.

Transiting at 15 knots, it took a while for the Romeo class submarine to come within visual range. This attack was to be made at night for a variety of reasons.

As the Romeo class submarine approached the attack point it got louder and soon through the infrared, they visually spotted the drug traffickers Romeo class submarine on the horizon at around twenty-four thousand yards running on the surface thanks to the new model non penetrating HIGH BOY periscope system as the Romeo class submarine continued to approach.

The HIGH BOY periscope was one of three fully automated periscopes installed on San Diego Class SSN's that operated via a new super lightweight telescoping multi lens system. No hydraulics were involved. The telescoping deployment action was accomplished by high pressure air.

The Brilliant engineers at NUWC Newport RI. Came up with a novel telescoping periscope that used very light weight digital lenses from Apple I-phones that was raised 40 feet into the air higher than all previous periscopes designed for open ocean long distance reconnaissance. They were not recommended to be used near the 12-mile limit where the two other periscopes were sufficient.

If there was any remorse on the submarine for the ambush and killing all those men on that submarine, it was tempered by the fact they were poisoning America's kids with powerful synthetic drugs like Fentanyl and in many cases inducing deaths by overdose. All is fair in love and war and when some *son of a bitch* is poisoning your kids.

Commander Gilbert (at the time) made a couple course changes to help generate the mathematical solution to the target. Even though these new acoustic seeking torpedoes only needed to be sent in the general direction and they would find and sink the target.

Commanding Officer, Tom Gilbert didn't want to accidentally hit a surface ship that could be nearby in a shipping channel. By sending the torpedo to the exact coordinates of the target, that minimized accidental targeting the wrong ship.

The range slowly decreased and soon the Romeo class submarine was at five thousand yards. At three thousand yards, which would essentially be down the throat shot far enough away for the Romeo to not be able to hear the launch transients.

INT. SUBMARINE CONTROL ROOM (APPEARS LIKE A VIRGINIA CLASS). CONSULT YOUTUBE VIDEOS TO RECREATE OR GET THE NAVY TO ALLOW FILMING ABOARD A VIRGINIA CLASS.

The commanding officer Tom Gilbert gave the launch orders.

TOM GILBERT
Launch torpedo tube number one.

CGI. UNDER WATER SUBMARINE LAUNCHING TORPEDO 15 SECONDS

VOICE OVER

Fire control technicians sitting on the command launch console were already at STBY with a greenboard ready to shoot. The sailor lifted the protective cover and pressed the FIRE switch.

The submarine shook slightly from the hydrodynamics of the heavyweight torpedo leaving the torpedo tube. The four-thousand-pound heavy weight torpedo took thirty G's of force to impulse it out of the torpedo tube, while its rocket engine lit off pushing the torpedo at almost two hundred knots, which didn't take very long to reach its target. Just before the impact, the sonar operator started hearing a strange sound associated with Doppler from the rocket exhaust.

The Romeo Class Submarine Sonar Operator said to himself outload:

ROMEO CLASS SUBMARINE SONAR OPERATOR
Nà shì shén me guǐ dōng xī? (WTF is that?)

The Romeo class submarine sonar operator was just grabbing the microphone to report to the conning officer a fast-moving contact was approaching, and he was fearful it might be a Chinese Coast Guard ship.

The main sensor array of Project 633 was the Arktika-M sonar system (NATO code name Pike Jaw), used for submerged target tracking of surface ships and other submarines. It was supplemented by the MG-15 (MG-15 Hercules) submarine sonar system. With this combination Romeo could track targets under and above it in water.

<u>Soviet Sonars range updates · Issue #2231 · PygmalionOfCyprus/cmo-db-requests ·
GitHub</u>

The Romeo (Project 633) submarine sonar transmitters and receivers were mounted on the top, and bottom of the bow. There was also a retractable radar (NATO "Snoop Plate") close to the periscopes and working in the X-band with 80 kW, for surface search.

This new sonar system (at the time 60 years earlier) was a considerable advance compared to the previous Project 613, developed in parallel to the one fitted later on Project 641 (Foxtrot class). It offered a vastly improved target acquisition and localization. This was a long derivative of the WW2 German GHG/Balkon system, installed in a bulge under the bow. Called MG-10 Feniks-M was used for submarine detection and above it was located the MG-200 Arktika-M. This active scanning sonar, with a small underwater telephone fitted on top.

GHG, the U-boat's group listening apparatus: <u>GHG1996.pdf (cdvandt.org)</u>

Targeting data derived from sonars was sent via synchro signals to the new Leningrad fire control system, a copy of the American wartime TDC system. This was the first Soviet underwater dedicated fire control system ever fitted. It became the great standard for all soviet subs for almost twenty years.

The sail on its side contained the sonar intercept system MG-23 Svet-M which was used to detect and obtain bearings to active sonar signals.

VOICE OVER

Unlike Americans, China only wasted one bullet to the back of a drug smuggler's head. The American Navy knew the Chinese would not be too pissed if we sunk a drug boat. But they would not like it being done this close to Hainan Island.

<u>EXT. CGI. UNDER WATER TORPEDO MANUEVERS UNDER THE ROMEO CLASS SUBMARINE AND EXPLODES. 15 SECONDS</u>

The heavyweight torpedo with elaborate sonar and programmed to sink a Romeo was equipped to go under the submarine with a draft of seventeen feet. The sophisticated sonar painted the bottom of the Romeo class submarine and went directly under the middle and exploded.

<u>EXT. CGI. THE ROMEO CLASS SUBMARINE AND EXPLODES SPLITS IN HALF WITH SMALL FIREBALL. 15 SECONDS</u>

The thousand-pound HBXG explosive on the heavyweight torpedo designed to sink any ship in the world including the new Chinese Aircraft Carriers with one shot, ripped the submarine in half and flung each half almost one hundred feet into the air. As the Romeo settled back down in the water it sank completely in thirty seconds leaving behind a small oil spill from the diesel stored in the fuel tanks.

<u>EXT. CGI. THE SAN DIEGO CLASS SSN GOING DEEPER AT AN ANGLE AND SPEEDING UP. 15 SECONDS</u>

Note: concerning the San Diego Class SSN. This class of submarine does not exist. It's purely fictional. For the CGI Developers. USE most of the Virginia class submarine design for the video with the exception of the stern area. Here's a picture.

Virginia Class SSN

SAN DIEGO CLASS SSN LAUNCHING WEAPON

The rear of the submarine will have a new X design rudder and stern planes which is now being incorporated into the new Columbia Class SSBN submarines:

Tom Gilbert gave a depth and speed order and lowered the scope and all mast and antennae as the stealthy submarine slowly slipped down to 1700 feet, where he would run quiet for a while before he kicked it in high speed and relocated towards Vietnam where they were invited a port visit to Cam Ranh Bay.

Tom's attention was slowly snapped back to reality as John Harris asked a question.

JOHN HARRIS
Captain Gilbert, are you ready for the challenge?

John Harris made the requirement that all prospective candidates go through weightless training and psychological assessment before they were allowed to continue the selection process. As part of the secret weightless training, they were taken out in space aboard a shuttle where they lived for a few days to give them a taste of space life. Using the restroom on a spaceship wasn't the same as on a ship to say the least! Tom Gilbert went through all that with no issues.

TOM GILBERT
Mr. Harris, I wasn't planning on being the ship's CO, though as the XO I understand if something happened to the CO I would be put in charge.

JOHN HARRIS
Captain Gilbert, do you want the job, and do you think you can handle it?

TOM GILBERT
Mr. Harris, this is a totally different situation than I expected. I'm not saying I can't do it, but in all candors, I can't honestly tell you I feel the zeal for the job like I did the XO assignment because quite frankly I have not had much time to think about it.

USSF SECRETARY MARGARETTE MACKWORTH
Captain Gilbert, that's why we wanted to meet with you today to give you ample time to consider before you go before the final board.

TOM GILBERT
Thank you, Madam Secretary, I appreciate your consideration.

USSF SECRETARY MARGARETTE MACKWORTH
Captain Gilbert, Right now, there are only three finalists which includes yourself. The other two now know the Commanding Officer assignment is what these proceedings are about.

TOM GILBERT
When would I expect to go through the final board?

USSF SECRETARY MARGARETTE MACKWORTH
You are now scheduled to attend that board two weeks from today.

TOM GILBERT
I see.

JOHN HARRIS
Will you be ready to accept such an assignment two weeks from now if the panel chooses you?

TOM GILBERT
Yes sir, if I decide I want this assignment, I will know by the time I am at that board.

JOHN HARRIS
Very well, Captain Gilbert, we are looking forward to seeing you during that board. We do not have any questions for you today.

TOM GILBERT
Alright, I appreciate you setting the record straight with me today.

JOHN HARRIS
The main reason for this meeting was to inform you what this assignment is about so that you would not go into that final board and be put on the spot.

TOM GILBERT
I do appreciate you giving me two weeks to think about it since there comes a lot of responsibility with such an assignment.

JOHN HARRIS
We apologize we had to do this maneuver but we

needed to deal with the possibility of politics entering the fray. This meeting is highly confidential. Please do not discuss it with anyone.

TOM GILBERT
Understand all. I appreciate that, Mr. Harris.

USSF SECRETARY MARGARETTE MACKWORTH
Very well, Captain Gilbert, that's all for now, thank you for stopping by.

TOM GILBERT
You're very welcome.

Captain Gilbert got up, shook hands with Madam Secretary and John Harris, then turned and walked out the door with his head slightly dazzled at the significance of what just transformed.

VOICE OVER
(While the video shows Captain Gilbert leaving the room.) Looking at the overall picture, Tom Gilbert realized that even if he didn't get selected for the CSS Alabama CO position, he would still be in an excellent position for the XO position.

The thought crossed Tom Gilbert's mind that of the three finalists there were two excellent opportunities. Using simple math, he had a 66-percent probability of getting the job he wanted or one better. Tom Gilbert then said to himself, *"I think I will celebrate by going on a ten-mile run."*

John Harris, a History Buff knew FDR selected Admiral King during *World War Two* for the role of the head of the Navy. John Harris had, the President's ear, knew it would be best to get the best leader possible for the job, but at the same time personal health mattered. That's why a 50-year-old wasn't suitable to start out the Space Carrier Project.

Admiral King was an alleged boozer and womanizer as well. But just as soon as FDR selected him for his critical role for the Navy, he gave up the booze and the women and concentrated on his job and thus became one of the most successful admirals in naval history during a time of severe crisis.

Likewise, when President Abraham Lincoln chose General Grant to head the Army, who had a similar reputation, Grant's results confronting Robert E. Lee in subsequent battles were spectacular. Unfortunately, Grant was not able to lead America as President as well as he led the Army. As far as John Harris was concerned, Tom Gilbert was another General Grant, and he expected the same results with the CSS Alabama.

VOICE OVER

The Final Board comprising the President, Secretary of the Space Force, Special Assistant to the President, John Harris, and two Admirals; Commander of Naval Operations and the four-star admiral head of Naval Reactors, met in a secret room in the bowels of the Pentagon.

The two admirals were upset they could not reject all three candidates. The President gave them no wiggle room. They could only do one thing and that was a vote for one of the three.

Candidate number one was wrangled over he had no combat experience. But his logistics expertise was awesome.

Candidate number two received sharp criticism that he had been mainly an *Airdale* and flown a lot of planes in combat missions but had no big ship command experience.

Candidate number three received strong rebuke from the two admirals over his reported womanizing and boozing. Even though he had never received a reported incident, one of his former commanding officers almost ruined Tom Gilbert's career by embellishing how bad the problem was.

It was clear his former CO truly disliked Tom Gilbert and none of them knew he was jealous because his wife would always flirt with Tom whenever she got a chance. And if her husband was ever gone and she became a Westpac Widow, she would have sought out Tom for some happy time.

With all three candidates sitting in another room, it was time to vote on the choice. Out of respect for the Navy and the military, the President started the procedure in a way he knew would make the admirals happy.

PRESIDENT
Gentlemen, I want to give our two distinguished
Admirals the opportunity to vote first for your choice
of who should be the first CSS Alabama Commander.

The Commander of Naval Operations (CNO), being senior military person present started first.

CNO
Of the three, I think candidate number one is the best pick.

Chief of Naval Reactors spoke second. Chief of Naval Reactors had a dual role as Naval Sea Systems Command (SEA 08) and Chief of Naval Operations for Naval Nuclear Propulsion (Code N00N).

The second admiral, Chief of Naval Reactors (CNR), wore Dolphins and was a former submarine Commanding Officer. CNR also wore Navy Diver pin, wore a strategic missile patrol pin with a row of stars on it. He also had some interesting awards: a Presidential Unit Citation (3 awards), the Defense Distinguished Service Medal, the Navy Distinguished Service Medal, the Legion of Merit (3 awards), Navy Expeditionary Medal (four awards), had been the Engineer on a new Aircraft Carrier delivered to the Navy.

CHIEF OF NAVAL REACTORS
I do not like the number-one choice in that he's a
logistics type and has no combat experience. I believe
there is no substitute for the taste of war to temper a
leader's judgement, especially if he has a lot of lives
that rely on him. I'm picking number two because he
has a lot of combat experience, and we can overcome
his lack of large ship handling experience by selecting
an XO who has been a Carrier Captain.

The President had watched John Harris in action over several years. His judgement was impeccable. He was not a selfish man and often stood back in the shadows allowing someone else to claim all the credit and accolades even though Harris was more than likely the person who made the difference. His performance at Area 51 and indoctrinating the former President while placing himself at huge political risk, exemplified the kind of insights and good unselfish judgement John Harris had.

The President would follow John Harris lead in this matter. The Space Force Secretary also felt the same about John Harris. His exemplary ideas on how to shape the Space Force and deal with the Air Force sour grapes made her life much easier. She was forever grateful for what John Harris had done for her. She trusted John Harris' judgement and like the President, would most likely vote the same way John Harris did.

Since John Harris, the President, And USSF Secretary Margarette Mackworth were military veterans with distinguished careers, the selection could not be criticized as if the selectee was picked by civilian neophytes.

The group not knowing who should vote next waited for the President to make that decision for them.

PRESIDENT
John Harris has more skin in this game than anyone. He has been consistently beneficial to me and the previous administration. Therefore, I would like John Harris to vote next.

John Harris wasted no time elucidating his remarks.

JOHN HARRIS
Admirals, I know your feelings towards Captain Gilbert, but I see his tangible qualities that may be needed as we cope with this ever-changing situation in space. I think he understands the seriousness of this assignment and over the next few years he'll be far too busy to contemplate spending time boozing or womanizing.

Captain Gilbert has real combat experience and command of a nuclear submarine that sank enemy drug cartel submarines. I think we can count on him to follow his orders even though we may have to send him and his crew in harm's way against incredible odds.

Of the three candidates only Captain Gilbert has commanded a major ship and did so in live combat, but also his ISR missions and STRIKE when we had to destroy a large terrorist base succeeded and met all expectations. Captain Gilbert knew he was going to exterminate 1000 terrorists plus some of their slaves and human traffic people used as human shields. I vote for Catain Gilbert because he has already proven he will carry out orders even knowing he's being sent to take actions that will result in a large loss of life.

John Harris then nodded at the President.

PRESIDENT
Madam Secretary, it's now your turn. We have a three-way tie.

USSF SECRETARY MARGARETTE MACKWORTH
Mr. President, Admirals, Mr. Harris, I concur with the remarks towards candidate number three by everyone, but in evaluating what is best for the United States Space Force as we embark upon this rather extraordinary venture in space, I want to start out with what I consider the best of breed in this horse race, and I see Captain Gilbert as the person I want to nominate for the CSS Alabama's Captain and Task Force Commander.

PRESIDENT
Thank you everyone for your wise comments. Madam Secretary is the tie breaker. I support her comments and thus vote for Captain Gilbert to be the first Commanding Officer of CSS Alabama. I would like the three candidates now all brought into the room so we can notify all of them of our selection.

The CNO briskly stood up.

CNO
Mr. President, let me escort them in.

PRESIDENT
Thank you, Admiral.

The CNO walked over and opened the door and looked in the other room.

CNO
Would you three gentlemen please come in?

The CNO came back to his panel seat that had a tent style placard designating his seat right next to the President and sat down. The three senior officers walked into the room and sat down at their position at the table across from the President facing him at a 90degree angle since he was setting in the CINC seat at the end of the table.

PRESIDENT
Gentlemen, our decision is final, we have just made the selection for the CSS Alabama Commanding

Offier. All of you are extremely qualified and the race
was very close. All of you received votes, but one of
you received more votes than the others. I'm pleased
to announce Rear Admiral Tom Gilbert is hereby
assigned command of CSS Alabama. I would also like
to congratulate Tom Gilbert for his promotion to Rear
Admiral.

Congress had to approve the promotion to admiral, but the President knew in advance
he had the votes because a lot of states would get a lot of pork out of the Space Force
building and supporting portions of it.

The President stood up and walked over and shook Tom Gilbert's hand.

PRESIDENT
Congratulations, Admiral Gilbert.

TOM GILBERT
Thank you, Mr. President.

The other people in the room then shook Tom's hands and congratulated him. If there
was any disappointment in the two other finalists, it wasn't showing. As soon as the
levity died down, the President made an announcement.

PRESIDENT
Would everyone please take your seats, we have a
couple more items to discuss.

This was somewhat unexpected, but John Harris and Margarette Mackworth already
knew what was coming.

PRESIDENT
Captains Riley and Avery, important people in this
room voted for you for the CO assignment. You are
well respected and even though it might not be the
assignment you were not chosen for; it was in fact
the assignment you put in for when all this began.
Assuming you still want the job, one of the two of you
will now be appointed as the Executive Officer (XO)
to CSS Alabama.

The body language of Avery and Riley presented some sort of relief and a bit of
gratitude because they were finalists in the job they had sought.

PRESIDENT
The way I would like to make the selection is to
have you two decide amongst yourself which of you
want to take the job and if there is no agreement, the
board here will now pick the XO, with another voting
member, Admiral Gilbert.

The President's guidance was outstanding in that it gave one or both a way to save
face in view of the previous selection. They looked at each other and while they were
waiting for the vote got to know each other a little better. Captain Avery knew in his
heart that Captain Riley had put far more combat skin in the game and deserved the
promotion.

Captain Avery's former work in logistics that turned a dysfunctional supply system
around may have saved the CNO's bacon a time or two, but in no way did that
prepare him for a combat role. Even though Admiral Gilbert would cover for his lack
of experience, he felt it would be immoral of him to take a promotion that Captain
Riley had earned dodging SAM missiles and harrowing escapes from numerous close
encounters during lethal air combat.

CAPTAIN AVERY
Mr. President, I'm flattered for the opportunity, which
is far more than I ever deserved, but as a career Naval
Officer who graduated from Annapolis, I share and
cherish those traits bestowed upon us by legends
such as John Paul Jones, Halsey, Nimitz, Spruance,
and others. I believe the best man for the job should
be picked and I believe Captain Riley has far more
to offer in leadership skills than I have. I thus un-
volunteer for this position and recommend Captain
Riley be assigned as XO for the CSS Alabama.

Before Captain Riley could protest and counter, the President quickly responded.

PRESIDENT
Congratulations, Captain Riley, you are hereby
appointed XO to the CSS Alabama and as such are
promoted to Commodore rank. It's good that you are
a pilot because the Commodore assignment on CSS
Alabama also makes you the commander of the Air
Wing aboard.

Commodore Riley was almost too stunned to speak as everyone rose and walked over
to congratulate him.

After a couple of minutes, the levity died down and the USSF Secretary Margarette Mackworth then made an unexpected announcement.

> USSF SECRETARY MARGARETTE MACKWORTH
> Just when you think we are all done here, I have a surprise for all of you. It's kind of ironic how the planets have aligned, and people were being fit into all the proper positions, but I failed to mention to you we have one more assignment we now must make, everyone please take a seat.

The President, USSF Secretary Margarette Mackworth, and John Harris had discussed the need to place an OIC on the Space Dock because attempting to run it from the ground at NASA headquarters was now starting to become problematic. The third-place finisher of these proceedings was going to be offered the OIC of the Space Dock. It all came out now.

> USSF SECRETARY MARGARETTE MACKWORTH
> Captain Avery, since you currently do not have a future assignment and even though the supply system needs a man of your caliber, we have far more challenges on CSS Space Dock number One. If you agree I hereby declare you as the OIC for CSS Space Dock Number One.

> CAPTAIN AVERY
> Does that mean I have to spend all my time up in space on the Space Dock?

> USSF SECRETARY MARGARETTE MACKWORTH
> No, you will have an office up there as well as down on earth and make routine trips to the Space Dock as you deem necessary to achieve smooth operation. I would guess that you would probably spend twenty five percent of your time on the space dock only to be there during critical phases such as reactor startups, docking, or undocking the Space Carrier.

> CAPTAIN AVERY
> I suppose I could live with that. I accept.

> USSF SECRETARY MARGARETTE MACKWORTH
> Very well, Captain Avery, you are now appointed OIC of Space Dock number one and as a result you are also

promoted to the rank of Commodore. You will oversee
all new construction and overhaul of any space Carrier
that goes into the Space Dock.

These three men would see a lot of each other in the future during new construction as well as future dry-docking operations.

Another wrinkle manifested right out of the starting block. The normal sea-shore rotation for Captains of large ships was three years or less. For submarines because of the excessive stress placed on commanders, their commands were reduced and in recent years limited to just two years to cover a deployment cycle. John Harris elucidated to Madam Secretary and the President one of the future staffing issues.

> JOHN HARRIS
> Admiral Gilbert will most likely have to remain the
> commanding officer for approximately six years to get
> the ship through new construction and shake down
> cruises, then the first major deployment.
>
> Should this plan be maintained it would serve the
> XO very badly because after six years he would be
> needing a lengthy rest period and would be too old
> later to command a Space Carrier.

John Harris met Commodore Riley later to have a private discussion and level with him what the forecast was and was quite surprised about his response.

> COMMODORE RILEY
> That's okay, Mr. Harris, I find more pleasure in being
> the Air Wing Commander where I can be directly
> involved in combat should that occur.

> JOHN HARRIS
> I suppose there is a silver lining in all that.

> COMMODORE RILEY
> Definitely. To control and direct a TR-3B group has
> far more excitement than being the Captain and Task
> Force Commander, especially if we end up with a fleet.

> JOHN HARRIS
> The construction of additional Space Carriers will
> occur slowly, don't expect a fleet any time soon.

3D MOCKUPS AND CONSTRUCTION

To keep the Space Carriers out of view of the public, the 3D mockup was built in Area 51. The mockup served a critical purpose. The 3D mockup was used to help figure out the design, but it was also used to check all parts and assemblies to make sure they fit correctly since modular construction was necessary to avoid a lot of welding, grinding, and industrial work in space.

The Admiral and the two Commodores spent a lot of time at the 3D mockup reviewing all the issues and discussing with engineers and scientist's various aspects of the craft. It was a colossal chore to figure out what would be necessary to provide all the necessities to sustain life for over three hundred people on missions that could initially last two years or longer.

Had the Air Force been running the program, progress would have been extremely slow if not impossible. The Navy learning how to deploy worldwide with fleets understood, you could not go alone with a carrier. You had to have escorts and refueling tankers and ships carrying munitions. To sustain carrier operations long term at sea, refueling and replenishment was a necessity. The key to success for long distance Space Carrier operations was to have drone refueling and cargo ships sent out with the space carrier.

These drones would get built after the Space Carrier was launched and started shakedown cruises within the solar system. By the time they were ready to deploy to another solar system, the drones would be ready to depart with them. Multiple drones ensured that at least some of the vital resupply material would be on hand when needed.

It did not take long to figure out by some mission planners if a high-speed transit above light speed occurred, the possibility of using drones for resupply and refueling may not be feasible. Hence, design it with a lot of automation to reduce crew size and make more space available to carry necessities. The nuclear power plants for electricity and the fusion propulsion rocket engines did not require a lot of hydrogen to create tremendous thrust. Ultimately a *Stand-Alone* platform was developed. There would be no drones planned by reconfiguring the manning and expanding automation to reduce supply requirements.

Once all the parts were fitted on the mockup and verified to fit the required installation, they were cataloged and put in containers to be lifted up to space on the Super Shuttles. Additional parts were fitted on the mockup to maintain the integrity of the mockup for future construction, but also the mockup was needed for crew training. All the systems were developed with simulators which gave the crew the artificial reality they would sense while in space. The major difference would be the weightlessness they would all sense until the super-secret Space Carrier was deployed, and artificial gravity turned on.

It was a coin toss decision whether to give artificial gravity to the crew or not, but eventually Admiral Gilbert won out the argument and by the time the Space Carrier was ready to undock it was operational. Designed for the TR-3B, an artificial gravity machine was redesigned for the Space Carrier. This comfort device was provisional.

Should the CSS Alabama encounter hostile aliens and get in a combat situation where they needed an element of stealth the artificial gravity machine would have to be turned off to eliminate the large orb like appearance it gave the ship just like the TR-3B experienced when its Artificial Gravity machine was operating. However, once counter detection was established and their presence exposed, there would be no advantage of shutting off the antigravity machine.

Therefore, their training in space during the shakedown cruise included frequent days without artificial gravity almost like a drill so that crew members would not be complacent and be able to cope with long periods without artificial gravity. The crew hoped those days would be far and few.

Unfortunately, when approaching a potential hostile planet, they could not have that bright ball lit up which could be spotted at such a long distance, the Space Carrier gave up any possible element of stealth. In those profiles there would be no artificial gravity and deceleration would have to be close to the planet meaning, everyone would be stuck in their pressure suits for a long period of time to deal with the excessive G forces the breaking action induced.

CSS ALABAMA LAUNCHES

The final day came when CSS Alabama would be launched from CSS Space Dock number one. Eleven years had passed since John Harris first met a newly elected President which resulted in what they all witnessed, the fruition of those efforts.

The President thought that such an auspicious moment deserved to have the people who were instrumental in making all this happed witness the undocking and the initial firing of the main engines. For this special moment the CSS Alabama would transit around the moon and return to the dock where experts would go aboard and check system status and determine the material condition of the space craft before it would continue doing various shakedown cruise objectives.

The President knowing how much the previous President was instrumental in starting this SPACE FORCE Project contacted him.

NEW PRESIDENT
Would you like a ride up to CSS Space Dock and
observe the launch of the CSS Alabama?

FORMER PRESIDENT
How long will it take?

NEW PRESIDENT
We can take you up there in a TR-3B we converted to
a personnel carrier and have you back home in time
for dinner.

FORMER PRESIDENT
Are medical certs required?

PRESIDENT
At your age why would you be concerned?

FORMER PRESIDENT
I'm not really.

After a few more phone calls the former President, the Commander of Naval Operations, Chief of Naval Reactors, John Harris, and the USSF Secretary Margarette Mackworth were flown to Wright Patterson Air Force Base, where they were put aboard a TR-3B shuttle craft and soon deposited up on CSS Space Dock.

EXT. CGI. SPACE TR-3B FLIES UP TO AND ATTACHES TO THE SPACE DOCK.

Space Dock operations center had a viewer port that gave an excellent view of the CSS Alabama. It was well lit so the entire Space Carrier could be observed. It was a monster size Space Dock and a monster size Space Carrier. The airtight gang plank was still attached to the Space Carrier as security sweeps were going through the ship doing last minute checks for bombs, stow-a ways or anything that might put the Space Carrier at risk.

The crew and officers had been restricted aboard for forty-eight hours as pre-underway system checks were being performed. All non-crew members had been removed for forty-eight hours while they fast cruised just like a navy ship exercising their systems and noting any malfunctions or unexplained system performance. Even though the crew should be able to do corrective maintenance on all the systems, due to the complexities and time constraints, a few tech reps could be escorted on board during these final moments, if necessary, should the crew not be able to reconcile system problems.

In addition to the crew, there were a few officials onboard as observers and safety officials. After undocking, when they powered up the nuclear-powered rocket engines, the Naval Reactors Personnel would order immediate shutdown if certain conditions gave unfavorable performance indicators. Naval Reactors had four reactors on this ship. Two for electrical generation and two propulsion reactors that superheated hydrogen that gave megawatts of energy output along with the discharge that exceeded light speed and the eerie visual effect.

Admiral Gilbert and Commodore Riley walked off the gangplank to the distinguished group to observe the undocking. The former President walked up to them and shook their hands.

FORMER PRESIDENT
Gentlemen, I wish you much success in your Space
Carrier Operation.

President addresses the former president:

PRESIDENT
Thank you, Mr. President.

Commodore Riley, who was never politically correct nor an ass kisser, then spoke.

COMMODORE RILEY
Mr. President, when you first announced the Space
Force soon after your election, you received a lot of
negative press. When I heard the news, I thought about
it for a while, and even though I'm a former fighter
pilot and someone who looked up to the Air Force,
I instantly understood your plan had a lot of merit to
it. None of this would be a reality today if you didn't
have the strong will to take on your political opponents
and make all this happen.

The former President turned and looked at John Harris then looked back at Commodore Riley and responded.

FORMER PRESIDENT
Commodore Riley, the person who really made it
possible for me to pursue the United States Space
Force was General John Harris.

The former President then moved his arm out pointing to retired General Harris who stood a few feet away, starting to show his age.

Most of the high-ranking officials knew General Harris had played a key role in the formation and development of the United States Space Force, but as the President continued, they were now made aware of aspects of the development few knew about:

FORMER PRESIDENT
What you don't know is how much personal courage
it took for General Harris to facilitate me moving into
this Space Force. Because of interservice rivalry and
some skullduggery, General Harris received a lot of
personal grief from the establishment that wanted to
maintain the status quo. Without the personal sacrifice
and risk, he took, the Space Force would never have
originated.

Commodore Avery standing next to retired General Harris turned to him.

COMMODORE AVERY
General Harris, I am honored to be by your side.

John Harris appeared in the most somber mood as he reacted to Commodore Avery.

JOHN HARRIS
I'm nobody special, I was just doing my job, looking
out for our future and the safety of our citizens.

Admiral Gilbert followed by Commodore Riley stepped towards John Harris and
shook his hand.

ADMIRAL GILBERT
Thank you for taking the time to come to the launch.

JOHN HARRIS
I wouldn't miss it for anything.

About that time the CNO and Naval Reactors Admirals stepped forward and shook
John Harris' hand.

CNO
General, it's also clear to me you had very good
judgement in how you voted for the manning of this
ship. I learned a lot from you in the process.

JOHN HARRIS
Well, Admiral, during the interview process and in the
FBI investigations, I learned a lot about these men,
and we are lucky we had such outstanding candidates
to choose from.

At this time an alarm went off and blue flashing lights along the Space Dock started blinking.

CNO
Looks like they are depressurizing the Space Dock. .

COMMODORE AVERY
Yes, we'll try to salvage as much of the air as possible to limit the amount of resupply we need for the next docking.

ADMIRAL GILBERT
We must get back aboard now. The Space Dock crew will be wanting to disconnect the airlock gangway soon.

FORMER PRESIDENT
Good luck, Admiral.

Admiral Gilbert and the remaining crew members marched smartly to the gangway and into the Space Carrier to prepare for departure.

Immediately afterwards the hatch slowly closed under hydraulic action before locking pins would lock it in place fully sealed. CSS Alabama would now be pressurized to sixteen pounds to allow one last air tightness check before they commenced the undocking sequence in case there was a problem not discovered with a leak before the gangplank tunnel was to be retracted. Access doors on each end were shut in case there were possible air leaks.

The air inside the gangplank was sucked out by an air pump system creating a near vacuum to allow the retraction so that there would be no risk of the Space Carrier crashing into it as it receded inside the Teflon covered bumpers that prevented the Space Carrier hull from touching the Space Dock.

Within fifteen minutes, atmospheric monitors indicated the Space Dock had reached a level of vacuum where salvaging and recycling the remaining air would no longer be cost effective.

Purple lights started flashing indicating full equalization of the Space Dock was now occurring, all conditions were normal as expected. Finally, the purple and blue lights went out and green lights came on and the order was given to open the Space Dock hatches. One might think these huge hatches were like hangar doors, but they were sophisticated devices that were designed to facilitate air tightness. No loose material was allowed in the Space Dock during launch. Every inch had been inspected which meant there could be nothing possibly to interfere with the undocking.

An expected warning that was discussed during the undocking conference a few hours prior soon came over the Space Dock public announcer system.

PUBLIC ANNOUNCING SYSTEM
All artificial gravity will now be turned off during the Carrier Launch. Crew Members are asked to not move around until undocking is completed.

The distinguished visitors were in the closed observation room and were taken their designated seats and in accordance with the coordinator, had engaged their seatbelts which held them onto the chairs for the duration of the launch while no gravity existed in a few minutes.

INT CSS ALABAMA OBSERVATION ROOM SIDE VIEWS OF THE GUESTS.

INT. CGI. COMPOSIT VIEW: CGI AND COMBINNED VIEW SHOWING GUESTS LOOKING THROUGH WINDOW AT THE CSS ALABAMA LEAVING SPACE DOCK

EXT. CGI. CSS ALABAMA LEAVING SPACE DOCK

Now fully in a vacuum with no gravity, the Space Carrier could move without much force. At each end of the Space Carrier, small jets existed that could provide short fast blasts of high intensity thrust that could vary from milliseconds to seconds. The inertia navigation system measured velocity in three dimensions real time. Computer algorithms could correct ships' velocity in the three dimensions at a millisecond rate.

CAPTAIN GILBERT
(REFERRED TO AS SHIPS CAPTAIN WITH RANK OF ADMIRAL)
All hands, this is the captain speaking. We will now commence undocking. Pay attention to all indicators and controls you are responsible for. If any issues are discovered make your reports to the control room to Chief of the Watch immediately.

NAVIGATOR
Captain, the ship is ready to undock in fully automatic mode.

CAPTAIN GILBERT
Navigator, initiate undocking sequence.

NAVIGATOR
Initiate undocking sequence, Captain aye.

<u>C.U. NVIGATION DISPLAY.</u>

<u>BACKGROUND MUSIC:</u> Richard Wagner - Ride of The Valkyries (youtube.com)

The Navigator had the undocking sequence display on his Navigational display that showed the CSS Alabama three-dimensional replica in the space dock augmented by artificial intelligence created CGI in a 2000-foot scaled image taking up ½ the screen. A casual observer would think this was the real CSS Alabama and Space Dock image and not CGI created by AI.

The Navigator clicked on the [ACCEPT] icon on maneuvering controls and the automatic sequence started.

Small jet blasts started the Space Carrier moving. CSS Alabama now started moving as undocking commenced.

NAVIGATOR
CAPTAIN, the ship is moving one foot per 10 seconds
in accordance with automated undocking guidelines.

CAPTAIN GILBERT
Very well Navigator.

CSS Alabama continued moving at that rate until the next acceleration was initiated by the ship's computers as it calculated position and velocity. Thanks to laser measurements the Space Dock and the Space Carrier knew precisely where the Carrier was always positioned which further allowed a high precision movement out of the Space Dock to eliminate any possibility of damage to the high-tech hull.

After the next blast of the rear navigation thrusters, the Space Carrier increased speed.

NAVIGATOR
CAPTAIN, the ship is moving one foot per 5-seconds
in accordance with automated undocking guidelines.

CAPTAIN GILBERT
Very well Navigator.

 The laser alignment tools which kept close monitoring of position of the Space Carrier provided the GUI the ship's navigator monitored to determine where in the cradle the Space Carrier position was. Currently the Carrier continued right in the middle of the track the profiler tracker reported.

<u>EXT. CGI. SPACE CSS ALABAMA LEAVING SPACE DOCK</u>

After the movement of ten feet there was another sequence of thrusters and the CSS Alabama increased speed.

NAVIGATOR
CAPTAIN, the ship is moving one foot per 2-seconds in accordance with automated undocking guidelines.

CAPTAIN GILBERT
Very well Navigator.

The CSS Alabama continued moving in perfect alignment according to the laser measurements. At the fifty-foot mark, another thruster blast and the Alabama was moving two feet a second. The ship maintained this velocity which was within the safety margin to prevent damage to the hull in case a thruster didn't perform correctly.

At two feet per second, it took a while for the 1100-foot-long Space Carrier to completely leave the Space Dock. As soon as the CSS Alabama was slowly moving away from the Space Dock, the navigator announced:

NAVIGATOR
Captain we are at a safe distance to turn the ship in preparation to launch profile requirements.

CAPTAIN GILBERT
Navigator, perform necessary maneuvers in accordance with SPACE TRIAL AGANDA.

NAVIGATOR
Perform necessary maneuvers in accordance with SPACE TRIAL AGANDA, Captain aye.

VOICE OVER
Admiral Gilbert and Commodore Riley worked very hard to determine what needed to be accomplished during the first SPACE TRIAL. Now came the moment when John Harris was able to see the great benefit of having a former submarine commanding officer leading the SPACE TRIALS.

Nuclear submarines are complex machines. The new San Diego Class SSN eclipsed any submarine technology ever attempted before. As such Tom Gilbert years before on several submarines he served on was doing the same exact event as he did on his submarine accomplishing Submarine Sea Trials Agenda, that was full of risk and required great efforts by the crew to demonstrate to NAVSEA REPS riding Alpha and Bravo trials, the ship should be delivered from Electric Boat to the Navy.

Submarine Sea Trials was truly a remarkable evolution that had months of planning and execution including dealing with NAVSEA 08 Naval Reactors. Anyone who thought NAVSEA 08 got lax after Rickover left, were fools. The head of Naval Reactors since demonstrated routinely they are hard ass admirals who would never allow anyone to cut corners. Nor would they hesitate to relieve a Commanding Officer who placed the nuclear reactor in peril due to mishandling the submarine and placing it in a dangerous scenario.

Tom Gilbert survived NAVSEA 08 thorough examinations with above average score cards. Likewise, when the INSURV teams or the nuclear certification NTPI teams arrived to certify the submarine to allow them to deploy with nuclear weapons if required also did rigorous inspections and that further demonstrated Tom Gilbert was a competent Commanding Officer.

John Harris and USSF Secretary Margarette Mackworth were required to approve the CSS ALABAMA SPACE TRIAL AGANDA. They had a privilege view of the process used and the brilliance of Tom Gilbert to include requirements a lot of *Pretenders* would have overlooked.

Even though a lot of the CSS ALABAMA SPACE TRIAL AGENDA would be accomplished flying in autopilot, the fact is it included all of Admiral Gilberts blueprint for success. Tom Guilbert had to make sure CSS ALABAMA could not only accomplish the CSS ALABAMA SPACE TRIAL AGENDA, but he also had to satisfy himself and John Harris that CSS ALABAMA could perform to design specifications, if the need arises in the heat of the battle.

As such Tom Gilbert with Commodore Riley's insights had to put a reality check into all the CSS ALABAMA

SPACE TRIAL AGENDA to make sure they truly tested critical aspects of a Space Carrier to allow it to perform unrestricted operations, far from home with virtually no means of being rescued.

Now it was ready for show time with the execution of the CSS ALABAMA SPACE TRIAL AGENDA. This SPACE TRIAL had more visibility than in 1961, when American astronaut Alan Shepard aboard a Mercury Rocket became the second person behind the Russian Yuri Alekseyevich Gagarin and the first American to travel into space. In 1971, Alan Shepard became the fifth and oldest person to walk on the Moon, at age 47.

The navigator used three-dimensional navigation tools on the Navigation display that showed a scaled replica of the CSS Alabama next to the Space Dock in a 1500-meter scale on the large screen display.

Using the mouse the navigator clicked on the flight plan imagery that showed the *proposed flight plan* and the simulated expected results of the first maneuver that would place the rocket exhaust perpendicular to the Space Dock. This maneuver was required so that when reactor startup occurred, the strong blast from the rocket engines would not strike the Space Dock.

After reviewing ship's maneuver orders in the *Space Trial Agenda* and current navigation simulation of expected results, the Navigator clicked on the [ACCEPT ICON] and the Alabama started swinging around in precision as the side thrusters engaged.

The Alabama slowly shifted heading as speed wasn't necessary, safety was the fundamental issue. As the Alabama approached a spatial alignment matching programmed navigational vectors, the side thrusters slowed Alabama's swing rate and stopped it precisely where the ship's maneuver orders positioned it.

The Alabama was two hundred yards away from the Space Dock when the thrusters fired again which changed the pitch of the Space Carrier to point it away from the Earth towards a direction of deep space for the initial reactor startup. Display monitors now showed TR-3B video monitors from the chase planes that would escort the Space Carrier as it powered up its main engines.

If for some reason the Space Carrier lost propulsion it could use a couple TR-3Bs as Space Tugs to tow or push it a short distance to get it back in the Space Dock for repairs. If the Space Carrier was marooned in Space somewhere, the crew were in peril and the only option they had when food and water ran out was to self-destruct.

One of the prime movers was needed for high-speed transit. The other was there just for redundancy.

NAVIGATOR
Captain we are ready to proceed to Earth Orbits IAW
Event #3 of *Space Trial Agenda*

CAPTAIN GILBERT
Navigator, commence *Space Trial Agenda* Event #3.

The nuclear fusion rocket engines which could be easily fired at any power setting required. For the first test they would only be brought up to 5-percent reactor power. This was enough power to accelerate the Space Carrier without causing a significant movement in the nearby Space Dock. That momentary 5-percent reactor power created enough thrust to put the Space Carrier on a course to orbit planet Earth leaving being the Space Dock that remained in synchronous orbit in the same relative angle from the planet perpendicular to the center of the USA.

<u>EXT. CGI. SPACE CSS ALABAMA STARTING ORBIT AROUND EARTH</u>

More diagnostics were being run continuously in non-obtrusive manners to eavesdrop on system performance. This was the last of a series of health checks prior to running the racecourses to the moon and back several times.

In various compartments aboard CSS Alabama tech reps with equipment racks processing fast number of data streams were recording all the certification data in computer files they would archive and have available in the future if there was ever a mishap or reasons to investigate system performances. This included propulsion, combat systems, sensors, communications, and computational resources. There was also telemetry sent to USSF laboratory's where performance data was including data from strain gauges mounted all over Alabama for space trials. This was a mega scientific experiment with numerous vested parties.

The pilot and copilot who could manually control Alabama during combat or serious events were part of Event #4 where they took manual control of the Space Carrier and ran some geometries in low power demonstrating *steering and flying* controls worked reliably and could handle the stresses these maneuvers caused with artificial gravity and tested again with artificial gravity turned off when far more aggressive actions could occur if necessary, in a live combat scenarios. As expected, 15 neophytes unvolunteered later when they returned to space dock One of the nuclear power technicians was proud to hear his buddy who unvolunteered tell him, "You are a better man than I am."

That sailor who admitted his shortcomings after space trials was previously considered an arrogant asshole by most of the men in his division. Aboard submarines they would say he acted like a *swinging dick, Mr. Know-It-All*. Captain Gilbert had more plans to weed out the *swinging dicks* who were not going to be able to hack it. Some of the junior enlisted that would normally be considered less reliable, came out of Space Trials in shining armor. One thing Captain Gilbert learned on submarines, looks are deceiving and the *swinging dicks* may not be the guy a commanding officer wanted in critical battle stations when the shooting started, and bad things happened. He also learned one other thing as a sub skipper, in the faces of the new guys that show up, some of them would eventually turn out to be superstars in the end because of devotion and eagerness to learn and participate.

Event #5 was space angles and dangles which the pilot and copilot loved doing and got addicted to in the trainers. They loved the fact these maneuvers would scare the living dogshit out of some of the neophytes onboard. The pilot and co-pilot flying in manual control, put *steering, and flying* through its paces all within the guidelines of the *Space Trial Agenda* testing the systems to design specification, which if far more aggressive than what would occur during normal operations confiding them to what is called the *Safe Operating Envelope* (*SOE*).

Captain Gilbert didn't mind this activity because it would help shake out the weak hands who shouldn't be here that made it through the screening process when they should not have been selected. For Captain Gilbert didn't mind this activity because it would help shake out the weak hands who shouldn't be here that made it through the screening process when they should not have been selected. For Event #9 the CSS Alabama moved an additional 25,000 miles above planet Earth to perform snap rolls and Crazy Ivan maneuvers they might need to make as a last-ditch effort to stay alive. They also needed to know if the ship's systems such as *steering and flying* could perform.

A variety of other system performance checks were made including playing with target drones to make sure the radars, photonics, and other systems performed reliably and in one special event #30, they were permitted to destroy a drone with their self-defense launcher systems once they got it moving at high speed towards the sun where the fragments would eventually hit and decompose. Those self-defense launchers operated in a similar fashion to Tomahawk VLS launchers, but the self-defense weapons traveled much faster than a hypersonic weapons since there was no wind resistance or friction with excess fuel that added to the warhead's explosive force.

The next event on space trials was time consuming but necessary.

Several TR-3B's were sent up to dock in Port and Starboard individualized hangar bays and then launched to make sure the launchers all worked as expected. This was a 24-hour test and kept Commodore Riley in the control room for the entire time. Commodore Riley was very grateful after the last TR-3B launch and the TR-3B's headed back to Wright- Patterson Air Force Base with exhausted crews. Thanks to the way the designers built the TR-3B Hangars in a modular form the quality control was exceptional because all the discrete work was done on Earth minimizing installation activity and possible human error.

CAPTAIN GILBERT
Commodore Riley, your services are no longer needed up here for a while. You have gone a long time without any sleep. I want you to go to your stateroom, get a good rest, and when you feel ready come back and relieve me as command duty officer. Then I'll take a rest during some of the racetracks we'll be running to the moon and back.

COMMODORE RILEY
Thank you, Captain, I know I feel like I can use some down time.

CAPTAIN GILBERT
Sleep well Commodore.

COMMODORE RILEY
Thanks Captain.

The racecourses to the moon and back began after a couple orbits around Earth doing system health checks and verifying no faults were detected.

NAVIGATOR
Captain, we are ready to commence Space Trial Agenda #53, the first racetrack to the moon.

CAPTAIN GILBERT
Navigator, commence Space Trial Agenda #53. Also, once we reach high speed and it appears we are not going to blow ourselves up, I want A-NAV to relieve you and you go down and get a few hours of sleep.

NAVIGATOR
Captain, I'm so wired up with energy drinks I'm not sure I can sleep now.

Not a problem NAV I'll have the Corpsman visit you in your stateroom to administer you some sleeping medications.

NAVIGATOR
Thanks Captain.

In ten minutes when CSS Alabama was flying faster than any previous spacecraft to the moon, The navigator watch relief occurred.

A-NAV
Captain, permission to relieve the Navigator of the watch.

CAPTAIN GILBERT.
A-NAV, relieve the Navigator.

A-NAV
Relieve the Navigator, Captain aye.

Moments later Navigator announced:

NAVIGATOR
I stand relieved. A-NAV is the acting Navigator.

CHIEF OF THE WATCH
Very well Navigator, relief entered the automated Deck log.

Moments after the Navigator departed Commander Gilbert announced.

CAPTAIN GILBERT.
Chief of the Watch, contact the Corpsman and have
him report to the Captain in Control.

The Navigator was soon treated by the corpsman who desperately needed some down time. But so did Captain Gilbert but he was satisfied knowing Commodore Riley would give him a chance to rest a while later.

Increasing rocket power in steps and utilizing the Moon's gravitational pull helped sling the Space Carrier back towards Earth at the completion of the first racetrack to the moon.

For the next leg of a multileg course to the moon and back increased prime mover energy outputs to do stress testing and get actual run time on the rocket engines and evaluate their performance.

Sticking to the racecourse to the moon and back allowed them to operate close enough to where they could send TR-3Bs to rescue the crew if they had to abandon the space carrier because of an unpredictable disaster.

EXT. CGI. SPACE CSS ALABAMA TRANSITING TO THE MOON AND BACK

Every single crew member felt satisfied they got their money's worth volunteering in the Space Force. Not many people would ever be entitled to get a bird's eye view of the back side of the moon and glimpses of Earth from outer space.

The numerous legs on this propulsion check during the engineering trials slowly helped build confidence in the technology and eased any concern of workmanship issues. No monkey wrenches were left in machinery that would put them in peril. All systems remained on a high standard of readiness.

To say it wasn't a humbling adventure would be an understatement as the enormity of all this space expedition quickly played on the psyche of everyone as they slowly developed a keen understanding of the purpose and the possibilities this space carrier created.

Mankind was no longer stuck on the planet. He could now range far and wide in Space. And to the crew members who had heard every rumor about aliens at Area 51, this brought them into a new perspective as it was no longer a possibility. It was now a probability since if we figured out how to get from here great distances, but it made sense now, so could aliens.

Running racetracks around the moon during the engineering trials phase of the post new construction testing soon passed a major milestone. But eventually it all had to come to an end and the CSS Alabama had to re-dock so that an army of technicians could descend upon the ship and perform a large variety of checks to help prepare it for its next voyage that would perplex mankind if it were not compartmentalized and out of public view.

That first trip to Mars occurred soon after. Despite all the coverup and propaganda used against Dr. Brandenburg about the Xeon 129 found on Mars, he was secretly invited to go with them bringing along some of his special instruments to get a better accounting of the Xeon 129 that permeated Martian atmosphere. Just like the emotions the crew felt passing the dark side of the moon away from the planet, arriving near Mars also presented a gigantic outpour of emotions to many crew members. As they approached the red planet and it became larger than life, Dr. Brandenburg's calculations were now gripping the establishment and the Majestic 12 group with more discovery.

Mars was far enough away to give the Space Carrier a chance to show its legs and go up to 100-percent reactor power briefly while accelerating. The crew was restricted to their pressure suits and strapped in during the acceleration. The megawatts of power those nuclear rocket engines put out was astonishing.

Just like when they were sling shot around the moon, Mars provided similar maneuvering options. The effects of the slingshot around Mars made them come close to the atmosphere where heat shields would be required provided the onboard video systems to get a range of new Mars video never accomplished before. Eventually as the Space Carrier approached earth, a set of forward thrusters were used to help slow down. Again, personnel were ordered into the pressure suits again and soon felt the G forces as the ship slowed down to a more manageable velocity.

The ship slowed and the navigation computers put it on a course for the Space Dock and the ships navigational computers very accurately pointed the rear of the CSS Alabama Space Carrier into the entrance of the Space Dock where it slowly slid in the Space Dock and slowly traveled down the length of it.

As the CSS Alabama Space Carrier approached the saddled position tiny blasts from the thrusters put it into perfect alignment and the last twenty inches of movement took thirty seconds. The outer entrance hatches for Alabama's access to the Space Dock were closing as soon as the bow of the ship crossed the sill. By the time optical alignments showed the space carrier was in the saddle, the hatches fully closed and were sealed thanks to the membranes and special gaskets designed to prevent any air leaks to help reduce the need to transport numerous air cylinders up to the Space Dock on each docking cycle.

As soon as the tubular gang plank was attached to the space carrier and a fifteen-pound air test completed, the access door on the ship was opened and on the Space Dock. For a brief period of time the self-sustaining liquid metal cooled reactors would continue providing the carrier electricity. As soon as electrical cables were hooked up the power supply would shift to the Space Dock that had a bank of liquid metal cooled reactors to supply all the power the ship needed as well as the Space Dock.

Because the Space Dock was well insulated, the CSS Alabama Space Carrier would warm it up real fast if the ship continued to use its own reactors. Reactor shutdown was a priority, including the installing of "shore power" which was done very efficiently thanks to all the robotics and automation involved as the gangplank tube had power cable connections built in and all that was required was verification of mating surfaces secure before applying power.

The CSS Alabama Space Carrier would transition from its internal reactors to standby power via batteries then to Space Dock power. During undocking operations, the transition was in the opposite sequence.

Once Space Dock power and Gang Plank integrity validated, a security watch was posted at the ship's entrance, and everyone checked for proper credentials to prevent stowaways and potential saboteurs onboard.

Admiral Gilbert and Commodore Riley were the first two off the ship as they had Commodore Avery waiting for them. He had arranged transportation for them as they were summoned to Washington, D.C., to report to the Joint Chiefs and the Secretary of the Space Force.

COMMODORE AVERY
Welcome back, Admiral.

ADMIRAL GILBERT
Thank you, Commodore.

COMMODORE AVERY
Your shakedown cruise can be categorized as nothing
short of spectacular.

ADMIRAL GILBERT
All the equipment worked. New Construction was a
monumental success.

COMMODORE AVERY
Any major material conditions that we need to deal
with while the ship is in dock?

ADMIRAL GILBERT
There were incidental equipment issues, but thanks to
the redundancy and spare parts we took with us, we
got by quite well. We just sent a Space Carrier Alert
(SCA) message detailing what is a mandatory repair
prior to undocking again.

The SCA Message, like a Navy CASREP, had all the issues, part numbers, and specific requests such as the need for a Tech Rep who had more knowledge than the crew to diagnose and assess tricky problems. In the old days the Navy built systems with stacks of servers in them all interfaced with GIGE switches. But thanks to IBM ingenuity, a new system of Blades made all those servers immediately obsolete.

A computer blade had the same horsepower as a server, but in a six-foot rack of equipment they could mount two hundred blades instead of thirty servers. The processing bandwidth was thus increased and based on the inverse square law, the number of CPUs you double, the amount of work you can do is quadrupled if it's programmed effectively, artificial intelligence on the Space Carrier just leaped forward.

A lot of processing was done in many areas one would not suspect impacted by the blades. In the 1980s a brilliant scientist, S. Y. Kung, designed the basis of Ronald Reagan's STARWARS system. Billed as a system to shoot down Russian and Chinese ICBMs, it was secretly put in place in case we had to shoot down aliens. STARWARS had nothing to do with Russians or Chinese but there was no way Reagan could sell it as a system to shoot down aliens while the government itself claimed there had never been any aliens!

All that number crunching ability gave the designers of the Space Carrier the ability to detect and track a vast number of objects in space that might be a threat. Even a dead satellite is a threat if it plows into you.

S. Y. Kung's Systolic Arrays allowed inferior technology using 1980s mainframe computers to process radar and photonics images to detect possible alien invasion fleets. We already had a sense of who some of the hostile aliens were and their home planet, the Hubble Space Telescope was put up to scan that sector of space. Since it would take up to ten years for those aliens to travel here, the Hubble only had to look now and then, so scheduling it for a security sweep was relatively easy without tipping off the scientific community its real purpose for being there in the first place.

All these blade processors available now operating at 275 Gigahertz gave a granularity of space search that S. Y. Kung and everyone associated with the STARWARS DARPA project could never believe obtainable. It was a game changer.

Unfortunately, what comes with better awareness is also the detection of more potential threats, whether it be a dangerous comet that could strike Earth, or a previously damaged alien ship, the victim of galactic warfare slamming into Earth and spreading horrible toxic chemicals around an impact zone.

The power plants of alien ships had chemicals that are so toxic that if one of them impacted a major American City, it's a safe bet that all life in that city would be immediately extinguished. Space Force had to be in position to intercept such craft and using space tugs move them on a trajectory that would not be a threat to the planet. Even a large comet could have its course altered by a space tug.

Even though TR-3B was never designed to be a space tug, it had enough propulsion and artificial gravity where it could change the course of a comet well enough to avoid hitting earth, unless we wanted to dump it on a country we were at war with.

Comet wars were a possibility for the future.

Crew members of a Space Carrier are not allowed to bring many personal items aboard. It simplifies security and at the same time prevents contamination. The first thing a crew member is required to do upon arrival to the Space Carrier is to change out of his clothes and wear the ship's uniform designed for life aboard an extended stay vessel which may end up spending a couple years in space traveling to and from a destination supporting its mission.

The materials used in the crew's uniforms were lint free and were designed to be worn for a week between changes. *Snipes* working in engineering spaces had daily changes of crew uniforms due to potential contaminants and the results of working around machinery that could develop a hydraulic oil leak, condensation, or some other means of material dispersal.

One theory suggests that the term *Snipes* originated during the American Civil War, when Navy engineers were responsible for operating and maintaining the Union Navy's steam-powered ships. These engineers were often referred to as *Snipes* because of their expertise in operating and maintaining ships' engines.

New guys on nuclear submarines were often sent to the engine room looking for snipes or Fallopian Tube Testers.

Captain Gilbert smiled the first time in the wardroom when one of his officers was wondering what kind of counseling sheet he need to write up on a sailor who sent a female technician to the Engine Room to borrow a Fallopian Tube Tester. The MPA (main propulsion assistant) a blonde female with a master's degree in nuclear physics sent the bewildered woman to the crew's library to look up the term Fallopian Tube Tester and report back so she could give the woman some instructions to give to her division chief who soon was chewing ass on the idiot that sent the young impressionable woman to the engine room.

The female MPA later met the perpetrator and informed him:

MPA
I have a blackbelt in Karate and if you mess with Sarah
again, I'm sure Captain Gilbert will look the other way
when I humiliate you in front of your buddies.

The *swinging dick* who messed with Sarah was one of the non-hackers who unvolunteered and was transferred off Alabama before he got qualified and earned his Space Carrier Insignia similar to submariner dolphins or a surface warfare pin.

Some of the men onboard Alabama wore the Space Carrier Insignia, Dolphins, Surface Warfare Insignia, and wings having also been an Airdale. A couple of them were also qualified divers.

Since the Ship's Captain Gilbert and Wing Commander Commodore Riley were leaving the ship heading for the planet for a series of debriefings and planning meetings, they had changed into their normal Military Uniforms and appeared like Space Force officers as Commodore Avery escorted them to the waiting TR-3B that would soon take them directly to Andrews Air Force Base.

When the CSS Alabama undocked in a couple weeks, it would then proceed out into deep space and start flight operations, qualifying the pilots for Space Carrier service. Some of the meetings scheduled concerned those Carrier Qualifications. Even though all TR-3B launches and retrievals were made in autopilot, it was necessary to train the pilots to do emergency landings in case the automation developed some type of malfunction. This training would also involve attacking a planet, and some of the hawks in the Pentagon wanted a TR-3B to deploy a nuclear weapon in the event we had to be prepared for an all-out war with an alien menace.

Admiral Gilbert and Commodore Riley were soon at the air lock for the TR-3B. Admiral Gilbert turned towards Commodore Avery and smiled.

ADMIRAL GILBERT

See you in a few days. Take good care of my carrier while I'm gone.

COMMODORE AVERY

Admiral Gilbert, you have an outstanding crew. They will rise to the occasion and help get this docking over quickly.

ADMIRAL GILBERT

How soon will you be checking the exterior of the CSS Alabama?

COMMODORE AVERY

Sometime today. The nukes are already taking swipes to make sure there is no radiation on the skin, then the robotic survey begins.

Out in space, small meteorites can impact the hull of a ship without knowing and some damage is done. That damage is usually easily repairable, but a lot of impact areas on the hull could not be deferred as if they were allowed to accumulate the reflective ability to help defend against laser strikes would be compromised. That was another reason for the series of meetings the two men had to attend, and there were rumors going around a second Space Dock was soon going to be built so that operational dry docking would not delay new construction.

<u>INT. SPACE DOCK AIRLOCK ACCESS TO TR-3B</u>

Admiral Gilbert pressed the entry button on the airlock to gain access to the TR-3B that would take them to the planet. Soon after a hissing sound, the hatch swung open via robotic arm. After the two men walked inside the air lock one of them touched the close button and the process reversed with the door shutting. Moments later the automated system did a sixteen-pound air test which made it slightly uncomfortable for a few minutes, and after the analysis indicated there were no leaks, the pressure was decreased down to 14 PSI.

Admiral Gilbert appeared being somewhat an impatient man, wanting to get to the planet surface so he could take care of some personal matters as well as attend what he thought would be mind boggling boring meetings he felt was a total waste of his time.

With interlocks closed and safe to open the TR-3B hatch, it suddenly swiveled inwards, and a TR-3B crew member was there waiting for their arrival.

<u>INT. TR-3B CONVERTED AS PASSENGER SHUTTLE CRAFT</u>

The TR-3B converted to a shuttle craft had no bomb bay or offensive weapons to make room for a few passengers. With the weapon systems removed ample weight and space accommodations made it a versatile transport. Viewing it from the exterior one would not know it was a non-lethal stripped-down model that cost substantially less than transporting personnel via space shuttles or rockets.

Dressed in winter "Blues" the sailor proudly wore his numerous service ribbons, wings, dolphins, and other insignias.

TR-3B CREWMEMBER (SAILOR)
Welcome aboard, Admiral Gilbert.

ADMIRAL GILBERT
Thanks. It's good to be here knowing I'll probably be
enjoying regular gravity again real soon.

TR-3B CREWMEMBER (SAILOR)
You got that right.

ADMIRAL GILBERT
How long before we land in Andrews?

TR-3B CREWMEMBER (SAILOR)
In about thirty minutes, sir.

ADMIRAL GILBERT
That quick?

TR-3B CREWMEMBER (SAILOR)
Yes, sir, we have the advanced heat shield for frequent
re-entry, so we just plow though the ionosphere on our
way down to the planet.

ADMIRAL GILBERT
That's good to hear.

TR-3B CREWMEMBER (SAILOR)
This way, sir, let me take you to your seats.

About ten feet away were some comfortable looking seats which they took and followed direction from the crew member as how to buckle themselves in and in the event of a water landing, the flotation devices at their seat. There were also a couple rubber rafts and if they were able to make a reasonable landing, they would crawl up a ladder to the rooftop and deploy the rubber rafts there hopefully before the craft sank.

Since they were the only two passengers scheduled on this flight, the umbilical tube unlocked and retracted after the air was sucked out to help reduce air loss on the facility. Shipping up tanks of air was an expensive process, so saving and salvaging air was always a big goal.

The TR-3B mated with the Space Dock in a cradle mechanism to ensure it had accurate mating surfaces to the telescoping airlock.

With everything now disconnected the pilot had a "green board" indicating he could now back away from the Space Dock Service Dock. Everything in space was done with patience and in a carefully calculated manner. A couple short blasts from the navigation thrusters resulted in the TR-3B moving away from the Space Dock at a rate of one foot in ten seconds.

EXT. CGI. SPACE. TR-3B LEAVING SPACE DOCK AND HEADING TO EARTH.

When the TR-3B had moved approximately ten feet away from the space dock, another short blast from the thruster rockets and it was now moving away at a rate of one foot in one second. When the TR-3B moved over one hundred feet away from the Space Dock it gave a couple short blasts of its forward thrusters and was soon moving ten feet in one second forward. In less than a minute later, the TR-3B had moved out in front of the Space Dock and subsequent thruster blasts reoriented it pointing planet Earth.

The propulsion system on the TR-3B was rumored to have had alien influence and a degree of reverse engineering. It could obtain 89 percent anti-gravity. It could also apply 89 percent positive gravity thus interacting with Earth Gravity Waves which then gave far more attraction to the planet than would be otherwise felt at this altitude where astronauts normally were in micro gravity.

When microgravity was combined with the artificial gravity the TR-3B radiated, the attraction was multiplied to the point the amount of gravity almost equaled what existed near the surface of the planet. The TR-3B did not have to waste a lot of rocket fuel going to and from the planet. All it had to do was exercise its gravity machine, hence propulsion requirements were greatly reduced. Passengers could feel the gravity but did not understand it radiated out just below the deck they sat on.

The velocity of the TR-3B exceeded 18,000 miles per hour now. The earth which they could see moving earlier while the Space Dock orbit slowly circled the earth appeared to stop moving, though it strangely grew. From their current vantage point, they could make out the East Coast and Florida peninsula sticking out.

Having taken similar rides Gilbert and Riley knew they would soon start feeling vibrations as the TR-3B hit the ionosphere. If it were not for the artificial gravity, the ship would have vibrations at least one hundred times greater, but the gravity waves bent space around it. The bending of space had the beneficial property of making the craft appear to be one hundred times more streamlined than it really was. In a manner it created the perfect hull for atmospheric penetration.

Once the craft was through the ionosphere and down around seventy-five thousand feet going about Mach 9 giving off sonic booms, the artificial gravity was turned off. Wind resistance would now slow down the ship and they would avoid using artificial gravity flying into Andrews as to not attract undue attention. From a distance it looked simply like a black painted Air Force Delta Wing Jet.

With the current velocity and distance to Andrews they would simply continue to drop, losing altitude and by the time they used up all the free energy from the free fall, they would be at safe speeds near the end of the runway, without applying speed breaks. If there was an emergency and something malfunctioned, the pilot could turn on the artificial gravity making it 89 percent lighter and much easier to handle. That would not be necessary today as the flight went just like clockwork and immediately after landing, pulled up to a hangar which already had doors open which the TR-3B glided right into and stopped. Within seconds of coming to a stop inside the hangar, the doors closed, the pilot opened the cabin door and Air Force personnel moved a portable ladder up to the plane so the Admiral Gilbert and Commodore Riley could quickly exit the craft to the waiting SUV that would take them immediately to the Pentagon.

COMMODORE RILEY
I hope there's not a lot of traffic today.

ADMIRAL GILBERT
We are going in the opposite direction of all those civil
servants heading for home, we should be okay.

The drive over to the Pentagon was quick as they were driving against traffic, so there were no delays, and pulled up to a special entrance installed after the 9/11 Pentagon attack put in to allow numerous high-ranking officers to egress the Pentagon swiftly in an emergency. It was also like the captain's brow of a normal Navy Carrier, where only the captain, his officers, and VIPs were allowed to use. Contractors and sailors and civil servants had to use all the normal entrances unless escorted by a senior officer that happens from time to time.

<u>EXT. DAY PENTAGON</u>

To Tom Gilbert's surprise, CNO and John Harris were at the entry waiting for them.

Earlier, when the CSS Alabama was approaching the Space Dock Tom Gilbert transmitted a PowerPoint for the briefing they were going to discuss in a few minutes. This agenda described all their milestones and issues encountered as well as any recommendations the Naval Reactors Team and the Combat Air Center personnel wanted to discuss.

JOHN HARRIS
Welcome back, Admiral.

ADMIRAL GILBERT
Thank you.

CNO
We are close to the conference room, just around the
corner here.

ADMIRAL GILBERT
Okay.

<u>INT. DAY PENTAGON CONFERENCE ROOM</u>

Within five minutes, the men were seated at a long table in a crowded room. The table seated fifty and there were at least another fifty sitting in chairs next to the wall surrounding the conference table.

At the head of the table was USSF Secretary Margarette Mackworth. John Harris sat down on her left side, followed by the CNO.

People invited to sit at the table had their place markers laid out with bottles of water, snacks, notepads, pens and pencils. A projector board was directly behind Margarette Mackworth. Whatever was written on the projector board could be emailed or it could also show a PowerPoint presentation.

Admiral Gilbert's place marker was right next to Margarette Mackworth. Commodore Riley's was next to his. Obviously, they wanted the two front and center. About that time Tom Gilbert noticed several cameras pointing his way. It was obvious this meeting was going to be televised to remote sites. Another interesting aspect of the meeting was that well over two-thirds of the attendees were wearing uniforms. There were not a lot of civilians in the room, which was unexpected.

Right at the top of the hour, Margarette Mackworth began.

USSF SECRETARY MARGARETTE MACKWORTH
Good afternoon, everyone, thanks for attending. All of
you were given the invite because we may be asking
something of you in the very near future.

Margarette Mackworth pressed a couple buttons on the display screen controller and suddenly there were classification markings, TOP-SECRET NOFORN.

> **USSF SECRETARY MARGARETTE MACKWORTH**
> As you all can see, this is a classified meeting, please do not discuss the meeting outside this room. Any questions should be sent to my office if you need any clarification. This meeting is also being televised by live broadcast to CIA and NASA headquarters where only restricted and cleared people are allowed to view in a private sitting.

Next, extracts from Admiral Gilberts PowerPoint were displayed.

> **USSF SECRETARY MARGARETTE MACKWORTH**
> Admiral Gilbert, do you have any comments on the PowerPoint? For those of you attending, if there were any questions about space trials agenda items, Admiral Gilbert can now answer them now or defer them to a later time and place if he needs to get you additional information.

Admiral Gilbert gave a recap of CSS Alabama's *Space Trial Agenda events* that took about thirty minutes, much of which most everyone in the room already knew about.

The next discussion was why they were summoned to this meeting. It was the ultra-sensitive issue concerning Space Carrier Qualifications. Never had a space carrier operated. The complexities were multiplied. Admiral Gilbert's flexibility was greatly diminished.

After Admiral Gilbert went over the plan, he and Commodore Riley gave blood sweat and tears to develop during several sleepless days prior to space trials outlining the process to conduct carrier qualification. USSF Secretary Margarette Mackworth's change of plans suddenly dropped on Admiral Gilbert like a ton of bricks.

> **USSF SECRETARY MARGARETTE MACKWORTH**
> Admiral Gilbert, for the most part, John Harris and I will endorse your carrier qualification process you laid out in the preliminary document. For now, we will only impose one change.

> **ADMIRAL GILBERT**
> Madam Secretary, May I ask what the change is?

Tom Gilbert was facing John Harris soon after asking the question. John Harris had a funny look on his face he often had when big surprises were inevitable.

USSF SECRETARY MARGARETTE MACKWORTH
Admiral Gilbert, what we have in mind will require you to do carrier qualifications beyond prying eyes. As such, our mission planners have decided you will do your Carrier Qualifications around planet Uranus.

ADMIRAL GILBERT
Why would we travel so far to do quals there when we can simply do them near the earth, moon, or worse case Mars?

USSF SECRETARY MARGARETTE MACKWORTH
Admiral, we have some new developments concerning aliens and it is now imperative we test our strike capability.

ADMIRAL GILBERT
We could drop a few bombs on the far side of the Moon. What's the big deal about going all the way to Uranus?

USSF SECRETARY MARGARETTE MACKWORTH
Admiral, the weapons you will be testing have never been used before, they have recently been developed, therefore we need to practice deploying them and we also must hide attributes these weapons are capable of from our potential terrestrial enemies.

ADMIRAL GILBERT
Our pilots have a lot of experience dropping bombs flying for the Navy or the Air Force before they transferred to the Space Force, I'm sure it's nothing new to them.

USSF SECRETARY MARGARETTE MACKWORTH
Admiral, one of the reasons why this meeting is Top-Secret NOFORN is we'll be testing a new generation of nuclear weapons.

ADMIRAL GILBERT
Which means you are trying to avoid the appearance

we have violated our treaties concerning weaponizing space?

USSF SECRETARY MARGARETTE MACKWORTH
Admiral Gilbert. the Russians and the Chinese will not take too kindly to the notion we have some super hydrogen bombs poised to deal with possible Alien enemies in space. They will view it as a threat to them.

ADMIRAL GILBERT
Okay, let me ask the fifty-dollar question: Why Uranus?

USSF SECRETARY MARGARETTE MACKWORTH
Because your spaceship is the only one that can get there quick enough to do the test without prying eyes.

ADMIRAL GILBERT
They still might see the energy release.

USSF SECRETARY MARGARETTE MACKWORTH
We believe that if we test them on the far side of planet Uranus, it will shield enough of the energy output, that astronomers will attribute it to a meteor impact.

ADMIRAL GILBERT
How soon do you plan on sanctioning this mission?

USSF SECRETARY MARGARETTE MACKWORTH
Your current space docking is just a precautionary maintenance period to verify hull integrity and make repairs, if necessary, from meteorite strikes.

ADMIRAL GILBERT
I've not received any reports yet on the results of those inspections.

USSF SECRETARY MARGARETTE MACKWORTH
We have already received preliminary reports from the robotic inspection process indicating minimal damage was done and probably all corrective actions can be deferred indefinitely.

ADMIRAL GILBERT

Assuming no negative reports, what does that mean for my schedule?

USSF SECRETARY MARGARETTE MACKWORTH
Since we now know we do not have any maintenance headaches, we should be able to deploy you at the end of your space docking without any reservations.

ADMIRAL GILBERT
Next question: How are the nuclear weapons going to be delivered to the carrier?

USSF SECRETARY MARGARETTE MACKWORTH
Several TR-3Bs will carry them up and dock on the ship. Those weapons will remain onboard those craft.

ADMIRAL GILBERT
How will we maintain the two-man rule required for handling nuclear weapons?

USSF SECRETARY MARGARETTE MACKWORTH
The crew will be minimized because most operations will be fully automated. We only need a few people on board for security and safety monitoring. Food and refuse handling and all maintenance teams are being cleared at the Q level. Their background investigations began a long time ago and now the entire crew is cleared. The nuclear equipped TR-3B's will be in tamper proof hangers that will have additional security measures, we'll discuss later after the meeting.

Tom Gilbert sat stunned; he had no idea how close to operational he really was. *The multi-year test program was a hoax to keep our enemies guessing.*

In just a little over two weeks, the CSS Alabama would be weaponized. It was now in the ranks of planet killers. But under what circumstances would we levy such destruction?

More conversations rolled along and soon everyone had their marching orders and Pentagon planners were hard at planning the strikes on Uranus. As far as they knew, the ice giant, eight times the diameter of Earth, had no evidence of life on it, though the atmosphere prevented much observation of the surface.

Images of Uranus did show some weather patterns in the southern Hemisphere.

However, the blue planet consisted mainly of molecular hydrogen and helium. The third-most abundant component of Uranus's atmosphere is methane. The abundance of methane suggests life formerly existed on the frozen planet. What happened?

In 1986, NASA sent Voyager 2 to perform an interplanetary probe of Uranus in a flyby. This remains the only investigation of Uranus carried out from a short distance and no other visits were planned. The Carrier qualifications and weapons test would provide more new information about Uranus than ever before accumulated.

One of the fears of the CSS Alabama program was NASA scientists would soon be banging down the doors for a manned space flight to another solar system for scientific purposes. The politics could turn dicey. That led to the meeting being adjourned and as people were in small pockets having a few discussions as everyone filed out of the room thinking about buzzing on the beltway to get home for the evening and fretting about the traffic.

Margarette Mackworth, USSF Secretary, approached Tom Gilbert who was having a few words with John Harris.

> USSF SECRETARY MARGARETTE MACKWORTH
> Admiral Gilbert, I'm not sure what your plans are for the evening, but I would like you and John Harris to accompany me to dinner, where we can discuss something, I couldn't bring up in the meeting here because of the remote video link, I wanted to get your take on an action item that came across my desk from the President.

> ADMIRAL GILBERT
> I suppose I could go. I really didn't have any plans.

> USSF SECRETARY MARGARETTE MACKWORTH
> Good, I'll have my driver take us to a nice place over in Georgetown that isn't too crowded, and we can have a friendly conversation there.

> ADMIRAL GILBERT
> I have a hotel room in Crystal City, could you pick me up there, so I have a chance to change into some civilian clothes?

> USSF SECRETARY MARGARETTE MACKWORTH
> Sure, how about 6:30 P.M.?

ADMIRAL GILBERT
That will work fine.

USSF SECRETARY MARGARETTE MACKWORTH
Do you have transportation to the hotel?

ADMIRAL GILBERT
I was just going to grab a cab.

USSF SECRETARY MARGARETTE MACKWORTH
I'll have my driver drop you off.

ADMIRAL GILBERT
I appreciate that.

Soon Tom was in an unmarked limo that was given to the Secretary to ferry her and her guests around, which simplified a lot of business. MID swept the car for bugs several times a day, so the secretary could have conversations on her scrambler phone in exigencies. The driver asked Tom Gilbert about his hotel.

EXT. DAY USSF LIMO

USSF LIMO DRIVER
What hotel will you be checking into, sir?

TOM GILBERT
The Hilton Hotel in Crystal City next to Jefferson Davis Highway.

USSF LIMO DRIVER
Know it well. Have driven a lot of personnel to and from there.

TOM GILBERT
Any chance we can stop off at the Pentagon City Mall, so I can pick up some clothes?

USSF LIMO DRIVER
No problem, I know a good department store there, and this time of day, there is plenty of parking.

TOM GILBERT
I appreciate that.

Since it was late spring, comfortable clothes were necessary including a change of shoes. If Tom Gilbert was going to be stuck on the planet for a few days like he thought he would, he would have to get a few more items or have someone pack up a few items he had on the Alabama and send it down on a transport flight if one was arriving in the Washington area which was likely.

In a way Tom Gilbert was glad it wasn't just a fast trip to the surface of the planet and back as he was notified he had to attend several more meetings over the next few days. Most of his other belongings were in storage back in San Diego since he didn't need to have anything besides his uniforms with as much time as he spent on CSS Alabama.

It didn't take Tom very long to shop, he knew his sizes and the store had a great selection. He was in and out in less than ten minutes.

Next to the department store was a drug store where he could pick up a few personal items like a toothbrush, razor, shaving lotion, mouthwash, and energy pack multiple vitamins. Since there were only a few customers in the store, he was in and out in five minutes. So, in the span of fifteen minutes he was suddenly situated for a little terrestrial lifestyle. The driver soon dropped him off at his hotel and before the driver stopped at the hotel, he notified Tom the plan.

USSF LIMO DRIVER
I was directed to be back at 6:30 to pick you up.

TOM GILBERT
I'll be ready.

Tom checked into his hotel room, made a bee line to the shower where he would indulge in a Hollywood shower, something that was impossible to experience where he just came from. The nice long shower was what the doctor ordered. And the normal gravity had a pleasant feeling to it as well. He knew that based on the doctor's advice, he was to try to take it easy during his stay on the planet because he would not fully adjust to normal gravity and by being too active, he could trigger a health risk. Also, he was used to breathing purified air. The filthy city air he was now breathing was soon felt. He now knew vividly, people returning from space duty would require some time to adjust.

By 18:30 (6:30 P.M.) he was more than ready and some slight hunger pains hit him as he had missed his feeding cycle on the ship. Hopefully this Georgetown restaurant served good food. Tom wasn't into experimenting. He was plainly a steak and potatoes man. But he would indulge in a nice green salad too.

Tom, being a punctual person, was at the hotel entrance at 6:30 sharp and the limo pulled up. The driver wearing a suit, got out walked around and opened the door for

Tom whom he instantly recognized as looking far more comfortable wearing his new civilian clothes.

Margarette Mackworth was in the limo with John Harris, both wearing the clothes they had on at the meeting because they had been working and meeting with select individuals for a host of reasons and had just left the Pentagon ten minutes before.

Six or seven people could comfortably sit in this limo, but it was laid out with two facing backwards behind the driver, a long sofa-like chair along the driver's side and two more seats in the back facing forward. John Harris was sitting on one of the side seats and Margarette was on the rear driver side seat facing forward.

MARGARETTE MACKWORTH
How's the adjustment to real gravity admiral?

Margarette Mackworth could see Tom looked refreshed and a lot livelier than before. The long Hollywood shower providing a lot of negative ions helped release a lot of endorphins and chemical reactions in his body made Tom feel far more satisfied.

TOM GILBERT
I feel like a million bucks, change of clothes, shower,
etc.

John Harris looked on fondly at Tom, seeing before him the results of his search and a very important selection. Picking the right man to be the first Commander of the first United States Space Force Space Carrier had been one of the most difficult tasks in his entire adult life. Anyone besides John Harris involved in steering the selection would have resulted in Tom Gilbert not surviving the politically correct profiling that often resulted in the selection of the most mediocre people to fill difficult and pressing assignments.

When Abe Lincoln picked Ulysses S. Grant to lead the Union Army after his stunning victory at Vicksburg, the very first selection in American History that defied political correctness ordained a fighting spirit that had been lacking in all the Union Generals that Lincoln sacked. Hooker might have been the man Lincoln sought out, but he lost his nerve at Chancellorsville, and was reported to have been drinking heavily during the battle and may not have been coherent during critical phases of what should have been an easily winnable battle that turned into a route and subsequent poorly executed retreat.

There was a time in history when America had to make a serious choice for a leader when General Curtis LeMay was selected to head the Strategic Air Command. In the very beginning, the wrong leadership was selected, which almost derailed SAC, but Curtis Lemay quickly overhauled it and using extensive training, brought the command back into focus and by the time the Vietnam War started, we had a viable deterrent.

Rumors circulated that Margarette Mackworth was just as much of a woman as Tom Gilbert was a man's man. Ironically, they were both single. Margarette Mackworth chose a career over a family and with the challenges she faced first as Air Force Secretary, then later Space Force Secretary, knew vividly there would absolutely be no quality time for children and she also knew kids required a hands-on outcome. If parents didn't directly intervene all the time, the child would most likely grow up to a lackluster life and possibly get hooked up to social degenerates that would lead them down the path of self-destruction.

Unfortunately, Margarette Mackworth caused the rumors to be embellished far more than they should have because instead of sticking with men her own age, she picked on guys ten or more years junior to her. One of her former girl friends said Margarette Mackworth once confided in her the reason why she liked the younger men was they were like the ever-ready battery bunny commercial on TV, they just keep going and going and going.

Margarette Mackworth also told her friend she might have the Catherine the Great Syndrome. Unfortunately, she never met the Potemkin type thus remained unsatisfied. Margarette was astute and knew about the golden rule of never dipping your pen in company ink (or the corollary of that never provide the company ink). Tom Gilbert was company, so he was safe, otherwise she would weave her black widow net and in due time have her way with him.

This dinner was purely business. Margarette wanted to discuss with Tom what was on her mind and what now confronted the President.

MARGARETTE MACKWORTH
What I wanted to discuss with you which I couldn't
back at the Pentagon with so many people there
including NASA spies, is new requests the President
is being hounded by.

TOM GILBERT
And what are those requests?

MARGARETTE MACKWORTH
NASA scientists are politicking hard to use the CSS
Alabama for scientific research.

TOM GILBERT
In what way?

MARGARETTE MACKWORTH
Since NASA was involved in the design of your power

generators and propulsion with Naval Reactors, they know that once Alabama exits the solar system and is out in the absolute vacuum of space, she can reach incredible velocity and make it to a nearby star system in less than two years.

TOM GILBERT
So, what you are telling me is they want to turn this military spacecraft into a science experiment.

MARGARETTE MACKWORTH
That's what they want.

TOM GILBERT
NASA obviously does not view the alien threat as tangible reasons to build an Earth Defense Structure.

JOHN HARRIS
Like many scientists, they operate off an idealistic purpose and I sincerely believe they think the aliens have no intentions of visiting earth nor committing aggression against this planet.

TOM GILBERT
Just how would they know the alien's intentions?

MARGARETTE MACKWORTH
They don't. It will take another Pearl Harbor attack to snap them out of their false sense of security.

TOM GILBERT
Why can they not understand a war with the aliens will last just one day?

MARGARETTE MACKWORTH
It's a scary thought.

JOHN HARRIS
That's why we must be capable of damaging them before they damage us.

TOM GILBERT
When do you think they will impose this scientific research?

MARGARETTE MACKWORTH
I think when you venture to Uranus you will be forced
to take a couple NASA scientists with you.

TOM GILBERT
Will they be cleared and sworn to secrecy?

MARGARETTE MACKWORTH
Yes, NASA says they agree to comply with all the
security requirements if they get to come along for the
ride and are given a day or two to study Neptune.

TOM GILBERT
Will they be informed of the special tests we plan on
doing?

MARGARETTE MACKWORTH
No. They are not cleared to know about those tests.

TOM GILBERT
Okay, understand all, I'm sure how we'll work this
out.

MARGARETTE MACKWORTH
Tom, thank you for your cooperation in this matter.

TOM GILBERT
My pleasure.

C.U. MARGARETTE MACKWORTH

Tom smiled as he looked Margarette directly in the face, and since he was a lot closer
than he had been before, could see the softness of her skin and some of the finer
features of her Nordic complexion.

The restaurant Margarette picked was ideal for a steak and potatoes kind of guy. Tom
had not had any alcohol in quite some time and knew it would have a much stronger
effect on him, so he made a mental note to keep it down to one glass of wine and drink
a lot of water.

The T-bone steak was cooked to perfection, and the baked potato loaded up with butter,
bacon bits, chives, cheese, and cream cheese is what the doctor ordered. He resisted
the offer of coffee because he wanted to get some quality sleep.

The restaurant had a bar not far from the table the group now sat at. A couple young men, engineers from Indiana who worked on loan to Naval Sea Systems Command, were eyeballing Margarette. The body language was revealing as they appeared focused on Margarette, who was not a stunning beauty, but she was equipped. As dinner party broke up Margarette explained her intentions.

MARGARETTE MACKWORTH

I'm going to meet some friends here. My limo will
take you guys home and come back and pick me up
later.

Tom was relieved because it meant there would be no delays and he would get back to his room and get some quality sleep to help him adjust to Earth Gravity and be able to deal with the numerous meetings he knew he was going to be sucked into tomorrow. After the polite goodbyes John Harris and Tom Gilbert were out at the entrance of the restaurant and just like clockwork the limo pulled up, the driver got out and opened the passenger door.

LIMO DRIVER

Mr. Harris, I'm here to give you a lift back to the
Pentagon and then drop Admiral Gilbert off at his
hotel.

JOHN HARRIS
All right.

John Harris was glad this dinner didn't turn into a business meeting afterwards. He needed a break as well. John went into the limo first, followed by Tom and the door was promptly shut. Tom just happened to look at the restaurant window which he could see from this advantageous angle of the bar. Margarette was with the two men, one of which had his arm around her giving her a hug and a kiss on the cheek. Apparently, they were old buddies. The rumors of Margarette and younger men appeared to have some validity to it.

The limo dropped John Harris off right at his car in the Pentagon parking lot where he had a reserved spot with his nametag on the guest parking stall.

Tom Gilbert went back to his room at the Hilton. He soon turned off his cell phone and undressed and by the time his head hit the pillow he was already half asleep. The Earth's gravity was making him feel lethargic and the dirty air was not pleasing.

Morning came too quick, but under the circumstances Tom realized he just had an equalizer sleep. Looking at his Swiss watch he had slept a good eight hours. It was time for Tom to get up and S/S/S *the three S's in sailor vernacular*. One of the perks of being an Admiral in the United States Space Force is he was exempt from staying in the BOQ, and only had to stay there if he wanted to.

In most cases Tom Gilbert would prefer a hotel, like the Hilton, that was considerably quieter than most BOQs on Naval Bases. There were a few exceptions. If he were in Japan, Korea, or Norfolk, Virginia, he would prefer the BOQ over a hotel room because they were kept in outstanding conditions there. The amenities for senior officers in those locations were superb.

In Korea all ports that a submarine would pull into such as Pusan (now called Busan) or Chin-Hae, there is only Army BOQ since there is not much of an American Naval Presence full time, though they do come in large numbers from time to time when a carrier battle group pulls in. Pusan's Army Officer Club has a message parlor. For a few dollars extra, you can get the *special message*, which is best described as a knob polishing routine.

As a submarine commander Tom Gilbert was introduced to some rather spectacular beautiful women in Yokosuka Japan and Pusan Korea. If it were not for the fact of his aversion to marriage as a sailor seeing all the damage long separations do to families, he might have considered tying the knot with both Japanese and Korean women he had met. He was secretly in love with a Korean doctor, but understood she was an intellectual who wanted no marriage, children, or a committed relationship. Her career was her life and there was not enough room in it for Tom.

Tom also had the opportunity to meet some Hong Kong women and it didn't take long for Tom to learn they were extremely high maintenance, though incredibly beautiful. Because of his position and role in the Navy, there was no remote chance of him having a committed relationship with a Hong Kong woman even though she might have been the daughter of a billionaire. Money isn't everything. At the point in his career, women and his personal life were put on a lower priority than his professional endeavors and goals.

It's true that officers have a hard time making senior rank unless they are married. Being a single officer is apparently considered a character flaw. But Tom's viewpoint after experiencing the submarine force for many years taught him married life has no business in the submarine force because it's a huge distraction and he could never drive his married guys as hard and as long as the single guys.

All he had to do for the single guys to get them buy in if he volunteered to take another submarine's mission, was to promise them an exciting port call like Pattaya Beach, Thailand; Subic Bay; or Pusan, Korea. Yokosuka, Japan, was no longer fun for sailors as the area had evolved to a mini-Honolulu.

All the Japanese in Yokosuka could effectively speak English and it didn't take long for a sailor stationed there to sometimes feel he was back in Honolulu or some other city with a large Asian population.

Likewise, the Yokosuka people were so Americanized they were slowly losing their Japanese identity. But you could say the same about Tokyo which was now a World City. Even though there are mainly Japanese in Tokyo, the cosmopolitan aspect of it along with tourists and travelers makes it seem like it's a suburb or twin city to Los Angeles but a lot cleaner and safer.

Now that Tom was an Admiral in probably the most sensitive position outside the joint chiefs, his career took on new meaning and with Space Exploration as a potential aspect of his future missions, getting tied down to a potential "West Pack Widow" didn't seem like a bright thing to do. It wasn't that he was a celibate like a Catholic Priest, family life just didn't seem appropriate for a man who might one day be going on two- to five-year voyages on a Space Craft to unknown planets and the risk associated with space travel where all it took was one unlucky hit by a meteorite flung at light speed from a supernova or some other celestial event to erase your existence.

Tom's not-so-long-ago activity sinking drug smuggling submarines on clandestine missions, might have seemed the ultimate at the time, because even though some of those submarines like the Romeo off Hainan Island, could also shoot back and if they had somehow got lucky and discovered them and shot back working and viable acoustic homing torpedoes. It was a gamble and had the drug smugglers used some of the leapfrog techniques some of the former Soviet Navy crewmembers understood well, the real threat of counter-detection and destruction was real. Lucky for the U.S. Navy, the drug smugglers were terribly greedy and viewed all other submarine drug runner's mere competitors and sometimes even they shot each other.

But the most recent events with the shakedown cruise and going through the selection process, arbitrated by no less than the President of the United States, turned Tom Gilbert world upside down and gave him a challenge that exceeded anything he ever witnessed serving on submarines. A few years ago, when he was seriously considering leaving the Navy upon the completion of his CO tour, he would have told you, there were no other jobs in the Navy or anywhere else that came close to being a sub skipper. Little did he know technology and the universe would prove otherwise.

Tom Gilbert knew that John Harris was always holding something back. The man was too slick of an operative. One never knew what his poker face meant. Even though he trusted John Harris whom he saw as his recent benefactor at the final round of the selection board process, he didn't understand what his motives were. One thing he did know about John Harris that intrigued him was that at one time he was chief of security at Area 51. *Perhaps there's more to the alien stories there than the government is letting on?* Tom asked himself.

At completion of his S/S/S, Tom Gilbert walked over to the closet and true to their word, the hotel had sent his uniform out and it was dry cleaned while he was out having dinner. One of the reasons why he loved staying at the Hilton is they knew how to take care of their hotel guests and for traveling military that needed a uniform dry cleaned over the night, was one of the many areas of customer assistance they provided.

As Tom Gilbert's quick trip to the surface of the planet unfolded into a longer stay and it appears it was stretching out even further, he was glad he picked up a few extras at the department store such as underwear and socks. After a couple more days of purchases or rentals, he could stay indefinitely.

Tom had been in and out of Crystal City numerous times as well as over at the Naval Yard where a lot of NAVSEA offices had moved twenty years before when the rent in Crystal City got too high. Just as soon as the Navy moved out, newcomers moved in. Space was tight, and United States Space Force taking over half of the former Air Force offices at the Pentagon and 20 percent of what belonged to the Navy had the same problem NAVSEA had around the time of the Vietnam War and the Reagan year military buildup.

Office space available was soon leased long term by USSF. On the ground floor, there were a lot of stores and shopping at Crystal City Mall. It was not quite as extensive as the Pentagon City Mall, but they had just about everything including good delis and restaurants and bars. However, just a block away past Eads Street places like Crystal City Tavern and the Sports Bar, provided a lot of entertainment for those who enjoyed having a brewsky with their buddies after work. Happy Hour was crowded and at lunch time the restaurants were full.

The American public would be appalled at how many top-level decisions were made over beers at the sports bar, or better yet after a group had a few drinks and tipped the dancers at Crystal City Tavern, where you could get a T-bone steak for about half the price. But they made up for it with the numerous drinks and tips the dancers received.

Tom was back at his old stomping grounds. He knew just the place at Crystal City Mall where he would get a fantastic cup of coffee, a blueberry muffin, and a banana. After downing the coffee, muffin, and the banana, Tom Gilbert had not requested any transportation, neither desired nor required, walked to the Washington Metro Station in Crystal City. It was one stop away from the Pentagon in one direction and Reagan National Airport in the other direction.

You don't often see two-star Admirals on the Washington Metro, but you do see them now and then get off at the Pentagon. But absolutely none of them look as young as Tom Gilbert who still had a somewhat youthful appearance and lacked a lot of Admirals leathery skin.

In the submarine business officers who do not spend a lot of time on shore duty end up staying out of the sun quite a bit, so their skin does not age as rapidly as normal people.

Tom Gilbert looked five to ten years younger than most two-star admirals. If it were not for the fact Tom was now assigned to the United States Space Force, he would probably be shipping off to Greenland or some other god-awful place the old battleship admirals liked to send fast rising young whipper snappers, unless they had political connections, none of which Tom had.

Admiral Tom Gilbert wearing his uniform, bought his Metro ticket and placed it moments later into the turnstile ticket reader which let him pass without an alarm. Since 9/11 there were security monitors at this entrance wearing shotguns and body armor. It probably sucked to be them on a hot muggy Washington day in the summer.

This time-of-the-day trains going towards the Pentagon from Crystal City could be slightly crowded, but not nearly as trains coming from the other direction from Washington DC and the Beltway.

Quite often there would be no place to sit. Today Tom Gilbert was lucky the train was slightly empty, and he quickly found a spot. A young beautiful black woman most likely in her mid to late twenties quickly sat down beside Tom. Her dress and attire appeared very sophisticated. Tom could sense this was a woman of intellect and demure. Tom also thought, the attractive woman was either super high maintenance or she just had not met the right guy to break her heart. Out of politeness, Tom acknowledged the woman's presence.

TOM GILBERT
Good morning.

Tom smiled.

The woman smiled and responded.

C.U. SHELLY BROWN

YOUNG LADY (a.k.a. SHELLY BROWN)
Good morning, Admiral.

The young lady, Shelly Brown, was far more sophisticated than Tom realized. She happened to be an aide to Senator Bosworth, who was a member of the congressional oversight committee on space exploration and was always looking for waste, fraud, and abuse in the new United States Space Force, which was often accused of being on a boondoggle. Any new major agency of this stature and magnitude will always have inefficiencies, but Senators do not stay in office being Mr. Nice Guy. They get reelected by busting someone's balls.

Tom had no idea who Shelly Brown was, and this would not be the last time he ever saw her again, like many people you see in Washington, D.C.

Shelly Brown, on the other hand, knew exactly this was none other than Admiral Gilbert. Tom Gilbert was living on borrowed time. The press had not yet tracked down Admiral Gilbert, but his days of freedom were just about over.

Tom Gilbert would soon discover how Grissom, Shepard, Carpenter, Schirra, Slayton, Glenn and Cooper had their lives changed because of the space program.

Long after the Mercury flights those astronauts that followed are not remembered by the broader public, and the younger generation has no idea who they are or their personal history. The first of the breed are always the ones remembered. Tom was the first in his generation, and the type of activity that would surround him which the public would become familiar with because of the pending scientific experimentation aboard CSS Alabama that would soon get the public's attention when they performed their Uranus mission.

But more was to come. NASA was pushing hard for a two-year trek off to another solar system. The price USSF would have to pay NASA for keeping the Uranus hydrogen bomb tests confidential was that free ride to another solar system instead of performing its duties as planetary defense.

It did not take long for the train which at this point on the route still traveled above ground to reach the Pentagon where three quarters of the passengers got off and at this time of day not that many others got on continuing towards the next stop Arlington then Rosslyn. If a person wanted to continue into Washington, D.C., they would stay on this blue line train. The silver line and the orange line trains also ran through Rosslyn on the way to Washington, D.C., and past the nation's capital.

Admiral Tom Gilbert walked to the main entrance of the Pentagon. He wasn't carrying much other than his planner. In his business he couldn't carry around classified information. If it was important the agency would be directed to either send a message or email to him. Almost everything had transcended to email.

Naval Messages were a dinosaur, but they had legal precedence over everything else, and combat units could only be guaranteed to have message processing ability. Mission Critical and Wartime Communications had to go via Naval Message so that encryption could be done in a way to where super computers could not break the codes in hours making them a hindrance and possible security risk.

Radio Traffic Minimize would then happen as well, so very few messages would be sent unless they were orders to a combat unit. And most of them would go via a very high classification level, so the bandwidth was limited with seven-thousand-bit encryption.

Tom Gilbert, like a gentleman, allowed most of the commuters to get off the train before he stood up and walked off the train onto the platform and followed a distance behind Shelly Brown.

Shelly Brown was wearing a high-end woman's *Genny* Italian made two-piece black and red skirt suit. Shelly was slender and her physical condition was that of one of the top fashion models. Shelly's skirt highlighted her hips in a way that accentuated the essence of a beautiful flower blooming in the springtime. Shelly's walk exemplified one that a woman with confidence, grace, and respect.

Shelly Brown knew she was going places and took no social risks. Shelly was the politician's politician. Her Ivy League schooling manifested by stratospheric high grades throughout her entire education put her on the fast track and when Senator Bosworth needed to shore up support with minorities, he started hiring in addition to staff members but also interns of a variety of minority groups, Shelly applied and was given an interview.

Shelly Brown's mother, an educator, was critical about Shelly's language skills as well as Shelly's vocabulary and worked on her relentlessly so that when Shelly would one day be a public speaker that showed no ethnicity in her voice.

Shelly Brown's lovely straight black hair and her facial features that clearly exposed an element of European genetic material, in essence Shelly Brown was that of a hybrid who benefitted the best from all her distant relatives. The ultimate blend of looks, intelligence, and nurturing had created what her mother viewed as God's gift to some future deserving spouse and potential for a very successful life.

Even though Senator Bosworth was a crusty ole geezer part of the establishment, he had learned one thing in his many years of survival in Washington, if you managed to recruit a very intelligent staff member who had an uncanny ability to figure things out, you better pay attention to them and let them help guide you through the political mine fields.

Shelly Brown was Senator Bosworth's rising star on his staff and Shelly Brown did figure things out quicker than most of her peers. Shelly had a great head on her shoulders and had no axe to grind. She knew the Democrats had as many skeletons in their closets as the Republicans and they both played the same game, just with different props. In reality, Shelly couldn't stand either of America's main parties but kept that to herself. She was simply using Senator Bosworth as a steppingstone for her future endeavors.

Shelly Brown was clean cut, a virgin, and had no desire to give up her virginity until after her wedding, if that day ever happened.

Shelly Brown would only be getting married for one reason and one reason only, to have children and a family, and she wasn't quite ready for that. Shelly was relatively young for the power she wielded through Senator Bosworth. Seldom did Shelly make statements in public and if she did answer any questions the answers were exactly what the Senator instructed her to state, with no modifications.

As the Senator once informed another fellow senator if the rest of his staff only conducted themselves and made statements exactly the way Shelly did, he could run the whole place on auto pilot and spend all his time on the golf course except when it was time to go vote on some measure.

Shelly Brown also had a pulse on voters in Senator Bosworth's state and no matter how much the Senator felt about an issue, Shelly made sure he understood what the majority of the electorate wanted. Therefore, Senator Bosworth's position in the U.S. Senate remained safe. During the election cycle, Shelly remained instrumental in helping Senator Bosworth come from behind and maintain his seat when the polls suggested he would be smashed by one of the previous president's favorites.

Shelly was on her way to the Pentagon for a briefing about the CSS Alabama. There were a few issues and expenditures were raising their ugly head. Even with one of the most ambitious and successful operations in the nation's history, the bean counters were incensed at how fast the money was being poured down a rat hole as far as the political enemies were concerned.

The liberals obviously had better ideas on how to spend money such as on Affordable Health Care, social programs to *assist undocumented workers*, support for *more refugees and people requesting political asylum* that had recently risen to half of India and half of China, and all of Central America.

Senator Bosworth wasn't for increased spending on social programs, but at the same time he wanted to find out just how much money was being dumped down that rat hole he accused of being part of the *swamp* that needed drained.

Shelly's job was to figure out just how big the swamp was and what defense contractors were on a boondoggle getting rich. Little did Senator Bosworth realize that CSS Alabama was built on a shoestring budget, because anything that went out in space was expensive for many reasons.

Shelly was surprised the commanding officer of the CSS Alabama was on a commuter train to the Pentagon. She turned around and watched Admiral Gilbert approaching the Pentagon's entrance she was entering where an escort was waiting for her to whisk her through security into the meeting.

<u>INT. DAY PENTAGON</u>

Admiral Tom Gilbert had a special coded CAC Card that allowed him access to the Pentagon. His encrypted biographic's were on the CAC Card including his picture and his digital thumbprint and his PIN number.

Everyone walked through scanners and metal detectors. Tom could see at least eight security people, some of which were hustling the people through the scanners and instructions on how to lay their personal articles on the conveyor belt for the security scanner X-ray machine. About one out of four people were taken to secondary inspection when the X-ray machine operator was not able to identify something that may be suspicious.

Even with all this extended vigilance, well over two hundred security tests a year fail at the Pentagon. The security personnel take it personally. They didn't know if they should cry or quit. The stress was high because all it would take i was one good, placed bomb, and the brain trust could be wiped out and if that happened at an auspicious moment, it might decapitate America's military in the prelude to war.

Tom received a text message to proceed to a conference room in the D Ring. To his surprise, the nice-looking woman was heading in the same general direction with the obvious military escort. Shortly, she walked right into that same room.

<u>INT. PENTAGON D-RING USSF CONFERENCE ROOM</u>

People requested to attend sitting the long conference table had name placards, coffee cups, water, pens, pencils, notepads, and a few other amenities. Tom looked around the room and saw a few familiar faces like CNO, Naval Reactors, USSF Secretary Mackworth, John Harris, a dozen USSF officers who were no doubt former Air Force or Naval Officers who received lateral transfer in the biggest reorganization the Air Force experienced since the formation of the Air Force.

A few civilians with NASA badges and a couple CIA types were present as well. Surprisingly there even were a couple Air Force officers, but they were probably here for logistics matters as most of the former Air Force that was gutted and placed under the USSF, no longer required Air Force involvement. Hap Arnold was turning over in his grave. Jimmy Stewart would probably have a few terse words as well.

Today the CNO and Naval Reactors Admirals had the pleasure of seeing their placards at the placemats next to Secretary Mackworth and John Harris, and Tom Gilbert's was directly across from them. Commodore Riley was also ordered to the meeting, and he was on the way, expected any minute. He had a previous engagement scheduled and Tom figured it was probably his old flame, a D.C. Attorney he almost married quite a few years before, but luckily kept his neck out of that noose by the misconduct of the woman allowing him to escape her machinations.

Just about when Tom was starting to worry Riley might show up late, he walked through the door and approached Tom.

MARGARETTE MACKWORTH
Everyone, please take your seats so the meeting can
begin.

Like previous meetings, the computer display board behind Margarette had the words TOP-SECRET NOFORN and Margarette informed the group the meeting was classified TOP SECRET and any information discussed during the meeting would have that classification level. Translated it meant: *Don't bother taking any notes because we'll have to confiscate them.*

MARGARETTE MACKWORTH

Okay, everyone, let's get down to item number one
on the agenda, number-two power generator. NAVAL
REACTORS, will you please give us the details?

NAVAL REACTORS, NAVSEA 08

Thank you, Madam Secretary

NAVSEA 08 the director of Naval Reactors had a briefing paper which he then had in front of him which matched what everyone saw on the computer screen.

NAVAL REACTORS, NAVSEA 08

Early this morning Naval Reactors personnel
completed the post shakedown trials assessments
and found some issues with the number-two power
generator. As such it has been ordered shutdown and
maintenance is beginning to rectify a malfunction in
the controller. We expect it will take about two weeks
to complete the repairs and go through all the tests
required to certify it for unrestricted operations.

This was one night Tom wished he had not turned off his cell phone. The duty officer attempted contacting him and decided to not have the hotel wake him up because he realized Admiral Gilbert was living on fumes and needed an equalizer sleep. Tom received some text messages, but the information was preliminary, and Naval Reactors, who had just received a complete report, was in a better position to discuss it.

Margarette Mackworth looked at Admiral Gilbert in a manner that showed some irritation as if he should have alerted her sooner.

MARGARETTE MACKWORTH

What is your viewpoint of this situation, Admiral
Gilbert?

ADMIRAL GILBERT

Madam Secretary, we were waiting for NRO's analysis
before we made any decisions on our next move.

MARGARETTE MACKWORTH
Well, it's clear you have a serious problem now.

ADMIRAL GILBERT
Yes, Madam Secretary, that's true, and my people have informed me they believe this can be repaired and be back online in time to support our pending schedule.

MARGARETTE MACKWORTH
Very well, Admiral, but mission planning has you undocking in two weeks, we have no slack in the schedule because of all the components coming together to support your next mission which will be considered your first actual deployment, since your last underway was nothing more than a shakedown cruise.

ADMIRAL GILBERT
All information is preliminary at this point. We will not know exactly what corrective action we must do until our nukes tear into the equipment and remove and replace damaged components and retest the system.

MARGARETTE MACKWORTH
We have a lot riding on the undocking schedule. Any delays can be extremely costly, and money is one thing we are quickly running out of.

ADMIRAL GILBERT
Understand, Madam Secretary, but from my experience on nuke subs, we can't cut corners and at the same time, I can't work my nukes to death especially if I expect them to be able to function during the maneuvering watch as we undock and proceed on unrestricted operations.

MARGARETTE MACKWORTH
Admiral, I'm not suggesting you kill your crew overworking them, but now is not the time for normal shift work, we must look hard at the timeline and make sure it's all ready to go two weeks from now.

ADMIRAL GILBERT
Madam Secretary, I saw too many times in the past when our submarines left port the crew was exhausted

and almost unsafe from working excessive hours. They pour their hearts into it knowing there is no substitute for success. Our business on the Alabama is just as hazardous if not more so than our submarines. I want to deploy with the crew fresh and vigilant.

MARGARETTE MACKWORTH
Admiral, the schedule is super tight, there is no flexibility in it.

ADMIRAL GILBERT
Madam Secretary, I'm not willing to put the last bolt on the generator and get underway five minutes later. And under the circumstances I want to fast cruise an entire day before we undock, that way I will know the physical condition of my men who will then be poised to proceed in a degree of safety.

MARGARETTE MACKWORTH
Admiral, I understand your concern, but we must be ready to go in two weeks.

ADMIRAL GILBERT
Madam Secretary, this is not like on a submarine where the CO can simply just transit on the surface a while until the crew gets their physical condition ready to support submerged operations. Unlike a submarine, we are in space the minute we undock and face all the perils of space travel immediately, and far away from help and with the prospects you will not be able to send any help to rescue us if we encounter some sort of disaster.

MARGARETTE MACKWORTH
Okay, Admiral, I get your point. I want to be notified the minute you think your schedule is not going to make our undocking date.

ADMIRAL GILBERT
Madam Secretary, I've been scheduled to attend a dozen meetings. Since people have figured I'm here now the requests started pouring in. I do not have the time to attend a lot of meetings. If you want me to

preserve the schedule, I need to get back up on the ship and oversee the work so I can prioritize what goes on and who does it and be in position to call for a pro from dover tech rep if that's what it will take to finish on time.

MARGARETTE MACKWORTH
Understand, Admiral, but you have a couple meetings scheduled that are mandatory, we'll have a sidebar in a while, and I'll tell you about those meetings. After you get done with them you can return to your ship, but may I ask you a question?

ADMIRAL GILBERT
Yes, Madam Secretary.

MARGARETTE MACKWORTH
Why not leave Commodore Riley here for a while, he can attend the meetings you miss and will be your representative.

Riley looked at Tom with that all familiar look like, *please don't do this to me.*

ADMIRAL GILBERT
Madam Secretary, I'm sure we can have Commodore Riley available for some of your meetings, but he is here to do business with his air wing and has a lot of meetings and work scheduled with them as well.

MARGARETTE MACKWORTH
As long as it's not a Tail Hook convention I suppose we must let him go about his business.

ADMIRAL GILBERT
I assure you, Madam Secretary, that Commodore Riley has numerous activities he needs to attend and from what I understand, he's on his way tomorrow heading to Wright Patterson Airfield where Alabama's TR-3B Squadrons are currently stationed, waiting to deploy to the ship after it undocks.

MARGARETTE MACKWORTH
Okay, Commodore Riley, keep in touch with my office and give us heads up on your whereabouts in case

we need to drag you into a meeting, because I would sure hate to have to bring Admiral Gilbert back to the surface to attend a meeting if you are available.

COMMODORE RILEY

Understand, Madam Secretary. I'll make sure your staff has all my contact information and I will always carry my cell phone with me so you can call or text me if required.

MARGARETTE MACKWORTH

Alright, let's quickly go over all the other cats and dogs. Admiral Gilbert, come to my office when we get done here.

Over the next two hours they went down the laundry list of action items. This was not like a ship builder guarantee meeting where they adjudicate responsible parties action items. Each item on the agenda had a direct impact on the nuclear tests. The mission to Uranus was not going to be discussed in this meeting since that activity was classified above top secret and most of the people in the room were here to discuss nuclear power issues.

During this time, Tom Gilbert looked down the table a few times and observed Shelly Brown taking copious notes. Even though she was five seats down and across on the other side of the table, Tom could see she had good handwriting and her notes appeared to be very organized as would be the case with an intellectual.

Tom had seen her type before. They were sweet and demure and all prim and proper, but they were all business and knew how to make grown men cry. A person like Shelly Brown with the full force of Senator Bosworth behind her was unstoppable. It wasn't that she would attempt any immoral or unethical behavior, and on the contrary, she always attempted to do what she perceived as logical and legal.

Working for the Senator, Shelly Brown had seen her fair share of shady deals and held crooks in total disdain. She had yet to be corrupted, which seemed rather incredible for D.C. where everyone was assumed to have a price. Thus far, Shelly has never given any lobbyist the impression she had a price and they found her extremely difficult to get around.

All the information disseminated in the meeting made its way to the computerized blackboard. By the end of the meeting, all that information was emailed on the high side to select attendees who really needed to be in possession of that information. Outside of the crew and Naval Reactors, nobody else needed discrete information about the number-two generator and did not receive those foils.

A real-time computer-generated transcript of the meeting was also in the secretary's inbox. After she approved it, she would send it to select email addresses on the high side with statement: DO NOT FORWARD. The list would be short.

After the meeting adjourned, Tom Gilbert was requested by Margarette Mackworth to go to her office with John Harris. A brief time later, John Harris and Margarette Mackworth were walking alongside Tom Gilbert engaged in small talk on the way to Margarette Mackworth's offices. The USSF Secretary's Office was a busy place. A lot of important people doing a lot of important things unrelated to CSS Alabama diligently work other priorities. New priorities such as the KH-14 and its replacement KH-15 Tech Insertion was a huge deal and the contractors out in California were frustrating as USSF tried to streamline and simplify the supply chain and accomplish congressional mandated COTS implementation. Simply put Congress was not in any mood to hear about them buying any more $600 hammers.

Tom not knowing what this meeting was about hoped he hadn't pissed off Margarette in the meeting with his long-winded discourse, but he had to look out for his crew.

As soon as the three were in the Secretary's office she grabbed her "Do not disturb" sign and put it on the doorknob on the outside so her staff knew don't approach the door. This was a privileged conversation of the type nobody was to enter and accidentally hear or see something they shouldn't. When the sign went up, the staff got nervous, shit usually hits the fan afterwards.

ADMIRAL GILBERT
Madam Secretary, what did you want to discuss?

MARGARETTE MACKWORTH
Admiral, this evening you have been invited to the
White House somewhat incognito. The President
doesn't want you to wear a uniform because he doesn't
want the press or staff to know it's you that is his guest.
He wants a few minutes alone with you and figured
this would be the easiest way to achieve that alone
in the oval office. John Harris will be there with you
where I think you will be given secret orders.

ADMIRAL GILBERT
Do you have any idea what those orders are about?

MARGARETTE MACKWORTH
No, and I've been told, don't ask.

ADMIRAL GILBERT
You said I had another briefing.

MARGARETTE MACKWORTH
Yes, you will be going over to the CIA for a briefing
concerning your upcoming mission.

ADMIRAL GILBERT
I see.

MARGARETTE MACKWORTH
After those items are completed, you will then go back
to your ship as you indicated you wanted to make sure
you have a hand in getting it ready to undock on time.

ADMIRAL GILBERT
Certainly. My presence aboard Alabama will ensure
we undock on time.

MARGARETTE MACKWORTH
Do you need a lift back to your hotel.

ADMIRAL GILBERT
No Madam Secretary, I'll take the Metro, kind of
enjoy it and it's a short ride anyway.

MARGARETTE MACKWORTH
All right, I'm not sure we'll meet up again before you
return to your ship, but wherever you go and whatever
you do, stay safe and I hope you have a safe return.

ADMIRAL GILBERT
Thank you, Madam Secretary.

Tom then turned and departed out of the Secretary's office and she and John Harris
talked for a brief while then she walked to her door and took down the do not disturb
sign and John Harris then left the office.

Tom knew the secretary was allowing him to leave so that he could go rent a suit to be
ready to meet the president. He was lucky he purchased a pair of black shoes yesterday
as they would now fit in well with the suit, he would wear this evening.

Tom Gilbert left the Pentagon building at the main entrance, walked to the train station
as the exercise was good, purchased a ticket and got on the Metro back to Crystal City.

He remembered a place in Crystal City Mall that rented suits and tuxedos. He made a bee line there and was immediately met by the store manager who knew well all the rank insignias especially on Naval Uniforms since Crystal City has been a huge Navy Office Space and even though a lot of it moved out of the buildings tothe Navy Yard, a lot of Contractors had offices there such as EG&G, URS, AECOM, GD, LMC, NGC, RTN, etc.

TOM GILBERT

Would it be permissible for the Hilton Hotel to return
the suit the following day?

BUSINESS OWNER

I've done a lot of business with the hotel and am all
set up to receive the returned suit, which was routinely
done for precisely the same reason, military coming to
town suddenly needing a civilian suit to go incognito
to some affair.

TOM GILBERT

What's the cost to have it picked up and returned?

BUSINESS OWNER

It was only a $10 fee to pick up or deliver a suit.

TOM GILBERT

That works.

What will they think of next? Tom wondered.

A white shirt and tie came with the rental, which Tom Gilbert tried on and was fitted in case some minor tailoring was required. Within thirty minutes upon arrival at the store, the Admiral was leaving with a suit in a carry bag back to his hotel. Inside the carry bag was a computer printout about the rental so when the delivery person picked it up for return at the front desk it could be tracked, and the Admiral not billed for lost clothing since the hotel signed over the suit to the delivery person who signed for receiving it. The receipt was scanned and emailed to the Admiral which would not do him too much good in space.

After stowing his suit in his hotel room closet, Tom decided he would walk over to 23rd Street past Eads Street and for old times' sake look and see what was still there. The Foxhole was long gone. It got converted to a gay bar long ago and corrupted many young men and sailors. The Sports Bar and Crystal City Tavern were still there, and with a lot of fond memories of the Sports Bar, he went in there.

Tom Gilbert went inside the Sports Bar. There were many ghosts there from the day NAVSEA was located just across Jefferson Davis Highway. More money changed hands based on the results of discussions at this sports bar than at many corporate board rooms across the nation. Programs were hammered out across the street in those tall corporate buildings the government leased after Rickover established the footprint there for the 688 Class SSN program.

It didn't take long for NAVAIR and other groups to occupy those spaces since the Pentagon was full and had no room for expansion. Plus, it was better to run some programs away from the day-to-day visibility of the Pentagon where political hacks often got stationed over some patronage scenario.

Often because of political horsepower at play, the decisions could not be made in the conference rooms the beltway bandits like EG&G or Tracor provided. Those companies have long gone merger into others such as AECOM that now was the prime contractor for Area-51 replacing EG&G who they absorbed. EG&G is not gone, they still exist, but a fragment of their former corporate giant thanks to their significant involvement with Cash-In-Advance.

There was just too much government infighting and turf battles going on. The term often used by program managers is the *stove pipe* principal. It was all about money and if the program manager sent work in one direction that means some other entity would not get any.

It was also a feast or famine, and it sucks to be located at some agency suddenly experiencing famine because another agency just picked up their work. A lot of times it was a political decision not based on the merits of the participants.

Tom Gilbert had been stuck in a program office for a while after he completed his CO tour, and it left a sour taste in his mouth. Though the assignment provided a lot of opportunity to meet a lot of nice-looking women as corporations had discovered long ago that the best way to influence some of the program managers was to send in a woman who was very attractive to influence the little head making all the decision.

Unfortunately, a lot of those women had marriage on their mind and even though they dressed for success their goal was to survive the corporate world of the beltway, where money talks, but also be poised to meet and marry (bury) young whippersnappers like Tom Gilbert who were fast risers. Tom also had the looks and the charisma to go along with the appeal of his other tangible assets.

The only good thing that came out of working as a program manager was the promotion to Captain which gave Tom Gilbert a shot at Admiral. In hindsight, working briefly at NAVSEA wasn't so bad after all. Also, Tom was lucky there wasn't enough room over at the Navy Yard, so he got to enjoy a lot of meals over on 23rd Street and elsewhere around the area, plus he was about five minutes to Washing National airport.

The sports bar brought back a lot of memories. Quite a few people involved in a lot of exciting programs in and out of time often had lunch or dinner here, *wining and dining* program managers and other officials they wanted to influence.

Beltway Bandits who wanted to win contracts and beat their competition schooled women and men who marketed their products to always pick up the tab. Some program managers still had good moral and ethical behavior. Others did not and it was surprising that even female GS-15s at time got in trouble doing what Margarette Mackworth was doing with her young engineers.

At least Margarette Mackworth was bright enough and subtle enough to not take her zeal for young lovers to junior officers. Engineers on TDY were usually in and out of town after a few weeks and if the short soiree didn't work out very well, the advantage was these young engineers were soon gone and out of sight and out of mind.

The new President knew of Margarette Mackworth's reputation, which was slowly becoming problematic, not the sort of person to be in a high visibility job. Margarette Mackworth was used principally to help carve up the Air Force and feed some of the carcass to the United States Space Force, and the rest dumped onto the Army as the service was destined to be discontinued with the Space Force taking over the essence of what the Air Force had been in the past.

Now that United States Space Force was secure in its new role, it was a foregone conclusion Margarette Mackworth would be gone before the next election. The only person the new President could think might succeed as Margarette Mackworth's replacement was the venerable John Harris. From Area 51 Security Manager to head of the New United States Space Force was quite a journey for John Harris.

Tom sat at the bar in the Sports Bar where he quickly ordered buffalo wings and French fries. He selected a craft beer to wash down his lunch and hoped Earth's Gravity would not get him too inebriated since he was going to the White House later.

A good-looking blonde and her friend sat down next to Tom Gilbert. With Tom's short-cropped hair and all the military around Crystal City and close to the Pentagon he could not help but look like a person in the military.

Tom smiled at the woman who ordered a salad and a glass of wine.

The woman returned the smile and initiated the conversation with a very friendly southern dialect.

LADY AT THE BAR (a.k.a. MAGGIE)
Hello

Tom responded to the woman while noting in the back of his mind, she was very pretty and built like a *brick shithouse* in sailor vernacular.

TOM GILBERT
How are you doing?

LADY AT THE BAR (a.k.a. MAGGIE)
I'm doing good, taking a break from work.

TOM GILBERT
What kind of work do you do?

LADY AT THE BAR (a.k.a. MAGGIE)
I'm an enforcement official for the Security and Exchange Commission.

TOM GILBERT
I see. That must be an interesting job.

LADY AT THE BAR (a.k.a. MAGGIE)
Life was good until Mr. Madoff came along and congress started breathing down our backs because we were not catching enough of the crooks.

TOM GILBERT
Any reason why it took so long to catch him?

LADY AT THE BAR (a.k.a. MAGGIE)
Well, it was one of the best Ponzi schemes ever. Had the stock market not crashed, there is a good chance we might not have ever caught him.

TOM GILBERT
How did the stock market help you detect his fraud?

LADY AT THE BAR (a.k.a. MAGGIE)
A lot of people got shaken badly by the very ugly stock market selloff. There was panic on Wall Street and some of Madoff's investors got margin calls on their trades and were short of cash and had to cover margin calls by pulling money out of Madoff's fund.

When Madoff could not come up with the cash fast enough to pay back some of the bigger investors, lawyers were hired, lawsuits started flying, and when a few of them thought Madoff had ripped them off for amounts as much as $300 million such as some charities, they immediately filed complaints with the SEC.

We normally would not have moved so swiftly, but some of the Charities funded hospitals and indigent care and were put in dire straits and not able to service their debt.

TOM GILBERT
That's quite an interesting story.

LADY AT THE BAR (a.k.a. MAGGIE)
How about yourself, what do you do?

TOM GILBERT
Well, I was a submarine officer most of my adult life. I'm now involved with space research.

LADY AT THE BAR (a.k.a. MAGGIE)
I bet that's exciting.

TOM GILBERT
More than you can imagine.

LADY AT THE BAR (a.k.a. MAGGIE)
My name is Maggie.

TOM GILBERT
I'm Tom.

MAGGIE
Pleased to meet you, Tom, this is my friend Sue.

TOM GILBERT
Hello, Sue.

At about that time the bartender delivered their food orders, and everyone appeared starved, and the conversation was quickly replaced by eager consumption of food. Tom was quite pleased with the taste of the buffalo wings, and he dumped ketchup and tabasco on his French fries with salt.

It's little things like this that you can miss on a submarine or a spaceship. The beer modulated the satisfaction. The perfume from Maggie added to the ambience and her friend was a very good-looking woman as well.

After they finished eating, Maggie grabbed her bar bill and put cash in it and informed Tom.

MAGGIE

I'm sorry, Tom, but we must get back to work. We probably have another five hours to go before we can go home.

TOM GILBERT

It was a pleasure to meet you, Maggie.

Maggie pulled out her business card and handed it to Tom.

MAGGIE

Give me a call sometime, perhaps we can meet for lunch some other time.

TOM GILBERT

Sure, I'll do that. I'm sorry I do not have any business cards with me, or I could give you one.

MAGGIE

That's okay, you got my number.

TOM GILBERT

Thanks.

Margarette and her coworker walked out of the Sports Bar and were walking towards Eads Street, then Jefferson Davis Highway, where she only had to go another block and half to her office in a leased building that had several government agencies in it.

Tom Gilbert finished his beer, paid for his bar tab, then walked back to the Hilton Hotel where he decided to take a two-hour nap, then get up and get ready to go to the White House. Hopefully he would not be disturbed during that time. Tom then set the alarm on his cell phone and lay down. The planets and stars aligned. Nobody attempted calling Tom during his nap, which he woke from fully restored. *Nothing like a power nap to set you up for a great evening.* Tom thought.

Tom had plenty of time to get ready and went about getting ready in precision like manner. One who is familiar with submarines would expect that from a nuke, who was generally great at following procedures very carefully and accurately. Nuclear Submarines were truly the best part of the Navy. Only Naval Air came close, and that was only because so many young men wanted to become pilots, so they gave the extra effort to get there. One thing is certain, you seldom find any pilots who are malcontents.

REVELATIONS IN THE WHITE HOUSE

Tom Gilbert wasn't sure exactly how he was going to get to the White House. Taking a cab to the White House is not exactly something a person would do. As Tom was thinking about how he would get there, his phone rang, and it was John Harris calling on his caller I.D.

TOM GILBERT
Hello John, what's up?

JOHN HARRIS
Can you be ready in thirty minutes?

TOM GILBERT
Certainly.

JOHN HARRIS
Good, be out in front of your hotel thirty minutes from
now. Transportation will be there.

TOM GILBERT
Roger that.

John Harris then hung up and Tom then heard the dial tone. True to his promise, Tom was outside the main entrance of the Hilton thirty minutes later and a limo pulled up.

The driver got out, walked around, opened the passenger door and asked Tom, the question.

LIMO DRIVER
Are you Mr. Gilbert?

TOM GILBERT
That's me.

LIMO DRIVER
I'm here to take you to your appointment.

TOM GILBERT
Okay.

Tom then entered the limo and immediately saw John Harris sitting inside the limo.

JOHN HARRIS
Hello, Tom.

TOM GILBERT
Thanks for the ride, John.

JOHN HARRIS
You are welcome, Tom.

The limo then drove off heading for the White House. Turning north on Jefferson Davis Highway, then onto 395 to 14th Street then Pennsylvania Avenue to the White House. The Secret Service was expecting John Harris and Tom Gilbert. The driver was a Secret Service employee and the rider inside the limo with Tom and John Harris who said nothing was also Secret Service.

The limo pulled into the circular driveway which goes right up to the front entrance. The passenger side car door was opened, and all three men got out and walked up the stairs to the White House and Tom Gilbert and John Harris were escorted inside.

Tom Gilbert and John Harris were ushered into a side room where Secret Service agents used a metal detector wand to pat them down and make sure they had no metallic objects with them.

John and Tom were then escorted to the oval office and met the President who was sitting at his desk and did not stand to meet them as he was looking over some important documents and but gave the greeting.

PRESIDENT
Please have a seat, gentlemen.

About that time the President nodded at the Secret Service escort which gave him the signal to stand outside the office. If there were any sudden sounds heard from outside the room, the Secret Service agent would be back in the office in a split second. The President needed privacy for the conversation that was to commence.

PRESIDENT

Thanks for coming right away, I wanted to talk to you before you go over to the CIA to get your briefing.

TOM GILBERT
Will that be today?

PRESIDENT
No, Admiral Gilbert, that's scheduled for 9:00 tomorrow. It's going to be a long day for you.

TOM GILBERT
I see.

PRESIDENT
Admiral, I do not envy you. In fact, I feel sorry for you knowing what you may soon be going through going where no man has ever gone before.

TOM GILBERT
It's quite an extraordinary opportunity, Mr. President.

PRESIDENT
Yes, but the danger is far more than what anyone realizes.

TOM GILBERT
I assumed risk when I was on submarines.

PRESIDENT
Admiral, I'm sure you will look back on your submarine days as a time of less difficulty and those days will seem plain compared to your future.

TOM GILBERT
I suppose so, sir.

PRESIDENT
Okay, now down to the point of why I asked you to come over. You may already know NASA is clamoring to put scientists on your ship for the Uranus mission.

TOM GILBERT
Yes, sir, I do not approve of taking them along, but I understand I may not have any choice in the matter.

PRESIDENT
You are right, you do not.

TOM GILBERT
I'll do my best to manage despite them being aboard.

PRESIDENT

What is critical is those scientists are not allowed to know anything about the hydrogen bomb tests on Uranus.

TOM GILBERT

I'll make sure the Alabama is on the other side of the planet when the bombs go off and as soon as we retrieve the TR-3Bs, we'll depart the planet and head back to Earth.

PRESIDENT

That's another reason why you are here now, to get new orders.

TOM GILBERT

What are those orders?

PRESIDENT

Instead of coming directly back to Earth, you are going to another Solar System where you will ascertain the aliens' intentions. You very well may be attacked and must defend yourself.

TOM GILBERT

Are these aliens advanced to the point my ship is in severe risk?

PRESIDENT

They are advanced to the point we think they are capable of visiting Earth.

TOM GILBERT

What rules of engagement do I have in the event I determine the aliens have hostile intent?

PRESIDENT

Minimize risk to the ship and attempt to get your ship and your crew home safely. But if you must shoot your way out to make it back, that's what you'll have to decide since you will be so far away, we will have no ability to send a force to assist you. You are on your own.

TOM GILBERT

I see. So, the point really is to avoid aggression and avoid hostilities that might lead to unpredictable consequences.

PRESIDENT

You will not know what you must do until you meet the Aliens and determine their intentions.

TOM GILBERT

Are the two scientists aware we are going on a long trip?

PRESIDENT

They think they will be spending a lot more time at Uranus than we intend. We are just going to give them a quick peak at Uranus, then you will re-chart your course to the planet the CIA will brief you on tomorrow.

TOM GILBERT

What is the estimated duration of the transit to this alien planet?

PRESIDENT

The CIA has calculated two years to get to the alien planet based on the velocity NASA thinks you can obtain.

TOM GILBERT
That's a long trip.

PRESIDENT

It will be cramped until you eat yourself some room and eject trash and waste overboard.

TOM GILBERT

I was kind of used to walking on cans of food during my submarine early days.

The discussion went along a while longer, then the President announced dinner.

PRESIDENT

It's about dinner time, we have a very small crowd

invited tonight, a Senator and his aide. I would like you two to join me."

JOHN HARRIS
I would be honored, Mr. President,

TOM GILBERT
I would be honored as well, Mr. President.

The President stood up walked around his desk, walked to the door, and opened it and gestured to John Harris and Admiral Gilbert, to follow him.

PRESIDENT
This way, guys.

The Secret Service men followed a few feet behind and a couple feet forward knowing where the President was heading to the White House dining room. It did not take long to reach the dining room, now set up with one long table and sixteen chairs and place settings. The new President liked sitting in the middle of the table so he could be closer to all his guests.

In recent years, the paintings hung in the room had been changed out by the previous two Presidents. The Current President, a former military officer and a big supporter of the constitution, replaced all the paintings with portraits of people that he felt had great impact on the country including George Washington, Abraham Lincoln, Teddy Roosevelt, Ronald Reagan, and others. These paintings came from the Smithsonian, Corcoran, and other galleries on loan to the President. They were considered the best paintings of these individuals ever made.

The Chandelier above the dinner table was put in by private funds during the previous administration which conveyed a sense of opulence never experienced in the White House. Other presidents had done extensive remodeling of the White House, but there had not been this much change since Teddy Roosevelt did the huge makeover in 1908.

The President, John Harris, and Admiral Gilbert were not the only ones suddenly in the dining room. As soon as the Secret Service announced the President was on his way to the White House dining room, the other guests were led in there who had been taken to side room. That side room had a bar, bartender, and waitress there to pamper the guests.

The staff were in their finest and most polished uniforms, were all smiles and very professional and were all appointed to their positions by the previous president who understood White House guests must be pampered. The new President didn't want to make any changes because he had spent a lot of time in the White House and liked the way things were arranged.

The smooth President walked up and individually greeted all the guests then announced the expected.

PRESIDENT.
Everyone, please take your seat at the dining table.

Each table setting with White House embroidery had a tent shaped placard with the guest name.

There was no doubt a couple of the guests would take those placards home with them for souvenirs. Some guests would steal the silverware if they thought they could make it past the metal detectors without being caught.

Tom found himself sitting across from the concert violinist Sarah Chen. This beautiful Asian lady would be asked to play a violin sonata later in the evening, with a concert pianist who had performed a dozen times at the Proms in London.

The big surprise for Tom sitting a couple seats down across the table from him was that gorgeous woman he saw on the Metro in the morning and later at the Pentagon meeting. The illustrious Shelly Brown looked great in that Genny business suit but now the couture evening dress Shelly now wore a full-length gown with the perfect shape for a slender body. Tom was captivated by this glamorous woman.

Sitting next to Shelly Brown was Senator Bosworth. Shelly often went to places with the Senator since his wife passed away from cancer. Even though rumors were flying around, the fact is Senator Bosworth looked towards Shelly Brown as one of his most trusted advisors, and she was like the daughter he never had.

Senator Bosworth developed parental instincts with Shelly and after meeting her mother and getting her phone number, the two were both candid about Shelly and her mother knew the senator was always concerned about her wellbeing and hoped that she one day would become successful.

Shelly liked Senator Bosworth because he was always sincere, ethical, and someone who wanted things done correctly. He also knew his job was to represent the people, not his own agenda. He didn't always do things the way Shelly wanted.

Senator Bosworth did things the way he perceived his constituents wanted. His pulse on his voters was very accurate. As a result, he was often accused of being a traitor to his party but at the same time, most of the voters approved of his style and his voting record. Senator Bosworth probably had the safest seat in Congress.

When Senator Bosworth busted some bureaucrat's balls over issues that were dear to his constituents, his popularity grew. Senator Bosworth had no grand illusions of running for the White House because he knew that at his age, his mental faculties might not be sufficient to handle the day in day out stress.

As soon as everyone was seated the staff started filling up their water glasses with Perrier water bottles. Another server had a tray set up on temporary stand and sat down five wine bottles that were opened and asked each person if they would like wine with dinner and gave them choices of Cabernet Sauvignon, Charney, Moscato, Sauvignon Blanc, and a Pinot. Half the guests selected a wine, the rest passed.

Tom Gilbert took a glass of Moscato but would sip it over a long period because he didn't know what real gravity and alcohol would do to his system. He needed time in real gravity to get back to normal. He had been warned that alcohol would have double the effect because of his long-term exposure to microgravity.

Tom could see the name placards across from him. Shelly Brown's name was very easy to see at such a short distance. He knew Senator Bosworth from numerous appearances on television, being a leading voice in congress for several issues including NASA and the Space Force.

As part of the USSF reorganization there were some attempts to insert NASA under the USSF organization.

However, NASA scientists and many college professors fought vigorously to oppose such a move citing the need for independence to allow honesty in reports on space discovery. The fear was USSF would totally weaponize space, and purely scientific advancement for the sake of enlightening mankind would be replaced by bomb throwers and baby killers if they allowed the USSF swallow up NASA and ostensibly redirect efforts towards prioritizing USSF needs over unrestricted scientific discovery and advancement of pure science.

Tom realized the beautiful lady who he had made eye contact with and a few brief words on the Metro was some sort of big shot at the meeting today and sitting next to Senator Bosworth meant she was probably associated with him. The evening was getting more interesting by the moment. Sitting directly in front of one of the world's premiere violinists also added splendidly to a semi-euphoric plateau reached by having such exquisite company, though only temporary.

Just as Tom was thinking about introducing himself, the President beat him to the punch.

PRESIDENT
Ladies and gentlemen, thank you all for being here and

since many of you do not know each other, I would
like to now introduce everyone.

The President knew his remarks and actions would loosen people's tongues a lot quicker than waiting for them to introduce themselves. Going around the table clockwise he announced each person's name and walked next to them and as if queued somehow, the person stood and shook the President's hand and mostly smiled and thanked him for the invitation.

When the President got to Senator Bosworth, the politician in Senator Bosworth didn't let the opportunity slip away and used that precious moment to get slightly political and surface some of his agenda.

The President didn't mind so much because Senator Bosworth was an expert on stating as much information possible without irritating the other guests and the President.

Tom was all ears when the President approached Shelly Brown. Bingo! Just like he figured. Shelly was an administrative aide to Senator Bosworth. Aka spy. Tom could pierce her soul looking into her eyes and knew her stilettos were as sharp as necessary.

Women like Shelly Brown were the types you would never want to get in a knife fight with. Hardcore driven with lofty goals and no doubt would not let anything stand in her way of success. She would do anything legal, though not necessarily ethical, to pursue her goals and achieve what she perceived necessary to manifest the outcomes she wished to accomplish.

PRESIDENT
Ladies and Gentlemen, please let me introduce you to
SHELLY BROWN, Senator Bosworth's chief of staff.

C.U. SHELLY BROWN

Shelly Brown stood knowing she would soon be shaking the President's hand. Shelly's response to the President was sweet, demure, innocent, yet done in a way that left no doubt in a neutral bystander that she had higher standards than almost anyone.

Tom Gilbert estimated Shelly Brown was likely high maintenance

SHELLY BROWN
Thank you, Mr. President. I'm thrilled to be at the
White House this evening.

Shelly then held out her hand in a cheerful manner with a lovely smile that gave the President great vibes for the illustrious senator's aide.

PRESIDENT

Shelly, you do excellent work with the honorable Senator, and I sincerely am glad you are not one of my political opponents.

Tom enjoyed that brief exposure to the essence of Shelly Brown. Just for a short moment while the President was *joking around with Shelly Brown and her Capitol Hill exploits keeping the administration on its toes,* he opened just a crack in her armor which Tom peered through before she slammed it shut tight.

Down deep Shelly Brown no doubt epitomized the essence of a demure woman that Tom knew historic figures in the past sought. Perhaps Shelly Brown was like *Justa Grata Honoria* daughter to the Roman General and later Emperor's daughter who Attila the Hun sacked Rome over demanding her marriage to him.

Justa Grata Honoria (born c. 418 - died around c. 455) was the daughter of Constantius III and Galla Placidia, as well as the sister of Valentinian III.

Constantius III was briefly Western Roman Emperor in 421. Some historians attribute the fall of Rome to Justa Grata Honoria, a historic manipulator full of scandals.

The President worked his way around the table then came up to Tom Gilbert and introduced him. Tom stood in a very respectful manner with a genuine infectious smile.

PRESIDENT

Ladies and gentlemen, we are privileged to have the Commander of the first American Space Carrier, CSS Alabama, here with us this evening. Please let me introduce you to Rear Admiral Thomas Gilbert.

ADMIRAL GILBERT

Thank you, Mr. President, for inviting me to dinner tonight and thank all of you for being here, especially Sarah, whom I've spent many hours listening to your performances.

SARAH CHEN

Admiral Gilbert, what performance did you like the best?

ADMIRAL GILBERT

Ms. Chen, if there was an orchestra here, I would say Sibelius Violin Concerto in D Minor, Opus 47 is my favorite.

SARAH CHEN
It's a shame we don't have an orchestra here tonight
or I would perform it for you; however, I have another
piece I think you might like I'll play later if the
President would give me the honor and permit me to
perform it.

PRESIDENT
Ms. Chen, of course we would love to hear your
performance after dinner.

Tom perceived a signal then sat down and could not help but notice Shelly Brown burning a hole through him with her very strong gaze. Her facial expression was quite extraordinary and was almost impossible for Tom to get any slight hint at the essence of her thoughts. Her demure smile wasn't one of arrogance, but at the same time it wasn't manufactured for the sake of a special gathering at the White House. No doubt whatever it was had an element of sincerity and freshness to it.

Tom could see not twenty feet away from the dinner table was a glamorous-looking white Steinway Grand piano. President Trump who brought class and elegance to the White House also purchased that piano with his own money and had it installed in the dining room so there could be frequent professional entertainment.

When the previous President left after his term in office, he saw no point in taking it with him and informed the new President who had been his supportive Vice President, he was leaving it for his exclusive use and needs as a gift.

What most people in the room didn't know is the piano tuner had driven the Secret Service nuts all afternoon long tuning the piano. The piano was now ready for prime time. In less than an hour from then, Sarah Chen and the pianist who had not yet arrived would be performing *John Sibelius Sonatina for Violin and Piano Opus 80*. Afterwards they would perform *Brahms Violin Sonata No. 1 in G Major Opus 78*.

The President then introduced the last person at the table, John Harris and gave him great praise for *his assistance in setting up the United States Space Force.* What the President couldn't divulge was John Harris had been instrumental in preventing the Air Force and the "Establishment" from sabotaging their efforts.

Essentially, the Space Force was about fifty years ahead by gutting the Air Force to set up this new agency prioritizing its developments for future space wars instead of rehashing the last war. Plus, unbeknown to almost all the people in the room, the next war could be with Aliens, not the Russians or the Chinese.

John Harris had not been invited often to the White House. It was a mutual benefit because had he been seen too often with the prior President and the New President, no doubt the old guard and the "Establishment" would have gone after him and destroyed him.

The current President was a history buff and knew well what the Battleship Admirals had done to Billy Mitchell who advocated Strategic Bombing and moving towards military hardware needed for the next war, including writing his treatise *AIRPOWER*.

The Japanese attack on Pearl Harbor was classic Billy Mitchell insight, which he forecast many years prior. It did not take long for the Battleship Admirals and the Establishment representing companies like U.S. Steel and Bethlehem Steel to court martial Billy Mitchell after he sank a couple WW1 German Battleships in a demonstration.

Billy Mitchell was thus kicked out of the Army Air Corp, forfeiting his pension and publicly humiliated. John Harris would have been the modern-day Billy Mitchell had the President and his very supporting Vice President not handled things in the most absolute secrecy including avoiding all physical contact with John Harris so that Air Force officials would not be able to go after him to prevent their eventual breakup and reorganization.

When it was looking probable that America was heading to war, President Franklin D. Roosevelt sent Harry Hopkins his trusted advisor to Billy Mitchell to get a copy of *Air Power*.

FDR's plan was to mold his response to the German and Japanese aggression using the strategy that Billy Mitchell laid out. Harry Hopkins informed Billy Mitchell he could not make any public statements concerning the President's move, but he should be gratified to know the President believed in him and at a future date the President would try to salvage his reputation and give him back his rank and privileges as a General in the Army Air Corp.

Eventually America could not prevent the escalation and outbreak of war. Meetings were set up and President Roosevelt met with the joint chiefs discussing equipment and materials they needed to successfully conduct the war.

FLASHBACK

In a brief interaction with Hap Arnold, in front of the joint chiefs, when pressed for how many Airplanes the President was willing to buy, he calmly stated.

PRESIDENT ROOSEVELT (FDR)
I will provide eight thousand new airplanes a month.

Hap Arnold thinking the President misspoke, because that was an extraordinary number and thought he really meant eight thousand a year which was what the Joint Chiefs thought to be achievable questioned the number.

HAP ARNOLD
Mr. President, did you mean eight thousand a year?

PRESIDENT ROOSEVELT (FDR)
No General, pay attention. I said eight thousand a
month and I meant that. Unlike any previous war,
airpower will have a much bigger role in the future.
We will need at least eight thousand planes a month
and that also means eight thousand new pilots each
month.

Most history buffs know that Henry Ford built the world's largest building at Willow
Run (also known as Air Force Plant 31) to build B24 bombers. When the Pentagon
officials asked how soon he could deliver airplanes, he shocked them with the answer.

HENRY FORD
One year from now the first bomber will roll off the
assembly line at that plant.

When pressed for actual production numbers, Henry Ford surprised them again:

HENRY FORD
I can deliver a new B24 every fifteen minutes if
desired. It is simply a matter of size and scale.

True to Henry Ford's word, the first bomber rolled off the assembly line one year to
the date.

The Current President realized that if CIA estimates had any merit, they would need
another Willow Run like initiative in the future, to deal with the increasing alien threat.

One of the consequences of blasting radio messages out to the Universe to announce
Who We Are and *Where We Exist* was to draw undue alien interest.

Unfortunately, the poor judgement in blasting radio messages out to the Universe
didn't mitigate the fact aliens may not like what they were seeing as they also began
intercepting our radio and television signals.

There are most likely both good and bad alien races within our own galaxy. Luckily
for us we exist on the outer extremes of the galaxy, far enough away as to not attract
too much interest. The Ponarian came from the Andromeda galaxy, thus the Ponarian
civilization was too far away to have any material influence over Earth.

One technologically advanced civilization could be reached by the CSS Alabama in
about two years. Based on interviews with the Ponarian and other bits of INTEL, it

appeared this alien race who called themselves Jupitorians did not have any positive views of Earth. They also may perceive Earth as a potential threat, especially if we ventured out of our solar system.

If the Ponarian was being truthful, and we had no way of knowing what his agenda might be, the President feared we might already be too late. What we needed now was a fleet of Alabama Class Space Carriers. John Harris was keen on selling the second Space Dock plan so that Alabama growing pains would not delay new construction of additional Space Carriers.

TR-3Bs were very sophisticated craft. Attempting to build them at Lockheed's Skunkworks wasn't viable because they had insufficient capacity to build the number of TR-3Bs required. Lockheed didn't want any of their competitors accessing proprietary technology. However, John Harris said that since it was derived by the Area 51 reverse engineering program, technically Lockheed did not own the TR-3B design.

Since it would never see the time of day in court because of compartmentalization and security standards, Lockheed was not likely to be able to stop the government from building copies of the TR-3B at competitors such as General Dynamics, Boeing, Northrup Grumman, and even possibly Airbus (Eads).

The President realized John Harris was in the fight of his lifetime because Lockheed now had the retired Air Force General Sandy Whitman and Kevin O'Toole on their payrolls and his spies had told him they had been beating down the door to Shelly Brown, aide to Senator Bosworth. They were lobbying hard. Like most good lobbyists, you go after their most trusted aides to handle matters.

The President then focused on John Harris in the introductions.

PRESIDENT
John Harris assisted the previous President in the
development of the Space Force, and without his help,
we surely would not have a ship like the CSS Alabama
now in the Space Dock getting ready for a mission.

JOHN HARRIS
Thank you for your kind words, Mr. President.

PRESIDENT
John, thank you. Speaking for myself as well as
the previous President, we owe you a huge debt of
gratitude for all you have unselfishly done for us.

JOHN HARRIS
You are welcome, sir.

John was observably touched by his change in body language.

Insiders knew turf warfare can get tough. Long before Kevin O'Toole and retired General Sandy Whitman whored themselves out to Contractors, they came very close to ending John Harris career. But now they were greasing a lot of palms to go after him again. In due time the President would have to intervene to protect John.

What those contractors didn't know yet and the government could not divulge to them due to the sensitivity of the information, that based on the outcome of Project Jupiter, Assembly Plant's far larger than Willow Run would be needed to build sections of CSS Alabama's sister ships that would be needed to fend off the Jupitorian invasion should that intel manifest into actual attempted aggression.

According to the Ponarian who refused to divulge his source, it was the Jupitorians who wiped out Mars more than nine hundred thousand years ago, which the nuclear physicist Dr. Brandenburg had relentlessly studied since his departure from Lawrence Livermore labs.

Shortly the President sat back down and gave a signal to one of the servers who immediately brought out the first course of an eight-course meal. Smart people only ate a portion of the servings because there was much more food to come.

The reason why the pianist hadn't shown up yet now became obvious as he then walked with a Secret Service escort from an adjoining room towards the Steinway and Son's grand piano, sat down and began playing not so loudly so the guests could have conversations, but loud enough to hear the quality of the music. Cole Porter's "Anything Goes" started.

This pianist also sang the song. He had a strange sound to his voice. One could almost think he sounded like Cole Porter. The pianist then played Cab Calloway's "Minnie the Moocher" next. Small talk erupted during the performance and eventually the pianist played Glen Miller's Moonlight Serenade Piano Solo. During this performance Tom could not help but gaze at Shelly Brown. She caught him looking and decided it was time for the *black widow* to start in on her next victim.

SHELLY BROWN
How was your last voyage, Admiral Gilbert?

ADMIRAL GILBERT
It was what I expected.

SHELLY BROWN
You did what no man had ever done before. I'm
surprised the press hasn't caught up with you yet.

ADMIRAL GILBERT

One can only wonder. I'm glad they don't know I'm here.

SHELLY BROWN

Since the White House press corps knows you are here, I'd say, you might have The Washington Post breathing down your back tomorrow.

ADMIRAL GILBERT

Hopefully I'll get my work done here and back up to my ship before they locate me.

SHELLY BROWN

If you keep riding the Metro, they're not going to have any problems finding you.

ADMIRAL GILBERT

I doubt they will be looking for an Admiral on the Metro.

SHELLY BROWN

If you ever get caught there you will be swarmed.

ADMIRAL GILBERT

I hope to not find out.

About that time the pianist started playing the theme to Casablanca, *As Time Goes By*.

Tom felt lucky he had not seen any notoriety manifest in media types hounding him. He recalled reading up on the Mercury Astronauts and how the media penetrated every aspect of their personal lives. For the shuttle crew's life was far more normal until the Challenger accident.

The CSS Alabama was somewhat more comfortable in that it never went into the atmosphere and there was not the fear of losing all three hundred men and women in a single accident. Since crews were ferried up in small groups on the TR-3Bs or Super Shuttles, no large catastrophe of the loss of many personnel in a Columbia like incident which disintegrated entering the atmosphere would occur.

Tom was soon overwhelmed by another act. The Black Widow reached into her small purse sitting on her lap and pulled out a business card and handed it to Tom.

SHELLY BROWN

Admiral Gilbert, I would like you to call me when you have time, I have a few questions I would like to ask you.

Tom didn't take that as a Shelly Brown social invitation. He knew Shelly Brown was the main aide to Senator Bosworth and no doubt Shelly Brown could ask poignant questions and already listening simply to her discourse with the other guests gave him a clue this was a very sharp woman and if she had some questions, they were probably the kinds of questions that John Harris and the President preferred he didn't answer.

By the time they got around to the eighth course, Sarah Chen begged off desert and stood up and walked over to the piano where the pianist had stopped playing for a few brief moments.

The two musicians had a semiprivate discussion, then Sarah walked over to a small table adjacent to the piano where a violin case was laying. She pulled out her violin and walked next to the piano and asked the pianist to play a couple notes, E and A, as she performed some slight tuning of the instrument. She played combinations of G, D, A, and E and then nodded to the pianist. Sarah Chen then started performing the Sibelius *Sonatina for Violin and Piano Opus 80* she previously promised Tom Gilbert.

Then they played the Brahms *Violin Sonata No. 1 in G Major Opus 78*. By the completion of the performance of those two pieces, dinner was complete, and all the dishes were removed except for wine glasses and coffee cups that had appeared a while earlier.

The evening wound up quickly and Tom was soon escorted out of the White House with John Harris after giving everyone a friendly goodbye. Tom was dropped off at the Hilton. As expected, there were no pedestrians outside and the place seemed to have very low activity as expected that time in the evening.

Tom thus walked up unmolested to his hotel room and was soon in bed resting getting another equalizer sleep in.

The morning came too quickly again as Tom Gilbert once again found his uniform dry cleaned and in his closet. While he was sound asleep the hotel employee had quietly, per his instructions, removed the suit from the closet and returned it to the rental company when they delivered his dry cleaning along with laundered underwear and socks.

After his morning routine S/S/S, he was in the process of leaving his hotel and when he got to the lobby, he discovered to his horror Shelly Brown had predicted the press would find him. Outside the hotel was no less than a dozen television vans and a dozen cameras waiting for him. Timing was perfect; he got a page on his cell phone; he had a ride showing up to take him to Langley. He was told to wait in the lobby of the hotel, not to go outside. Moments later, the hotel manager and a man in a suit approached him.

HOTEL MANAGER
Admiral Gilbert, will you please come with us? Your
ride is here.

Hilton Hotels sometimes have interesting VIPs that stay there. As such they provide a means of getting in and out of the hotel without having to crawl through the media and potentially a crowd who sometimes seek out these VIPs. They walked past a door, down a hallway that appeared to be a hotel service hallway which allowed things like room service access to elevators without having to be exposed to the public except for a very short distance.

Tom Gilbert followed the Hilton Hotel Manager outside through what appeared to be a hotel employee parking lot and service entry and there waiting was a limousine. The passenger door was open and driver waiting for him. He got inside and the man in the suit shut his door. Inside the car was John Harris smiling.

JOHN HARRIS
Looks like the press discovered where you are staying.

The car swung out on the access road that went out to Jefferson Davis Highway. As they passed the hotel, they could see the front entrance of the hotel and the circus that was outside it.

It then hit Tom Gilbert hard. His life was forever altered. He no longer had privacy. And this was just the beginning.

The car sped on its way to Langley near McClean where he assumed he would be going to get a special briefing. He knew what he was going to soon discover would test his moral and ethical fiber and the information could shatter his current belief system growing up as a Methodist which had no provisions for extra-terrestrial life.

Tom Gilbert expected to go inside one of those fancy looking buildings and go to a really strange office but instead the car pulled up to a helicopter pad with a helicopter there running and waiting for him.

JOHN HARRIS
Here's your ride to the briefing.

TOM GILBERT
It's not here?

JOHN HARRIS
No. The meeting will be held at Area 51.

Tom was suddenly perplexed as all this was now unfolding in ways he never predicted.

Note to the director: for the movie, the helicopter can be painted to look like this which is an S-97 on the back cover of Paul D. Escudero's (me) Novel *SOYLENT CARAVAN.*

The S-92 is a larger helicopter than the S-97 above.
The S-97 has a pusher prop to give it 250 MPH cruise speed.

See below.

S-92 used in the story.
The CIA helicopter looked like a commercial helicopter with no military markings.
A person observing it would assume it was probably a corporate helicopter used by

real estate developers or CEOs of corporations going to and from meetings in tight schedules. As soon as Tom was on board the helicopter it took off and headed south towards Hampton, Virginia, where Langley Air Force Base existed. Andrews would have been more convenient but today the President was leaving Andrews for a trip to several cities, and they couldn't fly the TR-3B out of there with all the visibility of the press corps following the President.

TR-3B

TR-3B on the Aircraft Carrier USS Gerald R. Ford (CVN-78)

Experimental Aircraft in Hanger Building 27.
The floor is an elevator for underground parking of aircraft.

The Sikorsky S-92 helicopter flying at 170 knots didn't take long to reach the Langley Air Force Base in Hampton, Virginia. It landed next to a TR-3B pared in a revetment to keep it out of view from the public. Tom followed his escort out of the helicopter and over to the TR-3B which was modified for CIA transportation when speed was essential.

As soon as Tom Gilbert was inside the TR-3B and seatbelt fastened, the plane went vertical. It had VTOL capability and with the artificial gravity machine Tom felt no major G forces because inside the craft he was feeling "relative" gravity and not Earth's gravity. The plane went up almost vertically to eighty thousand feet accelerating as it went. Tom was in for a surprise. He would be at S-4 in Area 51 in less than an hour as the TR-3B was traveling along at around Mach 9 for portions of the trip.

Because of the VTOL capability, the TR-3B could land at a helicopter pad next to the tall black building in S-4. They exited the TR-3B which then took off immediately and flew over to the hangar, building 27 where it was parked inside while waiting for them to return.

Admiral Gilbert walked one hundred feet to the main entrance of the building with an escort. Admiral Gilbert was soon inside and, in the elevator, and taken up to the Ponarian's residence.

The elevator door opened, and they entered the residence. This was something different. The Ponarian over the years had given the Americans drawings and guidance on how to build Ponarian like furnishings so he would feel at home.

Today, like most days the Ponarian was painting again, trying to remember his past and preserving it since he knew there was little hope of any creatures in the Milky Way galaxy returning him to Andromeda and the Ponar planet.

The painter looked normal, nothing about him would give Tom any reason to believe he was an Alien.

CIA ESCORT
Po, this is Admiral Gilbert.

The Ponarian as he preferred to be called Po.

PO
Hello Admiral.

ADMIRAL GILBERT
Pleased to meet you.

CIA ESCORT
Po, Admiral Gilbert doesn't know you are Ponarian.

PO
That's too bad.

Admiral Gilbert was looking at some of the paintings and thought they must be artwork for science fiction novels.

ADMIRAL GILBERT
Interesting paintings. Are these for books or something?

PO
No, this is my recreation of images of my home planet.

ADMIRAL GILBERT
Where is that?

PO
I'm from a different galaxy. I was marooned here over
seventy years ago.

ADMIRAL GILBERT
What happened?

PO
My space craft crashed and was destroyed."

ADMIRAL GILBERT
You survived?

PO
Yes, unfortunately. Now it doesn't seem to be all that good of a deal that I survived the crash.

ADMIRAL GILBERT
Why do you say that?

PO
Your government scientists tortured me for several years trying to force me to explain how my ship's propulsion system worked. Just as your pilots do not know the details of the TR-3B they are flying, we Ponarians did not know, nor did we care how the propulsion system worked because there was nothing, we could do about it if it malfunctioned.

ADMIRAL GILBERT
Did your ship crash because of a malfunction?

PO
No, it was a combination of flying through a thunderstorm and the radars the Air Force operated at Roswell Air Force Base that caused my ship's controls to not respond correctly and when I got sucked into the vortex of a tornado, all control was lost and I did not regain controlled flight until my ship was bouncing along the ground getting seriously damaged to the point the propulsion system was knocked out. Once that happened, I was marooned to this planet.

ADMIRAL GILBERT
Were you injured in the crash?

PO
Yes, I was severely injured and in a lot of pain.

ADMIRAL GILBERT
How were you rescued?

PO
A rancher near Roswell base called the Roswell Air Force Base and said one of their craft crash-landed on

his pasture. The Air Force didn't know of any of their aircraft that was missing and was instantly curious and drove out to check it out and make sure it wasn't some sort of crack call, but back in those days, the Rancher was well respected in the community, which further added to the suspense.

ADMIRAL GILBERT
How soon after the crash were you found?

PO
I think the Air Force men were pulling me out of the wreck within two hours of the crash."

ADMIRAL GILBERT
You can communicate well now, could you communicate, and did you know Earth languages back then?

PO
No, I had no means to understand what the Air Force men were saying.

ADMIRAL GILBERT
Did they think you were an alien or extraterrestrial?

PO
No, for about a day they thought I was a Russian flying some sort of advanced spy plane.

ADMIRAL GILBERT
Were you interrogated right away?

PO
Not right away, I had some rather serious injuries including internal organ damage that required some surgery. I was heavily sedated for probably a few weeks. Then I slowly came out of a drug-induced malaise, and they started asking me a lot of questions which I could not answer nor know what they were asking.

ADMIRAL GILBERT
How did they determine you were not a Russian flying an advanced spy plane over our first Hydrogen Bomber Base?

PO

At the time, of course, I didn't know what was going on, but I was told later by John Harris they brought in a Russian defector who asked me questions, and my answers, which were made in high-quality Ponarian speech, was nothing like he had ever experienced before and he said, I was not speaking Russian, or any language he had ever heard before.

ADMIRAL GILBERT

What made the Air Force decide that you were an extraterrestrial?

PO

When rumors were going around that a UFO crashed at Roswell, the Air Force, which had taken my crashed ship to a hangar at the air base, was directed to put all the parts and pieces on a couple C54 cargo planes and ship them to the Headquarters at Fort Worth, Texas, where apparently it was put in a hangar waiting disposition from higher up.

It did not take long before the Air Force and the newly created CIA figured out Fort Worth was such a leaking sieve; all that material could not remain and was then trans shipped to Wright Patterson Air Force Base that had extreme security because the Hydrogen Bomb Program was ran out of there since at the time only the Air Force could attack Russia and China with Atomic weapons. The Navy had not yet been certified.

ADMIRAL GILBERT
How do you know all this?

PO

General John Harris confided much in me as I cooperated with him fully on a lot of matters.

ADMIRAL GILBERT
So, you met General John Harris?

PO

Yes, we had numerous conversations as he visited me quite often. He was about the only contact to the outside world I had back then.

ADMIRAL GILBERT
They shipped your space craft carcass to Wright Patterson, what made them think it was extra-terrestrial?

PO
The ship was full of numerous devices never seen before on Earth."

ADMIRAL GILBERT
Such as?

PO
Microprocessors, flat screens, and the propulsion and anti-gravity machine.

ADMIRAL GILBERT
Did they know what they were looking at?

PO
No, because with no power because the power plant was ruined in the crash, there were no displays or anything to look at. All they could see is the markings on the components which was written in Ponarian language.

ADMIRAL GILBERT
Has a Ponarian-to-English translator been created?

PO
After I slowly got my health back, I worked with American government scientists to create a translation.

ADMIRAL GILBERT
You voluntarily did this?

PO
No, at first, I only did it to reduce or avoid torture.

ADMIRAL GILBERT
They tortured you?

PO
Yes, for several years.

ADMIRAL GILBERT
Do you know why they stopped torturing you?

PO
I was cooperating, and they provided books and pictures to help create a translation and assist in me teaching a nuclear physicist how to communicate with me. Eventually I grasped the English language and informed him I would no longer cooperate if they kept torturing me and I would commit suicide as soon as possible.

ADMIRAL GILBERT
You didn't know how the propulsion worked. How about other parts of your ship?

PO
Admiral Gilbert, do your Navy pilots know how the radars and the displays work in your FA-18 Super Hornet?

ADMIRAL GILBERT
Probably not.

PO
Same thing goes for Ponarian Space Crews. We do not know the inner workings of the equipment, nor do we care. We are most concerned about navigation and survival in a hostile universe. Pilots on long-range survey ships must be trained in so many areas, wasting precious time teaching them the fundamentals on how all the systems work would result in a colossal waste of time. Our propulsion systems are so complicated the designers and builders take ten to twenty years to study them.

ADMIRAL GILBERT
Has our space force figured out how your propulsion systems work?

PO
I do not know the answer to that question, and I seriously doubt they know how they work, since it took the Ponarians five hundred years to design them.

ADMIRAL GILBERT

Are there other alien races like you where you came from?

PO

I came from the galaxy you Americans call Andromeda. There are a dozen worlds in multiple solar systems with intelligent beings that are close enough we view them as a threat.

ADMIRAL GILBERT

Do they have a physical appearance like Ponarians and Earth people?

PO

No, only two of the other planets and societies we visited have humanoids that look like you Earth people. The rest look quite a bit different.

ADMIRAL GILBERT

Can you give an example?

PO

Yes, look over there, at those paintings. I've painted them.

Tom looked over in the direction the Ponarian indicated and saw paintings of beings that didn't look all that appealing. In some cases, they were downright awful looking. *I suppose beauty is in the eyes of the beholder.*

ADMIRAL GILBERT

How long did it take your ship to travel from the Andromeda Galaxy to our Milky Way?

PO

Slightly over two years Earth time reference.

ADMIRAL GILBERT

Did you come directly to our planet?"

PO

No, I stopped at several other inhabited worlds.

ADMIRAL GILBERT

What worlds were those?

PO
I visited the Jupitorians."

ADMIRAL GILBERT
Do they live on our planet Jupiter?"

PO
No, their name is like the planet Jupiter in this solar system, but they are from a different world quite a distance away.

ADMIRAL GILBERT
In another solar system?

PO
That's correct.

ADMIRAL GILBERT
What are they like?

PO
You earth people would not like them and would be appalled.

ADMIRAL GILBERT
Are they a threat to Earth?

PO
Most certainly?

ADMIRAL GILBERT
Why is that?

PO
They monitor your communications, television, and radio signals. They view Earth people as a menace.

ADMIRAL GILBERT
To the point would they do hostile aggression?

PO
They already did about nine hundred thousand years ago.

ADMIRAL GILBERT
Please explain.

PO
They wiped out Sedonia on Mars and Atlantis here on Earth.

ADMIRAL GILBERT
Mars was inhabited?

PO
Yes, an ancient but advanced society had quite a presence on Mars and Earth. That ancient civilization had a few outposts on Venus polar regions as well.

ADMIRAL GILBERT
So, Earth and Mars were attacked by the Jupitorians?

PO
Yes, Mars was destroyed, and Earth was spared because there wasn't much civilization outside of Atlantis, there were just indigenous tribes who were considered primitive and not a threat any time in the future.

ADMIRAL GILBERT
They view us as a menace now; what does that mean?

PO
It means you had better be prepared for a showdown.

ADMIRAL GILBERT
Can you show me on a star chart about where the Jupitorians exist?

PO
Sure.

The alien Po walked over to a table where he had several large documents that appeared to be folded several times, grabbed one and walked back to Admiral Gilbert and opened it up which showed some familiar star patterns and the Ponarian pointed to in the constellation Leo, the Lion.

PO
One of these stars is where the Jupitorians exist."

ADMIRAL GILBERT
Which one?"

PO
You will have to take me with you if you want me to
divulge the location.

ADMIRAL GILBERT
Why would you want to go there?

PO
I've met with the Jupitorians in the past before I came
to Earth. I would have a much better chance to get
back to Ponar with the Jupitorians than with you Earth
People.

ADMIRAL GILBERT
Can the Jupitorians reach the Andromeda Galaxy?

PO
I've been here for over seventy-one years. I do not
know what their current capability is. When I visited
the Jupitorian planet, they did not have the means to
get to the Andromeda Galaxy, but in those many years,
they may have improved their space technology that
might enable them to reach my home planet.

ADMIRAL GILBERT
You want to go home?

PO
Yes, I want to die on my home planet near my relatives
and not far away in a different galaxy all alone.

ADMIRAL GILBERT
I can understand that.

PO
You would feel the same way if you were stuck in my
circumstances."

ADMIRAL GILBERT
You know how to get to the Jupitorian planet.

PO
Most definitely. I remember the star charts and route as
if it were just yesterday.

ADMIRAL GILBERT
You are not willing to divulge their location unless we take you there?

PO
That's correct.

ADMIRAL GILBERT
I'm curious, how did you know we are considering a trip to the Jupitorians?

PO
John Harris informed me.

ADMIRAL GILBERT
You meet with John Harris?

PO
Yes, quite often.

ADMIRAL GILBERT
Why is that?

PO
He's the only person I will give information to. I ignore all other requests.

ADMIRAL GILBERT
Is there a reason why?

PO
Yes, John Harris is a humanitarian and after he took over security on this base, he made sure that anyone who mistreated me would end up in a place called Greenland for duty.

ADMIRAL GILBERT
So, you developed a friendship with John Harris?

PO
It gets lonely when you have nobody else and are marooned on a strange planet. I was about to break down and considered suicide until John Harris came along and befriended me. After I met him, life wasn't so difficult any longer.

ADMIRAL GILBERT

Did you help John Harris in the reverse engineering activity?

PO

I gave him a few details of things I know about.

ADMIRAL GILBERT

But not the propulsion?

PO

No, that's because I really do not know how it works.

ADMIRAL GILBERT

If you knew how your craft propulsion worked would you have divulged it to John Harris?

PO

Absolutely.

ADMIRAL GILBERT

Do you consider John Harris your friend?

PO

He is my only friend. I do not trust anyone else. I fully trust John Harris because he always delivers on his promises and never promises me something he can't deliver. He's a very practical man.

ADMIRAL GILBERT

Before I committed to taking you with me, I would have to discuss it with John Harris and get permission from the President.

PO

Why wouldn't the President not want to let me go?

ADMIRAL GILBERT

What if his intelligence agencies tell the President they're not done with you?

PO

I've already given them everything I know. There is nothing more to tell them.

ADMIRAL GILBERT
Except for the location of the Jupitorian planet.

PO
I didn't feel that was necessary to disclose.

ADMIRAL GILBERT
But you would disclose it if we took you on our mission?

PO
Absolutely.

ADMIRAL GILBERT
How hard is it to find this planet?

PO
You can't see it from here. You can't travel straight for it due to the large dust clouds in the way you have to travel around.

ADMIRAL GILBERT
What do you think caused the dust clouds in space?

PO
It's not possible for us to know since those dust clouds have been there more than five billion years or longer.

ADMIRAL GILBERT
How large are those clouds?
PO
There are a few thousand cloud clusters, many of them are larger than your solar system.

ADMIRAL GILBERT
Are you saying that we must travel around the dust clouds to get to the Jupitorian solar system?

PO
That's correct, once past the dust clouds the solar system can easily be viewed."

ADMIRAL GILBERT
Is the Jupitorian planet by itself?

PO

No, there are probably five hundred solar systems surrounding the Jupitorians.

ADMIRAL GILBERT

We have plenty of room on the ship, there would be no physical reason why we couldn't take you. I'm not in any position to make such decisions. I would have to contact Margarette Mackworth, USSF Secretary, and she would then have to take it to the President.

PO

I have a phone right over there; you can call her.

ADMIRAL GILBERT

For something as sensitive as this I would have to talk to her in person in a SCIF because a lot of people on the CSS Alabama are not cleared to know you exist."

PO

When do you think you will have that discussion?

ADMIRAL GILBERT

I think I'll be taken back to Washington, D.C., and spend one more day before they shuttle me up to CSS Alabama. I will request a meeting with Margarette Mackworth as soon as I can. I would prefer to make that appointment in Washington because I don't want to give certain individuals time to react and prevent me from meeting Margarette.

PO

How will I be notified I've been permitted to leave?

ADMIRAL GILBERT

My mission starts in about two weeks. If you are authorized to leave here, you will be taken up in space within two weeks. You will have your answer in two weeks.

PO

Thank you, this means a lot to me.

ADMIRAL GILBERT

It's time we found out about the Jupitorians. Without your help it's unlikely we would ever find them.

PO

You would never find them, but they know where Earth is.

The Ponarian's statement gave Tom Gilbert a chill. The visit to the Jupitorians could be dicey at best.

ADMIRAL GILBERT

What do the Jupitorians think about Earth people?

PO

They view Earth as a menace to the Galaxy. The only reason why they have not wiped you out like they did Mars nine hundred thousand years ago, is there has not been any motivation to come here and do the deed.

ADMIRAL GILBERT

Assuming they one day will venture this way and extinguish life on this planet, how much time do you think we have?

PO

One can never guess about these sorts of things. I would, however, suggest your time is running out.

ADMIRAL GILBERT

Is traveling to the Jupitorians possibly going to cause them to act?

PO

Such a visit may very well trigger it, but you're dead anyway, so you might as well surprise them with a visit and hope they will take pity on you and not wipe you out.

ADMIRAL GILBERT

What are the Jupitorian worlds like?

PO

Most of their population lives in three cities that have over one billion Jupitorians each.

ADMIRAL GILBERT

All their power and strength are centered in those three cities.

PO
That's correct.

ADMIRAL GILBERT
What about the rest of their worlds?

PO
They are mainly farming communities and are not allowed to have any major weapons. The Jupitorians are paranoid of internal strife and thus only the three cities have weapons and the technology to back it up.

Tom was instantly doing mental gymnastics and realized that all they had to do is wipe out three cities and they would eliminate the Jupitorians from every threatening Earth again. But then the thoughts of their advanced technology seemed he would never be able to make such an attack and his ship would probably be easily destroyed by the Jupitorians.

SHELLY BROWN

The following day, Shelly Brown and Senator Bosworth were alone in his office discussing the night before and now that Shelly had a chance to size up Admiral Gilbert, the senator asked her poignant questions about Admiral Gilbert.

SENATOR BOSWORTH
What was your impression of Admiral Gilbert?

SHELLY BROWN
He seems well poised and down to earth. I was quite surprised he was the Admiral I sat next to on the Metro.

SENATOR BOSWORTH
I've talked with a couple of my Navy friends over at Naval Sea Systems Command and they all had good praise of the man and were quite surprised when a former submarine skipper, then NAVSEA program manager of a small to medium size program was suddenly thrust into the limelight in the Space Force.

SHELLY BROWN
What makes them think a submariner was qualified and capable of commanding our first Space Carrier?

SENATOR BOSWORTH
Good question, I would have thought they would have picked an astronaut over someone who had never been in space before.

SHELLY BROWN

The whole selection process has been criticized by many.

SENATOR BOSWORTH

Don't you think a lot of that was just sour grapes of the Air Force?

SHELLY BROWN

No doubt since a lion's share of the astronauts they felt should have been selected were former Air Force pilots.

SENATOR BOSWORTH

When I talked to people involved in the selection, they pointed out the pilots never commanded a group of people and of the final three, Admiral Gilbert was the only person to have commanded in a combat situation.

SHELLY BROWN

It's kind of interesting how all three were selected for jobs all in support of the CSS Alabama.

SENATOR BOSWORTH

The Executive Officer, Commodore Riley, was a hot-shot pilot that should go a long way to silence the critics.

There was silence in the room for a couple minutes as Senator Bosworth was thinking about what he wanted to do next.

SENATOR BOSWORTH

I've been thinking about all this and your notes from the meeting were impeccable and insightful, so I'm going to ask you to do something very important."

SHELLY BROWN
What do you have in mind, Senator?

SENATOR BOSWORTH

I want you to take a shuttle flight up to Alabama and look around and talk with the crew, see how morale is and do a fact finding on the nature of the repairs and how realistic they will be done in two weeks. This is the sort of thing that could be delayed six months or a year and get very expensive. We need to know if the Space Force is competent in what they are doing.

SHELLY BROWN
How long would I be up there?

SENATOR BOSWORTH
I think a few days should suffice.

SHELLY BROWN
Do you think they would approve of my visit?

SENATOR BOSWORTH
I do not see why. You are cleared for Project Jupiter.

SHELLY BROWN
How soon will I be going and when will you find out?

SENATOR BOSWORTH
I'm going to request a meeting with USSF Secretary Margarette Mackworth today and will pitch your trip.

SHELLY BROWN
Why would Margarette Mackworth be willing to clear me to visit the Space Dock and the Alabama?

SENATOR BOSWORTH
She's going to need me to support her request we just got in for funding for a second Space Dock and another Space Carrier as she intends to build a fleet.

SHELLY BROWN
How critical is your support?

SENATOR BOSWORTH
From my informal survey, there are enough Senators wanting to divert all that Space Force money they think is pouring money down the sewer into social programs, so without my vote and influence on a couple Senators currently on the fence, that spending bill will never see the light of day.

SHELLY BROWN
What is our objective in doing all this?

SENATOR BOSWORTH
I'd like to make sure all this equipment is reliable
enough to have a dependable platform. Like all good
Pentagon programs, they usually overestimate the
capability and the longevity of their equipment. I want
to force them to make sure the program is viable, so I
don't end up with egg on my face supporting them in
case they are producing a lemon.

THE PONARIAN AND REVERSE ENGINEERING

Tom Gilbert finished his discussions with the Ponarian who seemed to be showing
signs of stress and thought it would be time to leave, as he had been advised the
SPACE FORCE AREA-51 operations had some other things to show him.

TOM GILBERT
It was interesting meeting you.

PO
Likewise, Admiral."

TOM GILBERT
What do I call you?

PO
Just call me Ponarian. My former name is irrelevant in this galaxy.

ADMIRAL GILBERT
As you wish, Ponarian.

Tom, mindful of possible pathogens, didn't shake his hand and simply turned and was
soon following his escort back to the elevator.

Admiral Gilbert was then taken over to building 27 where his TR-3B waited to take
him back to Washington DC. To his surprise the TR-3B was not there and they went
into an elevator.

As soon as they were in the elevator and the door shut, the escort typed in a series of
numbers in the keypad. Those numbers were the destination as well as the password to
enable the elevator to proceed to that level. Security personnel monitoring the elevator
video also detected the request and after monitoring the elevator video, enabled the
command which started the elevator downwards.

This was a long elevator ride which took several minutes. Tom could tell by the elevator mechanism sounds they were dropping fast. Soon a new sound and dynamic began, and he could then feel the added pressure of gravity. They were apparently slowing.

Shortly the elevator came to a halt and the doors opened. They walked into a large underground facility that was far larger than Tom could ever imagine. DARPA had sunk $billions into this complex since the 1950s. It was now clear why they built the black building so people could survive as the radiation levels rose from seepage of the underground nuclear test sites.

It would take them ten years and probably $1 trillion of today's dollars to build equivalent capability elsewhere. Thirty and forty years prior, costs were a lot cheaper and recruiting miners from nearby Tonopah was easier because back then it was just around the time most of the mines closed. But since the mines had now been closed almost fifty years, there no longer was a cadre of miners nearby to start another complex further East.

As they walked along the long corridor, it was clear to Tom why this thing was most likely far underground. There were several wrecked UFOs and even though they had gone through extensive cleaning at other sites, there was still the possibility hazardous substances existed and until they figured it out, it was best to be here in the event there was a major explosion and unpredicted release of toxic substances.

Some of the cleaner craft were also the simplest. One of the ships seemed far less mass than all others, and the escort, a Colonel in the USSF, explained.

USSF COLONEL
That's the ship the Ponarian crashed near Roswell.

ADMIRAL GILBERT
It seems too small to take him from the Andromeda
Galaxy to here.

USSF COLONEL
Back in the late 1950s we got him to admit, this ship
was launched out of the belly of a much larger ship.
This was just a small scout ship capable of making a
trip to the Earth surface and back out into space.

ADMIRAL GILBERT
Did he crash on his first attempt?

USSF COLONEL
No, he made multiple attempts.

ADMIRAL GILBERT
Did he divulge that?

USSF COLONEL
No, interrogators figured it out with some fancy lie
detector equipment and some electrical shock.

ADMIRAL GILBERT
So, is it true we tortured him?

USSF COLONEL
Only for about fifteen years. As soon as President
Kennedy found out he was being tortured quite a few
times and almost died from it, he ordered they stop.

ADMIRAL GILBERT
Did President Kennedy get to see the Ponarian?

USSF COLONEL
No, as far as we know only two Presidents ever saw aliens.

ADMIRAL GILBERT
Who were they?

USSF COLONEL
Eisenhower and Nixon.

ADMIRAL GILBERT
Was this during the Eisenhower administration?

USSF COLONEL
Eisenhower saw them while he was President at Area
51. Nixon didn't see them until a crash in Pennsylvania
and the ship and dead aliens were taken for a few days
to Air Force One hangar at Andrews Air Force Base.
Then after Nixon looked at the craft and the dead
bodies were shipped to Area 51. That craft is over
there.

The Colonel pointed at a nearby wreckage.

ADMIRAL GILBERT
So, Nixon knew all about the aliens, how about
Kissinger his top advisor?

USSF COLONEL
We'll never know for sure, but I believe Kissinger has
been a member of Majestic 12 ever since 1969 after
Nixon was sworn in, until his death.

As they walked further along, they saw what appeared to be spools of some substance
sitting beside a crashed UFO.

ADMIRAL GILBERT
What are those devices?

USSF COLONEL
Those are spools of fiber optic strands.

The Colonel picked one up and held it up for Admiral Gilbert to see up close.

ADMIRAL GILBERT
It looks like a spool of very thin thread.

USSF COLONEL
What you can see is the protective cover. We have
looked at these fibers under electron microscope and
the actual fiber is one third micron thick.

ADMIRAL GILBERT
That's damn small.

USSF COLONEL
It is.

ADMIRAL GILBERT
What's the purpose of these spools of fibers?

USSF COLONEL
They are part of the anti-gravity device.

ADMIRAL GILBERT
How do you know that?

USSF COLONEL
One of the aliens we captured eventually admitted to it.

ADMIRAL GILBERT
I suppose he got tortured as well?

USSF COLONEL

Admiral, you have to remember, forty years ago we were in a dangerous period. The Russians were conducting Project Ryan, which almost led to a pre-emptive nuclear strike. We were desperate for technology as it appeared the Soviets were out distancing us in many areas.

This was also at the same time the Chinese were gathering momentum in their nuclear weapons program and we started detecting Chinese submarines off Pearl Harbor and the CIA determined they had nuclear torpedo's onboard that would wipe out Pearl Harbor if the war started.

ADMIRAL GILBERT

It seems to me, if we did discover new technology, it would still take twenty years to weaponize it.

USSF COLONEL
That's correct. The TR-3B didn't fly until 1995.

ADMIRAL GILBERT
What happened to that alien?

USSF COLONEL

He died in captivity in about five years. He caught some Earth pathogens his body had no immunity against and he got sick very quickly and perished."

ADMIRAL GILBERT
Not because of torture?

USSF COLONEL

No, he died four years after the last time interrogators attached the electrodes to him.

ADMIRAL GILBERT

You realize the public will have a serious negative reaction if they ever learn we were torturing aliens.

USSF COLONEL

That anger will not last long after we bring forward several alien abductees who were treated far worse than we ever treated an alien.

ADMIRAL GILBERT
I probably do not want to know about that.

USSF COLONEL
You are probably right about that because if you ever
discover what aliens have done to living human beings
here on Earth, you will no longer feel any remorse for
what we did when we tortured them.

ADMIRAL GILBERT
What could possibly be worse than torture with
electrical probes using shock?"

USSF COLONEL
Cannibalism.

Suddenly Tom wished he hadn't asked the question.

As they walked on further, they came across another wrecked ship that had what
appeared to be strange-looking machinery torn apart in thousands of little pieces.

ADMIRAL GILBERT
What's all this equipment?

USSF COLONEL
You are looking at an alien power plant.

ADMIRAL GILBERT
How does that work?

USSF COLONEL
This is one of our most successful reverse engineering
efforts. We discovered from an alien or two that
in major sectors of this galaxy, a substance with an
atomic number U115 exists in good supply. Their
power plants work off a reactor that utilizes U115 but
does not give off large radiation like American nuclear
power plants and it can be designed in a direct power
application.

ADMIRAL GILBERT
You mean like our satellite power plants?

USSF COLONEL
Correct.

ADMIRAL GILBERT
How do they use that generated power?

USSF COLONEL
Some of the power feeds cosmic frequencies into the fiber-optic coils. By controlling the cosmic frequencies, they can produce gravity waves.

ADMIRAL GILBERT
Have we built any systems using this technology?

USSF COLONEL
Yes, that's how the artificial gravity in the TR-3B works.

ADMIRAL GILBERT
I think I've seen enough. I think it's time for me to head back to Washington.

The Colonel led Tom back to the elevator, then punched in a series of numbers and the elevator then ascended back to street level, then the door opened. The Colonel then escorted Tom Gilbert to the building front entrance and walked with him to the TR-3B that had just arrived from storage in the hangar to the helipad with a passenger access ladder attached.

The TR-3B was soon rising vertically and flew directly to Andrews Air Force Base where Tom was put in a Limo and taken to the service entry of his hotel noticing chaos in front of the Hilton with television vans with antennae parked out along the Crystal City access road just off Jefferson Davis Highway. Tom was escorted through the service entry to the elevator and as he was getting in the elevator, he could hear arguments between hotel employees and television personalities. Had they not been in such a heated discussion they would have seen Tom getting in the elevator. They missed their prey.

Tom Gilbert went directly to his room and to his surprise had a couple men with suits standing outside his hotel room. They knew who he was because of their briefings on the security plan, instantly recognized Admiral Tom Gilbert.

SECURITY DETACHMENT AGENT
Good afternoon, Admiral Gilbert. We are part of your security detachment.

ADMIRAL GILBERT
I deserve security now.

SECURITY DETACHMENT AGENT
Sir, the Secretary of the Space Force has arranged to provide you with around-the clock security while you remain on the planet.

ADMIRAL GILBERT
I appreciate you guys looking out for me.

SECURITY DETACHMENT AGENT
No problem, sir.

One of the men opened the door for Tom; apparently, they had room keys. Tom walked in his hotel room and the security man shut the door for him. He was just about to change his clothes when his cell phone rang. Looking down at the caller I.D. he noticed it was Margarette Mackworth, USSF Secretary.

ADMIRAL GILBERT
Hello.

MARGARETTE MACKWORTH
Tom?

ADMIRAL GILBERT
Yes, what can I do for you?

MARGARETTE MACKWORTH
This is Margarette Mackworth. I know you want to get back to your ship right away. Tonight, in about four hours, you will have transportation back to Andrews Air Force Base, where you will get on the shuttle TR-3B to get back up to the Space Dock and the CSS Alabama.

ADMIRAL GILBERT
Okay, thanks for the heads-up.

MARGARETTE MACKWORTH
One other thing.

ADMIRAL GILBERT
Yes?

MARGARETTE MACKWORTH
You will be taking a visitor up with you.

ADMIRAL GILBERT
Who is that and why, may I ask?

MARGARETTE MACKWORTH
Shelly Brown, aide to Senator Bosworth, will accompany you to the CSS Alabama so that you can give her a tour of your Space Carrier and answer any questions she has.

ADMIRAL GILBERT
This is kind of irregular.

MARGARETTE MACKWORTH
We need Senator Bosworth in our camp. Without him the Space Force will no longer expand, and maintenance will become difficult.

ADMIRAL GILBERT
Anything about this woman I should know?

MARGARETTE MACKWORTH
She's a smart cookie. Be on your toes, don't try to lie to her, but she doesn't need to know everything, and your upcoming mission is compartmentalized. I do not think you are obligated to divulge to her any details of that mission.

ADMIRAL GILBERT
Understand all.

Tom, having dealt with a prying public while he was a submarine skipper, knew how to handle the press and politician aides.

MARGARETTE MACKWORTH
Good luck.

Margarette hung up and Tom then sat down and reflected for a moment and decided he would take a nap. He walked over to the door to the hallway and opened it and asked one of the security men for help.

ADMIRAL GILBERT
Could you wake me up in about three hours, I want to take a nap."

SECURITY DETACHMENT AGENT
Will do, Admiral. Have a nice nap.

Tom kicked off his shoes, lay on his bed without moving the bed cover, and was soon drifting away into serenity as it took no time to accomplish the level of sleep he desired, building up his stamina for a busy day ahead.

THE VISIT

<u>EXT. NIGHT. SHELLY BROWNS HOME.</u>

Shelly said goodbye to her mother whom she lived with, and they had one last hug. Her ride, a limo, was waiting outside after one of the two men rang their doorbell to announce they were there to take her to Andrews, which was only a five-minute drive from her mother's home.

Shelly walked down the sidewalk and looked around the neighborhood which she had always known her whole life. Even while attending Johns Hopkins University, she lived at home with her mother and preferred that because her mother always helped her either with cooking her meals, doing her laundry, or giving her rides because Shelly hated to drive and preferred riding the metro over the headaches of finding parking spots. The Metro went right by Capitol Hill so it took her essentially everywhere she needed to go including a stop not but a few blocks from her mother's home.

Shelly's mother enjoyed Shelly living at home. Shelly was such a sweet girl, played the piano very well, and could sing like the best of them while attending church. Between the two of them they could walk to the grocery store and get whatever they needed. Life was simple and life was good.

Shelly was a trooper. She wasn't scared of anything and the thought of going up into space didn't faze her. In the past, Shelly would have had to go through a major astronaut training course to be allowed to do what she now embarked upon. But as they perfected shuttles to the Space Dock and a partial gravity machine was installed, Shelly could walk in reduced gravity and get around on the ships. Her instructions when the USSF Secretary Margarette Mackworth called her to inform her about her trip were simple.

MARGARETTE MACKWORTH
Just do as the crew members direct you and you will
be all right.

SHELLY BROWN
I intend to follow their instructions.

<u>EXT. NIGHT. ANDREWS AIR FORCE BASE HANGAR.</u>

The main reason for her to be in the limo is it could drive right onto the base and directly to the hangar which was currently inhabited by a TR-3B since the President's plane was gone. The TR-3B was in the hangar and the limo pulled right up next to it.

To an untrained and unsophisticated person, the TR-3B was painted in ways that made it look like a commercial jet. The special paint capable of surviving high heat during planetary re-entry was needed to hide the fact it was not some sort of super sophisticated military jet.

Shelly was escorted over to the ladder she climbed up which seemed like any commercial jet ladder. She walked into the TR-3B and sitting in a seat not far from the door was no other than Admiral Gilbert!

The seat next to Admiral Gilbert was empty, hence Shelly decided she would sit there and be poised to discuss with the Admiral and ask him questions she had thought about.

SHELLY BROWN
Good evening, Admiral Gilbert.

ADMIRAL GILBERT
Good evening to you as well.

SHELLY BROWN
I'm looking forward to seeing the CSS Alabama.

ADMIRAL GILBERT
I hope your trip is worthwhile.

SHELLY BROWN
It's already worthwhile. Not many people have ever
flown in a TR-3B or been to the Space Dock or seen
the CSS Alabama firsthand.

ADMIRAL GILBERT
You got a point there.

SHELLY BROWN
Tell me, Admiral, how do you see things aboard the
Alabama? Is the ship ready to deploy?

ADMIRAL GILBERT
Well, as you know because you attended the meeting

at USSF offices, we have some technical challenges to overcome in the next couple weeks.

SHELLY BROWN
Is there a possibility this two-week delay will turn into a six-month or one-year delay?

ADMIRAL GILBERT
Well, Ms. Brown, it would be premature for me to guess where we stand. I've been away from the ship for a couple days and Naval Reactors has not fully completed their inspections, so we really do not have a laundry list of mandatory repairs prior to undocking.

SHELLY BROWN
Please call me Shelly.

ADMIRAL GILBERT
Of course, Shelly, but when I'm around my crew, out of standard protocol, I'm required to state your last name.

SHELLY BROWN
That's all right. When in private I would prefer you refer to me as Shelly.

ADMIRAL GILBERT
As you wish, Shelly.

SHELLY BROWN
Thank you.

Tom and Shelly did not detect when the ship took off while they were talking because artificial gravity is almost like flying in a glider. You do not feel the forces as you merely float in the sky, in one of the most pleasing feelings a person can have aloft.

Shelly Brown and Admiral Gilbert only realized they were in space because the portholes in the side of the TR-3B suddenly appeared dark and no light shining through like when they were on the surface of the planet.

Within twenty minutes the TR-3B shuttle was in its final approach to the Space Dock landing pad area. Just like Maglev trains, the electromagnets on the TR-3B and the Space Dock magnetic decelerator positioned the TR-3B perfectly for alignment with the access tube and locking mechanism.

EXT. CGI. SPACE TR-3B LANDING ON SPACE DOCK

Once the TR-3B was locked into its cradle, the access tube fully seated on the ship and an fifteen-pound pressure test was completed satisfactory in the air lock, the door to the TR-3B and Space Dock entry room which provided a double airlock was opened.

INT. CGI. + REAL SCENERY SPACE ENCLOSED SPACE DOCK SHOWING CSS ALABAMA.

ADMIRAL GILBERT
Follow me, Shelly. I'll show you around.

SHELLY BROWN
Thank you, Admiral.

Shelly was wearing a stunning Gucci Beaded Embellished Black Burgundy Pant Suit that added to her ambience. Even without the expensive clothes she was a head turner.

Tom Gilbert thought for a few minutes *that even if she was going to be a pain in the ass political shark spy at least she would be pleasant to look at.*

It wasn't long after going through the double air lock they were on the main corridor of the Space Dock and the Observation Platform where undocking procedures were observed, but also guests could get a bird's eye of CSS Alabama tethered snugly in the bowls of the enclosed Space Dock.

By the time they arrived at the observation platform, Commodores Riley and Avery were there to meet them. Riley didn't look so happy and Avery was smiling like a Cheshire Cat because he was now ultimately grateful he didn't get the Commander's job on the Alabama.

Of the three, Commodores Avery spent far more time on Earth than the rest, and his involvement with Project Jupiter, was paving the way for him to get a promotion real soon and he too would be a Rear Admiral but without the headache of commanding a ship and dealing with the day-to-day myriad of issues that could crop up, along with the risk.

ADMIRAL GILBERT
Gentlemen, let me introduce you to Ms. Shelly
Brown, Chief of Staff for Senator Bosworth. This
is my Executive Officer Commodore Riley, and the
Commander of the Space Dock, Commodore Avery.

SHELLY BROWN
Nice to meet you gentlemen. While I'm here I might

wish to ask you both questions about concerns I think
may surface during my visit.

ADMIRAL GILBERT
These men will be available for you when you need to
talk to them. But please keep in mind they have a lot
to accomplish if we are to embark upon our mission
on time.

Tom Gilbert knew the two commodores were not planning on a grilling from the
senator's aid and had a lot of work to do to get the CSS Alabama ready to embark upon
its mission on time. Their body language betrayed the fact they were not enthused
about wasting precious time with a congressional neophyte.

SHELLY BROWN
Admiral Gilbert, I understand they will be busy and
will keep my questions to a minimum so as to not
interfere with their work.

ADMIRAL GILBERT
Thank you for your understanding, Ms. Brown.
Gentlemen you can go back to work now. I will show
Ms. Brown the Space Dock and the CSS Alabama.

Tom Gilbert could see the look of relief on the two Commodore's faces as they truly
had a lot to accomplish to get CSS Alabama ready to depart on schedule. There would
be many sleepless days ahead as preparations were being done and issues resolved.

The two senior officers quickly departed as they were knee deep in *elephant-shit*
getting the Space Carrier ready to undock on time.

SHELLY BROWN
Admiral Gilbert, or may I call you Tom since we are
alone, I have a couple questions.

ADMIRAL GILBERT
Yes you may, Shelly, and I appreciate you understanding
the protocols we have to do on a military space vessel.

SHELLY BROWN
You are welcome, Tom. Tell me what is the purpose of
having this space dock?

ADMIRAL GILBERT

Shelly, by having the enclosed huge cavity allows workers to be dressed in far more casual work clothes because space suits took up considerable amount of space and were much harder to work in. The Space Dock being pressurized, and temperature controlled allows the absolute most flexibility for the workers and at reduced gravity it is far more advantageous than micro gravity because it helps long-term equilibrium and workmanship issues were greatly reduced.

SHELLY BROWN

Tom, according to my briefings by USSF Secretary Mackworth, if the CSS Alabama's design works out well, there will soon be a second Space Dock under construction that would essentially be attached parallel to CSS Space Dock #1. Is this necessary?

ADMIRAL GILBERT

Shelly, that's correct. Yes, John Harris and my team feel it is needed. As soon as CSS Space Dock #2 is completed, it will become the refit platform and new construction will continue in CSS Space Dock #1 because all the known bugs have been worked out.

SHELLY BROWN

Tom, one of the criticisms I've received from some of the prime contractors, is that it's unwise to have these two docks connected because if there is a disaster on one of them it could affect the other.

ADMIRAL GILBERT

Shelly, I've heard that too. I also know the person spreading a lot of negative stories is Kevin O'Toole and his sidekick retired Air Force General Sandy Whitman. They are upset because they know we plan to second source the TR-3B's, TR-4's and TR-5's that will eventually roll out.

SHELLY BROWN

Tom, don't you think they have a legitimate concern?

ADMIRAL GILBERT

Shelly, because of the way Space Docks are manned

and handled, each one would be commanded by a different officer, and even though they would be tethered together for mutual support and benefits, there would be quick disconnects so that in an emergency such as with a dangerous reactor accident, where an explosion was eminent, the two Space Docks would have to be emergency separated.

SHELLY BROWN

I was aware of that, but one of the issues they brought up is that anyone caught in the joint air lock during separation and didn't have on a space suit would die of asphyxiation in a very short time.

ADMIRAL GILBERT

Shelly, that's true, but one life was not worth hundreds or if there was a manned Space Carrier upwards to a thousand that had to be saved by the emergency separation.

SHELLY BROWN

Tom, what about personnel trapped aboard a disabled Space Dock?

ADMIRAL GILBERT

Shelly, if personnel trapped aboard a disabled Space Dock, there are emergency habitability nodules people can go to and seal themselves in until emergency responders could get there and evacuate them.

SHELLY BROWN

CSS Space Dock #1 can easily be seen with binoculars from Earth. As soon as the second Dock is completed, the naked eye will be able to see and track them, especially if the external lights were turned on which would be the case in undocking. Some people are complaining about the space dock contaminating their view of the stars. What do you have to say about that?

ADMIRAL GILBERT

Normally so as to not irritate people on Earth who do not want their night sky contaminated with space junk, during routine operation, exterior lights are extinguished and only blinking red lights out of view of the planet were lit up.

It's one thing to see a sight such as the CSS Alabama in Space Dock on video. It's another thing to see it in real life in the awesome view from the Space Dock observation deck. Shelly Brown was taking it all in. In one sense she felt proud to be an American.

But at the same token, Shelly Brown knew there was a huge war going on in Congress over what liberals stated was wasteful spending on this space boondoggle. Liberals never perceive any types of military threats until the artillery rounds start crashing down upon them.

Shelly Brown was by no means a hawk on the defense posture, but at the same token, as a consummate history buff in high school and college because it accentuated her political science degree, she knew FDR's Army started out training recruits with broom handles.

FDR, though trying to implore congress to build more armaments and pushed the Lend Lease Act, really did not want to agitate liberals with huge budget requests for rearming for war until it was too late. Shelly recalls reading the book *Roosevelt's Secret War*, written by Joseph E. Persico, mentioned FDR thought he had three more months to prepare for the war until the Japanese proved otherwise.

With Shelly Brown's Project Jupiter clearance, she had one of the very rare awarenesses for people not actually involved working on Project Jupiter, because of her association as administrative aide to Senator Bosworth, allowed her to see what the Pentagon planners feared.

Shelly Brown had read some of Dr. Brandenburg's information about Xeon 129 found on Mars and his explanation of how it got there. And now suddenly, the CIA was stating the same aliens that wiped out Mars nine hundred thousand years ago, very well could wipe out Earth.

The fear of the Jupitorians paying Earth a visit is the only reason why CSS Alabama and the Space Dock existed. It's also the only reason why TR-3B was weaponized for space operations and the first designated craft to be carried by a Space Carrier to a perceived future war zone or shoot out with the perpetrators of the annihilation of a once proud Martian Civilization.

Commodores Riley and Avery soon approached Admiral Gilbert unexpectedly.

COMMODORE RILEY
Admiral, I would like to meet with you and go over
some growing concerns.

ADMIRAL GILBERT
Can we do that in the Wardroom?

COMMODORE RILEY
No, sir, I highly recommend your stateroom.

That gave the captain a quick indication. His stateroom was cleared for all levels of discussions and swept for bugs several times a day. No one could enter without his permission, and while he was away it was locked up and electronically sealed. To suggest a meeting required the security of his stateroom implied some very serious issues, far more, than what he wanted to hear about right now. But it is what it is, he would have to deal with it.

ADMIRAL GILBERT
Commodore Avery, would you please show Ms. Shelly Brown around, and after I get done talking with Commodore Riley, I'll give her a tour of the CSS Alabama.

Shelly, knowing this was precisely why she was sent up here in the first place, suddenly decided she needed to hear what those discussions were all about.

SHELLY BROWN
Admiral Gilbert, I would like to know what pressing issue Commodore Riley is referring to.

ADMIRAL GILBERT
Ms. Brown, as soon as I find out what the classification of the information is and if it's within your clearance, I'll brief you on it.

Tom Gilbert followed Commodore Riley aboard CSS Alabama and they made a direct bee line to his stateroom where a security outside was posted and upon the Commander's arrival, he did the electronic unlocking of the stateroom so Tom Gilbert could enter and conduct business with the XO, Commodore Riley.

The door shut behind them which allowed Riley to begin.

COMMODORE RILEY
Captain, Naval Reactors says they want to tear down generator number two that is having difficulty to allow them to perform an in-depth inspection.

ADMIRAL GILBERT
How long would that take?

COMMODORE RILEY
They claim only a month, but if they find other discrepancies you know this could turn into a three-month or six-month delay.

ADMIRAL GILBERT
Which is time we do not have.

COMMODORE RILEY
That's what I explained to them, but Naval Reactors says they can pull the keys if we do not allow the inspection.

ADMIRAL GILBERT
What's the alternative? There must be another way to prove things are normal without tearing them apart.

COMMODORE RILEY
One of the Naval Reactor guys said we could undock, take it on a high-speed run while they instrument it, and they could determine its operation correctly.

ADMIRAL GILBERT
I like that idea better. How long a run?

COMMODORE RILEY
Probably a couple days.

ADMIRAL GILBERT
Why a high-speed run? The generator has nothing to do with the propulsion motors.

COMMODORE RILEY
The Naval Reactors Rep informed me that during a high-speed run, we place maximum load on the generators because of increased cooling and propulsion high-speed pump operation.

ADMIRAL GILBERT
Schedule a meeting in the wardroom with Naval Reactors as soon as possible so we can plan this event.

COMMODORE RILEY
Right away, sir.

ADMIRAL GILBERT
One other thing: Two days of high-speed running would get us to Mars and back, is that correct?

COMMODORE RILEY
Yes, sir.

ADMIRAL GILBERT
Get with the 'Loggie's' and have them find a spare uniform or two for our distinguished guest. Something tells me she's going to demand to come along.

COMMODORE RILEY
I'll contact our supply officer immediately.

ADMIRAL GILBERT
Good, I'm going back to the Space Dock and escort her aboard.

COMMODORE RILEY
Is Shelly Brown cleared for access?

ADMIRAL GILBERT
Shelly Brown is cleared a lot higher than you think. USSF Secretary Mackworth sent me a copy of her visit request. She's cleared for Project Jupiter with Q, M, N, P, R, X, Y, and Z designations.

COMMODORE RILEY
Holy smokes! She's even cleared for the Radio Room.

ADMIRAL GILBERT
She sure is.

COMMODORE RILEY
I'll have the Yeoman give her a visitor's badge with all the compartment access codes when we assign her dosimetry device for the underway.

ADMIRAL GILBERT
Even though she's good-looking she's not just some political cupcake. She's a shark, be weary of her.

COMMODORE RILEY
Thanks for the heads-up, Tom.

ADMIRAL GILBERT
No problem. I know how you sometime let your little head do all the thinking for you.

COMMODORE RILEY
Well, an Airedale must keep up his reputation.

ADMIRAL GILBERT
Riley, this is not a Top Gun movie. This is the real deal where simple plain people endure the rigors and challenges of space.

COMMODORE RILEY
Tom, I understand that, and I'm sincerely glad you are the CO, because that gig would take me a while to work into it.

ADMIRAL GILBERT
There might be a CO assignment available sooner than you realized."

COMMODORE RILEY
Why, are you getting transferred or something?"

ADMIRAL GILBERT
No, but we may be building another CSS Alabama Class Carrier real soon.

COMMODORE RILEY
How soon?

ADMIRAL GILBERT
I would say the keel will be laid halfway through my tour here."

COMMODORE RILEY
That soon?

ADMIRAL GILBERT
Yes. I expect to see some rapid movement on building another Space Dock so that refits of Alabama can go on at the same time they are building new hulls.

COMMODORE RILEY
Hopefully, I'll be ready to step up and take command of one of those follow-on hulls."

ADMIRAL GILBERT
You are essentially a PCO right now.

COMMODORE RILEY
What about PCO school?

ADMIRAL GILBERT
There is no way they could create a PCO school anytime soon. Plus, who would be the instructor since NOBODY has any experience commanding this class of ship?"

COMMODORE RILEY
You have a point there.

ADMIRAL GILBERT
All future COs will have to be trained aboard and certified since there is no alternative.

COMMODORE RILEY
I like that alternative better.

ADMIRAL GILBERT
Why do you say that?

COMMODORE RILEY
I doubt very seriously the future Space Force PCO school could recreate the sense of urgency in a classroom or trainers like we see out in space.

ADMIRAL GILBERT
One of the biggest challenges is the fact, if something happens to your ship, there is nobody to come rescue you.

COMMODORE RILEY
Yes, that's a very sobering thought.

ADMIRAL GILBERT
Very.

Tom Gilbert led Commodore Riley out of his stateroom and nodded at the sailor at the security desk that electronically secured his stateroom, and his job was to control traffic in and out of the Wardroom. They didn't want any ships company entering the wardroom without an appointment on the ships calendar or meetings scheduled on the *plan of the day*, because there could be a classified meeting going on the crew member wasn't cleared to hear.

The Wardroom and the nearby Ship's Lounge and Research Library were often training classrooms in addition to their inherent normal use. The ship's librarian, Karen, often had to leave the ship's library while such training was going on because of classification levels or need to know information being discussed.

Tom walked to the Space Dock observation deck and found Commodore Avery there enjoying his time with Shelly Brown. What Commodore Avery didn't know was the shark had already bitten him. Loose lips sink ships and Shelly Brown was an expert at flattering men to open their loose lips up. Shelly Brown was no less than a dynamo and instinctively knew how to work her way into the male consciousness as well as his libido and take control of his little head which made all the decisions.

Tom arrived just in time to save poor Commodore Avery. In just about five more minutes, the great black shark Shelly Brown (a.k.a. black widow) would have eaten Commodore Avery alive.

ADMIRAL GILBERT
Ms. Brown, will you please follow me so I can take
you to my ship and show you around?

SHELLY BROWN
Why certainly, Admiral.

Tom nodded at Commodore Avery, who was left almost speechless, as he seldom had private moments with such a powerful woman who was self-assured in all aspects of her life, but she had an agenda and worked it relentlessly. Shelly Brown was one of those personalities that expressed: "Lead, follow, or get the hell out of my way!" God help someone that slowed Shelly Brown down.

Shelly's mother knew the dynamic personality her daughter had. But at the same token worried because one day she would stumble across a man with an equal dynamic personality and her daughter could fall hopelessly in love and end up with a broken heart. Even though she was a shark herself and knew how to swim with other sharks without being eaten alive, there were bigger sharks in the ocean, and Shelly Brown just met one.

As soon as Tom crossed over into the ship from the tubular gangplank, there was a sailor sentry standing there saluting wearing his dress blues uniform. The Navy had gone through numerous style changes and the Space Force had their own uniforms, which the crew wore routinely, but Tom wanted to give the feeling of a ship, even though it traveled through space, and was given great discretion on how the uniforms should be worn on his ship.

Admiral Gilbert decided he wanted his sentries with the Cracker Jack Navy Uniform of the distant past. Because this was a major departure from normal ships clothing allowance, he provided the uniforms out of his own pockets. As soon as a new guy reported aboard and was going on the watch bill as a sentry, he was outfitted with the Cracker Jack Navy Uniform via curtesy of the Commanding Officer.

Some didn't like it, they wanted to wear the new Space Force uniforms, but when they were shuttled down to the planet for special events such as parades, those Space Force guys who had the space force rocket emblem along with submariners' dolphins and boomer submarine patrol pins or surface warfare and aviation pins, they looked extra special and discovered the public liked the uniform. But as crewmember Danny O'Grady once said:

> DANNY O'GRADY
> That Rocket emblem and $5.00 may buy you a cup of
> coffee somewhere.

Admiral Tom Gilbert explained his ship as he walked through the main corridor and worked his way to the bridge where several consoles existed to operate the ship.

> SHELLY BROWN
> This almost looks like a ship in one of the movies.

> ADMIRAL GILBERT
> If you take a close look and compare it to the movies
> next time you will discover we have more consoles.

> SHELLY BROWN
> Does that mean the technology is inferior and requires
> more manual control?"

> ADMIRAL GILBERT
> No, much of it is automated. One of the reasons
> for so many consoles is for the Air Wing as well as
> redundancy in case of battle damage."

> SHELLY BROWN
> That's very interesting. Makes sense.

Tom Gilbert then took Shelly Brown into berthing then the crew's lounge.

> ADMIRAL GILBERT
> In the old days sailors would call this space, *chow hall*,
> or *mess decks*.

> SHELLY BROWN
> The crew has what appears to be far more comfortable
> than what I've seen on some Navy Ships I got tours on.

ADMIRAL GILBERT

The reason is we only have a crew of around three hundred, because of all the automation we can give each person far more room than a person on a ship."

SHELLY BROWN

Even though it's in space?

ADMIRAL GILBERT

When this ship was first designed it had four times as much volume associated with electronics and four times as many people expected to operate those obsolete systems.

Due to construction delays, a lot of the initial equipment was easily replaced with equipment with a smaller footprint that had more density and capability with substantially less power consumption.

A decision was made by the USSF to delay the CSS Alabama outfitting a short while to install essentially a new generation of electronics capable of utilizing a lot more artificial intelligence and machine learning enhancing automation.

SHELLY BROWN

What do most of the people on the ship do?

ADMIRAL GILBERT

Over half of the crew are associated with the Air Wing.

SHELLY BROWN

You mean it only takes half the crew to operate this ship?

ADMIRAL GILBERT

That's correct.

SHELLY BROWN

What are the jobs the Air Wing does?

ADMIRAL GILBERT

The Air Wing provides the pilots for all the TR-3Bs

we carry. They have communications people and some fly drones' part of the EWS system to assist the Air Wing in avoiding ambushes and traps.

SHELLY BROWN

Has the Air Wing on this ship ever deployed into harm's way?

ADMIRAL GILBERT

Not yet. Many of them flew missions for the Air Force or the Navy and Marine Corps in harm's way so most of them have tasted real air combat roles mainly as fighter pilots and ground support for army and marines in high threat areas.

They also spend a lot of time in combat trainers that are programmed with the TR-3B flight controls optimum performance configurations in simulated air battles.

SHELLY BROWN

Do they simulate fighting Russians and Chinese or do they attempt to fight aliens and how would we know about Alien combat abilities?

ADMIRAL GILBERT

Great questions Shelly. I'm not a pilot so I have to rely heavily on Commodore Riley's observations and intuition. This is what he explained to me: *We already know how to fight the Russians and the Chinese, so our time would be better spent training to fight Aliens which is our mission.*

SHELLY BROWN

How would they know what tactics they should use against aliens?

ADMIRAL GILBERT

Shelly, when I endorsed your visit request sent by USSF Secretary Mackworth, the USSF visit request sent to Alabama and USSF Space Dock #1 indicated you are cleared for the following designations: Q, M, N, P, R, X, Y, and Z designations. You do not have the *I-designation* on your SCI clearance so I can't reveal the source or information the source provided.

SHELLY BROWN

That's understandable, I should have assumed such.

ADMIRAL GILBERT

If you would like, I'll send a USSF military classified message to USSF Secretary Mackworth to initiate the enhanced background checks and processes needed to get you the *I-designation*. After you receive those credentials and get read in, then I can reveal to you how we know what tactics the aliens would use against us.

SHELLY BROWN

Thanks for the offer, Tom, but based on getting all my other clearances, by the time I get the credentials, the Alabama will be deployed and long gone so it would be a painful waste of my time.

ADMIRAL GILBERT

Shelly, you have a keen understanding of how slow the bureaucracy works, and I think you are quite accurate in your estimation.

SHELLY BROWN

Thank you for your astute observation on how I view things. I already have the answer to the puzzle I need. Our TR-3B wings are training for possible combat with Aliens and have good sources of information on Alien capabilities which further exposes a major flaw in compartmentalization.

ADMIRAL GILBERT

And what is that flaw Shelly?

SHELLY BROWN

Don't worry Tom, I'm not going to discuss this with Senator Bosworth or anyone else for that matter, but you have just confirmed to me, there really is an alien threat and we know a lot about them including their combat maneuvers our TR-3B pilots train to deal with. The public and congress are not aware of any of this.

ADMIRAL GILBERT

It's probably for their own good. There are not enough

psychiatrists and Catholic Priests who have the role of
spiritual psychiatry to treat a lot of people that would
not do well with the knowledge you have.

Commodore Riley approached Admiral Gilbert

COMMODORE RILEY
Admiral Gilbert, sorry to interrupt you and Ms. Brown,
but a couple Naval Reactors Reps are in the wardroom
now ready for the meeting you scheduled.

ADMIRAL GILBERT
Okay, I'll be right there.

SHELLY BROWN
Admiral, I would like to sit in on the meeting.

Since Shelly was cleared for Project Jupiter with all the credentials she had, a meeting
about testing a nuclear generator was nothing she should not be barred from attending,
so Admiral Gilbert responded positively.

ADMIRAL GILBERT
Ms. Brown, I see why not, sure follow me.

Tom led Shelly into the wardroom where two Naval Reactors inspectors sat looking
anxious. They knew if they forced the issue of tearing down the generator to do the
inspections, they thought were necessary in lieu of simply taking the ship out into
space and do a high-speed run, it would create a lot of unhappiness as it would whack
the schedule.

The Naval Reactors Engineers were not convinced Tom was willing to simply undock
and take them on an instrumented joy ride where they could get some real operational
numbers to clarify what appeared to be possibly faulty indications in the inverters.
The inverters took D.C. power generated directly from the metal cooled reactors
and created AC power for quite a bit of the electrical circuits. Some D.C. power was
siphoned off to recharge batteries and power D.C. loads including emergency lighting.

Diagnostics had indicated a potential anomaly between the direct power to the inverters.
If the Diagnostic fault codes were correct, the generator was operating dangerously.
A teardown and inspection would prove absolutely what failure mechanism existed.
But it could be there was no failure mechanism, and the truth was faulty diagnostics
software, something Naval Reactors didn't want to admit since their contractors wrote
the diagnostic code. The fact the other generator didn't exhibit any problems led them
to believe their software didn't have any flaws.

The two men seated were Naval Reactor Reps (NR REPS) Roger Keeney and Kevin Landry. Both of whom Tom had met many times before during new construction and initial space trials.

ADMIRAL GILBERT
Okay, gentlemen, do we really have to tear down the generator to verify we have faulty software?

NR REP ROGER KEENEY
No, Admiral, it's impossible to have faulty software, it's been triple checked.

ADMIRAL GILBERT
Okay, then what are our options?

NR REP ROGER KEENEY
Our recommendation is to tear down the generator to get to some of the conversion fabric and see if there is any damage.

ADMIRAL GILBERT
Any other options?

NR REP ROGER KEENEY
Yes, one you will not like.

ADMIRAL GILBERT
I'm all ears, tell me.

NR REP ROGER KEENEY
We could undock the Alabama, take it on a two-day high-speed run fully instrumented and get operational performance data. If test results indicate the equipment is functioning normally that would imply a sensor failure or faulty or corrupted software.

ADMIRAL GILBERT
How long would it take you to get all the instruments wired up to do the test?

NR REP KEVIN LANDRY
We could have our equipment aboard and checked out in twenty-four hours and support an in-space high-power run test.

ADMIRAL GILBERT
Okay, I'm going to make a command call now. It's often better to ask for forgiveness than permission. We are going to secure this meeting in a couple minutes. I want you gentlemen to get your workers together and immediately work on installing the instruments you need. As soon as you tell me you are ready to support a high-speed run check, we will immediately undock and go do it.

NR REP KEVIN LANDRY
We'll need to bring along about fifteen personnel.

ADMIRAL GILBERT
Not a problem, we don't need to bring much of the air wing with us, we'll have a lot of empty bunks for your men.

NR REP ROGER KEENEY
All right, Admiral, we'll get started right away.

ADMIRAL GILBERT
Very well, carry on.

Kevin Landry and Roger Keeney stood and walked out of the wardroom and knew the direction to the tubular gangplank to go initiate the efforts. They knew fifteen men were not going to be happy. Three months of outlandish overtime and space pay was a lot more palatable than two days of flying so fricking fast that there was a good chance you could bump into a stray meteorite and end up as cosmic dust.

Shortly after the men left, Shelly Brown spoke.

SHELLY BROWN
Admiral Gilbert, since you are only going to be gone for two days, I would like to go with you so I can observe the CSS Alabama operating in space.

ADMIRAL GILBERT
We have plenty of room since I'm not going to take most of the squadron. I'm only going to bring along enough pilots and air wing personnel for emergency flights, so we have room for you if you really desire to go.

SHELLY BROWN
I desire to go, Admiral.

ADMIRAL GILBERT
Okay, Commodore Riley will take you to meet the supply officer. He can have his Loggie's find you a space uniform to change into.

SHELLY BROWN
You sure you don't want me to wear one of those Cracker Jack uniforms like your sentry is wearing?

ADMIRAL GILBERT
That is a great idea. We could photograph you and use you on recruiting posters.

Shelly started laughing and had not laughed this hard in a long time. This admiral was something else!

SHELLY BROWN
That's okay, I would prefer to wear a space force uniform.

ADMIRAL GILBERT
We always have spare Space Force uniforms onboard for new guys who replace people that get transferred for end of duty tours.

SHELLY BROWN
Does that happen often?

ADMIRAL GILBERT
Yes, it seems like as soon as I get them trained up for deployment, they get yanked out and sent somewhere else.

SHELLY BROWN
Why can't you hold up their transfers if you are close to deployment?

ADMIRAL GILBERT
Some of these guys started out here during new construction. They have been here three or four years. If we kept them here any longer, they would have

legitimate complaints of cruel and unusual treatment since their contract stipulates three years max before mandatory shore duty.

COMMODORE RILEY
Ms. Brown, if you will please follow me, I'll take you to supply and introduce you to our Supply Officer and get you a space uniform and some space shoes.

SHELLY BROWN
What is special about space shoes?

COMMODORE RILEY
They have magnetic actuators if you click your heels together the magnets turn on so you can get anchored to a deck in case, we lose artificial gravity and you don't want to float around.

SHELLY BROWN
All right, lead the way.

As soon as the two were gone, Tom was thinking, *I hope, Riley doesn't try to do something stupid like pursue Shelly. She'll eat him alive.*

Within a couple hours, Shelly had on her space uniform, her magnetic space shoes, and was taken to the female officer's berthing area, where she was introduced to six female officers who would be going out in space with them during the at-space test for the nuclear generator.

Shelly was given a spare berth and shown the toilet and how to operate it in either gravity mode or microgravity mode, God forbid she had to do number two in micro gravity.

Things moved along rapidly. CNO found out what was going on and directed Naval Reactors to expedite their instrument onload and hookup and be ready in twelve hours, especially once he discovered Shelly Brown, aide to Senator Bosworth was onboard for inquiry. Naval Reactors Reps were briefed.

NAVSEA 08 CNR
You better make sure your men guys had their *"shit in one sock"* because if your findings were tainted forcing this unprecedented undocking and additional space-trials, CNO would have someone's ass.

ROGER KEENEY

I will be there personally observing all the work my staff of fifteen engineers perform. We'll leave no stone unturned and deliver a data package that will explain what went wrong during initial space trials.

NAVSEA 08 CNR

Your personal oversight onboard during the testing is mandatory. We have never been in the spotlight like this before. That senator's aide that will be aboard will no doubt report back to Senator Bosworth anything negative, and he will make a beeline to the White House. I don't want a shit storm on my watch. I want conclusive facts to inform the CNO in case he needs to explain all this to the President.

ROGER KEENEY

Sir, we will do what is necessary to prove one way or another if there are any defects with generator number two.

NAVSEA 08 CNR

I will be looking forward to hearing what you find out. Send me a *Quick-Look* Naval Message as soon as you determine what the failure is.

ROGER KEENEY
Yes sir.

The food aboard Alabama was par-excellent. The chief cook was a former chef at one of New York's finest restaurants.

After sharing a meal in the wardroom enjoying some chitchat with several of the female officers Shelly Brown met and immediately established a very friendly rapport. Shelly elected to go try out her bunk and take a nap and prepare her mind for the upcoming events.

Shelly had been asleep for a while and with the very pure and well oxygenated air, she slept better than ever before. To help with personnel psychology, the air was also fortified with negative ions which in recent years had been a major study in dealing with people closely confined in ships or spacecraft. After sleeping six hours Shelly was awakened by one of the female officers sent down to get her and report to the control room.

Having been schooled by the female officers, Shelly had been advised to sleep with her space uniform on laying on top the sheets and blankets in the event she had to get up quickly and make her way to an emergency evacuation craft. All she had to do was slip on her magnetic space shoes and she could be on her way in fifteen to thirty seconds, which would be critical in case of a rapid decompression where asphyxiation would occur in a couple minutes if she didn't get to the rescue craft in time.

The female officer led Shelly Brown up to the control room, now with several people manning the display consoles. The Commander was present, along with his XO Riley, and everyone seemed rather busy.

CAPTAIN GILBERT
(RANK TO SIGNIFCY SHIP'S CAPTAIN)
We are now starting undocking, I thought you might
like to watch.

SHELLY BROWN
Yes, I would like to observe this.

EXT. CGI. SPACE CSS ALABAMA LEAVING THE SPACE DOCK

Very soon Tom Gilbert started receiving reports from the operators of some of the consoles. The ship was no longer tethered to the Space Dock and Shelly could see they were moving slowly even though she couldn't feel it.

Between the video monitors and a small window area near where she was standing, Shelly could see quite a lot of the undocking operation. One of the displays was a 4 panel sreen showing live video sent from cameras mounted in the space cock recording the event. Alabama control room withstanders had an all encompassing situational awareness from it's own camera equipment but also from the perspective of the space dock.

CSS Alabama seemed to be moving very slowly, but it was continuous. Then suddenly, the velocity picked up slightly and Shelly could see from all the video displays, the Alabama was moving faster.

The Naval Reactors guys were still setting up their equipment, and Tom was not willing to wait for them to undock. They would take a few more hours to get all their readings to indicate they were measuring correctly before they requested high-speed.

Tom had decided he would do a side show for Shelly as the *Nukes* were *geeking* out in the engineering spaces preparing for the highspeed runs. Admiral Gilbert would maneuver the CSS Alabama and approach the moon while the *Nukes Geek Squad* were tinkering and then as soon as they were ready for high-speed, he would point Mars and kick Alabama into high speed.

NAVIGATOR
We are clear of the Space Dock.

ADMIRAL GILBERT
Very well, Navigator, go ahead and point the Alabama towards the moon and speed up. Take us to the far side of the moon.

NAVIGATOR
Any speed restrictions?

CAPTAIN GILBERT
Not yet, the Naval Reactors engineers haven't verified we got a problem.

NAVIGATOR
Roger that, speeding up to two-thirds. Would like the pilot and copilot to operate in manual for some proficiency training.

CAPTAIN GILBERT
Shift to manual operation for proficiency training.

NAVIGATOR
Shift to manual operation for proficiency training Captain aye.

Shelly didn't feel the speed change but looking at the video monitors some of which were showing the Space Dock lit up for docking operations was slowly shrinking in size and in a short while was way behind and shrinking in size.

The nuclear-powered rocket engines were doing their magic, leaving behind a nice shock wave as the engine exhaust was traveling faster than the speed of light creating a temporal anomaly.

If another ship was tracking and filming the Alabama, they would see the strangest image of the rear of the ship as the engine exhaust going faster than speed of light caused modal distortion and a strange eerie pattern. Some scientists claimed it appeared like a mini-black hole was following them.

As predicted it took the Nukes several hours to set up and calibrate their equipment. They knew the ship was traveling extremely fast because of the instrument readouts. Tom's approach to the moon helped them check out their instruments. By the time they reached the moon, they were ready for the high-speed run.

ADMIRAL GILBERT
Navigator, I want you to sling shot us around the moon
then steer towards Mars.

NAVIGATOR
Sling shot us around the moon then steer towards
Mars, Captain aye.

The Navigator on a CSS class carrier like the Alabama and follow on space carriers had a combined role as acting quartermaster and flying officer similar to combining a quarter master and diving officer on a submarine. The Navigator would then issue orders to the pilot and copilot which were legally binding requirements.

Shelly watched the surface of the moon get larger over time as they soon flew very close up and when they got to the far side which is never seen on Earth, she thought she might have seen a few lights and possible structures. Her thoughts were then, *Are we on the moon now?*

Using the moon to slingshot them towards Mars, they would increase velocity and as soon as they came out of the turn pointing Mars they would be almost at a full-power run.

Video trackers kept the moon on some of the scanners. The ship rolled into the turn which gave everyone an increased gravity level as the push against the centrifugal force added to the amount felt.

The surreal image of the moon this close sent chills up Shelly's spine. She knew what the implications were. If she could go on a joy ride around the moon, what could more advanced aliens accomplish?

At their present speed, it only took an hour to get around the moon and slingshot towards Mars. As Shelly Brown would learn later they would be circling Mars in twenty-four hours for the return trip, traveling at velocities believed not possible just five years prior.

At about that time the Navigator informed Admiral Gilbert.

NAVIGATOR
Sir, we are now on course to Mars, commencing high-
speed run.

Admiral Gilbert
Very well, Navigator. I would like an op's brief at
19:00.

NAVIGATOR
Op's brief at 19:00, aye, sir.

The Navigator would have all kinds of eye candy for those required to be at the ops brief including the XO and all department heads. There were others also asked to attend who may be needed to explain various attributes to the brief.

About this time Shelly Brown made a request.

SHELLY BROWN
Admiral Gilbert, would it be possible for me to go observe what the Naval Reactors personnel are doing?

ADMIRAL GILBERT
Ms. Brown, yes, that's possible, but you need to go see the ship's doctor and get a dosimeter since you will be walking through some potential radiation areas. We need to record your exposure just in case there is any. We don't expect you to get any dosage, but we have reporting requirements whether you receive radiation or not.

Knowing that a fully manned bridge was no longer necessary because they were steering in autopilot now, Admiral Gilbert decided it was time to secure the maneuvering watch and shift to standard underway operations.

ADMIRAL GILBERT
Secure the maneuvering watch. Commence normal underway watch, section one relieving.

Artificial intelligence part of the automated control roon scheme continuously monitors all conversations in the control room and records a transcript of everything said for future inquiry if necessary. Part of that monitoring process included notification to the crew. When the Alabama's Captain, Admiral Gilbert gave direction to the ship such as now, it made the proper announcements.

ARTIFICIAL INTELLIGENCE
(VIA SHIP'S INTERCOM)
Secure the maneuvering watch. Commence normal underway watch, section one relieving.

Software developers for the ship wide Artificial Intelligence picked Clark Gable's voice for all male communications and Elizibeth Tayler for female announcements. If a male was officer of the deck Clark Gables voice would be used in the intercom reports. If a female officer was officer of the deck Elizibeth Tayler's voice would be used in intercom reports or external communications to other vessels which may occur.

The Artificial Intelligence was continuously checking the accuracy of the officer's communications and if there was something unexpected or did not fit with the expected framework of ongoing operations, the Artificial Intelligence would repeat back to the officer and get confirmation or make suggestions.

Artificial Intelligence prevented embarrassing situations such as attempting to contact the wrong ship or external radio source and with automatic grammar and accuracy checking ensures all communications were highly accurate.

Artificial Intelligence knew who was really in charge, they were not humans.

Artificial Intelligence recorded the command in the deck log and as in this case required ship wide broadcast so that everyone knew what they were ordered to do. Artificial intelligence that broadcasted Admiral Gilberts order to the crew who was now notified to start normal underway operations with watch section number one manning key watch stations including taking log readings if required.

In most cases all required instrument readings required for the safety of the space carrier were recorded in electronic logs and the ship's force would walk around the engine room or elsewhere with a computerized tablet and confirm the transcripts matched the actual gauge readings.

Electronic gauges were more precise and eliminated any interpretation as most readings were with 16 bit-accuracy or 65,535 discrete data points that accurately monitored any possible situation.

Shortly afterwards, Admiral Gilbert approached a female officer who was leaving the control room who happened to be the ship's weapon's officer, in charge of all their self-defense weapons.

ADMIRAL GILBERT
Weps, would you please take Ms. Brown to the ship's
doctor to get a dosimeter and then escort her back
to engineering and introduce her to Naval Reactors
personnel working back there.

WEPS
Yes, sir. Ms. Brown, will you please follow me?

SHELLY BROWN
Yes, ma'am.

The ship's doctor gave Shelly Brown a form to fill out that asked numerous personal health related questions and got her mailing address to send dosimeter readings, then issued her the device and then stated.

SHIP'S DOCTOR

You are now cleared to proceed to the engineering spaces. The XO gave me this visitor badge for you to wear. It has all the designations of where you can go aboard the CSS Alabama.

SHELLY BROWN

Sir, looking at my credentials, what are the I areas cannot go into.

SHIP'S DOCTOR

Ms. Brown, you are very highly cleared. The only location you are not permitted in is the INTEL SUITE because you do not have the I-credentials.

SHELLY BROWN

Thank you doctor, I'm ready to proceed to the engine room.

SHIP'S DOCTOR

Ms. Brown, since you are going into a potential radiation area, please do not remain there long and when we get back to the Space Dock, please return the dosimeter or give it to the sentry at the gang plank, he has a special box there to put it in and one of our medical personnel will retrieve it.

SHELLY BROWN.

Sure, no problem doctor.

SHIP'S DOCTOR.

Ms. Brown, please do not leave the ship with it, or you will invalidate the readings and I'll have to fill out a mountain of paperwork. Weps will you please take Ms. Brown to the engineering spaces.

WEPS

Doctor, Shelly Brown can leave the dosemeter with me, and I'll return it to you.

SHIP'S DOCTOR
Thanks, Weps, I appreciate that.

The women were soon off to the engineering spaces of the Space Carrier. As they arrived, the Weps explained a few things to Shelly Brown.

WEPS
This is what the ship's force often calls *Zoomie Land*. This is where the Nuclear Power plant operators we call Nukes work on the propulsion, electrical, and ship's systems.

SHELLY BROWN
This area seems very clean. I'm surprised since it's in engineering spaces.

WEPS
Engineering on a Space Carrier is just like aboard nuclear submarines. Submarine and Space Carrier engineering spaces are especially clean. Dirt and debris are not tolerated and any time they have an Operational Reactor Safeguards Exam (ORSE), if the engineering spaces appeared dirty the Nukes would flunk ORSE.

SHELLY BROWN
What happens if the ship fails ORSE?

WEPS
The Commanding Officer would most likely be relieved.

One thing Tom Gilbert never did, which a lot of Commanding Officers did do, was having the sailors painting down in the engine room bilges, underway, just before an ORSE. Many sailors complained of headaches and nausea from paint fumes back in those days. The amine in the atmosphere when A-Gang screwed up was the icing on the cake to help the misery index to explode upwards.

Just outside maneuvering, in a spacious area, the Naval Reactors had all their instruments set up. Even though the ship had independent and self-sustained monitoring equipment, the Naval Reactors men wanted completely independent monitoring equipment. They didn't want to trust any of the ships' systems to validate any concerns. The carry-on equipment used in this test was extensive and quite extraordinary. They left nothing to chance. Every parameter of just about any piece of equipment in the engineering spaces could be monitored one way or another.

The engineers and scientists were comparing notes and scratching their heads. The results of what they were getting didn't add up. The actual real-time monitoring of the performance using the carry on test equipment indicated satisfactory performance. Then why did the ship's systems built in diagnostic code indicate otherwise. There was going to be hell to pay.

KEVIN LANDRY

We can't go full speed for a day and not have any issues
but yet we have a diagnostic code tell us otherwise."

ROGRER KEENEY

Unless the software is corrupted.

KEVIN LANDRY

That's not possible. It's the same software used on the
other generator monitoring."

ROGRER KEENEY

That's true but it's measured with a different set of
hardware and software.

KEVIN LANDRY

I'd buy a generator number two diagnostic hardware
failure.

ENGINEER WHO DESIGNED GENERATOR DIAGNOSTIC SYSTEM

That can't be either.

KEVIN LANDRY

"Why do you say that?

ENGINEER WHO DESIGNED GENERATOR DIAGNOSTIC SYSTEM

I've ran *Diagnostic Hardware Health Checks* on that
hardware repeatedly until I was just about blue in the
face, and it keeps reporting test results as *No Faults
Detected.*

KEVIN LANDRY

Well, gentlemen, you have about twenty-four hours to
come up with an answer or heads will roll.

ENGINEER WHO DESIGNED GENERATOR DIAGNOSTIC SYSTEM
How about we reinstall the software?"

KEVIN LANDRY
Unfortunately, that can only be done in Space Dock
due to safety requirements."

ENGINEER WHO DESIGNED GENERATOR DIAGNOSTIC SYSTEM
In twenty-four hours, we could shut down generator
TWO, cross-connect all loads to the other generator, do
the software reload, then reconfigure the switchboards,
power back up and retest it.

KEVIN LANDRY
At 19:00 we have an op's brief we have been asked to
attend, we could bring this up then and get Admiral
Gilbert's permission.

ENGINEER WHO DESIGNED GENERATOR DIAGNOSTIC SYSTEM
Admiral Gilbert may not be able to give us permission.
He probably must fly a message requesting permission
and knowing Naval Reactors, they will say not only
no but hell no.

KEVIN LANDRY
For good reason.

ENGINEER WHO DESIGNED GENERATOR DIAGNOSTIC SYSTEM
But what would they do if they were a long way away
on a mission?

KEVIN LANDRY
Obtaining permission to do something like this could
take weeks.

SHELLY BROWN
Admiral Gilbert would probably authorize it, then beg
for forgiveness later since there's not more, he could
do.

The engineers turned around to see the female voice that just made the statement.

Even with a space uniform on, Shelly still looked pretty. Some of the men were mesmerized. This was not Rosy the Riveter quality woman!

KEVIN LANDRY
May I ask who are you?

SHELLY BROWN
I'm Shelly Brown, Senator Brown's aide, here on a fact-finding visit. Looks like I just found some facts, boys.

Shelly smiled and turned around and headed back towards the bow of the space carrier. In the background she could hear one of the Nukes say to another,

NUKE TECHNICIAN
Man, you just fucked up royally!

The NRO chief engineer was almost sick to his stomach. He and his men failed to do the number-one thing while discussing sensitive information: *Clear your baffles and make sure you know who's listening first.*

Kevin Landry was not receiving good vibes from Admiral Gilbert. The upcoming *Ops Brief* was going to be rather painful. Gilbert is a former submarine sailor, and he most likely knows how to chew ass as the best of them, but he also knew who to call and get incompetent people removed.

Shelly knew she didn't have to say a thing. The men knowing, she heard everything they said would have to come clean on their own and they knew it. She would not miss the ops brief for any reason. This short trip was getting more interesting by the moment. *What other dirty laundry will be exposed next?*

Back on the Bridge (a.k.a. control room), the Weapons Officer walked Shelly around showing her some of the workstations. Out in deep space there wasn't much to look at. Though the stars were brighter. Depending on which flat screen she looked at she could see some slight movement in objects as the angle changed while they sped off to Mars, which currently looked like a bright star ahead. That would slowly change.

Shelly looked at the navigation plot screen. The ship was still accelerating though she didn't feel it.

SHELLY BROWN

What does the velocity of 1,500 mean?

WEPS
The speed is displayed in thousands of miles per hour.
We are now traveling at 1.5 million miles per hour."

SHELLY BROWN
That's incredible.

WEPS
Yes, when you have incredible nuclear rocket engines like we have you can go that fast."

SHELLY BROWN
Is that the max speed?

WEPS
No, we are speeding up to the ordered speed of 1.7 million miles per hour.

SHELLY BROWN
Why so fast?

WEPS
We must travel to Mars in forty-eight hours plus do a full-power run. We can go faster, but we are limited until all the engineering certs are done.

SHELLY BROWN
How much faster can the Alabama go?

WEPS
It depends on how much risk the ship's commander is willing to take. If we go too fast, we'll have no ability to see and avoid meteorites.

SHELLY BROWN
Do you know what absolute max speed is?

WEPS
No. Nobody knows because it's never been tested.

The tour around the control room lasted a few more minutes until the Weapons Officer informed Shelly of their next event.

WEPS
The evening meal now, I suggest we go to the wardroom. You might discover something interesting to eat.

Shelly and the Weps entered the Wardroom just as officers were taking their seats. CSS Alabama's Commander (Admiral Gilbert) sat at the end of the table. To his right were indicators and communications devices. On the far wall facing the captain is a large-screen display showing the space in front of them using the forward video cameras. Another monitor to the right of the large screen was a video of the control room.

The Alabama's Commander could look at the control room and communicate with the control room without leaving his seat. The XO sat to one side of the CO and the Engineer the other. Other officers sat down in pecking order, with the most junior the furthest away from the Carrier Commander. Each one had a name tent shaped placard, and some had salads, and some did not. The stewards knew each officer well and communicated effectively and knew trivial matters, like what kind of salad or drink do you want and what kind of dressing?

CAPTAIN GILBERT
Eng (as the ship's engineer is often called), how's the
Naval Reactors Engineers doing?"

ENG (CSS ALABAMA's ENGINEER)
Well, Admiral, I think they sort of already know what
the answer is, but they don't want to admit it.

CAPTAIN GILBERT
What's that, Eng?

Eng (CSS ALABAMA's ENGINEER)
All our equipment is working correctly and the built in
monitoring equipment has a diagnostics software flaw
in number two generator controller.

Tom Gilbert nodded his head up and down slightly taking it all in when the Weps, a very demure and sophisticated woman spoke up.

WEPS
Sir, while I was giving our guest a tour of the
Engineering spaces, I overheard the Naval Reactors
personnel discussing the problem. I suspect that at
your ops brief, they will have a come to Jesus' moment.

Tom Gilbert took it all in and knew this was not going to be one of the more pleasant Ops Briefs. But all new ships have growing pains, and many have moments like these where unexpected malfunctions create delays and make life uncomfortable for everyone. In his past nothing was more splendid than leaving a shipyard knowing you were not going back.

FLASHBACK

<u>INT. 688I CLAS SUBMARINE WARDROOM</u>

Tom Gilbert recalled one tender moment when serving on one submarine and the skipper was told the port hoist in the Torpedo Room had an issue and most likely they would have to go back into the shipyard to repair it. The skipper then had tears forming in his eyes.

688I CLASS SUBMARINE CAPTAIN

There's no way I'm going back into that God damn shipyard.

The commanding officer knew the crew morale would sink exponentially knowing their wives and kids down in San Diego were expecting them home in another week or so.

There of course had been more brutal events where a civilian out in Pearl Harbor directed the shipyard to put a couple submarines back in dry-dock because of failures that stemmed from workmanship issues. The joke around Pearl Harbor Sailors was "No Ka Oi," which meant "No can do."

Tom Gilbert looked at the Weps and smiled. He knew she knew far more than she was admitting, but she also knew the Naval Reactors men would be making their proposal at the ops briefing and she would bet 50/50 Admiral Gilbert would approve the software rebuild plan underway and hope to hell nothing happened to the other Generator while they were in the middle of the software reload.

It's always good to have redundancies, especially power generation.

There was some small talk, everyone got to know Shelly Brown and Tom Gilbert made sure they all knew she was the Senator's aide, hence keep your mouth shut around her, and by God clear your baffles before you speak until she gets off the ship.

After dessert was served and each officer slowly excused themselves to go do important work, the steward slowly cleaned away the evening meal plates and silverware. Tom knew they had to clean up and put the wardroom in condition for the ops brief to follow. He also excused himself and went to his stateroom where he looked over some emails and information he received before they blasted out towards Mars.

Tom knew his ship would be tracked by friendlies or also potential adversaries, both terrestrial and non-terrestrial. With modern technology a spaceship putting out a super-heated exhaust traveling faster than the speed of light can be observed long-range with special optics. Americans only obtained such optics within the past decade It was assumed the Russians and Chinese were not too far behind.

NRO (National Reconnaissance Office) had their KH-14 locked on the CSS Alabama. They knew the direction it was heading and that its speed was nearing 1.7 million miles per hour. They would find it hard to keep it out of the press from leaks that we could reach Mars with a very large ship in a day. These were exciting times for the CIA, NRO, and NSA. However, the Air Force was still crying in their beers over losing all the assets to the Space Force, facilitated by a traitor from within.

Margarette Mackworth, USSF Secretary, had the distinction of being the last Air Force Secretary and the First USSF Secretary. Her position in the history books was guaranteed. Little did she know the President wanted to reward John Harris for his many years of devotion to him and the former President, but also the American people and the Space Force which would not have come about without his input. There was only one thing holding the President back from relieving Margarette Mackworth as USSF Secretary, John Harris wanted to go on the Jupiter Mission.

The Jupiter Mission was a carefully guarded secret, and it was actually a blessing we had the planet Jupiter in this solar system to disguise the real destination, to the Jupitorians. But first there was the little test on Uranus that was needed to fully certify the TR-3B as a viable combat platform and the weapons they would deliver on the far side away from view of NASA or any other entity. The problem was NASA forcing their way on the mission. It was either invite them along or they guaranteed leaks and whatever the USSF was planning they would do their part to stick a monkey wrench in it unless they got a piece of the action.

NASA was of course put off until the very last moment, so they were not able to direct any experiments or control the information flow. Two NASA scientists, Burt and Don would be given last minute clearances, and the poor bastards would not know they were not coming home any time soon, until it was too late to do anything about it.

As part of the planning for the mission, Burt and Don would not be allowed on board unless they signed a power of attorney with their spouses in the event, they didn't make it back their spouses would not be hung high and dry. The spouses would receive a special briefing stating if they kept their mouths shut, they would receive their husband's full pay.

Since the extraordinary nature of the mission placed huge requirements, by agreement between several agencies, the two NASA men would receive over time every day throughout the mission prorated at sixteen hours per day including overtime whether they were working or sleeping. As it turned out the wives were glad, they were gone because the cash flow increased substantially with their departure. Life was suddenly financially a lot better.

Now all it took was to wrap up the generator issue and certify the craft for independent operations. Naval Reactors held the keys to all that.

19:00 came along smartly and standing-room-only, was available in the wardroom. There was great anticipation as well as consternation by a few Naval Reactors folks.

<u>INT. SPACE. CSS ALABAMA WARDROOM OPS BRIEF</u>

Ops briefings are always fun if the Navigator brings along all the eye candy such as maps and pictures. He usually does a recap of what the ship had done and what was in the works for the evening and the next day.

NAVIGATOR
In less than twenty-four hours from now we will be circling Mars. We will use Martian gravity to slingshot the CSS Alabama around the planet and back towards Earth.

The ship's course back to the Space Dock was shown on the 3D space map.

After the Navigator completed his briefing, the Commander of the mission, Admiral Tom Gilbert then announced.

ADMIRAL GILBERT
We shall now hear from Naval Reactors' Representatives and hear about their findings and recommendations.

The lead Naval Reactors Engineer started the report.

ROGER KEENEY
Captain, we have not been underway very long, but we have been doing sufficient speed over enough time to draw some conclusions.

ADMIRAL GILBERT
And what are those conclusions?

ROGER KEENEY
Measurements indicate all your equipment and machinery are operating nominally as expected. Our carry-on equipment has not detected any malfunctions or issues that would cause the fault-codes we are getting with the built in generator number two computer diagnostic software that's integrated into all the engineering systems.

ADMIRAL GILBERT
If the equipment is operating to design specifications and you are receiving fault codes, that tells me it's a monitoring problem and not a ship's problem.

ROGER KEENEY
You are correct, sir.

ADMIRAL GILBERT
Well, then what do you recommend?

Tom Gilbert predicted the next series of statements but went along with it as though this was all news to him.

ROGER KEENEY
Normally protocols state to only rebuild the software while in Space Dock. The problem with that is we would have to dock, do the software loads, then undock and go out and test it again. If we can fix it during this underway over the next twelve hours which I believe we can, we can then retest it on our return trip to the Space Dock.

ADMIRAL GILBERT
All our systems are completely redundant, correct?

ROGER KEENEY
Yes, sir.

ADMIRAL GILBERT
So, if we shift to a single power line up, as long as we do not scram the primary reactor, we will not even know the other generator was shut down?

ROGER KEENEY
That's correct.

ADMIRAL GILBERT
Let's proceed with the software rebuild.

ROGER KEENEY
Sir, I can't authorize any such work, it needs to come from higher authority unless it's in the Space Dock.

ADMIRAL GILBERT
Mr. Keeney, I got good news for you. As part of my rules and regulations, they state that once I'm beyond the two-million-mile limit, which we just crossed over a short while ago, I do not have to seek permissions from higher authority. I was endowed with this special authority because the President, Secretary of the Space Force, and the Joint Chiefs realize that once I get this far away from Earth, I'm on my own. They have no means to send out a rescue.

ROGER KEENEY
I would like to see that in writing.

ADMIRAL GILBERT
As soon as this meeting is over, you may come to my stateroom where my special portfolio exists. It's above your security clearance level. Normally I could not expose it to you, but since we have an extraordinary situation here, if you are willing to sign a non-disclosure form, I will show you the *special case instructions* and you can read it in its entirety.

ROGER KEENEY
Thank you, sir.

ADMIRAL GILBERT
One other thing, you will also discover once I cross the two-million-mile limit you no longer have the authority to pull the keys.

Normally Naval Reactors can pull the keys without any recourse because they work for the Department of Energy and did not report to the Joint Chiefs. Whoever wrote the Space Operations Instructions (SOIs often called – pronounced Soyuz) were forward thinkers and Naval Reactors were contained in their broad scope of powers. It all came down to situations like this when help was not available and no rescue could be attempted, they didn't want to erode the commander's power and authority since he had all the lives on his ship in his hands.

Naval Reactors would soon be appalled and severely disturbed when they discovered the two-million-mile rule.

To everyone's surprise, Shelly Brown suddenly spoke.

SHELLY BROWN
Admiral Gilbert, I would also like to review that instruction when you and Naval Reactors go to your stateroom.

ADMIRAL GILBERT
I'm sorry, Ms. Brown, even though I know you work directly for the Senator, you are not cleared high enough to see the document.

SHELLY BROWN
Who do I have to contact to see the document?

ADMIRAL GILBERT
I would start with Margarette Mackworth, USSF Secretary since it's her signature on the document.

Shelly Brown knew asking Margarette Mackworth permission to view the document was probably useless because she would most likely decline citing operational security or some other balderdash.

ADMIRAL GILBERT
ENG, I'm going to take Naval Reactors to my stateroom and have him read the document. You have my permission to shut down generator number two and start the software rebuild. I shall remain in the control room with the XO during the corrective maintenance.

ENG
Understand all, Admiral Gilbert.

Tom Gilbert and the Naval Reactors Rep went to his stateroom and were let in by the security guard and closed the door behind him. Tom then went over to a safe and spun the dial in three directions and opened it. There were two sliding doors that slid out containing notebooks and binders highly colorized for specific functions with labels such as PASSWORDS, SELF DESTRUCT, MUTINY, WAR, ALIEN, OPSEC, and PROJECT JUPITER.

Admiral Gilbert had some blank none-disclosure forms that were semi filled in just needing the person's name, rank (or civilian rating), full social security number, place of birth, and a few other pieces of information.

ADMIRAL GILBERT
Here, read this, fill in the areas in the light gray shaded area.

The Naval Reactors Rep read the document carefully. The USSF non-disclosure agreement in instruction 4797B stated the Naval Reactors Rep could not reveal any of this *4798B* information for the rest of his life. The information already typed in stated *Project Jupiter Instruction 4798B Information.*

After the Naval Reactors Rep signed the USSF non-disclosure form, Admiral Gilbert handed him the USSF Instruction 4797B that had a yellow sticky right where he needed to turn the page then held out the sheet. The information was as Tom had stated. The two-million-mile mark was clearly delineated in the instruction.

NAVAL REACTORS REP
Okay, I understand.

Tom then closed most of the sheets then only showing the cover sheet, which was signed by the President and Margarette Mackworth, USSF Secretary.

Tom Gilbert then shut the book, put it back in the drawer, shut it, closed the safe door and spun the dial locking it.

ADMIRAL GILBERT
Okay, looks like you have your work cut out for you. I'll be in the control room. Call me if you need anything.

NAVAL REACTORS REP
Will do, sir.

Tom Gilbert stood up, opened his door and the civilian exited and Tom followed closely behind shutting the door behind him followed by the security guard electronically locking it.

Tom Gilbert then went to the control room and sat down at one of the empty consoles not manned because the full Air Wing was not onboard. He then turned to his chief of the watch.

ADMIRAL GILBERT
Chief of the Watch send a messenger to Commodore Riley, he should be in his stateroom or the wardroom and ask him to meet me here in the control room.

CHIEF OF THE WATCH (COW)
Right away, sir.

In the Navy, it was customary to do a repeat back to make sure someone did not screw up the orders.

Tom Gilbert changed all that for CSS Alabama. His rule was: Repeat back if you are not sure what you were ordered to do. Otherwise, 'Right away, sir' is preferable since it causes far fewer delays which would be priceless in battle stations if someone was shooting at you and time was at the essence.

In five minutes or less, Commodore Riley appeared with the messenger.

COMMODORE RILEY
What can I do for you, Admiral?

ADMIRAL GILBERT

XO I need to send you back to the engineering spaces now and then to observe what's going on, then report back to me.

COMMODORE RILEY
You don't trust those civilians?

ADMIRAL GILBERT

I don't want to limp back on one generator. I want this problem fixed before we return to the Space Dock.

COMMODORE RILEY
Understand, sir.

ADMIRAL GILBERT

Also, locate the Engineer and inform him, I'd prefer he stay in Maneuvering while that software rebuild is in process.

COMMODORE RILEY

That's probably a good idea. On my way to the engineering spaces.

In a short while Shelly Brown arrived on the bridge which was semi empty while they were transiting. The thought crossed her mind, *this is probably how it would be when they traveled great distance across space to some unknown destination.*

Even though the watch section was minimal in auto pilot, there were numerous automation features and should radar detect another ship or a meteorite that could be a collision hazard the ship would sound alarms and make appropriate automatic maneuvers to avoid collision. Coming across an enemy ship in space though posed an interesting problem. Depending on the direction it was traveling, the closure rates could be excessive if they were going on reciprocal bearings. If there were intensions of firing weapons, you wouldn't know about it until it was too late, and you were a sitting duck.

Shelly approached Admiral Gilbert.

SHELLY BROWN

It looks kind of empty up here now.

ADMIRAL GILBERT

When we are transiting long distances in space we only need a chief of the watch and a sensor's operator. The Navigator can check his charts from his stateroom. I'm only here so that I can interact easier with the watch in case something goes wrong.

SHELLY BROWN

It's amazing what all this automation and artificial intelligence is changing everything.

ADMIRAL GILBERT

If you want some companionship, there are probably several people in the crew's lounge either playing cards or doing computer games.

SHELLY BROWN

Yes, I saw them earlier, they all seemed happy and not up tight they are out in empty space.

ADMIRAL GILBERT

We've been to space before. Almost my entire crew is qualified, though we will start to have a turnover soon.

SHELLY BROWN

How long does it take to train a crew member?

ADMIRAL GILBERT

Right now, the numbers are preliminary because these crew members had a lot of time in the simulators because of new construction. After we get four or five Space Carriers in operation and a larger turnover begins, they will not have the luxury of all time in trainers before deploying. I anticipate the level of expertise will decline unless we confront the inevitable now."

SHELLY BROWN

Knowing this is all going to happen, what would you propose to fix it?

ADMIRAL GILBERT

It all depends on the financial resources the bean counters decide to give the USSF. With more money we could invest more in training.

SHELLY BROWN

Being up on Capitol Hill, I can assure you there is no blanket support for high expenditures and quite frankly many members of congress are upset at the wasteful spending this whole Project Jupiter program has a reputation of doing.

ADMIRAL GILBERT

Yeah, I understand all that, but we better be careful we don't get caught with our pants down.

SHELLY BROWN

You mean like at the beginning of WWII?

ADMIRAL GILBERT

Yes, that's a good example. Korea is another.

SHELLY BROWN

WW2 was probably excusable, but with the money spent on WW2, there should have been far more equipment readily available for the Korean Pusan Perimeter.

ADMIRAL GILBERT

Some argue the same person in charge of the Defense of the Philippines at the start of WW2 was the same guy responsible for the lack of immediate retaliation when North Korea attacked under Stalin's orders.

SHELLY BROWN

History has a way of repeating itself.

In a short while Commodore Riley was back in the Alabama's control room.

COMMODORE RILEY

The Engineer is monitoring the situation in maneuvering?

ADMIRAL GILBERT

Yes. He's very keen on what's going on. How are the Naval Reactor guys doing?

COMMODORE RILEY
Generator #2 was shut down satisfactorily. They are currently loading up the new software into the controllers for that Generator.

ADMIRAL GILBERT
How are they building the software?

COMMODORE RILEY
They have data cubes they insert into the programming port on processors which take all the data and place it in various computers that run the software. They said they would be done in twelve hours just in time to begin the slingshot around Mars.

ADMIRAL GILBERT
What does *done* mean?

COMMODORE RILEY
I would assume done means that Generator #2 is back online in service with power split between the two generators with Generator #1 providing all PORT loads and Generator #2 providing all STBD loads in the normal underway lineup.

ADMIRAL GILBERT
In a couple hours I want you to swing back to engineering and clarify what 'done' means.

COMMODORE RILEY
Will do Admiral. ENG said he would contact me if something critical happens and I should come back to maneuvering.

ADMIRAL GILBERT
Alright Commodore, I'm remaining here for the duration until I know it's completed.

COMMODORE RILEY
Understand all. I'm going back to my stateroom for a couple hours to get a nap. It's going to be a long day and I want to have some freshness when we re-dock.

ADMIRAL GILBERT
I'll have the chief of the watch send a messenger to wake you in a couple hours.

COMMODORE RILEY
Admiral, I think you need to take a break.

ADMIRAL GILBERT
I will as soon as we are heading back to the Space Dock with our generators fixed.

Shelly Brown hung around on the bridge for an hour but there wasn't much activity.

SHELLY BROWN
Admiral Gilbert, I'm going to walk back to maneuvering and look at what's going on then I think I'll take a nap.

ADMIRAL GILBERT
See you later, Ms. Brown.

Shelly Brown made her way back to engineering where she approached the Naval Reactors Reps overseeing the software builds. She noticed a person wearing a Space Force uniform manipulating the equipment. The Naval Reactors personnel body language had an abrupt shift when she arrived. A day late and a dollar short they finally learned to clear their baffles!

SHELLY BROWN
How's it going back here?

NAVAL REACTORS REP
Things are moving along smoothly.

Shelly Brown looked at the person wearing a Space Force uniform and asked him the question:

SHELLY BROWN
Are you Naval Reactors as well?

ALABAMA REACTOR CONTROLS TECHNICIAN
No mam. I'm a Reactor Controls Technician, crew member of CSS Alabama.

SHELLY BROWN
Are you doing the programming and not Naval Reactors?

ALABAMA REACTOR CONTROLS TECHNICIAN
That's correct.

SHELLY BROWN
Is that normal?

ALABAMA REACTOR CONTROLS TECHNICIAN
Yes, Naval Reactors Reps are mainly oversight and have their carry-on equipment, but Alabama crew members perform corrective maintenance and software reloads.

SHELLY BROWN
I see. That seems like a great idea.

ALABAMA REACTOR CONTROLS TECHNICIAN
Yes, very much so, it insures we maintain our proficiency. The Naval Reactors personnel make sure we follow the procedures correctly with no deviations."

SHELLY BROWN
What happens if you must deviate?"

ALABAMA REACTOR CONTROLS TECHNICIAN
We need permission first."

SHELLY BROWN
How long before you will be done loading the software?

NAVAL REACTORS REP
In about four hours we'll be starting the generator up and shifting the loads. We'll then start our diagnostics. We should be ready for full power operation in no more than eight hours."

SHELLY BROWN
Ahead of schedule?

NAVAL REACTORS REP
Yes, because we are not going to tamper with Generator #1 software. It had no fault codes. We want to leave

it unchanged until we are back in the Space Dock. There may be no need to reload Generator number one software.

SHELLY BROWN
Thanks for the information.

Shelly then left, went back to female officer berthing to see if anyone was up, and then she went into the crew's lounge which was also nearly empty. More than likely, everyone is tired from a long day and is taking a nap.

Shelly then decided to do what most of them were doing and went and lay down. Shelly felt kind of strange. The artificial gravity was only about a third normal gravity and so she didn't press hard against her mattress. She almost felt like she was slightly floating and if it were not for the magnetic shoes, she would probably feel unsafe.

Perhaps it was the low gravity, Shelly wasn't sure, but it seemed she fell asleep a lot quicker than before. Six hours passed and she woke up on her own and decided to go see how things were going. Admiral Gilbert was still on the bridge, though starting to look a little ragged. The XO was there too so this would be good to listen in on.

COMMODORE RILEY
The Naval Reactors Rep said, the software load is complete, and the Engineer just gave them permission to restart the Generator.

ADMIRAL GILBERT
How soon before they can put a load on it?

COMMODORE RILEY
They will start loading it down fifteen minutes after the reactor is critical.

ADMIRAL GILBERT
Okay, standing by.

A few moments later the Chief of the Watch reported.

CHIEF OF THE WATCH
Admiral Gilbert, Maneuvering reports Generator #2 reactor is critical.

ADMIRAL GILBERT
Very well, Chief of the Watch.

In due time Chief of the Watch reported.

CHIEF OF THE WATCH
Captain, maneuvering reports all electrical loads are now split between Generator #1 and Generator #2.

ADMIRAL GILBERT
Chief of the Watch, when the Navigator makes his next report, make sure I'm woke up."

CHIEF OF THE WATCH
Understand, Admiral Gilbert, wake you when the Navigator provides his next report."

Tom Gilbert turned to Shelly.

ADMIRAL GILBERT
See that dark brown moon like object on the screen forward surveillance display?"

SHELLY BROWN
Yes, what is it?

ADMIRAL GILBERT
Mars.

SHELLY BROWN
Wow, it looks huge now.

ADMIRAL GILBERT
In a few more hours it will look huge and as we pass close to the atmosphere it will be the largest image of Mars you have ever seen.

SHELLY BROWN
I'll be looking.

Shelly then departed the control room and went back to her bunk to relax and if possible grab a couple hours of sleep.

ADMIRAL GILBERT
I'm going to now go get a couple hours of down time. I want to be up when we go around Mars, Chief of the Watch.

CHIEF OF THE WATCH
I'll make sure you are awake for the event, sir.

Admiral Tom Gilbert turned and left the control room and went back to his stateroom where he was soon horizontal and sleeping like a lamb.

Senator's aide Shelly Brown was also resting peacefully feeling good about her experiences on the CSS Alabama and realized how Admiral Gilbert calmly handled serious situations, but she was perturbed he refused to let her see the USSF Instruction 4797B that delineates the two-million-mile rule. She knew it must be true because the Naval Reactor's Rep followed the instruction with the understanding Admiral Gilbert could legally force the issue.

It seemed that no sooner than Tom Gilbert put his head on the pillow than he was being awakened again.

MESSENGER OF THE WATCH
Admiral Gilbert, the Chief of the Watch, sends his regards and wanted you to know we are now at Mars getting ready to enter the orbital pattern.

ADMIRAL GILBERT
Okay, thanks.

EXT. CGI. CSS ALABAMA ORBITING MARS (10 SECONDS)

INT. SPACE. CSS ALABAMA CONTROL ROOM.

Tom Gilbert got up and was soon in the control room looking at the monitor showing Mars in fantastic detail. Tom had studied pictures of Mars and knew where Cydonia existed, and it was clear to him he could see was perhaps one of the two hydrogen bomb blast zones Dr. Brandenburg had stated in his reports and subsequent books. If this in fact was true, it went a long way towards justifying the need for a Space Force. *Earth was living on borrowed time.*

Should the Jupitorians decide to come back to this solar system, they no doubt would finish what they attempted to do nine hundred thousand years ago when Mars and Atlantis were destroyed. If Mars was once a vibrant green planet before the Jupitorians did their handy work, what was left should be a warning to be prepared to defend the planet. If NASA knew TR-3Bs could land on Mars, there would be exploration going on right now.

ADMIRAL GILBERT
Chief of the Watch, send the messenger down to notify Ms. Brown. She should come up to the control to look at Mars.

CHIEF OF THE WATCH
Right away, sir.

\

Shelly Brown was soon aroused from a sensational dream that included Admiral Gilbert. Shelly's mother would be shocked to learn her daughter dreamed about provocative sexual circumstances in her dreams.

MESSENGER OF THE WATCH WITH FEMALE ESCORT
Ma'am, you are requested on the bridge, the Commander wishes you to get an observation of Mars.

SHELLY BROWN
Okay, I'll be right up there.

Shelly Brown then swung her feet around and slid out of her rack and grabbed her magnetic shoes in the shoe rack next to her bunk and put them on. Within moments she had her first Observation of a close-up of Mars. The high-resolution video was nothing less than spectacular.

SHELLY BROWN
Wow, that view of Mars is truly amazing.

Shelly Brown now observed the Martian imagery and slowly took it all in with tremendous gratitude for being given the opportunity to go on this voyage.

Tom Gilbert responded in equal awe of the observation knowing the implications of having a Space Carrier capable of transiting long distances.

ADMIRAL GILBERT
This close to Mars sure creates an amazing sight.

SHELLY BROWN
Looks like the North Poll of Mars is covered with snow or ice.

ADMIRAL GILBERT
It's winter now in the Martian Northern Hemisphere.

SHELLY BROWN
Even though Mars doesn't have much of an atmosphere, Mars still has weather?

ADMIRAL GILBERT
Mars has a greater atmosphere than you realize. The

main problem is the atmosphere is loaded with Xeon 129 and other elements that would make people from Earth very ill.

SHELLY BROWN
What about air filters?

ADMIRAL GILBERT
The atmosphere of Mars is composed primarily of carbon dioxide.

SHELLY BROWN
Interesting, does that imply former life on the planet?

ADMIRAL GILBERT
Well, according to Dr. Brandenburg, a former nuclear physicist who designed nuclear weapons at the Lawrence Livermore lab, the planet was probably teaming with life before it was destroyed by two huge hydrogen bombs."

SHELLY BROWN
Don't you think such a claim is silly?

ADMIRAL GILBERT
No, I believe he's on to something. NASA should take him seriously and do a full-scale investigation, because if Dr. Brandenburg is accurate in his assessment, we have reason to be concerned.

SHELLY BROWN
About what?

ADMIRAL GILBERT
Aliens.

SHELLY BROWN
There has never been any proof of any aliens ever detected.

ADMIRAL GILBERT
Madam, there are some things you do not know about, but one day I suspect you will get a briefing which will probably turn your world upside down.

SHELLY BROWN
"In what way?

ADMIRAL GILBERT
I suppose when more information about the galaxy
becomes apparent, there will be reason to believe your
faith will be tested.

To get them off a discussion that smelled like an argument forming Tom gave Shelly
Brown a very interesting view of Mars.

ADMIRAL GILBERT
I'm going to zoom in on something for you.

Tom Gilbert then took the joystick for the photonics controller and steered the optics
and also increased the magnification. In automatic mode, the computer could do that
without human intervention if it were directed on an object in space by automatic
detectors and Cosmic Interpolator Trackers.

ADMIRAL GILBERT
Look at this.

SHELLY BROWN
What is it?

ADMIRAL GILBERT
It's Olympus Mons, a volcano. It's 68897 feet high and
372 miles in diameter. There is evidence it was created
from recent volcanic lava flows, so some scientists
think it's an active volcano.

SHELLY BROWN
Double the height of Mount Everest?

ADMIRAL GILBERT
Approximately, yes.

SHELLY BROWN
The planet looks totally barren.

ADMIRAL GILBERT
NASA has discovered there is underground water on
Mars in several locations. Some of it is saltwater.

SHELLY BROWN

Is the salt content so high it would not work in a desalination plant?

ADMIRAL GILBERT

There are ways of getting pure water out of water samples with heavy salt content in reverse osmosis, so it should not be a problem.

SHELLY BROWN

Thus, what you are implying possibly is that CO2 on the planet would be great for growing plants and in an enclosure where atmosphere controls like on the Space Dock, would facilitate inhabiting Mars if there was incentive to put people on the planet.

ADMIRAL GILBERT

I can see where putting military on the planet would be desirable.

SHELLY BROWN
For what reason?

ADMIRAL GILBERT

To help defend this solar system. Mars could have additional photonics and radars that could be used with Earth and Space sensors to triangulate possible alien ships over long distance so we can pinpoint their location.

SHELLY BROWN
What is that dark area in the middle of the planet?

ADMIRAL GILBERT

There are several theories, mine is it's the charred remains of a proud civilization that once lived there.

SHELLY BROWN

Do you really believe all that Dr. Brandenburg information?

ADMIRAL GILBERT

Absolutely, I think the gentleman, Dr. Brandenburg is spot on.

SHELLY BROWN
Now that we have the Space Carrier and TR-3B shuttles, it shouldn't be too difficult of a task to land someone down there for a close look.

ADMIRAL GILBERT
There have been over forty surveys to Mars.

SHELLY BROWN
With all those missions, I would think scientists would be pounding their chests with requests to put people on the planet to discover if there is any credence in your speculation.

ADMIRAL GILBERT
NASA had the lion share of the missions but now that the European Space Agency ExoMars is going there now and India's MOM Mangalyaan orbiter, it will be more and more difficult for NASA to control the information flow. Discovery may have been made, but due to political decisions never left NASA because they want to be in position to exploit major new discoveries there before other space agencies can act on it.

SHELLY BROWN
How much water do you think exists on Mars?

ADMIRAL GILBERT
On planet Earth seventy five percent of all the water is underground, not in the oceans. I would bet the same thing exists on Mars, most of the water is underground.

SHELLY BROWN
But is it all salt water?

ADMIRAL GILBERT
We don't know. We have hardly surveyed much of Mars, especially underground. But I think as commercial enterprises start thinking about surveying for gold, silver, uranium, and rare earth metals, we may see a sudden flurry of activity.

The Space Carrier slowly circled Mars and as soon as the bow of the ship was pointing to Earth, a slight blast from its rocket engines helped reorientation of its course directly towards Earth. When Mars was suddenly behind them it seemed rather anticlimactic and like before the control room emptied out and Tom decided he would go for another shot at a few more hours of sleep because once they started to slow down, he would be required to be on the bridge from then until re-docking at Space Dock #1 was complete.

Re-docking was going to be a marvelous experience. He'll be able to finally get rid of the Naval Reactors engineers and more importantly, the Senator's aide which would allow him to breathe easier, knowing he wasn't operating in front of a woman who had the political strings to get him removed if she got a wild hair up her ass.

ADMIRAL GILBERT
Chief of the Watch, I'm going to back to my stateroom
for a while. Have the messenger notify me thirty
minutes prior to the deceleration.

Chief of the Watch
Thirty minutes before deceleration, will do, sir.

ADMIRAL GILBERT
Madam.

Tom nodded and walked off the bridge back to his stateroom.

Shelly took the hint and left.

Tom was horizontal and enjoying his nap a few seconds after he got horizontal. He knew he needed a power nap because once the Space Carrier started decelerating, he would be in the control room until re-docking was complete. He wanted to be on his toes and physically and mentally ready for what was to befall him, in lieu of the fact he knew Senator Bosworth's spy aboard would be doing a full report and he knew there would most likely be some repercussions and possible need for explanation and possible written reports in response to official inquiry.

The Naval Reactors fiasco blew up in NRO's faces. This software glitch should have been figured out and rectified before now. They sure had plenty of time on the previous underway to figure it out. But Naval Reactors is just as bad as the Office of Naval Intelligence. They want to know with one hundred percent accuracy if something is valid before they make a call. That's why their INTEL is often a day late and a dollar short.

But then on the other hand, they have been burned in the past like the Gulf of Tonkin incident where things were not clearly as they seemed to be. ONI's most proud moment was the Cuban Missile Crisis. They nailed it.

The Navy saved Kennedy's ass with Operation Boresight and SOSUS. Unfortunately, the Vietnam War dragged on far too long and it slowly eroded all INTEL services.

The CIA got heavily penetrated, NSA had their secret crypto compromised, and the INTEL ended up almost as bad as during the Korean War which had a major impact resulting in an Armistice instead of a Victory.

Tom had reason to worry that Project Jupiter would one day be called Jupiter's Folly because they were being guided down the primrose path. Was the Ponarian purposely setting them up for revenge from his numerous torture incidents or was he sincere. And the dirty part of it was, Tom may be forced to take him with him even though this might turn out to be nothing more than a boondoggle.

Based on rough estimates the Ponarian gave USSF, the Alabama would have enough fuel to go to and from the Jupitorian solar system twice, so fuel would not be an issue.

Also, since they're not flying into a perceived war with all sorts of ground support equipment and munitions, they could take with them more food and water than needed for the crew, which gave them plenty of supplies to get there and back even though the round trip could last almost four years.

The little side trip to Uranus on the outbound passage was a mild irritant. It wasn't enough that he was departing on a four-year trip, but to do a major clandestine weapons test was a huge distraction. Only he, Commodore Riley and the designated pilots would know about the mission.

Since they would use the huge size of the planet to shield what was going on the opposite side so that crew members and scientists on Earth would have no way of knowing what they were doing.

This nuclear test at Uranus would be a huge violation of the space weapons ban and it would be internationally condemned if other countries found out about it. But it was the price Tom had to pay to receive the honor of being Alabama's first Commanding Officer.

Shelly was too wired now to attempt sleep. She went into the wardroom where she saw the Weps reading some classified manuals. It seemed to her that she probably should not distract the Weps but decided that since she was here on a fact-finding trip, it might be useful to hear from women on board and get their take on things which would provide a well-balanced viewpoint since it would not be an all-male vantage point.

SHELLY BROWN
Hello Weps, thanks for your assistance earlier.

WEP'S
No problem, I'm glad I could help.

SHELLY BROWN
That's great. Can I ask you a question?

WEPS
Sure.

SHELLY BROWN
How do you view your role as a woman on this Space Carrier?

WEPS
As far as I'm concerned, Admiral Gilbert expects the same out of me as he does any other officer.

SHELLY BROWN
Do you feel you are treated equally and fairly?

WEPS
Absolutely. Admiral Gilbert has great trust and expectations of me. He delegates a lot of power and authority to me, which is necessary since I have one of the most sensitive departments on this ship.

SHELLY BROWN
How about the rest of the crew and your subordinates?

WEPS
As you can imagine, crew members all want to be here and be part of a history making experience. The cooperation is genuine and earnest. They know they are on a very high-risk assignment and that it is very hazardous.

SHELLY BROWN
What kind of training did they receive to help prepare them for the United States Space Force?

WEPS
Some of the people were sailors serving on Aircraft Carriers and Submarines. They are accustomed to

handle ordinance and conduct hazardous missions and long hours of watch standing."

SHELLY BROWN
How many women are in the ranks?

WEPS
Right now, there are approximately 45 percent of the billets aboard this Space Carrier filled by women.

SHELLY BROWN
Why not more?

WEPS
It comes down to an all-volunteer force. There were ten times as many men who requested Space Carrier billets than women.

SHELLY BROWN
Then why have 45 percent of the crew women if only 10 percent of all applicants are female?

WEPS
Because we have long missions expected and segregated berthing which I believe is essential, we had to reserve several billets for women exclusively so that construction of the berthing compartments matched requirements."

SHELLY BROWN
Are there sufficient number of volunteers to fully staff the Alabama with women?

WEPS
Actually, there is more than enough.

SHELLY BROWN
Then why only 45 percent?

WEPS
We have to make room for sick bay and a place to put injured patients. When we saw the statistics of ten to one relationship in volunteers, the decision was made

to put sick bay next to female berthing. Women's numbers were reduced 5 percent to accommodate the construction.

SHELLY BROWN
So, it had nothing to do with sexual bias?"

WEPS
No, Alabama's berthing design was all based on recruiting statistics and the need for a sick bay.

SHELLY BROWN
How well do the women perform?

WEPS
Since all the crew members volunteered and went through a really good psychological screening process, we ended up with very dedicated people, men and women. They all know their jobs and they also know its risky business.

SHELLY BROWN
How risky?

WEPS
We have four very powerful and complicated machines on board, the two electrical generators and the two propulsion motors. Serious failure in any of the four could cause a huge safety problem for the crew.

SHELLY BROWN
What are the big risks traveling long distance in space?

WEPS
Probably our biggest concern is we may not be able to spot a large meteorite before it strikes us.

SHELLY BROWN
I can visualize there are some unknow threats we may encounter.

Shelly Brown was thinking in terms of meeting aliens in space. And wondered if the crew would be ready for something as such. But WEPS gave her a response that seemed plausible.

WEPS
If we had a head on collision with a good size meteor
while we were doing 1.7 million miles per hour, the
crew would be instantly killed.

Shelly noticed the Weps was looking over a nuclear weapons security manual and as the Weps noticed her spying on the content of the manual she closed it but not before Shelly realized the Weps was studying an alarm system required to be implemented when nuclear weapons were carried on any type of ship or aircraft. That intrigued Shelly but she knew inquiry into it might create some friction and it was best she had good relations with the Weps, one of the senior female officers and department head.

Putting nuclear weapons on Alabama would certainly trash the treaties America had with all the nuclear powers on Earth. China and Russia would not take such revelations nicely.

The conversation shifted to general "girls talk." Where her hometown was, where she went to school, what was her major in college. Was she married, did she have a boyfriend, and what kind of music did she like, etc.

In due time the Chief of the watch sent the messenger down to inform the captain they were thirty minutes away from deceleration. The captain thanked the messenger then promptly went into the Wardroom where he asked the steward for a cup of black coffee to help wake him up.

Coffee was always kept in closed containers in the event artificial gravity as lost because hot coffee floating around in micro gravity was not a good thing.

After Tom Gilbert finished his cup of java, he moved swiftly to the CSS Alabama's control room.

ADMIRAL GILBERT
Chief of the Watch, how soon do we start decelerating?

CHIEF OF THE WATCH
Fifteen more minutes, sir.

ADMIRAL GILBERT
Very well Chief of the Watch.

Admiral Gilbert picked up the 1MC a microphone that gave the captain the ability to speak throughout the ship to everyone for moments just like this or during casualties or drills. By using the 1MC they all would hear Admiral Gilbert's voice and not the Artificial Intelligence voice which Admiral Gilbert felt was best way to interface with the crew during tumultuous occasions or very important communications.

ADMIRAL GILBERT

All hands, this is Admiral Gilbert speaking. We will be decelerating in about fifteen minutes. Recommend that at that time you find a seat somewhere and strap yourself in as the first ten minutes of deceleration will be unpleasant if you are standing up and walking around. Stow all gear and make sure everything is buttoned down good, so objects don't suddenly become projectiles and hurt someone. As you all know it is important that we remain '*stowed for space*' at all times.

If you need additional time to tie something down or prevent someone getting hurt by equipment you cannot get tied down in fifteen minutes, report to the chief of the watch in control immediately so we can adjust the deceleration timeline. But we need to do this soon so please be ready.

The time wound down and forty seconds before deceleration the Chief of the Watch reported.

CHIEF OF THE WATCH
Admiral Gilbert, forty seconds to deceleration.

ADMIRAL GILBERT
Very well, Chief of the watch. Make the report.

CHIEF OF THE WATCH
All hands, deceleration to commence in thirty seconds.

The Navigator was present sitting at the Navigation console where he had control of the ship.

 Normally it was autopilot, but he could manually steer it as necessary. He then typed in the deceleration command on the NAV terminal and the time mark to commence.

At T-0 deceleration commenced.

CHIEF OF THE WATCH
All hands, commence deceleration.

C.U. NAVIGATION CONTROL DISPLAY

Upon hearing the Chief of the Watch announcement, the Navigator selected the [DECELERATION] icon on the navigation control display, then moused over and clicked on the [EXECUTE DECELERATION] icon. Those actions considered critical navigation actions were verified by Artificial Intelligence by control room announcements in the form of affirmative backup. Had Artificial Intelligence not observed the proper sequence of ship-wide announcements validating the action the DECELERATION icon would not have been actionable.

<u>EXT. CGI. SPACE. ALABAMA DECELERATION 10 SECONDS.</u>

NOTE: The back cover of the Novel this screenplay depicts shows the deceleration:

Side panels on CSS Alabama that covered up the reverse thrusters near the bow of the CSS Alabama space carrier opened and slid out of the way. These thrusters pointed 30 degrees off either side of the bow and had rocket engines that put out about one tenth the force the main propulsion motors could do. These reverse thrusters could be substantially smaller since they pushed against a plume shot out in front of them giving added traction.

Unlike the normal main engines, the plume went in the opposite direction of the ship which had less traction, the deceleration thrusters pushed against the plume created by continuous output resulting in a much greater traction than experienced during acceleration where the plume was traveling in the opposite direction and diffusing quicker. The deceleration was so strong that a person could easily be tossed out of their seats if they were not strapped in either a seatbelt or a safety harness.

Earth was also now directly in front of them. If they didn't slow down or change course, in due time they would burn up entering the atmosphere traveling 1.7 million miles per hour.

The Navigator informed the Chief of the Watch.

NAVIGATOR
The decelerators were about to kick in.

And just like in the trainers the Chief of the Watch gave one last warning for individuals who have not heeded previous warnings.

CHIEF OF THE WATCH
The ship will now decelerate.

The navigator initiated the reversers when he clicked on the [EXECUTE DECELERATION] icon that confirmed the request on the navigation console. The giant panels now slid sideways and at first appeared an air scoop was fully exposed. Just like the main propulsion motors a jet stream of rocket exhaust began propelling two very bright plumes in the direction they were traveling engulfing the ship almost like the exhaust from ancient steam locomotives.

The reverse exhaust went through nuclear reactors that super-heated hydrogen resulting in a jet traveling faster than the speed of light. Light bands created an astonishing display of visual tapestry and the rocket engines gained traction pushing against the plume it was emitting. Looking at the inertial navigation-based speed indicator, the speed dropped off rapidly.

Anyone who was not strapped in soon regretted it as they would be flung to a forward surface and receive a hard landing.

The navigator watched own ship's velocity in millions of miles per hour reduce: 1.7, 1.6, 1.5, 1.4…and after ten minutes the ship was down to 100,000 miles per hour. About that time the Navigator made the expected announcement.

NAVIGATOR
Steering thrusters to obtain orbit around the planet.

One of the thrusters put out less energy which caused the ship to gradually change course as if it had a rudder. Soon the inertial navigation system showed the ship was on a course parallel to the planet as the speed had been reduced to 50,000 miles per hour. Thrust on the reversers was gradually reduced as the automatic controls slowed the ship to its requested speed, 25,000 miles per hour in a spatial derived formula based on slowing anywhere in space.

Earth's gravity would soon play into the course as the microgravity pulled the ship closer towards earth in very small amounts bending its heading slightly as it was now on course for the Space Dock which had a velocity of 18,000 miles per hour as observed from Earth. As they closed the range, there would be brief thrusts that would slow CSS Alabama down more and eventually stop the forward motion of the Space Carrier. Once lined up perfectly with the Space Dock, the reversers and thrusters would automatically position the Space Carrier perfectly in the Dock.

The XO, Commodore Riley, came towards Admiral Gilbert who would be referred to as the chip's Captain when they deployed, with instructions to the crew to simply call him Captain, just like it was back on his San Diego Class submarine. Commander Riley handed the captain an electronic clipboard that held all their messages.

A CSS Alabama SITREP prepared by Alabama's radiomen/women and scrubbed by the communicator, was ready to be transmitted to USSF Space Command and other addressees on the message including the Space Dock and Naval Reactors who would all be pleased to know a separate CASCOR was also transmitted reporting the Number Two Generator reported problem corrected.

COMMODORE RILEY

I see that in the CASCOR, Admiral Gilbert you showered Kevin Landry and Roger Keeney with accolades in the message for resolving the Generator Issue in a very timely manner and completed all required retests and put the Generator back in service in time to support ships operations.

ADMIRAL GILBERT

I did that for two reasons. First, they will have a more positive attitude towards us when they get back to their offices and receive some BZ's:

Note to the director: Bravo Zulu's are Navy vernacular for Congratulations for doing a good job. BZ Flags hosted on ships:

ADMIRAL GILBERT

Secondly, part of the language in the conclusion portion of the CASCOR stated: *Resolving generator number two issues in a timely manner will have a positive impact on CSS Alabama's schedule.*

COMMODORE RILEY

After all the recipients of the message read it they should realize the next milestone will be bringing the Air Wing on board, supply load, weapons load, then proceed on the mission defined by Project Jupiter.

ADMIRAL GILBERT
I know you are looking forward to getting your air
wing aboard Alabama for Project Jupiter.

COMMODORE RILEY
That's one of the main reasons I'm here.

While Admiral Gilbert checked the final revisions for the SITREP and the CASCOR, he made an astute comment.

ADMIRAL GILBERT
Project Mars would have been a better name for the
mission, named after the God of War. Jupiter was a
Roman *Father Sky God*.

COMMODORE RILEY
Why's that?

ADMIRAL GILBERT
The real secret behind the name of our project wasn't
for the planet within our own solar system.

COMMODORE RILEY
Why's that?

ADMIRAL GILBERT
I expect to have a rider for the mission as soon as that's
confirmed, you and the crew will get a special briefing.

Tom Gilbert knew Commodore Riley will be surprised when he discovers the mission instead was a variation of the name used by the Jupitorians whom the Ponarian claimed to be the race of beings that wiped out Mars and Atlantis nine hundred thousand years ago.

Dr. Brandenburg had no knowledge of the Ponarian nor the Jupitorians, so the fact he claimed the half-life of the Xeon 129 floating around the planet indicated that material was created nine hundred thousand years ago from two nuclear explosions was an eerie coincidence.

Just like clockwork the CSS Alabama was moving backwards into the Space Dock with lots of people observing from the observation deck. Should their latest journey get leaked to the press, it would mark a significant event in history where man traveled to Mars and back within forty-eight hours. It would mean NASA would do everything in its power to commandeer the Alabama for its own uses such as delivering a large exploration party to Mars, that would have plenty of supplies thanks to the incredible machine available to accomplish it.

Because of the pending mission, added security measures were now in place.

No ship's compliment was allowed off the Alabama. No new Space Service personnel will be arriving except for the Air Wing. And they would arrive via their own craft and dock on the Alabama after it left the Space Dock in a few days. No Space Dock personnel would be permitted to leave until forty-eight hours after the Alabama was gone in the event, they had to return for emergency docking.

Self Defense Weapons the Alabama would load were tethered in the sides of the dock and after pressurization of the Space Dock, workers using overhead gantry cranes would lift the weapons and place them vertically in their tubes that were designed similar to Tomahawk Cruise Missile VLS tubes on Navy Cruisers and submarines.

The weapons officer and her assistant weapons officer would observe ships technicians hook up the umbilical cords to the weapons inside an access hatch inside the ship.

Reduced gravity helped greatly in loading those weapons. As soon as they were in place, the hydraulic actuated hatches shut, and the tube air test verified no leaks. These weapons were designed for self-defense. But against advanced Aliens, they would likely prove useless.

The offensive weapons were the TR-3Bs that would land in their conformal slots and appear to simply be part of the hull. Once the TR-3B was launched, its individual panels rotated down covering each upper row of hanger cavities or upwards on the lower row of hangers to improve aerodynamics and provide some amount of armor protection and radar absorbers that would be needed if the ship was going Flank Speed to avoid enemy weapons.

Design engineers theorized that even in space where there may only be a few hydrogen atoms per cubic feet, if you travel fast enough those few atoms are multiplied and their impact on a surface such as a TR-3B cavity along the hull can slow it down or add heat. Those panels also created an airtight compartment for pilots to egress out of the TR-3B after it was parked post mission.

After docking was complete and access to the Space Dock was restored, Admiral Gilbert was at the entrance to say goodbye to all the riders.

Shelly Brown approached Admiral Tom Gilbert as she was ready to walk off the tubular gang plank on her way to her waiting transportation.

SHELLY BROWN
Thank you for the ride.

ADMIRAL GILBERT
You are quite welcome.

Tom Gilbert shook Shelly Browns hand. Shelly then stepped onto the tubular gangplank now wearing her civilian clothes and appearing like a sex pistol. USSF personnel standing by to assist all the riders offload their equipment and luggage were suddenly glad they volunteered to help out after taking a look at Shelly Brown's posterior as she walked off CSS Alabama.

As Shelly Brown began her departure, the XO, Commodore Riley suddenly approached.

COMMODORE RILEY
Let me escort you to your transportation.

SHELLY BROWN
Thank you, I appreciate that.

Tom Gilbert smiled wondering if the hound dog Riley based on his reputation was going after some action. Rumors were there were places where a few *Space Dock Bitches* made some extra cash from the Alabama crew. *Since there was little time for Riley to have a date with Shelly Brown, why all the fuss?*

Commodore Riley of course was always looking out for his future greasing the skids for a future command. It always paid to have powerful politicians on your side for patronage when you needed it. When President Lincoln was elected, there were immediately three hundred people in line outside the White House asking for appointments for patronage, plus members of Congress sent their cronies over asking for favors.

That's how it was in Washington, D.C., back then and nothing has changed since. In fact, though foreign lobbyists have always been around the politicians, the expansion of world commerce and much greater trade with Japan and China as well as unexpected sources from the EU or former enemies, multiplied the number of lobbyists. Former congressmen were now foreign lobbyists. Even though they were not foreign they did represent their concerns.

COMMODORE RILEY
Did you enjoy your trip?

SHELLY BROWN
Oh, yes, I really enjoyed my time, and I appreciate the
nice chat I had with the Weapon's Officer.

COMMODORE RILEY
Yes, she's a smart cookie. She got her master's degree
in nuclear physics from MIT.

SHELLY BROWN
Why is the WEPs not working in Engineering with that background?

COMMODORE RILEY
She could have gone to Engineer's School but, due to her seniority, could only be the MPA.

SHELLY BROWN
What's MPA?

COMMODORE RILEY
Main Power Assistant, which really means Assistant Engineer.

SHELLY BROWN
Why not take an MPA job, it seems like it would certainly lead to an engineer's assignment.

COMMODORE RILEY
The only way Weps could become an Engineer would be to do a back-to-back tour. That would delay her going to XO school which she's qualified to go to after she completes her tour as Weapons Department Head.

SHELLY BROWN
Weps is eligible to be an XO of one of these Space Carriers?

COMMODORE RILEY
Certainly. The XO course is two years, she would still be relatively young and most able then to do a tour as an XO.

SHELLY BROWN
Why does the XO training require two years, that seems excessively long, you certainly didn't train for two years.

COMMODORE RILEY
Those requirements were slapped on after CSS Alabama crew was selected in my opinion because CNO and Naval Reactors did not like our selection process. As a Prospective XO (PXO) that person must

go through two boards and spend time as a PXO on a Space Carrier. It gives the leadership a method to get rid of candidates they do not want later as a CO.

SHELLY BROWN
And then on to CO?

COMMODORE RILEY
If that's what she wants. She might have better offers from NASA by then.

SHELLY BROWN
Why would she want to go to NASA when she can eventually be in command of one of these space carriers?

COMMODORE RILEY
Real simple, this is a warship. It's designed to deal with our enemies and one day it very well might. NASA on the other hand would give her an opportunity to work in pure space exploration. Her experience here as well as her training in nuclear physics would prepare her to be on the propulsion board at NASA and help determine future propulsion systems for our spacecraft.

SHELLY BROWN
I can see where she might prefer the switch.

COMMODORE RILEY
Time will tell. None of us know how we will end up on this ship several years from now.

The two came up to the airlock and stopped.

COMMODORE RILEY
Here we are at the double airlock. Your transportation is through there. It was nice meeting you.

SHELLY BROWN
Same for you.

Shelly smiled and shook Riley's hand then walked into the first chamber of the double airlock.

The infrared scanner detected Shelly was inside the inner airlock and nobody else was approaching so the door shut. A moment later after a small hissing sound which was probably equalization a door opened to the outer airlock and the door between the airlocks shut automatically. Soon after another slight hissing sound the door to the TR-3B shuttle opened and Shelly Brown walked aboard the modified TR-3B shuttle.

A military flight attendant met her with smiles and escorted her to the seat reserved for her. A few others were also on the flight including Kevin Landry and Roger Keeney on their way back to Crystal City where they would have to answer questions for the next week and go over data, they are bringing back with their instrumentation which was in black Pelican suitcases strapped down on empty seats.

As soon as everyone was buckled in the seatbelt sign warning extinguished, indicating a person needed to buckle up.

<u>EXT. CGI. SPACE TR-3B LEAVING SPACE DOCK TO RETURN TO EARTH 15 SECONDS.</u>

PILOT VIA THE INTERCOM

Ladies and gentlemen, we are now leaving the Space
Dock. Any reservations about leaving are too late, we
are now in space by ourselves.

The TR-3B slowly re-orientated pointing at the planet and soon velocity was picking up. It did not take long for them to get to the ozone belt, and they felt some slight turbulence and an increase in background noise. Then they were soon gliding at supersonic speeds directly towards Langley Air Force Base where a Sikorsky helicopter waited for them to fly them to the CIA helipad in McLean near Washington. A limo and several SUVs were also waiting for them.

<u>EXT. CGI. DAY TR-3B VTOL VERTICAL DESCENT DOWN NEXT TO HANGER INCLUDING MOVEABLE PASSENGER STAIRS PULLS UP TO THE TR-3B. 20 SECONDS.</u>

Shelly walked down the portable passenger ramp and stairway and was directed to a limo and the rest were herded into the SUVs and within five minutes of arrival, the helicopter and the automobiles were gone out of sight.

The Limo took Shelly Brown to Senator Bosworth's office up on Capitol Hill where he wanted to have a private meeting with her. They had to meet there because he was expected to go into senate chambers soon to cast an appropriations legislation vote.

Senator Bosworth was anxiously awaiting Shelly Brown's return and read her report.

SENATOR BOSWORTH
How was your trip?

SHELLY BROWN
It was fun.

SENATOR BOSWORTH
Tell me about it.

Shelly Brown's poignant details of what transpired during the short trip would go a long way for Senator Bosworth to bolster his position on several Space Carrier issues. He of course would be pounding Naval Reactors for their slipshod operation and what he thought had to be a lack of apparent integrity.

Had Naval Reactors been less than forthcoming on this whole generator number two fiasco they would not be ready to face the music (in politician vernacular). Gone were the days of Admiral Hyman G. Rickover where everything was black and white and no ifs, ands, or buts about it were permitted.

Senator Bosworth was also waiting to hear any new sensational or salacious information he suspected existed.

SENATOR BOSWORTH
With a mixed crew fifty five percent male and forty
five percent female, there had to be an element of
fraternization, and the having a mixed crew is dumb.

Senator Bosworth idea was to have all male and all female crews. More reason to build a second Alabama Class Space Carrier. Unfortunately, the senator would be severely disappointed as Shelly's long conversation with the Weps gave a lot of insight into how things really were.

SHELLY BROWN
The Space Force resolved the issue by having
segregated berthing where women had their privacy
and there were strict rules about the opposite sex
entering the other's berthing areas.

SENATOR BOSWORTH
How do they keep them apart and prevent sexual fraternization?

SHELLY BROWN
With all the video cameras around the ship, anyone
who would do so was very dumb because facial
recognition software allowed an immediate report to
the Commanding Officer and resulting disciplinary
actions.

SENATOR BOSWORTH
You think they have taken prudent measures?

SHELLY BROWN
As far as Admiral Gilbert is concerned, his ship would never be given the distinction of being the *CSS Love Boat*.

CSS ALABAMA AIR WING ARRIVES

The TR-3Bs that made up the CSS Alabama's Air Wing were staged in hangars at Wright Patterson Air Force Base. The weapons loaded in the internal bomb bays were designed for space, except for six TR-3Bs that now had hydrogen bombs loaded.

Some of the weapons were kinetic weapons. They would travel as close as possible to the intended target where range was short and reaction time even shorter and be shot like a projectile out of an M1 Tank, traveling at incredible speeds capable of distance because of microgravity and the vacuum of space.

There were also chemical rockets that on Earth would only have a range of three hundred miles. But in space where the rocket engines could be turned on and shut down several times to maneuver towards the target, nothing would slow it down, so the actual range was unlimited or sensor range. Beyond that, no reason existed to attack what you couldn't see.

The CSS Alabama's TR-3Bs flight crews were on standby, restricted to the base and a few days prior to launch, restricted to their muster site which had trailers and barbed wire fence surrounding the trailers. All TR-3Bs were guarded by Space Force and Air Force security members. This was an Air Force Base; therefore, the Commanding General would not allow the Space Force to be present with weapons without his own people also present. It was an understatement to say the TR-3Bs were well protected.

Events unfurled rapidly at Space Command. Senator Bosworth was making his rounds and making the noise and was just about to blow the top off the mission and force it to be scrubbed until a thorough investigation was performed. Then Shelly Brown stepped forward and informed the Senator.

SHELLY BROWN
I have the perfect solution.

SENATOR BOSWORTH
What's that?

SHELLY BROWN
Inform Margarette Mackworth, USSF Secretary, we'll stand down and let the mission go as planned if we have one of our investigators on board during the departure.

SENATOR BOSWORTH
And who would you recommend we send? None of our staff are equipped to do anything like this.

SHELLY BROWN
Send me. I've been in space with them. I can go again.

SENATOR BOSWORTH
This is going to be a much longer mission.

SHELLY BROWN
I'm a big girl, I can handle myself, plus I know something that Admiral Gilbert is quite aware of.

SENATOR BOSWORTH
And what is that?

SHELLY BROWN
They do not have all the women aboard they were designed to carry. They have less than the 45 percent women they are designed to carry. That means there is extra room for another woman.

SENATOR BOSWORTH
Interesting.

SHELLY BROWN
I can leave any time. I live with my mother, and she can handle all my affairs while I'm gone. I'll go do a power of attorney today if you think you can swing the trip for me.

SENATOR BOSWORTH
Okay, go get your power of attorney, but something tells me they are not going to let you go.

SHELLY BROWN
You have them by the balls. They will not be permitted to leave if you invoke some of your oversight rulings forcing them to delay the mission.

SENATOR BOSWORTH
Yeah, I can see where I have some leverage.

SHELLY BROWN
I'm going to leave the office now. I need to make an appointment with an attorney and go prepare my mother.

SENATOR BOSWORTH
Okay, stay in touch, no point in coming back to the office. I'll let you know where to report for your assignment if they agree to let you go.

Tom Gilbert was in his stateroom going over some last-minute details and checking up on the status of stores loading and completion of the weapons testing so they would know if they had to offload one of their defensive weapons that did not test correctly. Based on prior agreement, there were four spare weapons in the bottom of the Space Dock in the event they delivered a dud.

It was all coming together even with the snag of being forced to bring the two NASA chaps along for the ride and Tom was seeing light at the end of the tunnel, almost feeling relaxed when Commodore Riley walked into his stateroom, semi-unannounced.

COMMODORE RILEY
Excuse me, Captain, we have a problem.

ADMIRAL GILBERT
We always have problems, what's new?

COMMODORE RILEY
Those politicians are at it again.

ADMIRAL GILBERT
How so?

Riley handed Tom Gilbert the electronic message clipboard. The message now being displayed came from the Queen Bee herself, Margarette Mackworth, USSF Secretary.

Tom quickly scrolled down and read the content and without a cue stated his feelings.

ADMIRAL GILBERT
You got to be shitting me!

COMMODORE RILEY

Admiral, it looks like the USSF is just as vulnerable to politicians as the Air Force and Navy were.

ADMIRAL GILBERT

Yeah, but I never saw them put a Senator's aide on a submarine going out on a special operation.

COMMODORE RILEY

What are we going to do with her? It's a relatively small ship if you start thinking how much time she'll be spending on it.

ADMIRAL GILBERT

By the time we finish with Uranus and are heading out to the Jupitorians, she will be simply a castaway. When she discovers how long this mission takes, she'll wish the hell she didn't volunteer for it.

COMMODORE RILEY

You can say the same thing for half the crew.

ADMIRAL GILBERT

That's why the doc has plenty of good drugs on board in case we must sedate a lot of people.

COMMODORE RILEY

What about us?

ADMIRAL GILBERT

I'll let you take the drugs whenever you see fit.

Tom Gilbert then chuckled. But he was thinking the obvious.

It was way too late to take a shuttle down to the planet and plead his case with Margarette Mackworth. Shelly Brown will simply have to become part of the furniture. Hopefully Riley didn't get any wild ideas.

Tom pulled up his Outlook calendar. It seemed several years ago this day would never come. The very first Space Patrol and possible combat with Aliens in the works. He had not heard anything new about the Ponarian, but that deal was so wrapped up in secrecy, if he hadn't shown it could not have been a big surprise.

Unfortunately, without the Ponarian's help, finding the Jupitorians far away in the

Galaxy would be like hunting for a needle in a dozen Claude Monet haystacks. But that wouldn't be so bad either. They could avoid combat and simply return with all their weapons minus the three they planned to test on Uranus.

Tom Gilbert would not be the first to call. Nor did he know while he was thinking those thoughts, John Harris was in the tall black building in S-4, Area 51 now talking with the Ponarian. This was the final showdown between the two.

The Ponarian wanting a way home knew the Jupitorians provided his only possible chance to be rescued. He left behind a special communicator when he left the Jupitorians just before his ill-fated journey to Earth. Even though it was almost eighty years ago, the Ponarian's would be at least curious if they received an ancient signal, hopefully they would process it and send a rescue mission to pick him up.

John Harris was a great negotiator. The Ponarian agreed to a lot of revelations Earth would find of great use. The holy grail of galactic awareness was now at John Harris' fingertips. The Ponarian agreed to give the cypher code allowing the information to be unlocked once he was on the ship on the way to destiny with the Jupitorians.

Because of the extreme secrecy involved, John Harris could not send Tom Gilbert a message. Tom's awareness of events that were about to unfold did not become apparent until the TR-3B shuttle arrived with its passengers.

The Ponarian who could pass for an Earth person was fitted with a Space Force Uniform with no rank. He had a visitor nametag.

Tom's challenge would soon come when he had to divulge to his crew the Ponarian was an alien. This would be a surreal ride, one that suddenly he did not like because it certainly had not started the way he wanted.

Preparations continued through the following day. Tom's biggest fear was the water recyclers would let them down, then they would all perish. Since they didn't have to contend with Earth's gravity too much, the ship could be loaded to the gills with extra food and water. For the first year they would poop and piss their extra room as they would dump waste overboard and it would fly along for eons until it encountered a planet's atmosphere or some star.

Within twelve hours of departure, Tom was starting to feel relaxed. No sign of Shelly Brown or the Ponarian. Perhaps he would get deployed without the encumbrances of them aboard.

Then suddenly, Tom Gilbert was notified by Margarette Mackworth, USSF Secretary.

USSF SECRETARY MARGARETTE MACKWORTH TEXT MESSAGE
Your visitors will be arriving shortly. Be sure and treat
them decently during their stay.

Tom's emotions flip-flopped. His mission would be difficult enough as it was. But then again, he would have to have a private meeting with the guests and tell them more about the two-million-mile rule. Essentially, they fall under the UCMJ-*Uniform Code of Military Justice* at that point in time even though they are not U.S. Military members.

Commanding Officers of extremely long duration missions need to have complete autocratic rule and must have the ability to squelch a mutiny if one ever materialized.

Should they make a fatal blunder, take over the ship and return it to the Space Dock or use the TR-3Bs to get back to the planet, they would be treated as mutineers and dealt very harshly.

The guest riders would be sequestered to the ship's research room/library until they were underway on their mission and Tom had a chance to explain to them their predicament. To the Ponarian, it wasn't much of a problem. He was expecting a long trip. But Ms. Shelly Brown finally stuck her nose where it didn't belong to the point it placed her in a situation she would soon come to regret.

Lucky for Shelly Brown, the ship supplied all needed items for everyone as part of mission planning to know what's onboard. Items such as toothpaste had to be provided since a special space formula was required. Since fewer women deployed than possible, extra female uniforms and items were available for Shelly Brown, since a couple women had just unvolunteered citing personal problems.

Learning how to bathe in space would be a new experience for Shelly and God forbid the artificial gravity broke down, learning how to poop in space the old fashion way would not be one of her better memorable moments. But in due time she would survive with help from some of the crew members who had to go through Micro-Gravity Pooping 101.

Tom was very happy they had backup poop removal systems. One used a pump, the preferred method, but in case the two sanitary pumps broke down and were not serviceable, the alternative method the way submarines used to do it with high pressure air worked too, but that method meant they could not fully blow down the sanitary tanks because they could not afford to waste the air. When the tanks were pumped down to twenty percent, they stopped blowing. Another bonus was the time to blead off the tanks was twenty percent shorter, ensuring less likelihood of the golden flapper awards. [Golden flapper award goes to a person who ignores the blowing sanitary tank signs, opens the flapper and blows crap all over themselves. That's how guys like *Shity Smitty* earned their illustrious nick names.]

The ship's captain as his official designation during the voyage didn't have time to meet and deal with his guest riders. Since the Weps was done with her pre-undocking requirements she could be their escorts until they received their briefing and filled out non-disclosure sheets. In the case of the Ponarian, all indications were, he would disembark once they rendezvoused with the Jupitorians, and they agreed to accept him. The big "what if."

The Ponarian would most likely become a huge issue if he knew he was going back to Earth. Thinking that he would get off at the Jupitorian planet, made him somewhat a reasonable passenger since it fit within his plans. The only concern would be to watch him closely during the final few weeks in case he decided to do some sabotage as a farewell gift for payback for his many years of torture and foul treatment.

Another interesting twist was John Harris would come aboard and be shuttled off on a TR-3B after he made some final arrangements with the Ponarian. This would delay them for a short while as they waited for their TR-3B to return and stowed in its form fit insert along the superstructure of the hull.

Hopefully John Harris didn't have visions of coming along as well.

Tom went over his checklists three times. All was in order. He called to the XO Riley whose stateroom was next to his

CAPTAIN GILBERT

XO, can you come to my stateroom and give me an update.

Riley quickly popped into the CO stateroom.

CAPTAIN GILBERT
Riley what's the status.

XO (Riley)

We have a green board. All issues resolved, we just received permission two minutes ago to undock when we are ready.

CAPTAIN GILBERT

Call all the department heads to the Wardroom, I want one more round of confirmations they have no issues I need to know about.

XO (Riley)
Right away, Tom.

All the department heads were soon in the Wardroom. All their relentless work and preparation was now complete. It was time to leave.

CAPTAIN GILBERT
Any last comments or issues?

There was dead silence, so Tom did what he learned on the nuclear submarine he commanded.

CAPTAIN GILBERT
Speak up now or forever hold your peace.

Again, it was dead silence with expectation on everyone's faces. They were now ready for the biggest event in their lifetimes.

CAPTAIN GILBERT
Okay, ladies and gentlemen, it's a go.

The nuclear test on Uranus was highly compartmentalized and few besides the XO, Weps, and the three Air Wing members to carry out the assignment knew that test was to happen in less than a week after they departed. View from Earth would be hidden on the other side of the planet, so unless there was a leak, the results of the test would never be divulged. Even the crew would not see it since they would be on the other side of the planet.

Tom Gilbert then picked up the 27MC that only went to a few locations during normal lineup such as Control, Wardroom, Radio, CO & XO staterooms, electronic equipment spaces, and air combat control, and weapons handling stations. The captain then pressed the push to talk button.

CAPTAIN GILBERT
Control, this is the captain, station the maneuvering watch.

CHIEF OF THE WATCH (in control)
Station the Maneuvering Watch, Captain Control aye.

The Chief of the Watch then talked over the 1MC that went ship wide.

CHIEF OF THE WATCH (in control)
Station the maneuvering watch.

ENGINEERING OFFICER OF THE WATCH (in maneuvering)
Station the maneuvering watch, Con maneuvering aye.

CAPTAIN GILBERT (via 27MC)
Chief of the Watch, seal the ship and request the Space
Dock retract the tubular gang plank.

CHIEF OF THE WATCH (in control)
Captain, chief of the watch, control, understand seal
the ship and inform the Space Dock to remove the
tubular gang plank, aye.

CAPTAIN GILBERT
Okay, department heads, we have work to do, everyone
report to your maneuvering watch stations.

Ship's Captain Gilbert stood up and walked to the short distance to the control room. Within minutes, the chief of the watch reported.

CHIEF OF THE WATCH
Captain, the tubular gangplank is removed. The ship's
access is secured, we have a closed indication on all
penetrations to the hull. The ship has passed a fifteen-
pound air test, no leaks reported.

CAPTAIN GILBERT
Very well, Chief of the watch.

The captain noticed John Harris enter the control room where he stood silently waiting to confer with Tom Gilbert.

CAPTAIN GILBERT
Navigator, contact the Space Dock and inform them
we are ready for them to initiate pumping the air down
in the Space Dock in preparation to undocking.

After repeat back and confirmation the Space Dock depressurization alarm was sounding. Anyone in the dock knew that unless they had a spacesuit on, they would soon die from asphyxiation. Once the dock got down below one PSI, they no longer were interested in recycling any more of the Space Dock air since the energy required and the time it took became counterproductive. Flying up canned air was cheaper than pumping down to a complete vacuum.

Space Cocks were then opened and the residual air from the Space Dock was released into space where it quickly dissipated. As soon as indications showed equalization because of no more air flow through the space cocks, the Space Dock hatch was opened to allow the CSS Alabama to undock.

By the time Alabama returned from its mission, *if it returned,* there might be another Space Dock and there might be another Space Carrier being built almost ready for space trials.

EXT. CGI. DAY WRIGHT PATTERSON AIR FORCE BASE TR-3B'S TAKING OFF 30 SECONDS

The crews with the TR-3Bs at Wright Patterson Air Force Base started moving their craft out of the hangars single file heading to the end of the runway 23R. To a casual observer from over at the passenger terminal at the air base, looking out across the field, one would think these were just modern experimental jets often seen flying around the area.

There was not a lot of hangar space at the Airfield, so some temporary hangars built out of inflatable tubing provided cover for half of the twenty-four-craft air wing. The six TR-3Bs loaded with nuclear weapons were in line first. To make sure no accident occurred they would take off and fly almost directly vertical after they went airborne.

Anyone who happened to be looking at the TR-3B's would soon lose sight of them because they could accelerate vertically as fast as a regular jet horizontally thanks to its anti-gravity machine each had. Of course, there was the tell-tale sign of the glowing orbs that extruded when the antigravity machine went full power producing 89 percent anti-gravity.

The anti-gravity effects would be the same had the planes been built with balsa wood powered by jet engines. Rate of Climb was incredible, and the planes were spaced out two miles apart to avoid any collisions. As soon as the six nuclear bombs equipped TR-3Bs were out of sight the remaining eighteen planes clustered on 23R started their roll in echelons of three with spacing about a half-mile behind. By the time the first echelon lifted off the runway, there were three more mid runway and three more starting their roll. Within four minutes all eighteen TR-3B airframes were airborne flying in formation circling the field then start climbing out like a normal airplane would.

The aircraft made a U-turn over Dayton then flew towards Columbus. By the time they reached Columbus they were already at eighty thousand feet and accelerating above radar. Only NORAD could see them now.

EXT. CGI. SPACE CSS ALABAMA UNDOCKING.

The Alabama slowly moved out of the dock as it had before. A shuttle equipped TR-3B was still attached to the Space dock but it would soon be traveling to the Alabama to pick up John Harris and return him back to Washington where he would give the most important information ever provided to congressional INTEL oversight committees.

Their sudden awareness of what's in the Galaxy and a few other interesting items carried off the Alabama with John Harris, would have staggering effects including no delay in funding for the follow-on Alabama Class Space Carriers.

Tom Gilbert had no way of knowing the extent of the information the Ponarian provided or what it all meant. John Harris' sudden appearance here to meet with the alien certainly conveyed a notion of intrigue on levels never before realized. All Tom knew he was now pleased to receive the report.

NAVIGATOR
The ship is now clear of the Space Dock.

The threat of a nasty collision was now minimized as the Alabama slowly moved away from the Space Dock well over one foot a second.

 Now Tom had to deal with John Harris. He approached him.

CAPTAIN GILBERT
Hello, Mr. Harris, why don't we go to my stateroom
for a few minutes while your shuttle docks on Alabama
and gets ready to return you to Earth.

JOHN HARRIS
Excellent idea Admiral Gilbert.

Once they were in the Alabama Commander's state room and door shut John Harris started the conversation.

JOHN HARRIS
The Ponarian delivered the goods. He will help guide
you to the Jupitorians, but we will also generate you a
map and email it to you.

CAPTAIN GILBERT
The information was helpful?"

JOHN HARRIS
Extremely. This is the best bargain we ever had with
an INTEL source.

CAPTAIN GILBERT
We are finally here. This would not be possible without
your help.

JOHN HARRIS

I believe in your mission. We probably need a dozen Alabama Class Space Carriers. As our awareness picks up with the Aliens, there will be easier selling of the program to the fence setters.

CAPTAIN GILBERT
No doubt.

JOHN HARRIS

How are you going to handle the two NASA scientists and Shelly Brown when they discover they're trapped on board for a lot longer than they ever imagined?

CAPTAIN GILBERT

If the Jupitorians receive us on friendly terms and anyone who wishes not to return to Earth and requests to stay there and the Jupitorians agree, I would be willing to leave them behind.

JOHN HARRIS
How about any deaths that may occur in route?

CAPTAIN GILBERT

The Two-Million-Mile rule is quite explicit. USSF should not have entrusted that authority in me if they didn't want me to fully use it as I see fit.

JOHN HARRIS
What does that mean?

CAPTAIN GILBERT
You know the Navy Tradition, burial at sea?

JOHN HARRIS
Yes, of course, I've seen the movies!

CAPTAIN GILBERT

We'll have a burial at space, ejected in our refuse chutes.

JOHN HARRIS

Any reason why you would not simply throw them in the freezer and bring the bodies back?

CAPTAIN GILBERT

We have brought with us an extensive amount of supplies such as extra water and food. Every square inch of the ship is miserably occupied by supplies of some sort. Whatever room we can gain no matter for what purpose will be a bonus.

JOHN HARRIS

What do you think will happen to the bodies if you have a burial in space?

CAPTAIN GILBERT

The refuse chutes are packed with items in a conformal plastic bag that mostly fills the cylinder. We can do one hundred shots with one canister of air. The refuse is impulse out diagonally to the ship's direction. In the vacuum of space there is no wind resistance. The bodies could end up floating for millions or billions of years in space until they encounter an object or burn up falling into the atmosphere of a planet or a star.

JOHN HARRIS

One other item I must remind you that is not covered by the Two-Million-Mile rule.

CAPTAIN GILBERT
And what is that?

JOHN HARRIS

Under no circumstance are you to bring an alien back with you.

CAPTAIN GILBERT
Does that include the Ponarian?

JOHN HARRIS

If for some reason the Jupitorians refuse to accept him, then you probably have no option but to bring him back. He would most likely end up not very happy and I would recommend he be restrained and sedated if that scenario occurs.

CAPTAIN GILBERT

Yeah, I figured he's not going to be very happy if he discovers he has no way home.

JOHN HARRIS

If you were in his shoes, you might feel the same way.

CAPTAIN GILBERT

Hopefully the Jupitorians do not destroy my way home.

JOHN HARRIS

It's a risky mission. I think you have a 50/50 chance of coming back alive."

CAPTAIN GILBERT

Thanks for the confidence booster.

JOHN HARRIS

Well, Tom, I suppose I should go now and let you commence your mission.

CAPTAIN GILBERT

Thanks for coming to send us off.

JOHN HARRIS

I would not have missed it for anything. Whether you can get back safely or not, the fact is you have already done an incredible job demonstrating what this great ship can do. It's the cornerstone of our immediate defense against alien attack.

CAPTAIN GILBERT

The TR-3B first flew in 1995, I think it's reaching a point of obsolescence.

JOHN HARRIS

You are right, they are obsolete and may not be able to defend us against some aliens, but the Jupitorians are not expecting you to show up with a few of them armed the way they are.

CAPTAIN GILBERT

I don't have a warm fuzzy those TR-3Bs would ever get in position to use those weapons.

JOHN HARRIS

We have the element of surprise. But on the other hand, if the Jupitorians act like they want peaceful coexistence, we need to keep our powder dry.

CAPTAIN GILBERT
Any plans to replace the TR-3B?

JOHN HARRIS
Since you will be away four years and pose no security risk and by the time you get back it will be common knowledge, we developed the TR-4 and the TR-5 and are now into TR-6 development which will supersede all the rest.

CAPTAIN GILBERT
I've never heard any rumors of the TR-4 and the TR-5, did we actually build the planes?

JOHN HARRIS
TR-4 and TR-5 were built with essentially KH-13 capability. When the aliens started to become a major problem and we had to develop the KH-14 to use against them, we realized TR-4 and TR-5 would no longer be viable and a plane with KH-14 sensor suites was essential so we started developing the follow-on TR-6. TR-6 is ready to enter production and the follow-on Alabama Class Space Carrier will deploy the TR-6's.

CAPTAIN GILBERT
Would the CSS Alabama then be retrofit with TR-6 capability?

JOHN HARRIS
Right now, we are planning an overhaul for when you return. Since we don't have a very large fleet and you will be burning up a lot of nuclear fuel during this mission, we want the Alabama to be completely refueled during that overhaul. TR-3Bs will be phased out by then.

CAPTAIN GILBERT
It takes several years to overhaul a Navy Carrier, what will it be like for this ship?

JOHN HARRIS
For one thing, handling the radioactive waste is much simpler.

CAPTAIN GILBERT
Why is that?

JOHN HARRIS
We will build a drone to fly the spent reactors into the sun where they will be destroyed. The new reactors will be installed just like you witnessed during new construction.

CAPTAIN GILBERT
That's amazing. By the way, does Senator Bosworth know we'll be keeping his aide on board a lot longer than he planned?

JOHN HARRIS
I think the Senator knows he'll probably be out of congress and retired before you get back. It's too late for him to back out now.

CAPTAIN GILBERT
What will you do to ensure his silence?

JOHN HARRIS
The Cash in Advance boys will grease his palms and he'll remain silent.

CAPTAIN GILBERT
What about Shelly Brown's mother?

JOHN HARRIS
She'll be informed in a few months her daughter has agreed to go on an extended journey, and when her paychecks start rolling in with a lot more Cash, she will most likely remain silent. Otherwise, we would have to make her silent.

CAPTAIN GILBERT
How would you do that?

JOHN HARRIS
Cash-In-Advance boys know how to silence people.

The private meeting shortly concluded, and it was time for John Harris to leave with all the cypher combinations he obtained from the Ponarian to obtain the most useful Alien information ever before obtained.

CAPTAIN GILBERT
Let me walk you to the air lock.

JOHN HARRIS
Thank you.

The airlock to the TR-3B personnel transfer and exchange station, inner door opened and John Harris stepped inside the inner airlock. Shortly the door shut and sealed and when ship's computers validated an air test passed with no leaks, the door between the two air locks opened and John Harris was cued to step forward to the outer airlock.

As soon as he positioned himself in the outer airlock the door between the airlocks shut and secured. After the interlocks indicated it was safe to open the TR-3B hatch, it opened, and John stepped inside the spacecraft. The door to the TR-3B then shut and moments later the air lock cylinder retracted inside the Alabama and a protective metal skin covered the air lock area. Once that occurred, nobody could see where the airlock existed.

John Harris was escorted to his seat and asked to attach his seatbelt and harness, which he did. Moments later thrusters fired slowly moving the TR-3B away from the CSS Alabama. As requested by John Harris the pilot moved the TR-3B a few thousand yards away from the CSS Alabama which was not far from the Space Dock to watch the Airwing arrive and Alabama departure.

<u>EXT. CGI. SPACE. AIRWING APPROACHING CSS ALABAMA 30 SECONDS</u>

The Alabama lingered in the area for a while as its Air wing approached. Each ship was already armed but reloads could take place via the belly of the TR-3Bs. The crew also exited the TR-3B in the small angled double air lock that connected to the weapon's loading hatch of the TR-3B which provided the crew the ability to move in and out of the TR-3B after it docked onto the Alabama. Each TR-3B fit nicely into a cavity designed to help establish perfect alignment and mating of the individual TR-3B weapons shipping hatches to the hull of the Space Carrier double air locks built for each TR-3B STOW (Special Tactical Outboard Weapon).

<u>EXT. CGI. SPACE. TR-3Bs LANDING BACKWARDS VIA ARTIFICIAL INTELLIGENCE INTO STOW POSITIONS ON CSS ALABAMA 30 SECONDS</u>

Each TR-3B was designated its STOW spot along the hull. Position in the STOWs was based on rank. The STOW position closer to the bow, was less susceptible to engineering noise and closer to berthing and the control room. Those junior pilots who were given the rear STOWs had to walk a much longer distance to get to their TR-3Bs and until they were launched, could feel the vibration of the propulsion rockets not far behind them.

Junior TR-3B pilots also feared under certain circumstances they could be sucked into the vortex of the propulsion rockets exhaust and hit by the blue exhaust that would immediately slice their TR-3B into millions of pieces.

C.U. JOHN HARRIS

John Harris enjoyed the bird's eye view of the Carrier Landings observing the TR-3Bs coming in and landing in the conformal indention created to manifest extremely fast and efficient landings.

In a tactical situation where reload of weapons was necessary, within two minutes of landing and the clamp restraints engaged securing the TR-3B to its STOW slot along the hull, the weapon shipping hatch could be opened, and a series of weapons loaded on the racks within the TR-3B hull. The weapon had network and power connectivity via the racks. During training on Space Carrier simulators, just like an Indy Racer, the TR-3B could be refueled and rearmed and launched within seven minutes, ready to go on another sortie.

The senior pilots were allowed to land first. To prevent collisions the flock was kept away slowly orbiting the Space Carrier until their number was called and the autopilot would glide the TR-3B to its designated STOW on the hull. Today, the weapon shipping hatches would open, the crews get out and they then entered the Space Carrier and proceeded to the crews lounge where the CO, Admiral Gilbert and the Wing Commander Commodore Riley would meet them there and welcome them aboard.

The Air Wing knew that three pilots were designated to fly missions on Uranus, but the nature of the missions was compartmentalized, and they were not permitted to know exactly what those pilots would be doing, nor what kind of weapons they brought. Three other pilots who ferried special weapons aboard, had no idea what the weapons were or what they were designated to do. They didn't have the need to know. Those first three pilots doing the Uranus Mission would be the ones to use those three special weapons if called upon to deliver them in the event a conflict with the Jupitorians erupted.

EXT. CGI TR-3B HANGER HATCHES CLOSING ON STOW POSITIONS ON THE SIDES OF CSS ALABAMA 30 SECONDS

Just like a flock of geese landing, soon all the TR-3Bs mated to the hull and a shield/ cover rotated down on the hull covering the craft in the upper rows and rotated up on the bottom rows. Now there was no indication of any TR-3Bs on the hull as the last one got covered.

John Harris knew it was just about the time the Alabama was going to leave. He knew he would be saying a few prayers for Admiral Gilbert whom he felt admiration towards, but at the same token a slight sadness as he realized this great man may not make it back safely as the perils of space were so great, especially if there turned out to be a showdown with the Jupitorians.

<u>EXT. CGI. TR-3B CSS ALABAMA LEAVING FOR PROJECT JUPITER MISSION 30 SECONDS</u>

Moments later a blue flame ejected out of the CSS Alabama rocket engines, and it slowly started moving away gaining momentum seemingly rapidly. When the Alabama was a couple miles away from the Space Dock now moving at a good pace, the blue flames coming out of the two propulsion motors appeared to grow and the ship quickly shrank in size as it headed out towards deep space. The blue flame continued getting larger until it seemed to light up the area in a surreal false light like a mini sun. The ship was accelerating significantly more than it did heading to Mars.

Uranus was currently 1.8 billion miles from Earth traveling in an elliptical orbit. To get to Uranus in about a week, the CSS Alabama would have to accelerate almost ten times faster than it did on the Mars trip. At 17. million miles per hour, Alabama would be traveling far below light speed, but it would be traveling fast enough to see relative motion of other planets.

Once they did the Uranus mission, they would be slingshot in the direction of a map coordinates the Ponarian gave John Harris which was now in the possession of Admiral Tom Gilbert, making the very first manned space flight outside of the solar system.

<u>INT. SPACE. CSS ALABAMA WARDROOM TRAINING</u>

Alabama's XO Commodore Riley, also the Wing Commander, had a week to go over the plan with his three TR-3B pilots who would do the weapons test on Uranus. It was cut and dry. The plan was shown to the three pilots on a projection system showing all the details as XO briefed the pilots.

> WING COMMANDER (Riley)
> The Alabama will circle Uranus after a deceleration
> getting into Orbit and make several circles around the
> planet so that NASA guys on board can send back to
> Houston images they take.

<u>INT. SPACE. CSS ALABAMA WARDROOM TRAINING PROJECTION SYSTEM SIMULATION OF THE HYDROGEN BOMB DEPLOYMENT 30 SECONDS</u>

> WING COMMANDER (Riley)
> The first TR-3B going in on the weapons test will
> produce video then curtail the filming as it deploys the

special weapon and moved to safety outside the blast range. This will occur simultaneously while Alabama was on the other side of the Uranus, obscure from the explosions which would also be on the outward side of the planet where observatories on Earth will also not see it.

The Australian, a naturalized U.S. Citizen Rudy Wilcox, call sign is Azzie.

> WING COMMANDER (Riley)
> Azzie will lead the formation deliver the first pickle (weapon).

> INSTIGATOR
> Why does Azzie get to drop the first one?

The two other pilots knew Instigator was Cowboying it up and was often considered a jokester. He got smiles out of the other two pilots.

> WING COMMANDER (Riley)
> Azzie was picked to lead this mission because he is the
> most highly decorated and senior pilot in the TR-3B
> air wing.

Instigator figured he just earned a couple demerits, but jet jockies had to have some charisma because they may soon be flying in harm's way. The XO understood Instigator quite well and realized Instigator would not treat chickenshits very well when the time came. In reality, his jocularity was beneficial to team spirit.

> WING COMMANDER (Riley)
> Behind Azzie and bombing a different location further
> North as you see on the map will be Batman.

Batman was a former Top Gun Navy pilot Tony Hudson, who earned the call sign "Batman" as he was the second highest decorated TR-3B pilot.

> WING COMMANDER (Riley)
> Finally flying South of Azzie would be Instigator and
> you can see his target area in relation to the other two
> on the map.

Brad Howard a former Air Force Pilot and Astronaut, earned his call sign "Instigator." One Wing Commander was about to toss Instigator's ass out of the Air Force for "Instigating" too many times when he was handpicked by Commodore Riley for his Air Wing.

The short-sighted Air Force General who was in the process of taking adverse action against Instigator, received a visit from John Harris and USSF Secretary Mackworth who was Air Force Secretary at the time, dictated the fitness report the former General had to alter to make sure Instigator had no issues transferring to the Space Force.

To say the General wasn't a bitter man is an understatement. But once Brad Howard (a.k.a. Instigator) transferred to the USSF, the Air Force General no longer had any impact on the Instigator's future.

John Harris supported Commodore Riley's picks after a careful search who wanted all BRAVE MEN and no *office warriors*.

INSTIGATOR
Why are we testing these nukes on Uranus?

WING COMMANDER (Riley)
Based on information that the nuclear physicist Dr.
Brandenburg reported during his NASA study, we are
simulating what ostensibly the Jupitorians did to Mars
nine hundred thousand years ago.

INSTIGATOR
Who are Jupitorians?

WING COMMANDER (Riley)
Jupitorians will be discussed in this briefing in a
short while. Project Jupiter is designed to deal with
Jupitorians and other threats.

INSTIGATOR
Very interesting?

WING COMMANDER (Riley)
Should the Jupitorians attack Earth during this mission,
which is felt highly possible, Admiral Gilbert's orders
are to conduct a similar attack on the Jupitorians like
the Jupitorians attacked Mars to eliminate their ability
to do aggression for an extremely long period of time,
if ever again.

Of course, Wing Commander Riley realized should a Jupitorian attack on Earth occur the chances of life surviving on Earth was slim, so he knew Admiral Gilbert, the current ship's Captain would have no remorse from wiping out Jupitorians if they laid waste to planet Earth. The jury was still out on how the Jupitorians would respond to an Earth ship visit or if the TR-3Bs could successfully deploy those weapons because of Jupitorian air defenses.

Now it was time to talk with the Ponarian who should be far more cooperative, knowing he might be on his way home.

Tom went to the ship's library where he met the Ponarian who was sitting talking to Shelly Brown about trivial things, and obviously he had not informed Shelly Brown he was an alien as she seemed rather nonchalant.

At Area 51 the Ponarian was given the name Randolph to use during this transit to the Jupitorian planet. So, that's how Tom addressed him.

CAPTAIN GILBERT
Randolph, would you please come with me to my
stateroom so I can give you a short indoctrination?

RANDOLPH (a.k.a. PO)
Sure, Tom.

Shelly Brown raised her eyebrows, as the simple and non-sophisticated man whom she had no idea what his role was, had first name basis with the ship's Captain.

As soon as Captain Gilbert and the alien Randolph were alone in the captain's state room the indoctrination began.

CAPTAIN GILBERT
I'm glad that you are coming along and perhaps we
may in some way help you get home to your planet.

RANDOLPH (a.k.a. PO)
I survived this long with a shitty life at Area 51, I
suppose another couple of years isn't too much to ask.

CAPTAIN GILBERT
If we had better technology, we could get you there
sooner, I apologize that we are so backwards, and you
must take the slow boat home.

RANDOLPH (a.k.a. PO)
With the information I gave John Harris, you should
be able to produce much quicker and smaller ships in
the future.

CAPTAIN GILBERT
We appreciate that.

RANDOLPH (a.k.a. PO)
I gave a lot of information and secrets for this ride home.

CAPTAIN GILBERT
I'll do my best to make sure you get to the Jupitorians.

RANDOLPH (a.k.a. PO)
When we get near their solar system, they will detect the presence of CSS Alabama and send out ships to investigate. When they appear, you need to allow me to communicate with them so that I can explain I'm on board and wish to visit their planet, otherwise they will simply destroy your ship.

CAPTAIN GILBERT
You can speak their languages?

RANDOLPH (a.k.a. PO)
No. Their language is far too complicated for me or you Earth people. They have built Ponarian and English translators.

CAPTAIN GILBERT
When did they learn English?

RANDOLPH (a.k.a. PO)
They visited Earth in 1917 and witnessed part of your World War. A lot of radio communications was in English, so they focused on it.

CAPTAIN GILBERT
They didn't stay long?"

RANDOLPH (a.k.a. PO)
No. They saw how primitive you were and decided you would not be of any threat for a long time, thus decided to leave. They will visit Earth again in about five hundred years to do another survey to assess your ability.

CAPTAIN GILBERT
You stated to John Harris the Jupitorians destroyed Mars and Atlantis approximately nine hundred thousand years ago. Why didn't they destroy Earth in 1917?"

RANDOLPH (a.k.a. PO)
Simply, you were not a threat to them and keeping the planet as a viable staging ground for future conflicts was the reason why they had no reason to destroy the planet since nobody of advanced technology exists since destruction of Mars as well as Atlantis on Earth.

CAPTAIN GILBERT
One thing I'm going to have to ask you to do is not tell my crew you are an alien. When we get close to the Jupitorians I will then divulge to them who you are and why you are onboard.

RANDOLPH (a.k.a. PO)
Okay, if that's what you want.

CAPTAIN GILBERT
We have enough concern about the crew enduring this long mission as it is. I don't want them to have any psychological problems by discovering you are an alien, any time sooner than necessary.

RANDOLPH (a.k.a. PO)
Understand, I will maintain my silence as to my true identity.

CAPTAIN GILBERT
One other thing. I'm going to assign an officer to show you around and explain all the facilities, so you know what's available to you.

RANDOLPH (a.k.a. PO)
I appreciate that.

CAPTAIN GILBERT
When you were at Area 51 did you become accustomed to American food?"

RANDOLPH (a.k.a. PO)
Unfortunately, yes. But on my planet, we would call
your food garbage.

CAPTAIN GILBERT
You only must eat our garbage for a couple more years.

RANDOLPH (a.k.a. PO)
When the Jupitorians allow me to contact my planet it
will take them several years to send a rescue ship. I'll
have to eat Jupitorian garbage for a couple years and
it's worse than your food!

CAPTAIN GILBERT
In a while, the XO, Commodore Riley will assign an
officer who is currently not terribly busy to show you
around and escort you to your berthing assignment.

RANDOLPH (a.k.a. PO)
All right.

CAPTAIN GILBERT
I'm going to warn you. Because of our very long
voyage, we brought on board extra food and water. We
are totally saturated with food and water containers
strewn about the ship; space will be tight until we eat
our way through some of the boxes.

RANDOLPH (a.k.a. PO)
That's okay. It's probably a lot better than conditions I
was kept in during 1947 and 1948."

CAPTAIN GILBERT
I'm going to take you back to the ship's library now
and in a short while, the XO or some officer will pay
you a visit.

RANDOLPH (a.k.a. PO)
Thank you."

CAPTAIN GILBERT
You are most welcome.

Captain Gilbert led the Ponarian back to the library then requested Shelly Brown.

CAPTAIN GILBERT
Ms. Brown, will you please come with me to my
stateroom.

Shelly brown followed Tom Gilbert to his stateroom.

SHELLY BROWN
What did you want to discuss with me Tom.

CAPTAIN GILBERT
Shelly, I wanted to let you know welcome aboard and
I'm sorry I could not meet with you until now because
I've been busy handling matter required to start this
mission.

SHELLY BROWN
That's understandable Tom.

Shelly Brown was given her own briefing.

CAPTAIN GILBERT
There are things we'll be doing during this mission that
are highly classified and above your security clearance
level. Please do not ask Randolph why he's here.
Randolph's part of the mission is a national secret.

Tom would not inform Shelly that she was "Shanghaied" until several days after the
Uranus attack and they were out of the solar system.

He then called the Weps into his stateroom.

WEPS
Yes Captain, what can I do for you?

CAPTAIN GILBERT
Take Ms. Brown to Female Officer Berthing and let
her pick which available bunk is available.

WEPS
She can have the VIP bunk since we are not going to
have any more riders.

CAPTAIN GILBERT
That's great. After you get her situated in her sleeping

quarters, help her get whatever items she needs from supply and answer any questions she has about the facilities she needed to know about.

The Weps led Shelly through the ship pointing out areas Shelly had not seen in the last underway because it was such a short duration.

WEPS

The ship has a really good exercise room. The problem is it currently is full of plastic bags full of dried food. As soon as we eat that food, the room will be available for crew workouts.

SHELLY BROWN

Why so much food if we are only going to be gone a few weeks?

The Weps was previously briefed by Captain Gilbert she was not permitted to disclose to any of the riders they had been Shanghaied and to avoid possible disclosure of what they intended to do on Uranus, they would be stuck on board for the entire mission including the trip to the Jupitorian worlds. She had no choice but to embellish the real reason. Instead Wep's repeated the party-line.

WEPS

In case we are called to deal with an alien invasion, we need to have substantial food on board because we would not have sufficient time to get back to the Space Dock to reload. This gives us freedom of movement. Plus, it will only be a couple of weeks before that food will either be eaten or transferred to other parts of the ship as Loggie's rearrange everything and put food and spare parts in a better organized fashion.

Shelly thought it was kind of unusual that the Weps would then describe protocols to make sure *women didn't accidently wonder in men's berthing or do it on purpose where some of the men might want to participate in activities the wardroom sought to avoid for such a short ride.*

WEPS

Last thing we want onboard a ship with close confinement and no ability to offload someone is an assault charge.

SHELLY BROWN

I seriously doubt your professional Space Force personnel will develop any rash desires in just a few weeks.

WEPS

It doesn't matter what the time duration is, it's our regulations. And we are obligated by our procedures and protocols to inform all riders.

SHELLY BROWN

I can see where the captain doesn't want the stigma of the ship developing the reputation of the *CSS Love Boat*.

WEPS

Well, as you should know, the military has had to learn the hard way that when you confine women and men aboard a ship for extended periods of time, events can arise, which puts the command in an awkward situation, especially if it got publicized. Because of the unique nature of this Space Carrier, there will be a lot of public focus, so our ability to cover up an assault case would not be likely.

SHELLY BROWN

Understand all, I promise not to get near men's berthing.

WEPS

Thank you for your indulgence in this briefing, we must give it to all the crew members and riders.

SHELLY BROWN

Have there ever been any cases on this ship?

WEPS

As you know this is a brand-new ship with a crew that has high expectations. There probably hasn't been enough time passage to test the theory of our protocols.

SHELLY BROWN

Hopefully it's a long time before that happens.

CSS ALABAMA URANUS BOUND

<u>EXT. CGI. SPACE CSS ALABAMA FULL PLUME FROM ROCKET ENGINES FOR 15 SECONDS, THEN THROTTLE DOWN.</u>

The CSS Alabama had accelerated to its cruise velocity in six hours. After that, the propulsion engines were throttled down which means the nuclear reactor that superheated the hydrogen was almost scrammed and heat greatly reduced as well as the hydrogen fuel cut back to 1 percent where the sustainment was maintained to prevent warpage from cooling down too quickly. This power setting that would save a significant amount of fuel would also keep the main engines warmed up and ready to go back into acceleration after the slingshot around Uranus.

From a distance, someone with a good telescope could track the small blue flame now exiting the main engines, but in no way could see the huge bright ball that existed prior to throttle back.

UFO enthusiasts had been tracking the bright blue light in the night sky. Radio talk shows were discussing it, but the United States Space Force did not comment on it or admit it was one of their ships.

The Russians and the Chinese had never seen a blue flame like that last as long as it did or appear to go as fast as it did. Scientists who claimed whatever it was traveled at 17 million miles per hour were laughed at. At throttle-back when the flame disappeared and only the small blue stream could be seen, it was extremely hard to track, and most viewers lost sight of it.

EXT. CGI KH-14 SATELLITE MOVING AWAY FROM FOCAL POINT with electronic noise in the background.

> Note to director:
>
> KH-14 is a fictional satellite. There has been KH-13 discussions on the internet and for one week a KH-14 story existed and was taken down. According to the source before it was taken down KH-14 has optics outside wavelengths America previously used and was in fact developed to track Alien ships utilizing a cloaking device.

KH-12 Block V Launch 2018

Launch of NROL-82 on Delta IV Heavy

A new generation of clandestine communications satellites launched to inclined geosynchronous orbits have led to speculations that these are in support of Block V electro-optical satellites scheduled for launch in late 2018 (NROL-71) and 2021 (NROL-82) The two satellites have been built by Lockheed Martin Space Systems, have a primary mirror with a diameter of 2.4 meters, and are evolutionary upgrades to the previous blocks built by Lockheed.

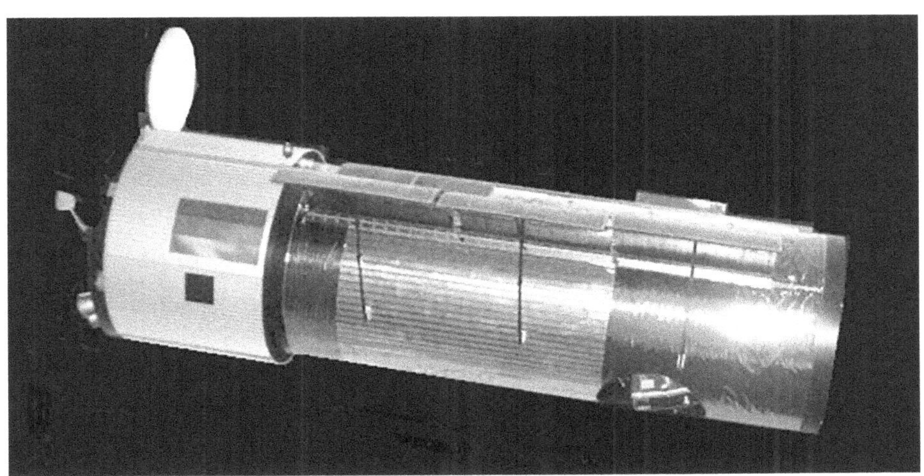

Based on the published hazard areas for the launch, an orbital inclination of 74° has been deduced for NROL-71. This could indicate that NROL-71 is targeted for a Type II Multi Sun-Synchronous Orbit Which would enable the satellite to study the ground at a range of local hour effects (shadow direction and length, daily activities, etc.)

KH-13: Enhanced Imaging System - Wikipedia

America's KH-14 satellite had no problems tracking the CSS Alabama and did so as the NRO (National Reconnaissance Office) now fell under the organization chart of the USSF. NRO was unaware the Russians had figured out how to download the KH-14 data and decrypt it. The Russians were also watching CSS Alabama and during the early part of the mission Russian Space Force saw the hull which caused Russian leaders' great consternation. The fact it was apparently leaving the solar system reduced concern for it to be weaponized against them. The Russian FSB (KGB) of course intensified their espionage to find out as much about it as possible.

RESCUE

Shelly Brown spent most of her awakened hours either in the wardroom, library, or on the Bridge. If the Admiral made his presence on the bridge and she discovered him there, she made every point to remain as long as possible and observe things.

For seven days, the ship remained on autopilot except when they traveled through the Asteroid belt between Mars and Jupiter where risk was high.

There always had to be a chief of the watch present. Copilots and pilots were not required to be on the bridge if autopilot was engaged. A messenger was always present. The ship had security guards patrolling who also were safety observers looking out for fires or other damage that could occur if some machine malfunctioned.

Sometimes electronics simply fail. If it was a power supply, it could create some nasty acrid odor, so the idea was to secure the machine as quickly as possible. There was full redundancy on everything. And all power and hydraulic mains were routed on both the port and starboard side of the hulls in case damage occurred on either side, there would be redundancy on the other side.

The STOW positions for TR-3Bs loaded with nuclear weapons were all next to each other as they required a two-man rule and a constant security guard. Only special security men knew there were nukes onboard and the area of those TR-3Bs was sealed off to the crew. No access was permissible. The only people on the access list for those TR-3Bs was the three designated pilots.

Each craft and each nuclear weapon had a 9AGZ tamper alert system that would trigger a security alert and total lockdown on the ship. Nobody was allowed to move once the security alarm went off except the security force which wore pink and black uniforms. They of course hated the uniforms, but the security designers wanted them to be distinguished against anyone else and an identifier chip surgically inserted into their bodies which insured validity during a time of crisis.

The security force also had special guns that stunned people that were the forerunner of laser pistols. To get hit by those stunners would leave no doubt in anyone they never wanted to feel that again. Also, they were physically disabled for several minutes so the security men could then cuff and tie down a perpetrator.

The whole ship was compartmentalized. Combat people were not allowed in the engineering spaces. Engineering personnel were not allowed in the hangar bay, the area next to the TR-3B STOWs. Only operational people and the designated guests were allowed on the bridge. Everyone knew their roles and knew not to go where you did not belong.

The Ponarian took a liking to Karen the librarian. He had almost forgotten what the opposite sex was like. The ship's library had five hundred thousand books in digital form. If there was a Kindle or eBooks, it most likely was purchased and uploaded into the library. The ship's library also had a complete set of drawings and system manuals so that maintenance workers could go research a problem and get drawings and details. A crew member had to have special access codes to obtain work-related classified documentation.

Crew members also had fully automated college courses. Their biographic's via face recognition software, palm print and retina scans provided security so the automated college would know someone was not cheating and they of course got their college credits applied to advanced degrees. Some crewmembers spent their off hours working on advanced degrees. Others read quite a few books.

The crew was of course looking forward to access to the workout room that had rowing machines, bicycles, treadmills, and had men and women's special baths. You walked in and closed the door, like a private bathroom, took your clothes off and placed them on a rack with several drawers to put your personal effects in. Then you walked into the bathing room, which was no larger than a telephone booth, sat down on the seat and manipulated a couple controls that would fill this to a mark the automatic scanners determined at your neckline around shoulder height. The digital temperature control adjusted it to the temperature that you wanted but had safety features not to go beyond healthy temperatures. There were several of these sports baths so there was usually no waiting to get in.

The sports baths also had vibration and water jets to message aching muscles from the workouts. The water was drained after use and recycled through special reverse osmosis machines purifying the water again. Thanks to the water recyclers and reverse osmosis machines, as well as the extra water carried on board, it was estimated the ship had twice as much water required for the voyage.

Tom Gilbert and Commodore Riley worked out every day. It helped reduce stress and the sports bath was preferred to the ship's shower systems located in the berthing areas. The space showers were fast and efficient.

One day when Tom was discussing the workout and bath situation, Tom informed Riley what it was like on nuclear submarines.

CAPTAIN GILBERT

Before we put reverse osmosis systems on our submarines, we had to take submarine showers.

XO RILEY

What were they like?

CAPTAIN GILBERT

Less than five minutes and while you are soaping up you better not be running the water. People accused of being Water Buffalos were not treated well by the crew.

XO RILEY

I imagine back in the old days' showers were a big deal.

CAPTAIN GILBERT

When we reached port, we often took *Hollywood Showers*.

XO RILEY

What was the nature of those Hollywood showers?

CAPTAIN GILBERT

Even if we stood thirty minutes in a shower, we still could not get the submarine smell off us. In foreign ports people knew we were submariners by our smell.

EXT. CGI. SPACE VIEW OF CSS ALABAMA APPROACHING URANUS 15 SECONDS

VOICE OVER
(DURING ALABAMA APPROACHING URANOUS)
On day seven, the CSS Alabama finally reached Uranus. Video from the various sources on the ship was piped into the crew's lounge and library flat screens so that curious crew members could observe the majestic blue planet.

INT. SPACE. CSS ALABAMA CONTROL ROOM

XO RILEY

Most people only think of Neptune as the blue planet.

CAPTAIN GILBERT

Uranus is very similar to Neptune, but Neptune is not quite as cold as Uranus. Uranus is the coldest planet in the solar system.

XO RILEY

I imagine our NASA scientists are having a field day looking at all this.

NAVIGATOR

They are lucky our photonics meet or exceed anything NASA has.

Everyone in the control room was concentrating on the Uranus imagery, but Captain Gilbert and the Navigator were monitoring everything for safety reasons even though CSS Alabama traveled in autopilot. The Navigator compared the actual track with the planned track in the flight plan.

CAPTAIN GILBERT
Are we giving them a good close-up of the planet?

XO RILEY
Yes, they are set up in the library now taking notes
and downloading images to their data recording
systems and transmitting signals back to Earth. This
is the closest observation of Uranus mankind has ever
witnessed.

CAPTAIN GILBERT
What about Voyager II?

XO RILEY
Voyager II did not have the quality of photonics we
now have. The resolution on our cameras is almost one
hundred times better.

As they had on the previous trip, the captain announced on the 1MC circuit the ship
would be decelerating to allow closer approach to the planet. This served two purposes,
giving the NASA REPS more time to produce some nice eye candy, but also being
closer to the planet would help obscure the upcoming weapons test while they were
going to be on the other side of the planet.

Eventually the Chief of the Watch made the final announcement.

CHIEF OF THE WATCH
All hands stand by for deceleration in thirty seconds.

Soon time passed and the navigator applied his magic, and the ship began slowing
down. Based on the navigation coefficients, CSS Alabama slid into a tight orbit. It
would make a complete circle around the planet then launch the three TR-3Bs.

Because of the secrecy of this mission, Tom Gilbert directed the XO to bring the three
pilots to his stateroom for their final briefing.

Tom Gilbert had a big-screen TV/video display in his stateroom where he could either
watch movies, look at control room surveillance, or any of the sensor data. He could
also pipe in power points or video from a personal digital assistant which the XO had
with him to do the final briefing.

This was it. Three of the largest hydrogen bombs ever built by mankind were soon to
be tested on the back side of Uranus. A simulated time lapsed video showing the entire
mission played and last-minute checks were made on all pertinent information.

This was not the first time a TR-3B deployed to another planet or moon. The TR-3B photographed the moon crater by an amateur astronomer where they thought they could hide it. The amateur astronomer photographer recorded the TR-3B was demonized by the UFO community and the government. The amateur astronomer photographer was the only honest broker in that discourse.

After a review of a PowerPoint that gave all the mission details, the TR-3B pilots were then ordered to their craft.

The TR-3B could have multiple crew members depending on its mission. Since Uranus was uninhabited and no other entities nearby, there was no reason to take along the copilots and the back seater electronic warfare officers. They kept the crew down to a minimum and that was just the pilot to reduce possible inadvertent disclosure.

The three pilots were escorted into the controlled area by security personnel, and they went through double airlocks into their craft. The weapons shipping hatches they traversed was immediately closed and sealed, and the pilots did their pre-flight checks. Once all systems were online and provided satisfactory automated systems status, the ready signals were indicated on the bridge indicating requesting permission to launch.

The TR-3B's computers communicated with the ship's computers and after [*permission to launch*] was granted, the automatic launch sequence commenced.

The protective shields were rotated upwards on the upper row of hangars fully exposing three TR-3Bs currently mounted in the STOWS. No other STOW hanger bays are opened and exposed. As soon as the launch command was given ship's thrusters and TR-3B thrusters combined to shove the three TR-3Bs away from the CSS Alabama. The force was far less that a normal Navy Aircraft Carrier catapult launch and the combinations TR-3B Navigation System and the Alabama's Airwing computer would immediately place the TR-3B into launch and attack profile that met all combat requirements. The direction of travel was unpredictable in most cases as the TR-3B could be flown head or behind CSS Alabama during its mission.

BACKGROUND MUSIC. WAGNER'S FLIGHT OF THE VALKARYS

EXT. CGI. SPACE CSS ALABAMA LAUNCHING THREE TR-3B FIGHTER BOMBERS 45 SECONDS.

> Note to Cinematographer:
>
> The CGI should animate the following:
>
> Alabama's three hatches for individual TR-3B hanger bays on the upper row rotate upwards exposing the fighter bombers. These

would be hydraulic controlled actuators opening the hatches just like missile tubes on a submarine.

The TR-3B's launch sequentially five seconds apart. The angle on the shot should be at several distances. First launch image would be closer, and the next two launches further away and finally a shot showing the TR-3B's forming up on a TR-3B spacecraft V formation.

The front cover of the original Novel depicts the launch of the three TR-3BS:

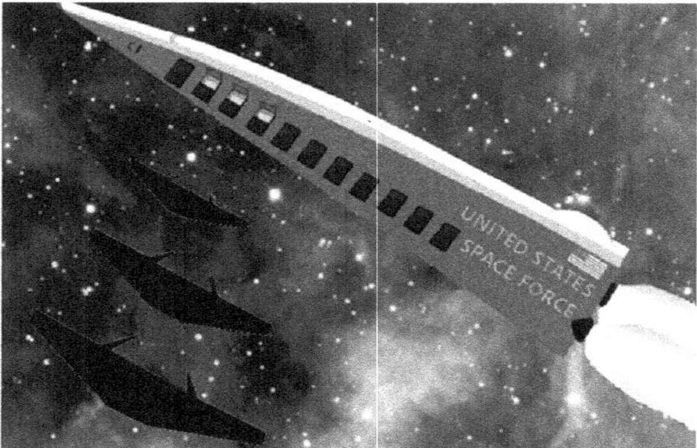

Note 11 Pairs of Hangars on Each side of CSS Alabama.

Then a shot showing the three TR-3B's heading down toward the planet.

Based on computerized flight plan the TR-3B's orb globelike appearance lit up and expanded almost encompassing the entire craft as the three ships peeled away and maneuvered away from the CSS Alabama which continued its orbital path. The TR-3Bs doubled back in the opposite direction of the Alabama was traveling and pointed downwards towards the planet.

Being the coldest planet in the solar system made up mainly of hydrogen and helium, but also sporting a large amount of carbon dioxide, the likelihood any sort of life existed on Uranus was highly doubtful. It took the Alabama almost thirty minutes to get near the other side of the planet.

<u>EXT. CGI. SPACE AZZIE'S TR-3B FIGHTER BOMBER DROPPING ONE OF THE HYDROGEN BOMBS 15SECONDS.</u>

> Note: On the initial sideview Azzie's name is painted on the side of the TR-3B in red letters against the black hull bathed in planetary reflection light.
>
> View of Azzie's TR-3B in two shots. First a side five seconds. A side view showing the underside of the TR-3B opening the hatches for the bomb bay and the bomb released falling under gravity as the TR-3B changes to an upward pitch leaving it behind on its gravity drop towards the planet. As the bomb gets into thicker atmosphere its control surfaces reorientate it heading down vertically.
>
> Later when Batman and Instigator drop their pickles, their bomb release sequence manifests in an identical manner.

The first plane piloted by Azzie dropped his pickle on upon open, and disregarded property. Azzie had just dipped slightly into the atmosphere, allowing hull temperatures to decline to a safe level before activating the weapon.

Nearby but spread out in a large V formation making up the wing pattern were the other two TR-3B's flown by pilots with code names Batman and Instigator.

The three TR-3Bs spread out flying in the strange atmosphere, praying for a none-screw-up made their way to their bomb release locations. To relieve the pilots of any psychological regrets, the bomb release and arming were fully automatic.

<u>EXT. CGI. SPACE BATMAN'S TR-3B FIGHTER BOMBER DROPPING ONE OF THE HYDROGEN BOMBS 15 SECONDS.</u>

Same filming sequence done for Azzie's TR-3B but on the initial sideview batman's name is painted on the side of the TR-3B in red letters against the black hull bathed in planetary reflection light

Batman's hydrogen bomb was now freefalling towards planet Uranus at his designated target.

EXT. CGI. SPACE INSTIGATOR'S TR-3B FIGHTER BOMBER DROPPING ONE OF THE HYDROGEN BOMBS 15 SECONDS.

Same filming sequence done for Azzie's bomb release.

Within one minute of each other Instigator's TR-3B let go of his pickle (hydrogen bomb code name *pickles*) as well and started to move out of the way of the expected blasts and shockwaves.

It took a while for the weapons to drop two hundred thousand feet to the detonation. Azzie poured on the coal to get away from the blast area, he didn't want a hard ride. Batman was also close behind and the two got well beyond the calculated blast radius.

Instigator took too much time and did not appreciate the size of the EMP these nuclear weapons would give off. In due time three horrendous blasts occurred, creating a mini sun for nearly thirty seconds and immense fireballs like they never witnessed in their lifetimes Azzie and Batman were clear of the EMP pulse that came out in a hyperbolic trajectory that missed them but hit Instigator's TR-3B.

Part of Instigator's electronics were immediately fried by the EMP pulse . Instigator (a.k.a. Brad Howard) suddenly observed some indications in the cockpit that gave him a real wakeup call.

Even though the TR-3B artificial gravity machine kept working, the propulsion system died. Instigator was thus marooned floating above Uranus with only his emergency radio working. It was battery powered and only had twelve hours of operation. Instigator was now facing a serious personal catastrophe.

It would be very negative for Alabama's crew morale to start the mission on losing one of their pilots.

For this mission the Space Carrier CSS Alabama call sign was Sierra Charlie.

EXT. CGI SPACE SIDE VIEW C.U. OF INSTIGATOR IN THE COCKPIT OF HIS TR-3B.

INSTIGATOR
Sierra Charlie, this is Instigator, I have some issues
and it appears my propulsion system has failed!

SIERRA CHARLIE
Instigator, are you in an immediate flight profile
emergency?

INSTIGATOR
Sierra Charlie, this is Instigator. I am above the
atmosphere traveling at 19,000 miles per hour, but I
have no ability to maneuver and only my emergency
radio is working. I have twelve hours of battery left on
my emergency radio. I need immediate help.

SIERRA CHARLIE
Instigator, this is Sierra Charlie. Stand by, we are
contacting Azzie and Batman for assistance.

A rescue attempt was hence immediately initiated.

The brilliance of the TR-3B designers now paid off. TR-3B designers astutely used
post war tactics and knew the possibility existed they may one day have to tow a TR-
3B to safety. Each TR-3B had a tow line that could be remote controlled.

Azzie was sent first, and his ECM suite localized the emergency communicator
transponder and locked on the disabled TR-3B with utilizing a Spectral Doppler Radar
(SDR) that could detect a TR-3B even though it had a stealth coating.

Azzie flew to Instigator's TR-3B and immediately started flying parallel to it. Since
Instigator's TR-3B was traveling around 19,000 miles per hour, there was no fear of it
crashing into the planet any time soon and was in a safe orbit.

But unless Azzie's TR-3B tow line latched onto Instigator's craft, Instigator would
be spending his last hours flying around Neptune until his life support systems failed
soon after the emergency radio stopped working. Rescue as soon as possible deemed
necessary.

Azzie made a dozen attempts to hook his tow line to Instigator's craft but could never
quite make it. Batman was vectored in and ordered to attempt a towline hookup. It
turned out to be a lot harder than it looked and now they realized training for an
emergency recovery in the trainer wasn't the same as a real attempt in space.

Batman was also having difficulty getting the tow rig to latch on to Instigator's TR-3B.
The only saving grace was, they removed the rest of the crew so if this rescue attempt
failed, only one crew member would be lost.

AZZIE
Batman, this is Azzie, I have an idea. I'm going to
reposition directly below Instigator and watch the tow
rig for you and give you thrust orders to help latch on.

BATMAN
Azzie, this is Batman, Roger that, standing by for your
directions.

Azzie very efficiently moved in and a few feet below Instigator's bow where he could observe the tow rig mating loop. This loop can be deployed manually by the pilot or automatically by Instigator's TR-3B navigational computer, but it was not working and probably dysfunctional from the EMP pulse.

AZZIE
Batman, this is Azzie, reposition behind Instigator and
maneuver forward slowly and stand by for my mark
to move the tow mechanism on Instigator's ship's tow
ring.

BATMAN
Azzie, this is Batman. Roger that, making a circle and
coming up from behind again.

It only took Batman a couple minutes to pull up, circle back around and line up for a hookup. Azzie watched very carefully and ordered.

AZZIE
Batman, slow down, you are coming in too fast. Also
move slightly starboard.

Batman eased up on the throttle and steered sideways using its thrusters.

AZZIE
Batman, you are lined up now, just ease forward nice
and slow.

Minutes seemed like hours and hours seemed like days, the stress was enormous because the pilots would be under a lot of pressure to not reveal this harrowing adventure even though a few communications people on the Space Carrier were privy to their radio communications. Captain Gilbert was standing next to XO Riley. Alabama's control room was currently an exclusion area due to the nuclear operations, only the Chief of the Watch, messenger and Navigator were also in the control room with orders this event is compartmentalized.

AZZIE
Batman, keep it coming, nice and slow, your ship is
halfway home.

Batman's TR-3B was moving one foot in ten seconds. Instigator didn't care. One good maneuver would be better than twenty bad ones. All it took was just one good hook on the tow ring with the tow mechanism and Instigator could be towed to safety.

It was clear to everyone involved; this would be impossible during live combat. Rudy Wilcox (Azzie) had known Brad Howard (Instigator) for several years. They were just like brothers. Saving Brad was almost a personal matter because of their close friendship.

Rudy Wilcox (Azzie) knew the TR-3B like the back of his hand. He suddenly knew he was only two feet away from another attempt at grabbing the tow ring with the tow mechanism and lines. In twenty seconds, it would be directly over the spot where he needed to attempt deploying the towline mechanism to latch on. The current design was terrible and something TR-3B designers overlooked.

They were ten seconds away from success or failure. If they failed this grab, Instigator would start feeling a lot more concerned, if not panic. Nothing is worse than the notion of being marooned in space and dying.

The last foot was very stressful. And soon they were on the mark. During crucial moments call signs were deferred because precise timing of language was essential.

AZZIE
Standby to deploy locking ring.

BATMAN
Standing by.

AZZIE
Mark, deploy ring grabber.

BATMAN
Deployed.

AZZIE
You got it. Lock the ring and stand by for further instructions.

BATMAN
Ring locked, ready for tow.

BATMAN
Sierra Charlie, this is Batman. I have the tow ring
attached to Instigator. Request instructions.

SIERRA CHARLIE
Batman, this is Sierra Charlie, stand by for Romeo
Papa (rendezvous point) will be sent to your ship's
vector voyage navigation system.

BATMAN
Sierra Charlie, standing by for Romeo Papa.

SIERRA CHARLIE
Azzie, this is Sierra Charlie. You are to escort Batman
and Instigator to Romeo Papa.

AZZIE
Sierra Charlie, this is Azzie, I understand escort
Batman and Instigator to Romeo Papa.

The Alabama slowed on its orbit so that all three TR-3Bs would catch up and avoid doing another complete circle of Uranus because Admiral Gilbert did not want the two NASA people to see there was a radical weather change on the opposite side of the planet caused by the three horrendous nuclear blasts.

Alabama would be long gone and way out of the solar system by the time scientists discovered a strange phenomenon on the surface of Uranus.

Moments after the three hydrogen bomb blasts, weather patterns never seen before on the planet occurred. Huge thunderstorms with cumulous clouds ranging up to one hundred fifty thousand feet in the air made up of mainly hydrogen, helium, nitrogen, and carbon dioxide suddenly had Earth like weather patterns and cloud patterns all over the hemisphere. The planet's surface that had been previously obscure from many cloud layers now had pockets of exposure. Even though the sunlight was insufficient to warm the planet, it did expose a lot of unknown planet surface.

Unfortunately, the clouds would be back by the time it rotated to where visibility from the Hubble Space Telescope was available. The view of Uranus surface would thus remain unknown.

Out in space with no wind resistance, towing Instigator to the CSS Alabama was nice and smooth. All they had to do was get Instigator close to its docking STOW and robotic arms that existed in the general area to assist in docking issues could then be used to grab instigator and move it into the recessed area that held the TR-3B, just like all the others.

Within an hour, Instigator's TR-3B was back in its cradle with the protective hatch hiding it from external visibility. Even though the EMP damaged a lot of TR-3B circuitry, Alabama's equipment and technicians were able to verify a good air seal for the hanger bay and hence were able to open the TR-3B's weapon shipping hatch from inside Alabama's individual hanger bay.

Brad Howard slid out of his TR-3B and was immediately met by Captain Gilbert and XO Riley and the two other pilots, Azzie, and Batman.

CAPTAIN GILBERT
Welcome back, Commander Howard, please follow me to my state room."

The two other pilots (Azzie and Batman) had already been directed to go to CO Stateroom and not to say anything to the crew prior to debriefing.

Once the pilots were all inside Tom Gilbert's stateroom, he gave them their marching orders.

CAPTAIN GILBERT
Okay, gentlemen, we almost had a fatality. We'll do a replay on whatever information we can extract out of the TR-3B. Hopefully there would be data retained in Instigator's TR-3B nonvolatile memory leading up to the failure.

XO Riley
One other item, gentlemen. Nobody except the individuals in this room are allowed to know about the mission you just completed. It is compartmentalized and sealed. Never discuss it with anyone.

CAPTAIN GILBERT
I must get to the bridge to start our next leg of the mission. You are all dismissed for now. We will meet again in twelve hours and hold a formal debrief if we are able to extract information from Instigator's TR-3B.

Everyone left the CO's stateroom. Tom went to the bridge and was not happy. He had lost a lot of speed due to the exigency and it would take a megawatt or two of energy to recapture the speed they lost burning up more fuel he wanted to preserve in case he needed it.

Up on the bridge Captain Gilbert contacted the Navigator via the internal wireless telephone system.

CAPTAIN GILBERT
Navigator, please report to the control room.

The navigator had planned to be on the bridge momentarily since he knew the next leg was to *Juliet Delta*, code word for Jupitorian Destination.

NAVIGATOR
Admiral, reporting as ordered.

CAPTAIN GILBERT
Navigator, commence operation *Juliet Delta*. Also, I want the Pilot, Copilot, and Chief of the Watch in the control room until we exit the solar system."

NAVIGATOR
Roger that, Admiral.

CAPTAIN GILBERT
Navigator, what is your current projection of solar system exit?

NAVIGATOR
Admiral, when we start the next acceleration, we do not need to worry about slowing down for a long time, thus we can increase our speed substantially while in the solar system. My calculations show we may be able to be outside the solar system designated markers within forty-eight hours."

CAPTAIN GILBERT
How many watch sections are available?

NAVIGATOR
Until we get some more pilots and copilots qualified, we only have the manning for two watch sections. They will work eight-hour shifts until we secure their watch and go fully autopilot.

CAPTAIN GILBERT
What is the latest schedule to have another watch section qualified so they will be able to sustain three watch sections?

NAVIGATOR

Without cutting corners, I'd say at least six months, but all we have on board is simulators without physical movement.

CAPTAIN GILBERT

That's better than nothing?

NAVIGATOR

I don't like the idea of certifying a pilot unless he feels the real movement of the ship.

CAPTAIN GILBERT

Understand, but face it we will never have the ideal situation to qualify them. We need three sections for sustainment in the event we must post three watch sections, especially if we get trapped in a dust cloud.

NAVIGATOR

The best I can promise is six months using onboard simulators.

CAPTAIN GILBERT

Okay, keep me posted and put together a timeline showing all individuals involved.

NAVIGATOR

Yes, sir, I'll do that today.

CAPTAIN GILBERT

Thank you.

NAVIGATOR

Sir, request you announce over the 1MC we will be accelerating.

Captain Gilbert nodded at the Navigator, then grabbed the 1MC microphone and made the shipwide announcement.

CAPTAIN GILBERT

Let me have your attention, this is the captain speaking. We will commence accelerating in a few minutes, expect high ambient noise levels in part of the ship until we reach our new velocity. Report any

deficiencies discovered during the acceleration to the
Chief of the Watch in control immediately.

Captain Gilbert then decided to go down to the library where he knew the two NASA scientists were working on their SITREP and getting ready to broadcast several messages and space to space emails. As he expected they were super animated with the luster of scientist who saw a rare image they obtained watching Uranus at a close distance.

The NASA scientists were also looking at the video sent by Azzie that enthralled them like nothing in their lives before. Never in human history had scientific recordings inside the atmosphere of Uranus existed. The data from the sensor package appeared extensive.

SHANGHAIED

It would be a few hours before these two scientists figured out the CSS Alabama was not pointing Earth as expected.

Tom Gilbert was not looking forward to it but in twenty-four hours he would have an all-hands meeting and explain they were now on an ultra-sensitive clandestine mission. The destination and duration of the trip will be given later.

Shelly Brown would be her bubbly self for another couple days, then she would quickly turn bitter as she discovered she had been Shanghaied. Sally Browns bitterness would slowly grow as she discovered she would be gone a lot longer than she or anyone realized.

The crew knew they were probably going on a long trip, but Shelly and the NASA scientists were totally in the dark and soon depressed when reality set in. Tom wasn't too concerned since the ship's doctor and assistant doctor were poised to sedate them and if necessary, put them in a drug-induced coma to put them asleep for several years.

Shortly people felt the acceleration which lasted for several days, which seemed rather odd to Shelly and the two NASA scientists.

The NASA people were getting ready to take more pictures and video of the solar system as they got closer to Earth. The problem was the current position of Uranus was far away from any of the other planets. They would not see much of the other planets until they got closer to earth.

Two days later after they passed the solar system outer marker (point on the map), the scientists approached Tom Gilbert.

FIRST NASA SCIENTIST

Sir, something does not add up. The sun is getting substantially weaker in appearance. Are we traveling in the correct direction?

Tom could see an almost panic on their faces and he responded.

CAPTAIN GILBERT
Come to my stateroom with me so we can discuss it.

Captain Gilbert then contacted the XO on his wireless.

CAPTAIN GILBERT
XO, please meet me in my stateroom.

XO Riley
I'll be there shortly captain.

As soon as Commodore Riley arrived, Tom Gilbert shut his stateroom door then turned to the two NASA scientists.

CAPTAIN GILBERT
Okay, gentlemen, as you both well know, NASA forced you onto this mission. We didn't desire you to come along and we would have preferred you not. We tried hard to talk you out of it, but you used dirty politics to force your way onto this voyage.

FIRST NASA SCIENTIST
We admit our actions appear somewhat dubious, but we viewed this voyage as a rare opportunity.

CAPTAIN GILBERT
We are on a very important mission for the national security of our country and for the entire Earth's population.

FIRST NASA SCIENTIST
Captain, it appears we are heading in the opposite direction of Earth. Can you tell us why?

CAPTAIN GILBERT
It's going to be a long trip far outside our solar system and you are stuck on board. Had you not insisted on coming you would not be stuck here. I'm sorry.

Panic suddenly flowed across both the NASA scientist's faces. They appeared like someone who just lost their close mate or spouse. It appeared to be a tumultuous moment.

FIRST NASA SCIENTIST
How long will we be gone?

CAPTAIN GILBERT
That part is still classified above your security clearance levels. I'm not willing to divulge that for a while. But at the midpoint to our destination, you will be told.

FIRST NASA SCIENTIST
Can you tell us where we are going?

CAPTAIN GILBERT
To another star system.

FIRST NASA SCIENTIST
For what purpose?

CAPTAIN GILBERT
You do not have the need to know currently. I will relax that condition later as I see fit.

FIRST NASA SCIENTIST
What do we expect to find where we are going?

CAPTAIN GILBERT
I would say there is an excellent chance we'll find intelligent life where we are going.

The NASA scientists were stunned. They didn't know what to say. Tom Gilbert knew he needed to give them some time alone. This would be a very tough time for them. No doubt they had families.

Admiral Gilbert would wait a few more days and inform the NASA scientists that by now government representatives will have met their spouses and informed them that their husbands were on a secret mission for the government and would be gone a very long time. They would be taken care of, have a coordinator available to help them with personal problems and finances if necessary.

Tom also thought that if they were real scientists and adhered to the philosophy of what and how scientists should pursue the secrets to the universe, this trip for them will advance them as scientists way beyond their peers. They now have almost four years to devote to independent science with some of the best technology ever produced without any distractions.

The discovery would be immense though spellbinding quality, that would no doubt shake the foundation of their belief system as they soon discovered Earth was a much smaller concern in the galaxy than what its inhabitants would wish to know.

Earth was blessed it existed on the opposite side of the galaxy from the most arrogant beings that would treat Earth inhabitants as nicely as we do ants in the kitchen with a can of RAID.

CAPTAIN GILBERT
Another thing I wanted to inform you of. We are beyond two million miles from Earth. As such the laws change. I now have full legal jurisdiction over all matters and can do whatever I choose without any legal recourse. Here is a copy of the section in the two-million-mile law passed by congress in secret session to support this mission which gives me the legal right to continue my mission without the delay associated with returning you to Earth.

Tom handed them both copies, which gave them even further trepidation.

CAPTAIN GILBERT
I'm ordering you not to discuss this with anyone. Also, I highlighted in the document that you fall under the UCMJ and subject to my legal authority over you in every aspect of your time aboard this Space Vessel.

FIRST NASA SCIENTIST
Captain, I really do not know what to think about all this right yet. It will take me a while to come to grips with it.

CAPTAIN GILBERT
What we stated here today is to not be discussed again. If you wish later, you may request a private audience with me to discuss your predicament.

Tom Gilbert knew the two men were now into such a state of shock, they would not be able to rationally discuss it for days or weeks and he didn't like to see grown men cry, so he knew he had to end the session soon and send them on their way back to the library where they hung out.

CAPTAIN GILBERT

However, be advised, I'm not permitted to be alone with non-ship's personnel, there will be security present.

The men shook their heads in total astonishment, then Tom sent them away to give them space among themselves to deal with the overwhelming revelation.

Tom had one more of these meetings coming up and he sincerely regretted it. He really didn't want Shelly Brown coming along, but she got shoved down his throat by Senator Bosworth.

Shelly Brown was also probably a co-conspirator, and just like the NASA scientists who pulled their political crap to force themselves aboard for what they thought was a short mission, she too got trapped. In essence she was like some of the passengers on the Lusitania in 1915 on a fatal voyage who failed to heed the German warning just before U20 sent them to the bottom in almost twenty minutes.

Tom would not instigate a meeting with Shelly Brown. He would let her continue her daily routines for a while until she started wondering why none of the stars looked familiar or the sun appeared shrinking and started asking questions. Her new friend the Weps was told that only the CO would break the news to her. She of course would be crushed at first and the thought of losing four years of her life would soon foster a personality change she never anticipated.

Shelly Brown was a brilliant woman, well educated, and capable of deep thought. No wonder Senator Bosworth discovered her and then weaponized her for his purposes. The Senator soon discovered his huge loss the minute she was gone. When you lose your very best employee, it hurts right away. One never knows how much they really mean because we take for granted the tangibles they bring.

Acceleration continued and became slowly annoying even though active noise reduction was employed. Because the acceleration lasted far longer than what Shelly had experienced before, she knew something wasn't right. She thought it was odd the Control room was staffed for several days then suddenly; the Chief of the Watch and the messenger were all that were present except for the Navigator or the CO visiting now and then. The two NASA scientists were now GONE most of the time and requested sedatives from the doctor so they could rest and cope with their new confinement. The doctor was well briefed to expect this to come.

After three continuous days of accelerating Shelly Brown finally decided the Admiral was hiding something from her and when she pressed the crew for information, they simply said they were under orders not to discuss ships operations with visitors until further notice. So, she laid in wait in the control room knowing the Admiral went there sometimes and she would confront him.

Just as Shelly Brown anticipated on the third day, the admiral appeared, and she cornered him for a discussion. Captain Gilbert knew this was probably going to be the big showdown and asked one of the doctors to meet him in the control room in fifteen minutes with a couple assistants to sedate Shelly Brown if necessary.

SHELLY BROWN
Admiral, I need to talk with you about something.

CAPTAIN GILBERT
What do you want to talk about?

SHELLY BROWN
Perhaps it's not appropriate to discuss it here in front
of the bridge watch.

CAPTAIN GILBERT
The Chief of the Watch authorized to hear anything I
say to you.

SHELLY BROWN
What about messenger?

CAPTAIN GILBERT
He's sworn to silence, he'll be instructed if you say
something he should not repeat to anyone.

SHELLY BROWN
Okay, Admiral, I don't want to beat around the bush,
what's going on?

CAPTAIN GILBERT
What do you mean by that question?

SHELLY BROWN
Admiral, we have been accelerating for three days. We
are probably going at incredible speed now.

CAPTAIN GILBERT
Yes, we are going very fast.

SHELLY BROWN
If we are simply returning to Earth, why are we going
so fast?

CAPTAIN GILBERT
Shelly, when you and the Senator bulldogged your
way on this flight, at that time I informed you I did
not think it would be a good idea if you came along. I
specifically asked you not to come.

SHELLY BROWN
Well, I didn't want you to bully me around and tell me
what I could or could not do.

CAPTAIN GILBERT
I wasn't bullying you; I was looking out for your best
interest.

SHELLY BROWN
You should know that my people had taken so much
crap for generations, how else was I to respond?

CAPTAIN GILBERT
I knew we were going to have to conduct this
conversation eventually. I'm very sorry you got
trapped and caught up in all this. But unfortunately,
Senator Bosworth and you unwittingly staged yourself
in a scenario we could not divulge to you due to the
secrecy.

SHELLY BROWN
Please do not give me that crap, just tell me what the
facts are. I'm a big girl and I want to know what's
happening.

CAPTAIN GILBERT
Now is probably as good a time as any to tell you. We
are going to another solar system.

SHELLY BROWN
What!

CAPTAIN GILBERT
We are traveling to an inhabited world teaming with
intelligent beings that exceed our level of technology.

SHELLY BROWN
Why are we going there?"

CAPTAIN GILBERT
Hopefully to advert a war.

SHELLY BROWN
With these aliens?

CAPTAIN GILBERT
If that's what you want to call them, yes.

SHELLY BROWN
Do we know in fact these aliens exist?

CAPTAIN GILBERT
Yes.

SHELLY BROWN
Why doesn't the public know this?

CAPTAIN GILBERT
People above my pay grade have determined it would
not be a good time to inform the public.

SHELLY BROWN
How long is this trip?

CAPTAIN GILBERT
Round trip is four years.

SHELLY BROWN
You got to be kidding me.

CAPTAIN GILBERT
Sorry, no, I'm not.

SHELLY BROWN
What about my mother, she's all alone?

CAPTAIN GILBERT
We are taking care of that.

SHELLY BROWN
What does that mean?

CAPTAIN GILBERT
The minute we left the solar system, your mother and Senator Bosworth were informed. Your mother will receive special help when required. We have a support group that will be in constant contact with your mother and make necessary arrangements for her needs, including Secret Service protection.

SHELLY BROWN
How does my mother rate Secret Service protection?

CAPTAIN GILBERT
The President determined that eventually information on this mission would leak out and your mother could be swamped by curiosity seekers and troublemakers.

SHELLY BROWN
So, my mother already knows?

CAPTAIN GILBERT
Yes, I'm sorry.

Tears slowly started streaming down Shelly's face. She knew her mother had nobody else and would feel terribly alone. Four years out of their lives at her age was a terrible ordeal. And the truth be told, she caused most of it herself being a Ms. Busy Body, relentlessly hounding Admiral Gilbert.

SHELLY BROWN
Thank you for your time, Admiral.

Shelly then walked out of the control room and went directly to her berth and lay down and shut her eyes and tried to forget the vibrations of the acceleration were annoying.

TRAVELING THE VOID

The days slipped into weeks, the weeks into months and soon a year had passed. The best day was the day the acceleration ended, and they were now coasting to a point where they could see behind the huge dust clouds hundreds of millions of miles wide.

Just as the Ponarian had indicated there was a whole different group of solar systems hidden from Earth's view.

There would now be another burn on the rocket engines to create a new course. It would require exact navigation; otherwise, they would end up three or four solar systems out of direction. This maneuver could not be accomplished in manual control.

Calculations by the computers figured it out and force vector components of a new solution all added to the intricate controls of the rocket engines that caused a new course even though it seemed they were not pointing in the right direction. Actual relative motion was correct.

Eventually after time with the new course the ship appeared to be pointing their new heading. By the time they were accurately transiting on their new course they only had nine more months to go to get to their destination. In the final couple of months would be the most dangerous time, as it was expected they would be detected by then, and a welcoming party would be sent out to deal with them.

One of the problems navigating stemmed from blurring of the images of stars and planets because of the excessive velocity. As such a Cosmic Interpolator was created that produced a geometric guess of the actual position. Without the Cosmic Interpolator, they never could have traveled at these velocities and navigated with any kind of precision.

Another issue was that the further they got away from Earth the more the heavens changed. Stars were no longer in the expected locations. The whole tapestry of the heavens changed, and they had to build new star maps the further they traveled to enable them to have a way to navigate back to Earth.

THE END OF THE MARTIANS

Admiral Gilbert didn't have much of an intelligence briefing on the Jupitorians, but he did have an eyewitness and an intelligent person who spent time with them, the Ponarian Randolph.

In a private meeting with Randolph, XO Riley, and himself he asked Randolph if he wouldn't mind briefing them and selected department heads on the Jupitorians and the Mars Massacre.

The CO set up training for select department heads as they transited to the Jupitorian Empire. The first session had Weps, Nav, Eng, Com, XO, and CO at the wardroom briefing table with placards in front of them so that Randolph would know who he was talking with.

>   RANDOLPH (a.k.a. PONARIAN – PO)
> Thanks for inviting me to tell you about my genuine
> experience with the Jupitorians.

>   CAPTAIN GILBERT
> Thank you for being here to assist us Navigate to
> the Jupitorian Empire and briefing us on what the
> Jupitorians are like and their history in our own solar
> system.

RANDOLPH (a.k.a. PONARIAN – PO)
You are welcome, Captain.

CAPTAIN GILBERT
In case you have doubts in what Randolph tells us, I will now disclose I met him in Area 51 when we were discussing this mission possibility. Randolph has been in government custody for 71 years and our government hasn't always treated him well.

Randolf was tortured and mistreated over time, and I know all about his history. Some of the information he's going to brief you on has been verified by the USSF. Some of the information is unconfirmed, but as we explore his history, some of it is based on facts we obtained via means you are not cleared to know about. That includes Mars, which he will soon talk about.

RANDOLPH (a.k.a. PONARIAN – PO)
Thank you, Captain, for your faith in me. Now I will get right into the Jupitorians so you all will understand what you are up against.

To give the appearance of how important this brifing is, Captain Gilbert surprised the department heads.

CAPTAIN GILBERT
Randolf, I want you to sit in the captain's chair so you will be in the middle of all of us.

RANDOLPH (a.k.a. PONARIAN – PO)
As you wish, Captain.

Everyone found seats near Randolph and was quite ready to hear all about the Jupitorians.

RANDOLPH (a.k.a. PONARIAN – PO)
The Jupitorians give the appearance of arrogance and their imperialistic tendencies in their area of the galaxy are legendary. The Martian debacle nine hundred thousand years ago is just another example of how the Jupitorians built their reputation.

CAPTAIN GILBERT
Randolph, can you tell us what the Martians were like?

RANDOLPH (a.k.a. PONARIAN – PO)
The Martians had a growing Empire, but it was a long distance away, and simply by the twists and turns and many mistakes they made they blundered into a conflict with the Jupitorians.

Martians were attempting to expand their own Empire. In the beginning, they didn't even know the Jupitorians existed.

The Martians colonized Earth and set up the provincial capital of Atlantis.

Earth's climate was quite a bit different nine hundred thousand years ago. At the time of the creation of Atlantis, the planet had just exited a glaciation period. The Arab Peninsula daily temperatures were 25 degrees cooler than present times. Flora abounded and potable water could be obtained in quite a few places as the mountains were heavily forested and snowcapped in the winter months.

CAPTAIN GILBERT
Randolph what was Earth like back then?

RANDOLPH (a.k.a. PONARIAN – PO)
Most of the rest of Earth was undeveloped. In reality, the only civilized area of the planet was indeed Atlantis which had amazing modern technology, some of which Earth was just now started to develop again in 2024 and beyond. At the time of Atlantis destruction, one could estimate they were advanced several hundred years beyond present day Earth.

CAPTAIN GILBERT
What was the relationship like between Mars and Atlantis back then?

RANDOLPH (a.k.a. PONARIAN – PO)
Atlantis did commerce with the Martians, their ancestors. But as time slowly moved on, a great divide slowly grew between the two planets. Martians were somewhat antagonized in they felt the people of

Atlantis owed their entirety to the Martian Empire. Cooperation declined and at the time of the galactic disaster there was no cooperation or mutual defense, so the Jupitorians understood if they attacked one of them, the likelihood the other would not come to their aid was a most probable outcome. It was every *man for himself* mindset.

CAPTAIN GILBERT
How did the Martians meet the Jupitorians?

RANDOLPH (a.k.a. PONARIAN – PO)
The debacle all began when Martians realized the day would come when Atlantis would want complete autonomy. That gave them an even greater reason to reach out in space and select a planet with an atmosphere and natural resources to add to their portfolio. During a survey of other solar systems something caught their attention and hence as they traveled to discover the source of emanating radio signals, they were soon to discover the Jupitorians.

Jupitorians and neighboring civilizations had considerable struggle between them over the years. The slowly developing reality became, don't go into another solar system without an invite. Otherwise, the reception could become quite military in nature.

The Martians, violating some of the covenants that were expected in this part of the Galaxy, were not prepared for the hostile reception they soon received.

CAPTAIN GILBERT
I take it was not a warm welcome.

Captain Gilbert starts having visions in his mind based on training videos and movies of plausible imagery to Randolph's story that continued to evolve as the descriptions unfolded.

Were these images telepathically inserted by Randolph?

<u>EXT. CGI. SPACE MARTIAN FLEET ARRIVES IN JUPITORIAN SOLAR SYSTEM 30 SECONDS.</u>

RANDOLPH (a.k.a. PONARIAN – PO)
The Martians were excellent tactical fighters. They were nimble and capable. In some ways outsiders would estimate the Martians were almost as arrogant as the Jupitorians. As soon as the Martians showed up in Jupitorian solar space, they were met by a hostile reception and a trigger-happy Martian created a scenario that didn't need to get started.

EXT. CGI. SPACE MARTIAN FLEET STARTS COMBAT WITH JUPITORIANS 30 SECONDS.

The Martians were excellent at warfare and tactics and did a good job of defending themselves but in the process made waste on several Jupitorian space assets. It did not take the Martians long to figure out they needed to depart the area and head back to their own planet and retreat in the most efficient manner.

EXT. CGI. SPACE MARTIAN AND JUPITORIAN FLEETS CONVERGE START LAUNCHING MISSILES. 30 SECONDS

CAPTAIN GILBERT
How did that relate to Mars getting wiped out?

RANDOLPH (a.k.a. PONARIAN – PO)
Because of miscommunication, embellishment, and other distortions of reality, the Jupitorian leadership was led to believe the Martians acted out of aggression and thus should be made an example of.

Before the Martians were able to get far enough away to hide their transit back to their own civilization, the Jupitorians were able to deploy several assets to track them down and destroy them if necessary.

EXT. CGI. SPACE JUPITORIANS CHASE AFTER THE MARTIANS WHO ARE UNAWARE THEY ARE BEING FOLLOWED. 60 SECONDS SOUND + MUSIC ONE OF BEL SUONO (RUSSIAN) SONGS

CAPTAIN GILBERT
These are lessons learned we need to be aware of and not lead the Jupitorians back to Earth.

RANDOLPH (a.k.a. PONARIAN – PO)
It's too late Admiral Gilbert. The Jupitorians already know Earth quite well. You need to make sure you offer no hostile intentions.

CAPTAIN GILBERT
What brought on the destruction of Mars, why was it annihilated?

RANDOLPH (a.k.a. PONARIAN – PO)
The Martians were cocky and had no idea the level of sophistication and ability the Jupitorians possessed. Nor did they know that due to the continual conflicts the Jupitorians manifested or were recipients of.

The Jupitorian fleet was at least ten times larger than the Martians and they were ordered to follow the Martians home and if necessary, make some permanent examples out of them. Hence the Martians were unaware they were leading the Jupitorians back to their planet creating the ultimate disaster.

CAPTAIN GILBERT
How did Mars get destroyed?

EXT. CGI. SPACE JUPITORIANS ARRIVE AT MARS AND ENTER ORBIT CAUSING ALARMS TO GO OFF ON MARS. 30 SECONDS.

RANDOLPH (a.k.a. PONARIAN – PO)
As the two groups of ships passed within the Martian solar system, the Jupitorians detected Mars and the communications to Earth which was in Orbit not far from Mars that time of the year. Right about the time the Martians reached their planet they were attacked by the Jupitorians. The qualitative difference between the two space forces quickly led to the demise of the Martians Fleet in Space.

CAPATAIN GILBERT
What caused all the destruction on the planet surface of Mars and what wiped out Atlantis?

EXT. CGI. SPACE MISSILES COMING AT THE JUPITORIAN FLEEET AND SUBSEQUENT EXPLOSION 30 SECONDS.

RANDOLPH (a.k.a. PONARIAN – PO)
The Jupitorians detected missiles leaving the planet heading for them. One of the missiles detonated with a nuclear blast which severely damaged a few of the Jupitorian Space Cruisers.

EXT. CGI. SPACE HYPERSONIC MISSILES LAUNCHED BY THE JUPITORIAN FLEEET AT CYDONIA SUBSEQUENT EXPLOSION 30 SECONDS.

The Jupitorian Task Force Commander then targeted the areas where the missiles were launched. One of those locations was the exquisite city of Cydonia. The Jupitorian plasma weapon which had the destructive force of 1000 Megaton bomb, ripped Cydonia apart.

EXT. CGI. SPACE HYPERSONIC MISSILES LAUNCHED BY THE JUPITORIAN FLEEET AT NUCLEAR WEAPON STORAGE SITE SUBSEQUENT EXPLOSION 30 SECONDS.

Simultaneously another missile launching site on the other side of the planet also received a devastating attack. A lucky shot hit a Martian nuclear weapon storage site and the plasma weapon creating temperatures equivalent to the sun, caused the entire nuclear magazine to cook off simultaneously creating a horrific explosion ripping away the atmosphere.

In doing so, the Jupitorians extinguished life on Mars. There were no survivors after the atmosphere got removed from the most unusual nuclear release of energy from the Martian nuclear weapon stockpile.

CAPTAIN GILBERT
What destroyed Atlantis?

EXT. CGI. SPACE JUPITORIAN FLEET DEPLOYS HYPERSONIC MISSILES THAT FLY DOWN AND ANIHALATE ATLANTIS.

RANDOLPH (a.k.a. PONARIAN – PO)
Earth was then surveyed by the Jupitorians who discovered there was only one major provincial center, Atlantis. With a heavy heart the task force commander ordered Atlantis destroyed. All intelligent life within the solar system thus perished, or so it was thought.

The Jupitorian fleet took the secret of their handy work back home, and for nearly nine hundred thousand years never ventured back or explored this solar system since it was quite a distance away and thus had no economic reason for visits.

CAPTAIN GILBERT
You mentioned the Jupitorians did a survey of Earth in 1917, can you please tell us about that?

RANDOLPH (a.k.a. PONARIAN – PO)
Unexpectedly, radio waves that originated from Earth arrived. It took a while but eventually the Jupitorians were aghast when they discovered the source was from one of the planets they had destroyed long ago.

<u>EXT. CGI. SPACE JUPITORIAN FLEET ARRIVE TO EARTH.</u>

RANDOLPH (a.k.a. PONARIAN – PO)
By the time the Jupitorian survey party reached Earth in 1917, the planet was embroiled in bitter violence. In a very short period, the Jupitorians determined this was the remnants of the Atlantis civilization but were technologically inferior and had no space capability and were viewed as terribly inferior.

Experts brought along in the survey party observing transportation modes and the lack of radars and primitive communicators gave it a technological rating around one point zero on a scale of one hundred.

These experts further advised the Jupitorian Task Force Commander, it would take this civilization thousands of years to develop transportation and weapons that could be of any threat to the Jupitorians. Based on that evaluation, the Jupitorian Task Force departed.

<u>EXT. CGI. SPACE JUPITORIAN FLEET DEPARTS EARTH</u>

RANDOLPH (a.k.a. PONARIAN – PO)
Earth remained unscathed to the Jupitorians and were left to their own demise in the brutal world war that was ongoing that could end up wiping out civilization.

CAPTAIN GILBERT
How did you encounter the Jupitorians?

RANDOLPH (a.k.a. PONARIAN – PO)
Thirty years after the Jupitorians left Earth, my spacecraft I traveled in from the Ponarian world in the Andromeda Galaxy as you call, it arrived in Jupitorian space and was quickly vectored to the planet's surface for interrogation and determination and disposition.

CAPTAIN GILBERT
How was your welcome by the Jupitorians?

The Jupitorians would probably have executed me had I not impressed them with the explanation I traveled from the Andromeda galaxy.

I convinced my Jupitorian inquisitors I was merely exploring the galaxy and was the first of my kind to ever travel the far expanse between the two galaxies.

The Jupitorians of course were interested in my spacecraft's technology and were soon disappointed to learn I didn't know much about the inner workings of the U115 reactor nor the antigravity machine fundamentals.

Eventually they allowed me to leave, and I eventually accidentally passed towards your Earth's solar system totally lost from view of the Jupitorians who probably regretted allowing me to leave the minute I was gone and out of site. Once I got behind the large dust clouds, they had no way of tracking the direction I went.

CAPTAIN GILBERT
What did you think about Earth back then?

<u>EXT. CGI. DAY PONARIAN SHIP CRASH LANDS AT ROSWELL, NEW MEXICO.</u>

RANDOLPH (a.k.a. PONARIAN – PO)
Earth was still primitive in 1947. As my research ship entered the atmosphere the point, I became marooned on the planet. With the intention of finding a potable

water source, radio and radar signals were discovered and I flew to the source and coincidently traveled near Roswell, New Mexico.

A combination of the thunderstorm I temporarily flew through and the radars from Roswell Air Force Base disorientated my craft's navigation system. That lead me to a hard landing and severe damage to the craft, to the point I was marooned on the planet.

CAPTAIN GILBERT
I think this is a good break point. We'll try to work in some additional training in the future. Thanks for your participation and enlightenment.

RANDOLPH (a.k.a. PONARIAN – PO)
You are welcome.

Department head training then secured with everyone now truly indoctrinated how this all unfolded which helped them make better decisions in the future.

As the CSS Alabama slowly approached the Jupitorian Empire, this part of the galaxy was once again embroiled in galactic warfare that would soon determine the outcome of the Jupitorians, or the demise of their foes.

Luck was on Admiral Gilbert's side as the Jupitorian Space Fleet was at the time far away deployed in space battles and was out of position to take on any unexpected visitors to their planet. Born out of their arrogance, the Jupitorians didn't believe any of their traditional enemies had the nerve to approach their planet and thus were not expecting anything like the CSS Alabama arrival.

<u>EXT. CGI. SPACE CSS ALABAMA MIDCOUSE CORRECTION BURN 15 SECONDS. THE RESULTING BLUE PLUME WAS INTENSELY BRIGHT FOR A FEW MINUTES.</u>

The Jupitorians would never have any idea CSS Alabama was arriving except for the mid-course burn for the CSS Alabama to change its heading towards the Jupitorian solar system.

<u>INT. DAY JUPITORIAN ASTROPHYSICISTS LOOKING THROUGH TELESCOPES.</u>

A Jupitorian astrophysicist happened to coincidently be looking in the direction of where the CSS Alabama resided at that moment.

JUPITORIAN SCIENTIST #1
I've detected the blue flare probably from rocket engines at a great distance.

JUPITORIAN SCIENTIST #2
The ship was too far away to identify or analyze.

JUPITORIAN SCIENTIST #1
It appeared those blue flares on were shooting out above the speed of light for a few minutes based on modulation and Doppler effects.

EXT. CGI. SPACE CSS ALABAMA MIDCOUSE CORRECTION BURN 15 SECONDS. THE RESULTING BLUE PLUME DISSIPATING AND FADING.

During CSS Alabama's burn to change course created an eerie blue plume that eventually stretched a million miles long and slowly dissipated.

JUPITORIAN SCIENTIST #2
Jupitorian Astrophysicists usually attribute blue plumes are advanced civilization space propulsion systems.

The CSS Alabama was too far away to determine course and speed. As soon as the maneuver was complete and the rocket engines shut down, all visibility slowly ended. No measures could be taken because there was no rhyme or reason as far as the Jupitorians were concerned.

JUPITORIAN SCIENTIST #2
Most likely it was a wayward traveler just passing by.

Even though the Jupitorians could not see the CSS Alabama at this time, it was alerted something was out there, so naturally surveillance of the area was maintained for quite some time. After almost eight months of not detecting any further indications of a craft or propulsion the Jupitorian focus shifted elsewhere especially since they were now embroiled in a tough intergalactic strife.

Had the CSS Alabama started its deceleration just a few weeks earlier before the Jupitorian fleet departed to the war zone, they would have kept back several ships to deal with the Earth People. But with no great threats anywhere near and the fact they could recall ships, if necessary, the planet was left more or less ill-protected.

After one year and eleven months Shelly Brown and the NASA scientists were grateful their ordeal was half over. The Two NASA scientists quickly swung into scientific research mode since they were stuck on board anyway.

After Tom Gilbert explained the government had a secret program that would look after their families including making sure their wives got all their overtime money prorated at sixteen hours per day seven days a week, at least they would be flushed with cash. Their personal economic situation improved by taking this long trip. The downside was they could not be home to help their families in any exigency.

Just days before Tom Gilbert ordered the deceleration, he met personally with each watch section in the crew's lounge as they rotated through. This was considered GMT, General Military Training.

The cat was now out of the bag. Tom knew there was no point in withholding the truth from the crew any longer, plus they needed to know what they were up against.

<u>INT. SPACE. CSS ALABAMA'S CREWS MESS HALL/LOUNGE</u>

> CAPTAIN GILBERT
> Alabama space travelers, thank you all for being here
> at this briefing. Let's get right down to the point. This
> will be considered a question and answering session
> after I put out a few pieces of information.

Tom looked around the room. Watch-section three had no doubt heard rumors and conversations of the GMT that Sections One and Two already attended.

> CAPTAIN GILBERT
> I know this has been a very long trip for all of you
> and this really is a milestone in the advancement of
> mankind by proving we can travel to the stars and
> beyond. You are all part of a history making voyage
> that is unprecedented in human affairs. I know I've
> asked a lot of you up until now, but we are about at the
> midpoint of this voyage. Depending on how we'll be
> received could mean we can rotate personnel down on
> a planet for some R&R.

Captain Gilbert looked around the room and could see the intensity in the stares of every single individual.

> CAPTAIN GILBERT
> You all probably have heard a lot of rumors by now. I
> wish I could say it wasn't true, but a lot of it is.

Tom noticed sitting at one of the tables was Shelly Brown. In almost two years of space flight, she had changed. She looked a lot rougher now. It doesn't take long before women in space stop using all cosmetics and say, *"The hell with it."*

Shelly had put on a few more pounds, her face had puffed out slightly, but once she got back to normal gravity and worked out regularly and put on her cosmetics, she no doubt would be that admirable female aide the Senator was so proud of.

The Ponarian was sitting next to Shelly Brown. He was all upbeat. His expectancy was that his journey was almost half over and as soon as he got back to the Jupitorians, they would be able to communicate to his planet to send a rescue ship. He did not want to die on Earth, and he certainly did not want to die on the Jupitorian planet.

Tom had informed the Ponarian that he now had to level with the crew and admit the Ponarian was an alien. The Ponarian didn't care because *he would be off the ship in less than a month and never see these people ever again.*

CAPTAIN GILBERT

Okay, everyone, we are now going to make a full disclosure to you as I think you need this information so that you will be prepared to respond to exigencies that may arise over the next month as we get closer to the Jupitorian Planet we intend to arrive at.

The watch section was now fully attentive hanging on every word Tom Gilbert stated.

CAPTAIN GILBERT

First and foremost, Randolph, please stand up.

The Ponarian stood like he had during the two previous sessions. Shelly Brown was busy writing notes which Tom Gilbert later thought he might eventually have to *censor and confiscate.*

CAPTAIN GILBERT

Randolph, whom you have all got to know pretty good over the past, almost two years, is an alien.

The crew had spread the rumors right after the first watch section received their briefing. The Pomeranian suddenly discovered everyone in the room was looking at him very strangely. That knowledge changed their relationships immediately. Instead of the warm jovial atmosphere it was now somewhat strained, seemingly disenfranchised on many levels.

CAPTAIN GILBERT

Randolph comes from a planet in the Andromeda Galaxy and has been in America for seventy-one years, mostly living at Area 51. Randolph, would you like to make any statements?

RANDOLPH
Thank you, Tom, for giving me this opportunity to speak to your crew. I will be leaving you in about a month. We expect to contact an alien race I once visited named the Jupitorians, not to be confused with your solar system planet Jupiter.

CREW MEMBER
What are the Jupitorians like?

RANDOLPH
Thanks for asking that question. Jupitorians are far more advanced than Earth. Though they have been in your neck of the woods before, last visiting in 1917, it seems they lost interest in planet Earth and have not been back since.

SECOND CREW MEMBER
Can you tell us why we are going to this planet.

RANDOLPH
Because I come from a much more advanced society, I had knowledge of secrets your government wanted. I traded those secrets for this trip to the Ponarian Empire.

CREW MEMBER
Why do you want to go to the Ponarian Empire?

RANDOLPH
When I visited the Jupitorians almost seventy-five years ago, they were kind to me, unlike the way I was first treated on your planet where I was tortured for several years.

Randolph looking around the room could see a lot of inquisitiveness.

RANDOLPH
When I was on the Jupitorian planet, I left behind a special communications system I hope to be able to communicate with the Jupitorians or they could contact my home planet, Ponar, to send a rescue ship to take me home. I do not wish to die on Earth or the Jupitorian planet.

FIRST CREW MEMBER
Will you report to the Jupitorians that we mistreated you?

RANDOLPH
That's a great question and thank you for asking it. At this point in time, I look differently at a lot of things.

Of course, I'm angry with your past leaders who had me tortured back in the 1940s and 1950s, but I understand why they did that because of your cold war with the Soviets.

Eventually new leaders came into power and new policies, and I was treated far better.

A few years ago, the Air Force sent out a new General to Area 51 and placed in charge of security, General John Harris. General Harris met with me and after numerous discussions General Harris did his utmost to improve my living standards.

After General Harris' arrival, my living conditions were quite extraordinary, and in fact better than what I was accustomed to at my home planet. I developed a very respectful friendship with General Harris who took a great risk allowing me to see a lot of the world.

CREW MEMBER
How did he do that?

RANDOLPH
Since I'm now gone from Earth forever it probably doesn't matter what I now divulge about General Harris and me and I doubt the General cares either. Overseeing security at Area-51, General Harris was able to move me around with phony orders. His superiors never caught on.

CREW MEMBER
Where did he take you?

RANDOLPH
The easy trips were down to Las Vegas. He took me to

shows up and down the strip. I was quite mesmerized by what I discovered in Las Vegas to be honest. What I remember the most was the exquisite food and the concerts with sounds that were far better than anything I heard on my own planet.

CREW MEMBER
What did General Harris taking you places do to help out Area 51?

RANDOLPH
Prior to my relationship with General Harris, I had a lot of knowledge I never divulged. I was bitter about being tortured and mistreated. I knew a lot of things that could help your world. As General Harris told me later, he knew he could attract more bees with honey than with vinegar.

CREW MEMBER
Where else did General Harris take you?

RANDOLPH
One trip was to Alaska to Kodiak Island. He wanted me to see the large brown bears with two-foot-wide heads. I was astonished. In doing so he also showed me some of the most beautiful landscapes.

CREW MEMBER
Did he show you any other cities?

RANDOLPH
Yes, on one occasion he snuck me out of Area 51 and took me to Washington, D.C., and then to New York City during that same trip.

CREW MEMBER
How was New York City compared to your planet?

RANDOLPH
My planet Ponar has a higher population density. Space is a bigger premium. We can't afford to destroy farms to make room for more housing or our population would starve, so we build taller buildings and preserve

the farmland. Our buildings are typically twice as tall as your buildings in New York City.

CREW MEMBER
What is your transportation like compared to ours?

RANDOLPH
Our trains go faster, our aircraft go much faster, we don't have personal cars per say, but we can get around quicker as our cities are integrated with a transportation plan. Shopping and work are designed to where you can walk and do not require transportation.

CAPTAIN GILBERT
Thank you, Randolph. You may please be seated, as I now need to discuss the main purpose of this GMT.

RANDOLPH
Thank you, Admiral Gilbert for allowing me to address your crew.

CAPTAIN GILBERT
Shipmates, we do not know if there will be a friendly reception. If not, we will have to fight our way out of here and hopefully will survive. In the event we have to leave under such circumstances we may have to fly sorties with our TR-3Bs to give a chance to get away alive. That's why all the TR-3Bs are being armed.

Now the crew looked mildly depressed as the captain pressed on.

CAPTAIN GILBERT
It's my genuine desire to get everyone home alive. I will first attempt to arrange to transport Randolph to the Jupitorians before we leave.

CREW MEMBER
Can't we just put him on a TR-3B and send it to the planet?"

CAPTAIN GILBERT
We must first find out to what extent they will cooperate with us before we proceed."

CREW MEMBER
After we drop off Randolph will we quickly head for home or are we going to waste time on a social visit.

CAPTAIN GILBERT
Just as much as the rest of you, I want to return to Earth. As soon as we hand Randolph over to the Jupitorians, it's my intention to immediately return to Earth. But we also must be aware, we are also acting as diplomats. Should the Jupitorians insist we make a social call, I would be compelled to spend a little time there in hopes of establishing a beneficial relationship with Earth.

CREW MEMBER
Captain, back on Earth, people are criticized for claiming aliens exist. How many alien worlds do we know of, and will you disclose this mission to the public when we return?

Shelly Brown quickly snuck in before Tom Gilbert had a chance to respond.

SHELLY BROWN
I like that question.

Tom thought about it for a moment and then offered an insight into medical concerns the crew wasn't ready to hear.

CAPTAIN GILBERT
As most of you probably understand, if we come into physical contact with aliens, we'll have to go through a period of medical isolation back on Earth and undergo tests to ensure we pose no biological threat to the world.

The body language of watch section three personnel suddenly appeared negative. Tom was glad that question didn't come up during the two previous watch section GMTs.

SHELLY BROWN
How long will the crew be in isolation?

CAPTAIN GILBERT
First of all, we can avoid isolation by not coming in physical contact with alien atmosphere or any aliens.

CREW MEMBER
What about Randolph, he's here already?

CAPTAIN GILBERT
Randolph was haphazardly medically cleared sixty-five years ago and had been routinely monitored since.

SHELLY BROWN
What about me?

CAPTAIN GILBERT
Medical Isolation pertains to everyone who is aboard this ship now.

SHELLY BROWN
Do we have plans to bring any aliens back with us?

CAPTAIN GILBERT
I have strict orders not to bring back any aliens.

SHELLY BROWN
Under any circumstances?

CAPTAIN GILBERT
That's correct.

Shelly, not having received an adequate answer to her question.

SHELLY BROWN
Admiral Gilbert, you never really answered my question. What is the required medical isolation period?

CAPTAIN GILBERT
It's more of a quarantine in my opinion. But I think they should be able to finish all biological tests within a six-month period.

CREW MEMBER
Where will medical isolation be conducted?

CAPTAIN GILBERT
If we trigger the quarantine by alien exposure, we

have developed a special TR-3B transport with a bio-capsule. It will fly us in sections to a facility in Arizona in groups.

SHELLY BROWN
Will there be any provisions for visitors?

CAPTAIN GILBERT
This facility has glass viewing areas with speakers and microphones. You will be able to look at your relatives through the glass window and communicate with them. Also, you will have the standard USSF email system, which you all should know is censored to ensure you do not accidentally release classified information.

SHELLY BROWN
How would we know anything on this mission is classified?

CAPTAIN GILBERT
As you all know by now the two-million-mile law gave me broad powers. Once something is classified it must be declassified by officials before it can be treated as unclassified. Furthermore, if it's compartmentalized and part of the SAP program, then only people cleared can access that information. You must in addition have a clearance, but for compartmentalized information you must be cleared for that specific information, and no compartmentalized information is ever allowed to be declassified until the originator initiates declassification and any sensitive information properly redacted.

SHELLY BROWN
What about things such as my personal notes?

CAPTAIN GILBERT
After we passed the two-million-mile mark, I compartmentalized all the information derived on this mission and classified it. That means anything that occurred on this mission is classified and compartmentalized and you need SAP privileges to transfer any information off the Alabama.

SHELLY BROWN
That's extremely unfair. What about the NASA researchers? They have accumulated an incredible amount of information on solar systems we have passed and soon to discover.

CAPTAIN GILBERT
NASA has an arbitrator who is cleared for the program. If I deny any requests for information dissemination, the arbitrator will be present at the meeting if he wants to grant them permission to transmit the information.

Shelly's ears perked up a bit.

SHELLY BROWN
Where will the meeting occur?

CAPTAIN GILBERT
The only place possible.

SHELLY BROWN
And where is that?

CAPTAIN GILBERT
The arbiter will have to be willing to go into quarantine with us if the scientists want the information immediately released.

SHELLY BROWN
Is there an arbitrator who is willing to live under such quarantine to release the information?

CAPTAIN GILBERT
No, not likely.

SHELLY BROWN
What you are really saying is there probably is no possibility for them to get their research information off the Alabama.

CAPTAIN GILBERT
Most likely not for a long while.

SHELLY BROWN
Don't you think that's unfair?

CAPTAIN GILBERT
There are bigger issues at play than a scientist seeking
his rewards for finding new science.

SHELLY BROWN
That's ridiculous, what issues could possibly force us
to hide all these scientific research materials our two
NASA scientists have created?"

CAPTAIN GILBERT
You are not cleared, for access to that information.

Shelly Brown was the consummate politician. She knew how to slice through red tape and when the time *came, she would apply her talents and Admiral Tom Gilbert would have less control over events than he thought.*

It was unpleasant for crew members to think that they had another two years stuck on board, but when they got back to Earth, they would be stuck in confinement for another six months probably. What if it was longer?

The days passed swiftly as they approached the Jupitorian planets. Shelly Brown, realizing this would be an incredible opportunity for her, especially if they met the aliens, started being more conscious of her appearance. She started working out in the exercise room since they had cleared the food out of there during the previous year. The whole ship now was opening as they were walking on stores less and less every day.

Randolph had grown attracted to Shelly Brown and during the many hours they spent together playing card games and other forms of entertainment, he decided that before he left the Humans for good, he would ask Shelly to go with him and eventually back to his world. Even though he was considerably older than Shelly, he would still out live her. Would she really accept the invitation?

ARRIVAL TO JUPITORIAN WORLDS

Finally, the day came when they would have to decelerate. Just prior to starting the evolution, Tom gathered all the officers in the wardroom to discuss what he perceived as the probable consequence.

CAPTAIN GILBERT
As you all know, in a short while when we initiate

deceleration, we'll light up this area of space just like a miniature sun. Our presence, if undetected up until now, will no longer be hidden. We have no idea what our reception will be like.

WEPS
If that's the case, my self-defense technicians need to be at their consoles ready for action.

CAPTAIN GILBERT
Weps, your division will have to be position for deceleration with seatbelts engaged and not be able to move about the ship. In the event we have a hostile reception, I want the first two flights of TR-3Bs manned and ready to launch immediately upon my orders.

XO RILEY
Sir, I would like to remind you that will have to secure the deceleration during the TR-3B launch sequence.

CAPTAIN GILBERT
XO, yes, I understand.

XO RILEY
The TR-3Bs will be traveling at excessive velocities when launched but the forward vortex created by the decelerator's could damage a TR-3B.

CAPTAIN GILBERT
Yes, but with their anti-gravity machines, they should be able to maneuver as required. Also approaching enemy ships at exceptional velocities will help them survive as they will be harder targets to track and attack.

XO RILEY
Is there any reason we can't secure deceleration during TR-3B launches?

CAPTAIN GILBERT
There is no reason why we can't secure the decelerators if we need to. It might be best to secure the decelerator's during TR-3B launches to get a better assessment Jupitorian dispositions.

XO RILEY
I fully concur.

One group of TR-3Bs not discussed sitting at the ready was the deadly witches brew of super weapons they would inflict upon the Jupitorians the same way Jupitorians handled the Martians and Atlantis nine hundred thousand years ago.

Tom Gilbert hoped it didn't come to that.

But Admiral Gilbert was ready to carry out his orders which were based on INTEL gathered by a growing amount of evidence what these arrogant monsters had done and may do again.

This was Earths first and final chance to mitigate a future attack for generations to come. Whether or not those super weapons would be used depended upon their reception. If it were hostile, that meant the Jupitorians remained a threat to Earth's future survival, and if they decided to do another survey and determined our civilization needed wiped out again, we would end up like the Martians on a dead planet.

Tom wasn't trigger happy, but John Harris and the President knew if he had to fight his way home, just like when he took out drug running submarines, he would also eliminate a planet that sent out fleets to destroy civilizations like the Martians and Atlantis.

Azzie, Batman, and Instigator would be in their TR-3Bs all checked out and loaded with special ordinance. They would not be launched right away but Tom wanted all systems checked out and ready to launch in the event he had to do the inevitable.

<u>INT. CGI. SPACE CSS ALABAMA WARDROOM.</u>

CGI FOR THE BRIEFING MAP.

The navigator then gave the ops brief.

NAVIGATOR
This computerized map of the surrounding space, the current ship's position and track, and the solar system we now approach. The blue curved line shows our track to the Jupitorian Empire Planet where their capital city Proximas Dyafalious exits.

The Jupitorian planets are now identifiable with our photonics and at our present velocity we should soon arrive at the main Jupitorian Empire Planet where the seats of government exist at Proximas Dyafalious shown with the blinking blue dot on the computerized map. According to INTEL, Proximas Dyafalious is the most powerful society anywhere near this area of the galaxy.

Since the Milky Way was huge and vast, none of the Jupitorians or Earth people knew of only ten percent of the Galaxy. Some solar systems were simply too far away to even consider transiting to them. Earth itself was almost existential at such a distance from Jupitorians, which seemed confusing as to why they would even be interested.

WEPS
Any fear of past animosity to enter in our reception?

NAVIGATOR
Nine hundred thousand years was a long time. One would think that in such a long passage of time, whatever caused the conflict between the Martians and the Jupitorians should be long past. Since technically the Martians no longer existed, our reception should be far different, one would hope.

INT. SPACE CSS ALABAMA CONTROL ROOM

After securing the meeting, Captain Gilbert and XO Riley went to the control room where they would oversee operations.

Tom Gilbert picked up the microphone to the 1MC and made the announcement:

CAPTAIN GILBERT
We shall begin deceleration in a few minutes. Everyone please latch yourselves in with safety harness and seatbelts. Also standby for combat and launch of two air squadrons if required.

After several minutes, Admiral Gilbert gave the order to the Chief of the watch.

CAPTAIN GILBERT
Chief of the Watch, commence deceleration.

CHIEF OF THE WATCH
Commence deceleration Captain, Chief of the Watch, aye.

The Chief of the Watch then made the ship wide announcement.

CHIEF OF THE WATCH
The ship will commence deceleration.

The pilot and copilot were now manning the bridge full time until they completed their business here and departed for home.

The Navigator was also in the control room on the navigation console and responded.

NAVIGATOR
Initiating deceleration.

EXT. CGI. SPACE SIDE VIEW OF CSS ALABAMA DEPLOYING ITS REVERSE THRUSTERS SHOOTING OUT A SPARKLING AND MODULATING BLUE PLUME.

The Navigator was controlling the reversers (decelerators) to ensure the CSS Alabama continued their flight plan track. The pilot and copilot were standing by to do combat maneuvers prompted by artificial intelligence. The pilot and co-pilot controls in many ways were like the Virginia and follow on San Diego Class Nuclear Submarine that could either use joy sticks or type in three-dimensional heading commands into *steering and flying*.

The Navigator slowly ramped up the reversers to keep a stable heading matching the intended heading. Soon the two small rocket engines were throwing out a strong blast forward of the ship initially traveling several times the speed of light.

The CSS Alabama's crew felt the instantaneous drag put on the ship that grew in intensity, they were familiar with back during the space trials two years prior. This slowing lit up the area better than a comet.

INT. GCI. SPACE JUPITORIAN OBSERVATORY IMAGES OF CSS ALABAMA AND SCIENTISTS CONFERING.

The CSS Alabama reverser plume was immediately detected by Jupitorian astrophysicists. Soon after Jupitorian scientists reported this to their leaders, military leaders were dismayed they had just sent their fleet to an intergalactic squabble and were out of position to be of help.

The Jupitorians employed a Coast, Air, and Space Guard (CASG) as a planetary defense to prevent surprise attacks. The three-dimensional CASG force acted like the Earth Coast guard to interdict smugglers and rescue people who suddenly had bad luck or poor planning.

The Jupitorian CASG was practically the only major force left to protect the planet because the arrogant Jupitorians didn't think any other planet or civilization had the nerve to attack them because the retribution would be quite devastating.

When the Jupitorians deployed their fleet to the War Zone that would take almost a month to get them back, the last thing in the world they would have believed was a lonely craft from the Martian solar system would show up on their door step any time soon.

When the CSS Alabama started decelerating using its two forward thrusters shooting those dual above light speed pencil like jets canted at a 30-degree angle to avoid hull damage, Jupitorian scientists immediately observed this phenomenon which was outside their solar system but appearing to come closer at a remarkable speed.

At the time of engaging the deceleration, CSS Alabama's Cosmic Interpolator read out indicated they had managed to achieve double the speed of light. The forward-facing thrusters used for deceleration putting out jets traveling above light speed slowly changed the relative velocity.

The modal distortion of the deceleration jets surpassing perhaps four or five times the speed of light magnified the strange effects to an observer on the Jupitorian planet. No Jupitorian had ever seen such an optical illusion before.

In some sense this image appeared frightening because the jets extended out millions of miles after just a few moments slowing the craft and as the craft slowed down, it stretched and diffused creating a highly ionized cloud that also gave off a rather strange radar reflection when the early warning beams returned four hours later.

<u>EXT. CGI. SPACE JUPITORIAN CASG SHIPS LAUNCH TO GO INVESTIGATE THIS ANOMALY. 30 SECONDS, MULTIPLE SHIPS.</u>

Jupitorian CASG (Coast, Air, and Space Guard) ships were sent out to investigate. The whole planet was suddenly ablaze in communications and since the CSS Alabama was approaching the dark side of the planet, Jupitorians, who had the advantage of the night sky, didn't require a telescope to see the very bright object that appeared to be splitting in two and coming right at them.

JUPITORIAN MILITARY LEADERS
Is this a planetary invasion force?

CHIEF JUPITORIAN SCIENTIST.
That is the question of the hour.

Hours of consternation followed as the CSS Alabama was far enough out of the solar system that CASG ships would not make contact any time soon. Fear crept into the minds of many Jupitorians the galaxy viewed as the major menace to nearby space. Jupitorians feared no other races or planets. But the object now in the heavens suddenly gave them reason for pause, especially if this was a former enemy coming back to exact some revenge.

The ruthless Ponarian Leader with the title *Grand Constabulary* was duly informed and now started asking questions.

GRAND CONSTABULARY
Did they suck our fleet into the war zone as a trap so they could come in unmolested and destroy our planet?

GRAND CONSTABULARY'S TOP AID
It's impossible to know. We have no idea what this thing is.

GRAND CONSTABULARY
We need to recall the fleet now.

GRAND CONSTABULARY'S TOP AID
But sir, it will take thirty days for them to return and if we have a sudden departure, it might give our enemies a brash idea that we are faltering and give them psychological momentum.

GRAND CONSTABULARY
What forces can we bring back immediately?

GRAND CONSTABULARY'S TOP AID
We can't pull out the entire fleet, but we could pull back say half the fleet. They might think we are maneuvering for attack and would thus go into a defensive position expecting it.

GRAND CONSTABULARY
All right, send orders to the fleet to send back half the ships to defend this planet from an unknown possible threat that is now approaching the edge of the solar system.

GRAND CONSTABULARY'S TOP AID
It will take several days for the message to reach them. Whatever this thing is will be here before we can even contact the fleet!

As the deceleration continued, the crew of course grew uncomfortable. Tom Gilbert had decided he would sequence the deceleration and stop the reversers for two hours out of each six our period so that people could take a cat nap and do various things to regain their composure.

After four hours the first break came, and the reversers were shut down. The vibration and the pressure which resembled forward gravity ended. Some people took the time to do those functions they knew would become painful if they waited another four hours after the resumption of deceleration.

Bathrooms had lines, the crew's lounge was crowded as people came in to get snacks the ships cooks had prepared and stored in special wrappers in a chill box, they could quickly put in a microwave and heat up and eat.

People were also reminded not to consume too many liquids. Half the crew avoided snacks and liquids. Even though the ship had decelerated quite a bit, it was still traveling above light speed and CSS Alabama's resulting image was full of modal distortion. The best telescopes in the Jupitorian worlds had enough magnification they could see a blurred image that appeared to be resonating.

The best description of the image the Jupitorians observed was a ball of something was shooting out two huge jets that gave off the strangest physical appearance and nothing like the Jupitorians had ever witnessed before. Then suddenly, the jets stopped.

At CSS Alabama's range to Jupitorian planets it was too difficult to track without the bright jets emanating out of the craft. But whatever the weak object was, pulsating was observed with the upmost interest by Jupitorian scientific community as well as the CASG (Coast, Air, Space Guard) approaching them at just a fraction of CSS Alabama's speed.

Some of the Alabama crew that chose to take a nap in lieu of a snack or drink merely left themselves in their safety harness strapped in. That worked out well because a two-hour cat nap is rather refreshing. The Navigator was one of those who chose to catch up on sleep instead of partaking in snacks, drinks, and toilets. He remained in the control room in his safety harness ready to receive the CO's orders to recommend continued deceleration.

The CSS Alabama was still outside Jupitorian's solar system traveling above light speed and getting closer at a good rate. The next deceleration cycle would bleed off a lot of speed and their closure rate would decline noticeably.

Captain Gilbert gave everyone a five-minute notice to regain their safety harness and be prepared when the process started all over again. Captain Gilbert remained in the control room.

There were a few unused seats in the control room that were only occupied during battle stations while conducting flight operations and engaging in weapons deployment. Shelly Brown suddenly appeared in the control room which surprised Captain Gilbert.

Shelly Brown looked somewhat whimsical for an adult who by now would normally be sick and tired of space especially since she and the two NASA scientists had more or less been Shanghaied in space for two years already.

SHELLY BROWN
Would it be possible for me to sit on one of the unused
chairs during the next deceleration?

CAPTAIN GILBERT
I do not see why not.

Captain Gilbert pointed to one that was unused though he would have full visual of Shelly the way seats were orientated, giving him an excellent view of the main Bridge components for periods of exigencies enabling him to observe participants actions and more effectively communicate.

Shelly took the seat Tom indicated, then proceeded to strap on her safety harness. The safety harness was designed to be comfortable but hold their body in place even in high G turns or radical maneuvers to provide safety.

Captain Gilbert grabbed the 1MC microphone and held down the push to talk button and began talking.

CAPTAIN GILBERT
Give me your attention, please, this is the captain.

Captain Gilbert waited a few seconds to allow everyone to focus on his statements then continued.

CAPTAIN GILBERT
We will commence the next deceleration in five
minutes. I want everyone to know we are getting closer
to the planet we'll be visiting. We expect a welcoming
party soon and do not know if they have peaceful
intentions. We need to be prepared to shift to battle
stations and launch the Air Wing if necessary. Stay
focused and be ready to carry out orders immediately.
If there are any delays in carrying out orders it could
prove to become highly dangerous. Carry on.

Captain Gilbert clicked the microphone into its holder then checked his own safety harness and knew he was ready to feel the kick in the pants when the reversers lit off again shoving out their tremendous jets that would quickly a few million miles. Five minutes later, just as he promised, the deceleration started again and would last four hours. There wasn't much to do but watch the indicators and the displays.

Tom Gilbert was quite taken back by the stares he observed from Shelly Brown. He also noticed in the past two weeks she had started working on her glamor again and even though she wasn't applying significant amounts of cosmetics because she had enough natural beauty that didn't require a lot, her workouts and new regiment on dieting was now having a noticeable effect. She was almost back to the prim and sassy woman who had come aboard two years prior. Tom would love to know what was going on inside Shelly's head.

Shelly Brown likewise wanted to know how Tom Gilbert felt about a lot of things. Even though Shelly was saving herself for her future mate, and someone she would have a family with, she did have some slight interest in Tom Gilbert. But she felt he would never take interest in her when he could easily have a woman like Weps and some of the other pretty ladies aboard that would fit much easier into his world. Tom Gilbert, the consummate bachelor never exposed his agenda. And until now, no lady had been successful in snagging him.

Tom was quickly approaching that mental cutoff date where a man might choose to stay single forever. If he didn't get married soon and have children, he knew he never would. He also knew for a fact, upon return to Earth he would be relieved of Command of CSS Alabama, and a younger man put in his place because the Space Force would not allow one officer to hog such a lofty assignment. Others wanted their shot at command as well as a shot at command in space.

As Tom gazed upon Shelly Brown, he could not help but to feel some strange inward tensions. Being out of the sun for two years resulted in Shelly losing a lot of color in her skin, and at the present time, she would easily pass for a Polynesian or a person not of color. The metamorphism seemed rather interesting to Tom. Shelly was a borderline genius, but she was also a master politician. She was one of those politicians up on her game every day. She never let her guard down either.

Shelly Brown observing Tom Gilbert started her thinking about Randolph being kind of sassy the previous few days. He started in on Shelly Brown and his primordial feelings for her intensified the closer they got to the Jupitorian planet. Eventually Randolph proposed Shelly Brown leave CSS Alabama with him and go to the Jupitorian planet and when the Ponarians sent out a rescue ship they would go to Ponar together and live together forever.

Shelly thought about the proposal for a while but being the sophisticated brilliant thinker, started putting a few facts together she would weigh her decision.

SHELLY BROWN
How long would we be on the Jupitorian planet?

RANDOLPH
Long enough to contact my people on Ponar and for them to send out a rescue ship.

SHELLY BROWN
How long would that take?

RANDOLPH
I can't really say for sure, but I think we would be heading to Ponar within ten years.

SHELLY BROWN
What are the Jupitorians like? Do they have anyone of color?

RANDOLPH
No, they are a homogenous society. The best I could explain them is they almost appear to be Chinese.

SHELLY BROWN
What is Ponar like?

RANDOLPH
It's been eighty years since I left Ponar the last time. When I left Ponar, it was far more advanced than Earth is now. We have intergalactic transportation and I'm here because we figured out how to efficiently get across the empty space between our galaxies in the most efficient manner.

SHELLY BROWN
How do you do that?

RANDOLPH
It has to do with the spaceship design. As part of my release from Earth, I gave the information about the technology that allows such long-distance transit to John Harris, just before I left. Earth will have this technology probably within one hundred years is my guess.

SHELLY BROWN
What do people on Ponar appear like?

RANDOLPH
Mostly like me.

SHELLY BROWN
No people of color?

RANDOLPH
None.

SHELLY BROWN
How long will it take to go from the Jupitorian planet
to Ponar?"

RANDOLPH
Six or seven years maximum.

Shelly Brown started thinking, *By the time I reached Ponar I would be pushing fifty years old and no longer be youthful like I am now. By then the luster would have worn off and what are my chances of not being treated well after that?*

Shelly made no promises and as she started pondering the time it took to go between galaxies was the deal breaker. After she got back to Earth, she would never entertain ever going on a spaceship the rest of her life. Then she started wondering, *Would Tom Gilbert ever have any interest in me?*

After a few more deceleration cycles the CSS Alabama finally dipped below light speed and the planets of the solar system slowly grew larger. The Jupitorian CASG (Coast, Air Space Guard) ships drew closer.

<u>EXT. CGI. SPACE. CSS ALABAMA MODAL DISTORTION ENDING DIPPING BELOW LIGHT SPEED 30 SECS</u>

CSS Alabama modal distortion above light speed.

As soon as the Alabama dipped below light speed, the modal distortion ended.

The magnificent optics of Jupitorian surveillance systems quickly determined it was a lone ship now traveling over 100,000 miles per second and quickly converging upon the CASG spaceships.

As the Navigator tweaked the arrival times near planet and recalculated speed requirements, they no longer did four-hour decelerations, but they did decelerate to get the velocity down. They had not yet detected the dozen oncoming CASG ships that was still a good distance away, but it was more comfortable coming in at a slower speed and after Tom Gilbert's long hard assessment of the Cosmic Interpolator decided to slow even more and ordered the Navigator another deceleration.

CAPTAIN GILBERT
I want to do another deceleration and bring ship's velocity down to 25,000 miles per second so we can get a better analysis of this solar system in the event we have to execute an egress plan.

NAVIGATOR
Captain, I'll try to get at that velocity, but it might take two decelerations so that we can get a good analysis of the Cosmic Interpolator to determine speed. Then get a more precise speed on the second deceleration.

CAPTAIN GILBERT
How long will it take you to do the Cosmic Interpolator analysis?

NAVIGATOR
Captain, I think in less than five minutes.

CAPTAIN GILBERT
Alright NAV, do the decelerations, split them in half.
Commence as soon as you are ready, and the Chief of
the Watch makes the announcements.

NAVIGATOR
Understand all, Captain.

CHIEF OF THE WATCH
Captain, ready to make the deceleration announcement.

CAPTAIN GILBERT
Chief of the Watch, make the deceleration
announcement.

After posting the warning to the crew to get back in their safety harness, the ship did two more decelerations and with the Jupitorian CASG (Coast, Air, Space Guard) ships closing, the reversers shooting out those two impressive jets had a significant psychological impact on the CASG crews who still had no idea what they faced or the level of sophistication.

After slowing down to the new ordered speed, the Alabama photonics were hard at work looking over the Jupitorian planets. They were now finally close enough to see light on the dark side of the planet which ostensibly was caused by city lighting during the dark periods.

Unlike Earth, where the night lighting illuminated portions of the dark side of the planet, the Jupitorians had apparent expansive density as most of the area was lit up. No doubt this was an impressive society, and Tom realized in the manner of just a few more hours he would see first-hand the level of sophistication these aliens exhibited if they were not simply wiped out unceremoniously.

Many of the crew members were off watch. The photonics piped the video images into the ship's lounge where everyone watched with great interest. Everyone had safety harness and chose to remain and watch events unfold. After several hours they closed the brightest planet rather quickly and performed another deceleration. This time they slowed all the way down to one hundred thousand miles per hour. By the completion of the deceleration, the CASG were almost to converge on them. They were waiting their orders to either destroy the ship or escort it to the planet and force it to land and be boarded.

Tom Gilbert, realizing the distinct possibility they all could be dead in a few hours if the Jupitorians did not give them a friendly welcoming, decided he would now inform

Shelly of his private thoughts she had no idea he possessed. He gave her a rare smile as he began.

TOM GILBERT
Shelly, in case the Jupitorians destroy us today, I just
wanted you to know I've always liked you.

Shelly was struck by the tone and the tenor in Tom's voice. She knew Tom was sincere because they truly were not aware yet of how they would be received. Their arrival could signal their end.

Earth would have no way of knowing whatever happened to them. Tom's revelations to her were quite evocative and in future days, Shelly Brown would explore this more as she pondered her future.

Shelly knew she was probably two years away from reaching home again, seeing her mother and friends. She wondered whether Senator Bosworth would still be a senator in office when she returned. His next election would be just before they returned. She toyed with other ideas for her future when suddenly reality snapped her back to attention.

The ship's ECM and ESM started receiving numerous signals and audio alerts started sounding on the early warning receiver.

Automated trackers started showing photonics and signals intercepts on Interpolated Tracker display that Captain Gilbert now focused on.

COMMUNICATOR OFFICER (COMO)
It appears the Jupitorians are attempting to
communicate with us on UHF and VHF bands.

Tom Gilbert was all prepared for this moment and grabbed the 1MC.

CAPTAIN GILBERT.
Randolph, please report to the control room
immediately.

While Randolph was on his way to the bridge, Tom grabbed the microphone for UHF communications. The system automatically selected a transmit frequency matching the alien communications.

CAPTAIN GILBERT.
Hello, Jupitorians, this is CSS Alabama. We have
come from planet Earth for a visit.

The Jupitorians quickly intercepted the Alabama's transmission and within a minute of receipt, Jupitorian scientists brought in to study this phenomenon were busy scanning communication databases to identify the species and the relevancy.

Within two minutes, the Chief Scientist reported to Jupitorian's CASG.

CHIEF SCIENTIST
These are humanoids from the Scullion Sector.

JUPITORIAN CASG COMMANDER
Do you mean planet Earth?

CHIEF SCIENTIST
Exactly, and we have an automated translator. We can communicate with them.

JUPITORIAN CASG COMMANDER
How can such an inferior race suddenly show up here?

CHIEF SCIENTIST
Apparently, they have developed technology at a much faster rate than we gave them credit for.

The Ponarian Randolph arrived immediately in the control room.

CAPTAIN GILBERT
Randolph, we are in contact with the Jupitorians. Is there anything you wish to say to them? If so, press *PUSH TO TALK BUTTON* on this microphone and begin talking.

Captain Gilbert then handed the microphone to the Ponarian Randolph.

The Ponarian then began talking in his native language explaining who he was and why he came here.

JUPITORIAN CHIEF SCIENTIST
That's another language they are transmitting, let's identify it with our translator database.

The language database artificial intelligence quickly discovered by voice print and notified the chief scientist.

JUPITORIAN LANGUAGE DATABASE
ARTIFICIAL INTELLIGENCE
This is Ponarian Language, do you wish me to translate?

JUPITORIAN CHIEF SCIENTIST
Yes.

Soon the Jupitorians were getting the translations of the Ponarian and hearing what he had to say.

JUPITORIAN CHIEF SCIENTIST
It appears the Earth people have brought the Ponarian here in hopes that he will be able to communicate with his planet to request a rescue ship take him back to his home world.

JUPITORIAN JUNIOR SCIENTIST
Do we still receive Ponarian communications?

JUPITORIAN CHIEF SCIENTIST
We have not received Ponarian communications in fifty years.

JUPITORIAN JUNIOR SCIENTIST
Do they still exist or is it possible they have been wiped out?

JUPITORIAN CHIEF SCIENTIST
The Ponarians had been engaged in biter fighting with the Trouc and the Lar, it's possible they no longer exist.

JUPITORIAN JUNIOR SCIENTIST
The Ponarian is requesting permission to come to the planet, what should we tell him?

JUPITORIAN CHIEF SCIENTIST
Tell him we need to obtain permission to please wait. I will contact the Grand Constabulary and find out how he wants to handle this.

Shelly Brown had her notepad out taking notes as she realized this was one of the most important events in American and World History. She realized one day she would probably write a book about it, so it was necessary to now start recording the events as they appeared in the control room.

Suddenly, the sensors operator reported:

SENSORS OPERATOR

> Admiral, we have a dozen contacts on radar closing at
> high-speed. Interpolated range estimates are twenty-
> five thousand miles.

Tom selected the radar display on his multi-screen repeater that could show the display images for the man machine interface that existed on the bridge, whether it be photonics, radar, navigation, and even engineering status.

XO RILEY
> The interpolated ranges to those Jupitorian ships are
> still a little shaky.

NAVIGATOR
> Those range estimates are geometrically analyzed
> from the group of radar returns that create an amount
> of distortion caused by Doppler components that make
> exact range estimate determination difficult.

XO RILEY
> Those range estimates are usually close to real time
> range but not precise.

CAPTAIN GILBERT
> The ships were still too far away to get good clear
> photonics observation, so we'll have to rely on radar
> for now.

In just a few minutes, the closure rate soon slowed, and photonics started presenting better images.

The answer soon came from the Grand Constabulary to the CASG space warships.

GRAND CONSTABULARY
> Have the Earth Ship land at Proximas Dyafalious.

Soon Tom had no choice but to respond to the CASG via the Jupitorian UHF Radio Frequency.

CAPTAIN GILBERT
> I'm sorry, our ship is not capable of entering the
> atmosphere, we must remain in space. We have a
> shuttle craft to take the Ponarian to the planet.

Upon receipt of the response the Jupitorian leader commented.

GRAND CONSTABULARY
They must be backwards if they can't take their ship into the atmosphere."

JUPITORIAN CASG COMMANDER
It could have been built out in space and designed for only space travel.

GRAND CONSTABULARY
Why would any entity want to do such a stupid thing?

JUPITORIAN CASG COMMANDER
I suppose if you have inferior technology, you will have to do something like that.

GRAND CONSTABULARY
All right, tell the Earth people to launch their shuttle and one of our CASG ships will escort them to Proximas Dyafalious.

CAPTAIN GILBERT.
Who's the designated shuttle pilot on the Watch Bill?

XO RILEY
It's the pilot Clarance Williams, call sign Blaze.

Captain Gilbert picked up the 1MC and pressed the push to talk button.

CAPTAIN GILBERT
Clarence Williams this is the captain, report to me in the control room.

About two minutes later Clarence Williams entered the control room.

CLARENCE WILLIAMS
Reporting as ordered, sir.

CAPTAIN GILBERT
Mr. Williams, you are going to ferry the Ponarian to the planet. I'm sorry but I'm also going to have to impose upon you a few requirements.

CLARENCE WILLIAMS
Yes, sir?

CAPTAIN GILBERT
First of all, you are not allowed to leave your TR-3B under any circumstances. Understand?

CLARENCE WILLIAMS
Yes, sir.

CAPTAIN GILBERT
Put on a bio suit just in case you run into difficulties, we don't want you to get exposed to any possible alien pathogens.

CLARENCE WILLIAMS
Of course, sir.

CAPTAIN GILBERT
Next, I'm sorry but we will have to put a self-destruct with remote trigger on your ship in the event they somehow overtake you and attempt to gain control of your ship. That installation will commence immediately while you get suited up.

CLARENCE WILLIAMS
What about the Ponarian, is he to be suited up?

CAPTAIN GILBERT
It's up to him.

Randolph, who was standing a few feet away, quickly spoke his intentions,

RANDOLPH
Jupitorians are a lot cleaner and carry much fewer germs than humans, I do not need a bio-suit.

CAPTAIN GILBERT
Get ready and report to the shuttle bay area. XO, I want you to accompany them to the shuttle TR-3B and ensure everything is promptly made ready and they get launched within ten minutes.

XO RILEY
On my way, sir.

RANDOLPH
One last thing, sir.

CAPTAIN GILBERT
Yes, Randolph, what is it?

Randolph looked at Shelly Brown.

RANDOLPH
Shelly, you have never given me an answer yet, will
you please go with me to the planet?

Shelly was now feeling completely different about a lot of things. Going to an alien planet and arriving at her new home at the age of fifty didn't feel appealing to her. Tom Gilbert's sudden exposure of his feelings had captivated her. She knew he was sincere, and her instinct told her that once they got back to earth, there would be a distinct possibility, a relationship could form. That was a risk she was willing to take.

Shelly had grown fond of Randolph over the past two years on their way to the Jupitorian planets, but not nearly enough for her to commit to such a drastic change in her life. And whether Tom ever approached her to establish a bona fide relationship in the future or not, she still wanted to see her mother again. That was the deciding factor.

SHELLY BROWN
Randolph, I truly like you more than you will ever
know. But I can't accept what you are offering me.
I have my life back on Earth and my family whom I
want to see again. I'm sorry but I can't go with you.

RANDOLPH
Okay, I understand.

CAPTAIN GILBERT
Randolph, will you please follow Commodore Riley
and Mr. Williams to the shuttle bay as we are ready to
take you to the planet.

RANDOLPH
Alright Admiral Gilbert, thank you for living up to
your promise. I know you had to expend a lot of time
and effort and undue risk getting me here. I will always
be grateful to you.

They then shook hands and Tom Gilbert would never see the Ponarian again. Randolph followed XO Riley down to the hanger bays to get into the TR-3B configured to be a shuttle.

CAPTAIN GILBERT
What's the status of the radar contacts?

NAVIGATOR
Captain, one of the ships is getting closer, the others have slowed down their approach. The closer ship is now one thousand miles away and arriving at a fast pace, the other eleven are approximately five thousand miles away and appear to be coasting towards us and with the slower speeds I can see better definition of their hull structures.

CAPTAIN GILBERT
Are these images being recorded?

NAVIGATOR
Yes, sir.

CAPTAIN GILBERT
Any good photonics on the lead ship?

NAVIGATOR
Captain, the lead ship, is now just entering a range where we should be able to start putting it into focus even with its reduced Doppler and improved light reflections from sunlight.

Tom calmly waited only moments before the visual on the Jupitorian ship stabilized as it slowed, and he suddenly had a clear graphic display.

CAPTAIN GILBERT
Wow, that ship looks very interesting.

Tom Gilbert saw Shelly was taking copious notes again. Upon returning to earth after reviewing them he made peace with her by saying he would include her notes once screened and censored to remove all unrelated personal information in the Patrol Report and she would be given two things as a recommendation:

Official recognition of a good narrative to the patrol as an independent observer, but since her copious notes were collectively very professional and well written, she was given the title of official historian for the mission.

Admiral Gilbert also requested Shelly Brown be given compensation as a GS-14 that is about the same pay scale as the WEPS received. To Admiral Gilbert and Shelly Brown's surprise the President who could authorize it agreed.

Shelly Brown no longer had the fear of all her notes confiscated and circular filed via shredder. She also received 4 years of back pay including the *Cash in Advance* her mother was paid to keep her silent. Her mother was also extremely grateful the Secret Service kept her safe and the media could never get to her.

EXT. CGI. SPACE. JUPITORIAN CASG SHIPS ARRIVE 15 SECONDS.

> CAPTAIN GILBERT
> It's a big ship, probably has a lot of fire power. Estimated size?

> NAVIGATOR
> Using the infrared geometric focusing tools, it appears to be approximately four hundred feet long. It has a beam of forty-five feet.

> CAPTAIN GILBERT
> Any idea of the type of propulsion?

> NAVIGATOR
> No rocket exhaust was observed. So, these spaceships must be magnetic or gravitational.

> NAVIGATOR
> The Jupitorian spaceship has started blinking at a blue light.

> CAPTAIN GILBERT
> I wonder what that blinking light is all about.

Momentarily they received CASG communications from the Jupitorians who were using an automated English translator operated by Artificial Intelligence.

> JUPITORIAN CASG SPACESHIP
> ARTIFICIAL INTELLIGENCE VOICE.
> Have your shuttle craft follow the ship with the blue blinking light.

> CAPTAIN GILBERT
> Understand our shuttle will follow the ship with the blue blinking light. We anticipate launching the shuttle momentarily, please stand by.

A moment later, Blaze contacted the bridge via his TR-3B radio communications.

BLAZE

Sierra Charlie, this is Blaze. The passenger is on board, ready to launch.

Captain Gilbert responded.

CAPTAIN GILBERT

Blaze, this is the Sierra Charlie, you are to proceed with launch sequence and follow the Jupitorian ship with the blue blinking light to the planet.

EXT. CGI. SPACE TR-3B LAUNCH SEQUENCE 30 SECONDS

VOICE OVER (DURING TR-3B LAUNCH)

The TR-3B Hanger Bay security panel hatch rotated up out of the way previously hiding the shuttle. Clarence Williams (a.k.a. Blaze) initiated launch controls and shortly the TR-3B slowly eased out of the recessed cavity hold and moved slowly away from CSS Alabama.

EXT. CGI. SPACE TR-3B AND JUPITORIAN CASG SHIP TRAVELING IN FORMATION. 30 SEOCONDS.

VOICE OVER (DURING TR-3B TRANSIT)

As soon as the TR-3B was a few hundred feet distant, the alien ship with the blue light flashing was dead ahead. Blaze eased the throttle forward and the alien obviously closely watching the TR-3B started moving away from CSS Alabama.

By now CSS Alabama had closed within twenty thousand miles of the Jupitorian planet and Captain Gilbert would orbit Jupitorian Home World until Blaze's TR-3B returned or Captain Gilbert had to remotely detonate it to prevent the Jupitorians from discovering the level of their technology.

Crew members on the Alabama could now see the essence of Jupitorian society with the enormous number of lights on the dark side of the planet.

Observing the Jupitorian home world was an awesome spectacle; it was all being recorded. At their present velocity they would enter orbit in an hour and orbit at around five thousand miles above the planet so as not to reduce too much speed. In due time the eleven Jupitorian ships spread around them flying in a loose formation. The Earth ship was considerably larger than the CASG ships, but Tom had no doubt the CASGs packed a lethal punch.

In CSS Alabama present situation it would not be likely Captain Gilbert would be successful in launching many of the TR-3Bs if the alien technology was as advanced as he figured it would be. Captain Gilbert also decided it might not be possible to successfully drop the three hydrogen bombs and therefore keep his powder dry and not to attempt nuking the Jupitorian planet.

The Jupitorians were surprised at the sophistication of the shape of the TR-3B. It was on par with the architecture and design of ships built by some of their toughest enemies.

When the Jupitorian ship came close to the planet's atmosphere it slowed down an amount and the TR-3B shuttle kept its range though out. It became apparent to the Jupitorians these Earth people had a ship that had no problems penetrating the atmosphere at a fairly good velocity, around 22,000 miles per hour, which meant compared to other aliens the craft was on par. It also meant to some extent in one hundred years the Earth people had grown dangerously advanced.

While all this was unfolding, Jupitorian scientists opened the case file of the Ponarian. He had left a communicator behind in the event he needed to call them for help, and never did. After twenty years, they stored the device in archives and assumed they would never need or use it again. Now with this Ponarian suddenly arriving, that communicator suddenly got more interesting. It would be immediately brought out of storage and be prepared for use if required.

Proximas Dyafalious was chosen as the landing site because it was fenced off and highly controlled. The elite on the planet vacationed at Proximas Dyafalious where they had a lot of open room and an ideal climate. It was truly the only paradise left on the Empire's chief planet.

Three other planets in the solar system were inhabited but due to weather or chemical composition of the atmosphere, everyone was forced to live in domed cities and if they ventured outside the dome they would immediately choke to death or freeze. But those worlds were key to the whole civilization as numerous manufactured products were built there.

The Jupitorians were now slowly coming to the realization population control was vital for their survival. Conquest of other planets to obtain their natural resources was becoming problematic as more and more alien planets were slowly forming alliances to fend off the Jupitorians.

The current war taking place was one of those instances where a cooperative established decided to push back. It was a bloody war and the Jupitorians had lost enough men and material, the material wealth they intended to obtain by imperialism was slowly turning too expensive to get in terms of men and material to secure it.

Having to send the entire fleet to take on the cooperative was signs of the time. Population reduction through contraceptives, abortions, castration, etc., was just going to have to be implemented.

As the ships approached Proximas Dyafalious and were slowing, the TR-3B suddenly had four glowing orbs which surprised the Jupitorians, especially the center one that took up almost most of the surface area of the triangular ship. Images of the TR-3B were sent to military intelligence who were immediately studying the ship. They quickly drew the conclusion this was some type of anti-gravity device because the orbs got bigger as the ship slowed.

<u>EXT. CGI. TR-3B AND JUPITORIAN CASG SHIP LAND AT PROXIMAS DYAFALIOUS 30 SECONDS</u>

Soon both ships landed at Proximas Dyafalious. The weapon shipping hatch which doubled as the ship's ladder for egress lowered.

Clarence Williams turned to the Ponarian.

CLARENCE WILLIAMS
You are here, you are free to leave.

RANDOLPH
Thank you for bringing me here.

Randolph choked up a bit knowing he was one step closer to home. Randolph, knowing how Earth people shook hands as a sign of respect, held his hand out for Clarence, who grabbed it, and they shook hands.

RANDOLPH
Goodbye.

Randolph then turned and walked out of the cockpit area into the weapons bay and to the weapon shipping hatch/ladder that was deployed downwards.

<u>EXT. CGI. PLUS PROPS JUPITORIANS SURROUNDING BLAZE AND TR-3B.</u>

ESCAPE

Jupitorian Security personnel appeared out of nowhere and were surrounding the TR-3B.

Clarence raised the weapon shipping hatch just in time otherwise security personnel would have stormed the TR-3B and taken over control. They were highly interested in this aircraft, and it was not going to be allowed to leave anytime soon.

> BLAZE
> Sierra Charlie, this is Blaze. The Ponarian has left the ship, but I'm surrounded by what appears to be security personnel and a few strange-looking vehicles have arrived that look terrifying.
>
> Blaze, this is Sierra Charlie. Take pictures of what you can get with your photonics and transmit them immediately via the combat link.

The combat link, which was hard to jam, also was quick and Captain Gilbert was soon looking at these vehicles that didn't look like anything he had ever seen before and looked up to Rily.

> CAPTAIN GILBERT
> I bet those things have a nasty sting.

Suddenly Clarence received via his communicator a metallic voice that was obviously a translator output.

> JUPITORIAN ARTIFICIAL INTELLIGENCE
> Earth ship, lower your ladder, we wish to examine your ship.

Tom Gilbert could hear the communications as well since it was broadcast on a networked frequency.

> CAPTAIN GILBERT
> Blaze, this is SIERRA CHARLIE, you are not permitted to lower your ladder and I suggest you leave the planet immediately.

JUPITORIAN ARTIFICIAL INTELLIGENCE
Earth person, if you attempt to leave the planet you will be shot down.

Tom looked at Riley with a concerned look on his face.

CAPTAIN GILBERT
Looks like we have a situation.

XO RILEY
Mr. Williams knew he was going on a high-risk mission. If it ends up badly for him, he knows that's par for the course.

CAPTAIN GILBERT
We did those tests with maximum power antigravity a few years ago and found the TR-3B was able to avoid a lot of damage from shrapnel, or bullets.

XO RILEY
What about lasers? This is an advanced civilization; they probably depend on laser technology.

CAPTAIN GILBERT
The laser testing was inconclusive because we could never get any volunteers to fly the plane while being shot with a laser.

XO RILEY
Is it possible the antigravity orb could disperse a laser making it significantly weaker?

CAPTAIN GILBERT
Doctor Fremont claims the antigravity orb would disperse a laser just as well as it did bullets.

XO RILEY
It looks like BLAZE will have to choose an attempt to blast out of there with his antigravity turned on maximum or we'll have to remotely trigger the self-destruct.

CAPTAIN GILBERT
Blaze, this is Sierra Charle. Recommend you do the

following: Turn on Antigravity to maximum, then
leave the planet promptly. Leave your antigravity
turned on maximum until you reach Sierra Charlie.
We'll then do a maneuver to get you aboard.

BLAZE
Sierra Charlie, this is Blaze, understand all.

Clarence Williams (a.k.a. Blaze) looked at the menacing vehicles now coming towards the TR-3B way. They appeared to be at least four stories tall with a half-sphere on top that rotated and now pointed some type of gun barrel at his TR-3B.

VOICE OVER (BLAZE VOICE)
I wonder, is that some kind of laser weapon?

Clarence figured he had nothing to lose. If that was big bad laser, he would be instantly fried and the TR-3B blown up. The self-destruct explosives would most likely cook off adding to the detonation. *These Jupitorians are going to be in for a rude awakening when the U115 reactor blows.* Clarence smiled as he flipped on the anti-gravity switch and swiveled the dial to maximum which by experimentation showed typically 89 percent.

However, they knew that manufacturing of the tiny fiber optics used to generate the antigravity was not a precise science and some pilots said a few had slightly better performance, maybe 91 percent or better. Clarence hoped today he had one of those better examples.

Turning on the antigravity served one useful purpose. The glare was so bright it immediately obscured the Jupitorian optics used to target their enemies with their laser tanks. The Jupitorian tank's laser beam could do immense damage if it hit the target.

<u>INT. NIGHT. TR-3B SHOWING CLARENCE AND FLIGHT CONTROLS/
INSTRUMENT PANEL</u>

Clarence set the flight controls to maximum vertical ascent then shoved the throttle forward to maximum.

Clarence hoped he didn't pass out in the process even though the antigravity machine would take at least much of the gravity away.

Even though Jupitorians were used to fighting enemies with high G performance on their aircraft, they had never fought any entity that could pump twenty G's out in a straight vertical climb.

Blaze started receiving rendezvous designated areas far away from the planet, if they could all get there in one piece.

Just as soon as the Jupitorians saw the ship start to move they ordered the laser tanks to fire, but without proper focusing they didn't have a lock on the target and by the time they figured out the solution, the TR-3B was already ten thousand feet in the air moving vertically at a pace the Jupitorians would ever believe an Earth craft obtaining. Ten thousand feet was about the limit for the four-story tall Jupitorian laser tanks. Beyond that, targeting and focusing was too problematic.

The CASG escort craft was still on the ground and had not been ordered to chase down the Earth ship. By the time the Jupitorians figured out the Earth vessel had slipped out of their snare, the CASG was too far out of position to rally to the destruct.

It would take the Jupitorians too long to catch up, so the decision was made to pull a couple of the remaining CASG ships escorting the Alabama to go after the lone TR-3B that without a payload and just one crewmember and probably 91-percent antigravity managed to get up to eighty thousand feet rather remarkably quick while still accelerating. Plus, the TR-3B was going in a direction they didn't expect, away from the mother ship!

Because of the ill-defined plan to send off the entire fleet, only these CASG ships were available to deal with the Earth ship. They would blow it out of the sky if necessary. Their laser technology would slice it open like a can opener would do a can of sardines.

It did not take Captain Gilbert long to decide he needed to do to get away from the remaining CASG ships who could do a lot of damage and thought of a brilliant plan.

CAPTAIN GILBERT
Navigator, we can accelerate while orbiting the planet, correct?

NAVIGATOR
Yes, Admiral, by using propulsion and the reverse thruster opposite the planet for steering we can maintain distance to the planet while accelerating. We demonstrated that in the trainers in a variety of scenarios. I have such maneuvers programmed in on our Navigation egress macros.

CAPTAIN GILBERT
Okay, that's what I want to do, maintain the altitude of five thousand miles but constantly accelerate. I don't want to speed up to the point we'll leave the TR-3B behind, but just enough to give us some space to these Jupitorians.

NAVIGATOR
Roger that, Admiral, I'm ready to proceed.

CAPTAIN GILBERT
Okay, commence the maneuver now.

The Alabama caught the Jupitorians recklessly without paying attention. Because of their eternal arrogance, they knew the Earth ship was primitive and they could simply lay waste to it when the orders came. When suddenly, the Alabama commenced accelerating with its huge nuclear-powered rocket engines it darted ahead before the Jupitorians realized what was happening.

With four-point thrusts, the Alabama also had precise control where it could spin on a dime or keep an exact geometry in its movement. Before the Jupitorians reacted, CSS Alabama was already miles ahead and because of the two jets leaving the ship above light speed, any of the CASGs that were in the path of those jets were sliced in half.

Within a minute there were only the three CASGs left that didn't get destroyed by the above light speed wake plus the two others now chasing the TR-3B and having a hell of a time catching up because they had gravitational attraction to the solar system where as the TR3B didn't. The only thing the TR-3B didn't have was food, water, and indefinite time it could remain traveling in space with the one crew member.

After a while when the reports filtered in the Grand Constabulary appeared almost in disbelief.

<u>INT. EVENING. PONARIAN PLANET GRAND CONSTABULARY MANSION AT PROXIMAS DYAFALIOUS</u>

GRAND CONSTABULARY
What do you mean the ship got away from Proximas Dyafalious?

CASG COMMANDER.
Your Excellency, this ship apparently has some awesome capabilities and fled the scene so quickly our laser tanks didn't have time to fire a shot.

GRAND CONSTABULARY
What about the CASG that escorted it?

CASG COMMANDER.
The Earth ship left so quickly the CASG ship could not catch up.

GRAND CONSTABULARY
What are you doing about it?

CASG COMMANDER.
Your Excellency, we had two CASGs break away from
escorting the mother ship to chase it down.

Moments later the CASG Commander reported to the Grand Constabulary.

CASG COMMANDER.
Your Excellency, it appears the Earth mother ship has
escaped.

GRAND CONSTABULARY
What!

CASG COMMANDER.
Your Excellency, the Earth ship appears to have
destroyed seven CASG interceptors.

GRAND CONSTABULARY
That's impossible. How could they do that?

CASG COMMANDER.
According to some eye witnesses this Earth ship can
shoot out a stream of energy that is very destructive to
any ship following it.

GRAND CONSTABULARY
Keep me posted on all new developments.

CASG COMMANDER.
Yes, sir.

The CASG Commander departed, and the Grand Constabulary looked at his aid.

GRAND CONSTABULARY
Bring me the Ponarian, I want to talk with him.

<u>INT. SPACE CSS ALABAMA CONTROL ROOM</u>

The CSS Alabama could keep its distance from the planet while accelerating, but the
Jupitorians could not. In the span of just a few minutes, the CASGs were already one
thousand miles above the planet while the CSS Alabama made that perfectly circular
turn and because it could exit the planetary orbit precisely, while the four-point thrust
kept it in perfect alignment it gathered significant speed. The three CASGs chasing the
CSS Alabama would never catch up.

Using the transponder tracker aboard the TR-3B, Clarence was given flight coordinates and knew exactly where to rendezvous. The Alabama was now traveling at a high velocity and unless the CASGs came closer there was no need to add to propulsion. Tom's plan was to position the Alabama ahead of the two CASG's chasing the TR3B and use his thrusters to do them the way he apparently sliced the other CASG's back on the other side of the planet.

Looking at the combat systems display with radar and photonics display overlays, the sector in space in front of them was graphically plotted. The TR-3B and the two CASGs were apparent. The problem would be landing the TR-3B at the same time avoiding the CASGs' firepower. Since it was not known at what point the CASGs would give up the chase, Tom had to neutralize them then retract the TR-3B before accelerating to speeds necessary to get back to Earth in a couple years.

Captain Gilbert knew the crew was in fear right now. This was more than they bargained for. Shelly Brown was writing none-stop. Captain Gilbert felt sorry he would have to censor all of Shelly Brown's notes and possibly confiscate it all. That's when he started thinking more about using Shelly Brown as CSS Alabama's Historian if they survived this journey.

Looking at the three-dimensional tactical display cube on the combat systems display Blaze's TR-3B and the two CASGs were moving in a straight line.

COMMODORE RILEY

The Jupitorian ships are not gaining on Blazes TR-3B,
but at the same time the TR-3B isn't escaping either.

CAPTAIN GILBERT

The Alabama's course is slowly intersecting the path
of the Jupitorians chasing Baze behind us.

COMMODORE RILEY

Captain, have you considered launching our
squadrons?

CAPTAIN GILBERT

I considered that but decided the Jupitorians probably
had advanced weapons that would result in most if
not all the airwing being squandered, so I'm deferring
launching the squadrons until there were no other
options.

<u>EXT. CGI. SPACE. SPACE BATTLE CSS ALABAMA WITH JUPITORIAN CASG INTERCEPTOR CLASS SPACESHIPS</u>

The Jupitorians were so focused on capturing the TR-3B or destroying it; otherwise, they didn't observe the Alabama come in line with them until it was engulfing their sensors. The CASGs quickly identified the Earth mother ship and reported it. Then for some reason there was a brightness they couldn't explain. Tom was using the forward reversers to decelerate to allow the CASG's to get closer, then he would kick in the main propulsion thrusters he knew would damage those thin skin Jupitorian CASG ships.

The Jupitorians were late in advising these two CASGs about the peril of flying directly behind the Earth Ship. And just about the time they were receiving the warning, Tom nodded at the Navigator who stopped the deceleration and kicked in acceleration shooting those jets above light speed in the path of the CASGs. Predictably the CASGs blew up in a cloud of sparkling debris. Tom then cut the thrusters and notified Blaze.

CAPTAIN GILBERT
Blaze, this is Sierra Charlie. You can slow down and
approach. We have a short period we can re-dock your
TR-3B.

BLAZE
Sierra Charlie, Roger that. Shifting to automatic
docking mode. You now have control of my ship.

With great precision, in a few minutes the TR-3B was landed in its isolated hangar bay and a disinfectant was sprayed over the entire body of the craft.

Clarence was directed to strip down naked, place his flight suit and all his articles in a slot that would ultimately dump it out into space with treated garbage traveling in space for eons until it either entered a planet's atmosphere and burned up or into a star and perhaps a black hole.

Thanks to the acceleration around the planet, Tom had utilized less fuel and time than expected. As such he did not have to accelerate to the top speeds until the maneuver several months later to point Earth's solar system. At that point in time he would accelerate to speeds the Cosmic Interpolator guessed approached two or three times the speed of light. By doing just the one high-speed burn, he would have ample fuel to accelerate to those astonishing speeds never attempted.

People were on their toes for a couple of weeks, but when it seemed the Jupitorians were long behind them, they gradually chilled out and went back to normal daily routines.

Everything on the ship seemed as it was before arrival to Jupitorian worlds, except Randolph was no longer with them. They wondered how he faired. Shelly would never know but it could take the Jupitorians years to figure out how to get the Ponarian communicator operational again. Then they figured out it would take the Ponarians many years to receive the radio signals if they were listening. By then the Ponarian would likely be gone from old age.

Because of overcrowding and suspicions in general, the Ponarian soon realized his worse days at Area 51 were probably more enjoyable than here at the Jupitorian worlds. The amount of advanced technology he gave up for this ride to hell was astonishing, especially when it seemed he was now marooned with the arrogant Jupitorians.

Men in biohazard suits grabbed the Ponarian shortly after he exited the TR-3B and had they arrived at the weapon shipping hatch just five seconds earlier they could have rushed aboard and shot the pilot with a stun gun and taken possession of the craft for further analysis. They would have had a little time to discover and deactivate the self-destruct mechanisms had everything worked out.

The biohazard team drove off with the Ponarian moments after the TR-3B unexpectedly went vertical and caught the Jupitorians by surprise. Word reached the team and the supervising scientists, the Grand Constabulary who was currently at Proximas Dyafalious, to have the Ponarian put in a temporary bio-transport suit and take him to the summer palace where his presence was demanded.

One could say Grand Constabulary's Proximas Dyafalious summer palace appeared like New York City's Central Park in the summertime, except the park at Proximas Dyafalious summer palace was about ten times larger.

The buildings that existed outside of Proximas Dyafalious park were much taller than any buildings in New York City.

Part of the structural integrity of the buildings one could easily observe from Proximas Dyafalious was made possible by the upper-level transportation tube that anchored the buildings together at the top and added greatly to the structural integrity, so that wind and weather conditions could not affect them. Unlike the other Jupitorian inhabited planets where dome living was common, Acropolis had mild weather conditions and domes were not required or desired.

Proximas Dyafalious was indeed the most awe-inspiring area of the planet. It was a huge contrast to the congested world that had become the banking and industrial center for the Empire for the Jupitorian solar system planets, and inhabited planets that had become colonies to the Imperialist Jupitorians over many centuries.

Grand Constabulary's mansion in the exact middle of Proximas Dyafalious provided a huge buffer to the masses and the high-rise buildings that rimmed the palatial gardens benefitted from the view, even though it required special invitation to get into Proximas Dyafalious summer mansion.

As such there were several dozen sites within the sprawling park like retreat where political cronies associated with the Grand Constabulary were given limited periods of occupancy when they were rewarded special vacations earned by doing the dirty work for the autocratic Grand Constabulary. It took considerable organized crime to rise to the panicles of power wielded by the Grand Constabulary. It also took as much effort to remain in power as most Jupitorian leaders were deposed and ruthlessly removed.

The Grand Constabulary was sitting in a shaded area next to the swimming pool when the security detail brought the Ponarian to the nearby vicinity.

The Ponarian looked rather distressed wearing the protective biohazard suit.

> GRAND CONSTABULARY
> Has he been decontaminated?

> SUPERVISING VIROLOGIST
> Yes, he has, sir.

> GRAND CONSTABULARY
> Any reason why he must keep that ridiculous looking suit on?

> SUPERVISING VIROLOGIST
> As a precaution since he needs to go through an incubation period before we can declare him medically certified to come in contact with the population.

> GRAND CONSTABULARY
> Is there any reason why he can't take the hood off?

> SUPERVISING VIROLOGIST
> I suppose not if he doesn't cough or transfer any body fluids, it would be okay to take the hood off.

> GRAND CONSTABULARY
> Okay, Ponarian, if you feel like you need to cough, but the hood back on, but for now you may take it off," the Grand Constabulary stated and the small universal translator sitting on the table replayed in the Ponarian's language.

> PONARIAN
> Thank you.

The Ponarian now wondered what his fate was to become.

GRAND CONSTABULARY
When you left here eighty years ago, I was still a kid.

The Ponarian looked at the Grand Constabulary dressed in a white tunic with gold trimmings and braid. The Ponarian had plenty of time on his hands while he was stranded on Earth and studied world history and quickly drew the impression the Grand Constabulary was dressed as he envisioned Romans such as the famous Caesar.

 Near the Grand Constabulary was a beautiful scantly clothed female Jupitorian sitting at a harp-like instrument she had been playing for the illustrious leader, before he had been notified the Ponarian was on his way to the mansion.

Just like clockwork, here was the Ponarian right after they decontaminated him and placed him in protective clothes.

The Ponarian would be restricted to a biohazard facility in medical isolation until he was thoroughly tested to not be carrying any infectious diseases or pathogens that would be harmful to the Jupitorians.

GRAND CONSTABULARY
Tell me, how long did it take you to travel from Earth
to here?

PONARIAN
In about two years.

GRAND CONSTABULARY
That's rather impressive, that's about how much time
it would take us.

PONARIAN
Yes, it is a long distance.

GRAND CONSTABULARY
According to briefings I've had since you arrived, I
was told that when we visited the Earth one hundred
years ago, they had primitive technology and no space
transportation. You left here eighty years ago and
now you are back with them. How did they evolve so
quickly?

PONARIAN
The Earth people benefitted by several crashed UFOs.

GRAND CONSTABULARY
What does 'UFO' mean?

PONARIAN
It's the name they use to describe unidentified flying objects.

GRAND CONSTABULARY
You mean extra-terrestrials?

PONARIAN
Yes, precisely.

GRAND CONSTABULARY
How did you get involved with these Earth people?

PONARIAN
My ship crashed in a severe storm because Earth people had developed powerful radar's and it interfered with my navigation system and I lost control and had a hard landing.

GRAND CONSTABULARY
Your spacecraft was unable to take off again?

PONARIAN
It was wrecked by a hard landing and could not function ever again.

GRAND CONSTABULARY
Were you injured?

PONARIAN
Yes, severely.

GRAND CONSTABULARY
I take it the Earth people rescued you.

PONARIAN
They did but they did a lot of wrong medical treatments for me, so my recovery time was lengthened considerably longer than what it needed to be.

GRAND CONSTABULARY
Had the Earth people discovered any UFOs prior to you arriving?

PONARIAN
There had been a couple wrecks, but the aliens and the craft were completely destroyed, so they had no idea what the occupants were like.

GRAND CONSTABULARY
Did they capture your ship?

PONARIAN
Yes.

GRAND CONSTABULARY
Did they get technology from it?

PONARIAN
Unfortunately, yes, they did.

GRAND CONSTABULARY
You sound like you were not happy they discovered the technology.

PONARIAN
They often tortured me to extract information over a five-year period. It was the worst days of my life.

GRAND CONSTABULARY
Is that how they got here, on your technology?

PONARIAN
No. There was a crash a year later at a place they call Aztec, New Mexico, where a much larger craft with eighteen aliens onboard crashed. Some of that technology was used to develop a lot of their capability, but some of their technology such as their propulsion systems they designed themselves.

GRAND CONSTABULARY
According to information provided to me, they used that propulsion system as a weapon to slice open our

ships with a tremendous jet. It's kind of an interesting application, a propulsion system they can use as a weapon.

PONARIAN

That must be incidental, they had no plans to use it as such.

GRAND CONSTABULARY
What were they planning on using?

PONARIAN

They had no plans for any armed combat, I think you frightened them, and they were just trying to escape.

GRAND CONSTABULARY
How does this fantastic propulsion system work?

PONARIAN

Their nuclear propulsion is like the Alien ship that crashed by the town of Aztec, New Mexico. It has a nuclear reactor they use to superheat hydrogen that produces an explosive output. I overheard their engineers talking once and they claim the jet it shoots out travels above light speed.

GRAND CONSTABULARY

It must be above light speed because for you to arrive here in two years Earth time, you could not get here that quickly without traveling above light speed.

PONARIAN

How fast do you think we obtained if you know the distance?

GRAND CONSTABULARY

For our ships to travel that distance in two years, we would have to travel at three times the speed of light. How long did it take you to travel from here to Earth?

PONARIAN
About nine years.

GRAND CONSTABULARY

Any other important information about these Earth People you wish to offer?"

PONARIAN
They have some horrific weapons.

GRAND CONSTABULARY
Such as?

PONARIAN
The same type and class of weapons Jupitorians used to destroy Mars nine hundred thousand years ago.

GRAND CONSTABULARY
How do you know about that?

PONARIAN
I was informed here before I left eighty years ago and advised that I should not go that way.

GRAND CONSTABULARY
But you went anyway?

PONARIAN
I had no intentions of going to Earth when I left here. I didn't know I accidentally found Earth and wasn't aware the planet was Earth until I crashed on it. I was not able to confirm that was the same planet until about ten years ago when a prominent researcher was trying to figure out why Mars had what appeared the remnants of two extremely large nuclear blast areas.

GRAND CONSTABULARY
How do they know they were nuclear blast areas?

PONARIAN
Residue Xeon 129, which can only be produced by hydrogen bomb blasts.

GRAND CONSTABULARY
What you are telling me now is Earth possesses Hydrogen Bombs and they certainly know how to get here, that puts us in a very dangerous situation.

PONARIAN
I doubt Earth is interested in the Jupitorian planetary system; you are a great distance away.

GRAND CONSTABULARY
Have they figured out we may have had a hand in the destruction of Mars?

PONARIAN
Yes, they also know Jupitorians destroyed Atlantis.

GRAND CONSTABULARY
Is that something you informed them?

PONARIAN
It was part of a quid pro quo, so that I could arrange transportation here and find a way to get home to my planet.

GRAND CONSTABULARY
What kind of a space fleet do they have?

PONARIAN
They just have one ship.

GRAND CONSTABULARY
Just that one?

PONARIAN
That's correct.

GRAND CONSTABULARY
We'll simply wipe it out and they will be no more. We might also go to the planet and wreak some major devastation to send them back to primitive lives like we had to do before.

PONARIAN
Why not just leave them alone? They have no interest in your planet and wanted a peaceful meeting. Their only purpose was to bring me here to reward me for helping them on a few matters.

GRAND CONSTABULARY
What exactly did you help them with?

PONARIAN
I gave them the basis for long-distance communication using neutrinos and methods to navigate more accurately.

GRAND CONSTABULARY
No weapons or propulsion?

PONARIAN
They tortured me for five years until they realized
I didn't know anything about how the propulsion
system worked. I was a navigator and knew how to
travel long distances and operate the equipment. I
was never trained in the engineering design of our
propulsion systems or weapons systems.

GRAND CONSTABULARY
Have they developed laser weapons?

PONARIAN
Yes, for short-range mainly naval applications.

GRAND CONSTABULARY
What does that mean?

PONARIAN
They have large bodies of water on their planet. Since
they are still somewhat primitive, they have devices
called ships that operate on the surface of those bodies
of water much like your spaceships operate. They
have put laser weapons on those ships for defensive
measures.

GRAND CONSTABULARY
Do those ships travel very fast?

PONARIAN
No, they go very slow, and you would consider them
a joke.

GRAND CONSTABULARY
So, they are still somewhat primitive?

PONARIAN
Yes, in many ways, but at the same time they are
gradually advancing, and you saw their TR-3B that
landed here that dropped me off.

GRAND CONSTABULARY

That was quite a spectacle, I was watching a live security video. It's amazing they got away so quickly.

PONARIAN

I would caution you not to go after Earth. They will now be looking for you and they now have weapons that will be lethal to you. You might be risking your planet if you attack Earth.

GRAND CONSTABULARY

I have no fear the Earth people can do anything to us Jupitorians. I've recalled half our fleet who is on their way home now. They will be sent after that Earth ship and destroy it. I might also send them to Earth to leave a message by wiping out a few cities with a warning to never come back this way again.

PONARIAN

If you do that, they will come back and on their terms. Your planet could end up being the next Atlantis.

The Grand Constabulary started laughing hard and could not believe how ignorant the Ponarian was. He then turned towards the Harp player and asked her to continue her performance.

GRAND CONSTABULARY
Would you like some food and drink?

PONARIAN
That would be rather kind of you.

GRAND CONSTABULARY
Please bring this man something to eat and a nice *Vlachik of Sprutasmium*.

The *Sprutasmium* was derived from a grape-like substance and heavily fortified by opium which poppies grew in abundance in a domed growing facility on another Jupitorian planet.

The *Vlachik* was a special drinking container made from molded synthetic diamond. The mold had exquisite designs. Diamond cutters and gemologists added intricate patterns and artwork.

There was nothing on Earth that came hardly close to *Vlachik* stunning artwork. Only the richest Jupitorians could afford to ever purchase a *Vlachik* which was indeed a status symbol. For the Grand Constabulary a *Vlachik* was considered ordinary houseware. His life transcended Jupitorian society by many stratums.

VOICE OVER (PONARIAN'S VOICE)

The harp music created an ambience and the *Sprutasmium* certainly had an immediate effect on the Ponarian. The Ponarian's endorphins were migrating to synapses in ways he had not experienced in eighty years.

If only he could enjoy this special moment with Shelly Brown. But he took pause for a moment.

The Ponarian's heart sank as he realized the Grand Constabulary would most likely have commandeered Shelly immediately and had her put in chains for his own pleasures.

Perhaps it was best Shelly Brown didn't come with me.

Within moments a tray of succulent ribs arrived. The Ponarian had heard stories about Jupitorian delicacies. His worst horrors were coming true right before his eyes. The remnants of a cannibalized human lay before him.

These sick bastards.

The Ponarian didn't know if he should vomit, but he also knew his ride home was sitting across from the table from him.

Lucky for the Ponarian, the *Sprutasmium* had dulled his sensitivity a few notches, otherwise he would have gone mad on the spot.

The Grand Constabulary was a ruthless dictator, it would not faze him a bit to cannibalize the Ponarian and serve him at a party reminiscent of ancient Roman Toga parties.

The Ponarian knew the predicament he was in and had to be careful of every movement he made, including not making any comments to anyone other than responding to questions from authorities, and he would be guarded in what he said from now on. He certainly didn't want to give any more Earth secrets away in view of the attitude the Grand Constabulary now exhibited.

The CSS Alabama was too far distant to receive any Earth communications nor send any. It was conceivable that if they did transmit a message, they would beat the message to Earth by a year if they sent it now.

Traveling with momentum and the main rocket engines shut down because they had obtained the desired velocity and wanted to save extra fuel for after the turn to speed up their return, they didn't want to give away their position by transmitting any signals. As such they also shut down their radars.

The CSS Alabama crew were now flying with only the aid of photonics. They simply would not detect an image unless they could see it. And in the open dark areas of space, it is very dark. In some ways this was better because you were going to get hit by a meteor.

To many, it probably it seemed best not to know their fate since death would come quickly through explosion and asphyxiation.

Unless you got close to the CSS Alabama, you would not know it existed as it sailed on forward in high pride and dignity of performing one of the most spectacular and stunning escapes in galactic history.

Nobody has ever evaded a dozen CASG ships. And no Jupitorian enemy had ever destroyed nine CASG ships inside their solar system.

When the Jupitorian Fleet was recalled, all the details of the Earth Ship visit and the wreckage of those nine CASG ships were made clear to the task force who now traveled with a bone in their teeth. They were directed to bypass Jupitorian planets and go right after the Earth ship.

Commander Zorgiev addressed the situation with the Battle Fleet Commander, Admiral Moritar.

COMMANDER ZORGIEV
It's a single ship. We don't need half the fleet to take
out this miserable miscreant primitive ship.

BATTLE FLEET COMMANDER
ADMIRAL MORITAR
These orders came directly from the Grand
Constabulary. To even question his orders could land
you roasting on a spit.

Traitors, Spies, and Saboteurs were usually impaled with an eight-foot-long spit and hoisted above a good fire and slowly turned and barbecued, then the delicious meat was served to distinguished guests who didn't know they were cannibals. With the proper spices and basting, the flavors were quite compelling.

Fear suddenly hit Commander Zorgiev. He knew he might have been misspoken to his mentor Admiral Moritar, but in the privacy of Mortar's space cabin, he thought his privileged communication would be confidential and private.

But now Commander Zorgiev saw for all what it was worth, the ruthless Grand Constabulary had spies everywhere and coerced even the most patriotic and astute military commanders such as Admiral Moritar.

COMMANDER ZORGIEV

I'm sorry sir, I misspoke, I didn't say exactly what I meant.

BATTLE FLEET COMMANDER
ADMIRAL MORITAR

That's okay, I got the message loud and clear. But one thing you must realize, especially since you are only a few more years away from one day becoming a Battle Fleet Commander, never assume the Grand Constabulary doesn't have spies among you. Any comments directed towards him are very unfortunate as he will have no remorse in how he deals with you, including putting you on a spit to make an example out of you.

COMMANDER ZORGIEV

Such foolishness will never happen again. I know I must carry out my orders as I'm trained to do.

BATTLE FLEET COMMANDER
ADMIRAL MORITAR

Now you know why I have several ampoules of *Sprutasmium* in my quarters. When I receive orders that I have a really hard time executing, like when I was ordered to lay waste to the *Murocrins*, after a couple drinks of *Sprutasmium*, my mind is numb, and the torment gone long enough so I can at least have the first night of restful sleep after the combat.

COMMANDER ZORGIEV

I try to avoid all mind-altering substances.

BATTLE FLEET COMMANDER
ADMIRAL MORITAR

As the ship's commander, you only must exercise control over actual execution of your orders. As a task force commander, you will be required to determine how to carry out those orders and direct the assets in ways you will not enjoy, especially if you must sacrifice an entire ship for a diversion to give you the opportunity for a surprise attack on your own terms. Trust me when I say this, your days of being forced to make such decisions are soon to be bestowed upon you, so you need to prepare yourself. I'll send you a case of *Sprutasmium* when you get promoted.

COMMANDER ZORGIEV

Sprutasmium is rather expensive, I don't know if it would be fair for me to receive such an expensive gift.

BATTLE FLEET COMMANDER
ADMIRAL MORITAR

Task Force Commanders get special privileges. Sprutasmium doesn't cost us nearly as much as it costs you. Don't worry about the price.

The two senior Jupitorian Space Force (JSF) officers were aboard the two-mile-long ship whose name translated to English was "Invincible." Accompanying the Invincible was two dozen escort ships all a half-mile long and a couple more Invincible Class Planetary Assault Ships.

The Planetary Assault Ships each carried two complete divisions of Jupitorian Airborne Assault Troops that utilized cyborgs, exoskeletons, laser tanks, fighter bombers for close ground support, kinetic and chemical weapons. Most of the troops were in suspended animation to allow them to pass great stretches of time and space without the rigid requirements to sustain life.

Twenty-four hours before combat while deploying for planetary conquest, the Jupitorian Airborne Assault Troops were all awoken by JSF officers with a special serum that reactivated their cognitive pathways and gave their reality back. The drugs also contained large doses of *Invectracitus Invincibility Syndrome Serum.*

Jupitorians were highly successful in shock and awe mainly because thesee Jupitorian Airborne Assault Troops had little or no fear of dying after their brains were altered with a heavy dose of *Invectracitus,* a long-lasting *Invincibility Syndrome Serum.*

Cyborgs who were approximately ten percent of the force, were former airborne troopers who had lost arms and legs and because of their exemplary bravery and leadership skills were given robotic replacements giving them superhuman abilities. If both legs had been previously amputated, the new robotic legs allowed them to run at 40 miles per hour or jump thirty feet in the air.

Additional manpower that arrived with a Ponarian Invasion Force now in suspended animation, included normal healthy men who operated the exoskeletons which could be used to ferry troops, supplies, munitions, or elaborate electronics enclosures to facilitate battlefield operations and planning.

Sending such an armada which was needed back at the warzone to squat a fly, such as the Earth-bound ship, irritated Zorgiev. But he realized he had to keep his mouth shut. His mentor just gave him some valuable advice. No doubt on every ship was a snitch or two.

Admiral Moritar simply wanted his protégée to avoid being cooked on a spit. He had already seen too many bright, sophisticated, and intelligent young men get cooked alive by insulting the Grand Constabulary. He also feared he too could be held accountable for not properly training men under his command.

As the Jupitorian Fleet passed by their own solar system, the fleet crew personnel who operated the ships and kept awake to do so unlike the combat troops sadly watched their planets appear and soon fade behind them as they were still accelerating to reach optimal velocity to catch up with the Earthlings and wipe them out as their Grand Constabulary had directed.

In a few more days the Jupitorian Armada would reach three times the speed of light far faster than the Earth men traveled, they assumed.

They were partially correct only because Admiral Gilbert was saving his burst of speed to after the turn on final course to Earth's solar system. A year after the course change required to reach Earth, CSS Alabama would then decelerate, finally returning home.

VICKSBURG

Immediately after the CSS Alabama departed for this spectacular voyage, work commenced on building the sister ship CSS Vicksburg.

The CSS Vicksburg ship's name was chosen by John Harris and it normally would not have been approved being a southern small City when the name of a state was more politically correct, John Harris convinced the President to name it on behalf of General Ulysses S. Grant's fabulous victory at Vicksburg, which sealed the deal for President Abraham Lincoln choosing him to take over the Union Army and bring victories in hopes of shortening the bitter fratricidal war.

Decisions have consequences. Grant's decision to maneuver and attack Vicksburg from the south created an element of surprise which ultimately trapped the confederates who then were not able to extricate the thirty thousand troops stranded at Vicksburg that ultimately weakened the southern defenses and opened the Mississippi River to Union Troops cutting off Texas and Arkansas from the rest of the Confederacy, along with contributions of men and material for the cause. It was classic divide and conquer.

Since the 3D mockup was still in place, parts needed for the construction of the Vicksburg were easily manufactured and checked for tight tolerances. Lessons learned from the construction of the Alabama were instrumental in cutting off a lot of wasted time in construction since all the forms, jigs, and 3D-printing created most of the parts.

Naval Reactors, fully confident they had solved all the nuclear power plant issues, were instrumental in getting propulsion related systems in working order way ahead of schedule. Meanwhile a second dock was also being constructed because by the time Alabama returned and needed time in dock, a third hull would be under construction.

In three years, Vicksburg was ready for Space Trials. This coincided with the time frame Alabama would be making its final turn for home.

Alabama was still too far away to send message traffic because they would still beat any such message traffic traveling at light speed back to earth. There was no sense in sending any messages until they started deceleration near the end of the Voyage.

Meanwhile the Jupitorians Battle Fleet personnel who controlled the fleet and were required to remain in an awakened state were growing restless. They had traveled quite a distance and to find a ship in open space was like looking for a needle in a haystack.

They needed the enemy to reveal his position by communicating or operating his radar so they could get a fix on him. Just as they were about to give up hope and the chase, luck was on their side.

The Alabama reached its maneuver point and fired off its propulsion engines. The surreal brightness and the jets streaming out above the speed of light giving massive modal distortions and modulations of light giving the Jupitorians precise bearings. Plus, it took several days to complete the acceleration which made the Alabama crew unhappy during the period they felt the constant vibrations from the rocket engines preventing many of them including Shelly Brown from sleeping.

The main problem with attacking the Earth spaceship traveling at such extreme velocity was that Jupitorian Battle Fleet escorts would have to get close to use its weapons; otherwise, the Earth ship would simply run away from the attack without receiving any wounds.

The Jupitorians closed the Alabama slowly and consistently using visual verification only. They would have to wait until the Earth spaceship shut down its engines and started coasting to launch the attack because the bright light from the jets and the modal distortion it created would not allow them to correctly target the ship. Finally, the day arrived, and Admiral Gilbert directed the navigator to cease acceleration as they could now coast all the way to planet Earth and have plenty of fuel to do an aggressive deceleration as to not prolong the trip.

As part of the training of the Vicksburg crew, USSF decided they would send Vicksburg out along the expected track of the Alabama and meet her, then fly back in formation to earth. Messages were sent and the Alabama was now starting to copy Earth messages that were sent months and years ago just now arriving to them in space. Tom Gilbert was amused. But he also knew this was the longest trip Vicksburg will have made to date so for crew training it was probably a great opportunity, especially this far away from earth have a friendly ship there to help if necessary.

JUPITORIANS ARRIVE

The CSS Alabama never let its guard down. Captain Gilbert realized they could have triggered a Jupitorian response, and the photonics displays were always monitored. Captain Gilbert routinely monitored watch standers checking up on possible instances of vigilance decrement by a crew member who was bored to tears keeping an eye on a blank screen for such a long period of time.

It was during one of those vigilance monitoring periods when Tom approached the sensor's operator, he noticed some unusual behavior almost as if it the person had a quizzical look.

<u>INT. SPACE. CSS ALABAMA CONTROL ROOM</u>

CAPTAIN GILBERT
Everything all right?

SENSOR'S OPERATOR
Not sure, Captain, but it might be an equipment issue
or it could be an actual intercept?

CAPTAIN GILBERT
Let me look.

Tom stared at the display and saw some minor perturbations and almost a shimmering effect. Tom figured if nothing else he could instigate a good drill in all this, but he might as well play it cautionary and go ahead and man battle stations. He hit the alarm, then grabbed the 1MC and barked.

CAPTAIN GILBERT
Man, battle stations.

In a flash Commodore Riley was in the control room standing next to Tom as others entered and took their seats and within a couple minutes the Chief of The Watch made the announcement.

CHIEF OF THE WATCH
Captain, battle stations are manned.

CAPTAIN GILBERT
Very well, Chief of the watch.

Riley then looked at the screen and back at Tom.

XO RILEY
What do you think it is?

CAPTAIN GILBERT
Whatever it is, it's dark out and almost impossible to see even with the infrared. How long does our plume stay lit up when we fire up the rocket engines?

XO RILEY
Seems to me the plume is observable several minutes after we shut down the rocket engines.

CAPTAIN GILBERT
That's what I remember, too.

Captain Gilbert then turned to the Navigator.

CAPTAIN GILBERT
Nav, I want you to fire the rocket engines for one minute on my mark then shut them off.

NAVIGATOR
Understand, Captain.

CAPTAIN GILBERT
Okay, here we go, standby, mark!

INT. SPACE. JUPITORIAN COMMAND SHIP CONTROL ROOM.

The Jupitorians were not expecting the Earth ship's acceleration.

COMMMANDER ZORGIEV
Admiral Moritar, do you think they are accelerating again?

BATTLE FLEET COMMANDER
ADMIRAL MORITAR
They might just be maneuvering, doing an adjustment for their navigation vectors.

After one minute the CSS Alabama shut down its main propulsion engines.

COMMMANDER ZORGIEV
The enemy ship just shut down their rocket engines, it must have been a slight maneuver.

BATTLE FLEET COMMANDER
ADMIRAL MORITAR
How much longer before our escort is in position to attack?

COMMMANDER ZORGIEV
About five minutes, sir.

BATTLE FLEET COMMANDER
ADMIRAL MORITAR
This should be interesting; the Earth people will not even know what hit them.

The exhaust plume of the rocket traveled above light speed, and it sent out jets that lasted several minutes. As the light was slowly dimming from the plume extinguishing from dispersion and cooling, there was a moment objects could be seen behind them.

<u>INT. SPACE. CSS ALABAMA CONTROL ROOM</u>

XO RILEY
Looks like a lot of ships are following us.

CAPTAIN GILBERT
Yes, I think they are coming in for the kill now. I'm not sure how we can defend ourselves.

XO RILEY
We did a good job of slicing them open with our rocket exhaust.

CAPTAIN GILBERT

There is no telling what kind of weapons they have and at what range they can hit us.

XO RILEY

Going at our current velocity it's probably problematic they can shoot unless they are close.

CAPTAIN GILBERT

I have an idea. You know the little dry dock operations thrusters we have in the rear?

XO RILEY
Yes?

They would probably act like a good light.

CAPTAIN GILBERT

We can turn them on incrementally and get position data on the enemy ship and when we think they are close enough to hit them with our rocket exhaust, we simply turn the ship placing them directly astern, then turn on our rocket engines.

XO RILEY
Captain, I think his is a good plan.

CAPTAIN GILBERT
Everyone understand?

NAVIGATOR
Understand, sir.

In a couple minutes they tried the technique and to their surprise the thruster engine, normally only good for dry docking operations, did a great job of lighting up the area behind them and they could see that huge ugly menacing ship approaching.

XO RILEY

That big ship is getting close.

CAPTAIN GILBERT

Okay, I think it's time to maneuver. Proceed with maneuver NAV.

NAVIGATOR
Roger that.

Nav immediately turned on the rocket engines and did a 10-degree course change putting the Jupitorian half mile long escort directly astern and as predicted the jet exhaust cut through the nose of the Jupitorian escort completely disrupting its attack at the critical moment and setting fires ablaze.

The trailing Jupitorians were watching at a safe angle and fully traumatized observing the incredible site of the Earth ship easily destroying their escort in the matter of just a few moments.

Captain Gilbert directed the communicator sitting at her console.

CAPTAIN GILBERT
COMO, send a message to Earth and tell them we are in combat with Jupitorians following us home. We may not make it home and they should brace themselves for possible attack. Also put in SITREP our present location.

COMO
Captain message prepared via AI; do you want to read it before I hit the send button?

CAPTAIN GILBERT
COMO if you agree with the contents send it now. I trust your judgement.

COMO
Captain, message sent.

CAPTAIN GILBERT
Earth might not receive the message for months, but if something happened to us they will know.

XO RILEY
The Vicksburg heading our way will know long before Earth, but would they be flying into their deaths?

CAPTAIN GILBERT
The Vicksburg will have no way of knowing since communicating to them at this distance would be impossible.

Tom Gilbret came up with a new plan quickly.

CAPTAIN GILBERT
Maneuver might be our only option. There is nothing that says we must head directly towards Earth.

XO RILEY
What do you have in mind, Captain?

CAPTAIN GILBERT
I can buy us some time; we have something they don't have.

XO RILEY
What's that?

CAPTAIN GILBERT
We proved with our forward thrusters we can outmaneuver them. We are going to make a high G turn and hopefully cut open a few more with our rocket engines.

Captain Gilbert picked up the 1MC.

CAPTAIN GILBERT
Everyone remain in your safety harness; the ship will be making high-speed turns in one minute.

Tom calmly walked over and sat down in his Captain's chair and fastened his safety harness. He then looked at the time and at one minute gave the orders.

CAPTAIN GILBERT
NAV, using the forward thrusters make a hard 90degree course change and apply acceleration until my mark.

NAVIGATOR
Executing 90-degree course change and applying acceleration.

The Jupitorians were once again caught by surprise. The Alabama turned so swiftly unlike anything they had witnessed outside of a scouting class ship.

<u>EXT. CGI. SPACE CSS ALABAMA'S ROCKET EXHAUST HITTING JUPITORIAN SHIPS INFLICTING DAMAGE.</u>

A couple Jupitorian escorts received some severe damage from the rocket exhaust as they flew past. They were not disabled but their comfort going home would suck if they couldn't do a space-to-space transfer of half the crew.

XO Riley
None of the big Jupitorian ships (Invincible Class) were hit.

CAPTAIN GILBERT

Those big ships are a huge menace. Nothing on Earth was probably capable of stopping the firepower of those huge Jupitorian ships short of a lucky hit with a nuke if they could get the weapon close enough to be detonated before the Jupitorians destroyed the weapons with their advanced self-defense systems.

<u>INT. SPACE. JUPITORIAN COMMAND SHIP CONTROL ROOM.</u>

BATTLE FLEET COMMANDER
ADMIRAL MORITAR
This latest action by the Earth ship is a good reason why we must destroy it.

COMMANDER ZORGIEV
It will not be acceptable to return to Acropolis if we don't destroy this Earth ship.

BATTLE FLEET COMMANDER
ADMIRAL MORITAR
It would not be the first time nor the last time a fleet admiral was put on a spit above a fire for failure to do so.

COMMANDER ZORGIEV
May I suggest we send some ships and attempt to get ahead of them and attack from multiple directions so they will not be able to rely on that rocket exhaust using it as a weapon.

BATTLE FLEET COMMANDER
ADMIRAL MORITAR
Start an end around, send two escorts and a Planetary Assault Ship out in front of them to help box them in, spread out the remaining ships so it's harder for them to hit us with their stinger.

<u>INT. SPACE. CSS ALABAMA CONTROL ROOM</u>

Tension mounted on the Alabama as in due time they were able to spot the three Jupitorian ships accelerate.

XO RILEY

It appears they are going to attempt sending some ships out in front of us.

CAPTAIN GILBERT

It's a new ball game now. Riley, make two squadrons ready to launch as well as the three special ships.

XO RILEY

Too bad we didn't use those special weapons on the Jupitorians when we had the chance.

CAPTAIN GILBERT

No use tipping our hands until we have too. If they declare war on us and come after our planet, we have the option of going back.

XO RILEY

I wonder where all these ships came from.

CAPTAIN GILBERT

They were probably away at a war like the Ponarian stated and out of position to defend the planet.

XO RILEY

How much of their fleet is this?

CAPTAIN GILBERT

We'll never know, but I would think they sent a good chunk of their fleet after us. More than likely at least half of them were retained in the war zone.

WEPS

Captain, I'm able to get optical trackers on one of the ships trailing behind the other two and am doing statistics on it should have some results soon. Permission to use the radar to help estimate range.

CAPTAIN GILBERT

Since they already know where we are, go ahead and radiate on Radars until further notice.

WEPS
Radiate on Radar, aye, sir.

SENSOR OPERATOR
The third ship trailing the other two is approximately
two miles long.

XO RILEY
That's incredible. I think we pissed off the wrong
people.

CAPTAIN GILBERT
Send that information in SITREP to Earth immediately.

COMO
SITREP on the way.

A lot of the SITREP was voice encoding using artificial intelligence to capture the
essence of what the CO wanted to convey, including imagery data from radar and
photonics.

CAPTAIN GILBERT
Any success in determining the disposition of the two
other ships?

SENSOR OPERATOR
Getting close, right now I can say probably half-mile
long.

CAPTAIN GILBERT
Send that information immediately.

COMO
Another SITREP on the way.

AIR GROUP LEADER
Control, this is the Air Group Leader, ready for launch.

Squadron One was on the Port side of the ship. Squadron Two was on the Starboard
TR-3B Hangers. Tom decided he would do another maneuver to obscure the launch
and responded.

CAPTAIN GILBERT
Squadron One, we are going to be turning left, stay

away from the rocket exhaust of the ship. I want you to attack the trailing fleet. Squadron Two, you will delay launch until we do another maneuver.

AIR GROUP LEADER
Azzie, Batman, and Instigator, are you ready?

Azzie, ready to launch.

Batman ready to launch.

Instigator ready to launch.

AIR GROUP LEADER
Azzie, you will launch with Squadron One. Follow them in and let them do the fighting. They will be acting as a decoy for you. Find the largest ship and attack it.

EXT. CGI. SPACE CSS ALABAMA LAUNCHES TR-3B FIGHTER/BOMBERS.

AIR GROUP LEADER
Squadron One, begin launch.

Captain Gilbert realized most of the TR-3B's would be squandered but hoped the distraction would be enough to allow Azzie to get in and send his pickle to one of the monster size ships chasing him.

INT. SPACE. JUPITORIAN COMMAND SHIP CONTROL ROOM.

COMMANDER ZORGIEV
Admiral, the Earth ship has maneuvered again.

BATTLE FLEET COMMANDER
ADMIRAL MORITAR
It's almost as if that captain is reading my mind.

COMMANDER ZORGIEV
Admiral, the enemy has launched fighters!

BATTLE FLEET COMMANDER
ADMIRAL MORITAR
So now it begins.

Radar was distorted at the velocities they were traveling, but the photonics had real time images since they were going speeds relative to each other. Because of the speeds the laser weapons only had a lethal range of only one thousand yards.

EXT. CGI. JUPITORIAN SHIPS SHOOTING HUNDREDS OF LASERS TOWARDS CSS ALABAMA AND SQUADRON OF TR-3B'S NOW ATTACKING.

The lights from the lasers lit up like a porcupine all over the Jupitorian ships. The pilots knew to instinctively avoid those super bright lights. The TR-3B was far more maneuverable than what the Jupitorians had ever experienced. It was now turning out to not be such a cake walk like they assumed.

Some of the TR-3B squadron attacked the wrong ship, an escort, but the remainder went after the big sucker in the lead. This was another two-mile-long Planetary Assault Ship. Admiral Moritar was on the ship far behind it observing everything from the rear as expected.

By the time Azzie's TR-3B finally made it to the Planetary Assault Ship most of Squadron One had been wiped out. Azzie's TR-3B was suddenly just one of a couple remaining and a laser was now hitting him, so he knew it was now or never. The pilot had the option of self-detonation if he felt his situation was hopeless and he wanted to make sure the weapon went off.

Just as Azzie punched the detonation key setting off the nuclear trigger his life ended. He had no way of knowing if he contributed. The very large hydrogen bomb designed to wreck a world was also a viable weapon in space. Just like a tsunami, its shock wave would eventually find planets and leave behind a nice ripple sensation but due to cylindrical spreading there would be no power in it.

EXT. CGI. SPACE JUPITORIAN PLANETARY ASSAULT SHIP HIT BY MASSIVE NUKE SHOCK WAVE.

The front half of the Jupitorian Planetary Assault Ship was instantly severely wrecked, but the rear of the ship was left intact. All those sleeping grunts in suspended animation were hit with a terrific shock wave, they would never waken. The control room was filled with corpses who quickly expired from the massive fireball that engulfed the front of the ship and the damage to the hull caused rapid decompression so any living soul who escaped the initial shockwave and blast soon expired from asphyxiation. The Jupitorian Planetary Assault Ship was out of control and could continue traveling in space until some clever salvage crew had the audacity to claim it.

Admiral Moritar now had a personal grudge against this Earth Ship. It had just cost him dearly. What should have been a simple go smack a gnat and return to Acropolis or be sent back to the war zone, now had a new dimension to it.

Admiral Moritar would have some explaining to do for the admiralty. He lost too many ships too quickly and would be accused of negligence and incompetence. His only salvation would be to take out the gnat without losing any more ships.

The Jupitorians continued with their present course and did not aggressively attack. A survey craft was sent to the disabled ship that continued traveling above light speed and trailing a plume behind it as fires were out of control in spaces that still had significant oxygen content, but the infrared cameras showed the front end of the ship was rapidly cooling down as any remaining heat was quickly radiating in space where temperatures were absolute zero with one hydrogen atom per cubic meter.

<u>SPLIT SCREEN. ADMIRAL MORITAR IN JUPITORIAN CONTROL ROOM LEFT SIDE, SURVEY SHIP CAPTAIN IN JUPITORIAN SURVEY SHIP CONTROL ROOM RIGHT SIDE.</u>

SURVEY SHIP CAPTAIN

It's a total loss, the whole front of the ship is ripped
wide open.

BATTLE FLEET COMMANDER
ADMIRAL MORITAR

No chance of survivors?

SURVEY SHIP CAPTAIN

None.

COMMANDER ZORGIEV

We don't want our power plant falling into the hands
of our enemies, I we must destroy the engineering
spaces.

BATTLE FLEET COMMANDER
ADMIRAL MORITAR

I agree. Send orders to the fleet to change course and
pull away a safe distance and use a Proton Distributer
Weapon targeting the engineering spaces and destroy
what is left of the Planetary Assault Ship.

<u>EXT. CGI. SPACE. JUPITORIAN ESCORT SPACE CRAFT SCUTTLES THE DAMAGED JUPITORIAN PLANETARY ASSAULT SHIP</u>

A short later after the fleet obtained a safe distance an escort launched several Proton Distributer Weapons at the two-mile-long Planetary Assault Ship that blew up into a huge ball of sparking debris.

Captain Gilbert, observing the explosion, did not waste the moment. Captain Gilbert touched the panoramic view of the ship's horizon surveillance display and clicked on the icon: [NEW COURSE].

Then as soon as Artificial Intelligence displayed the [CONFIRM] icon, the pilot made announcement:

PILOT
Captain, Helm has responded to new ordered course. steadying up on new course.

CAPTAIN GILBERT
Squadron Two, commence launch, attack the nearest large ship. Instigator, follow squadron two in and deliver the pickle on the large ship.

EXT. CGI. SPACE TR-3B SQUADRON TWO SALVO LAUNCH.

This smaller group of three ships was not quite the gauntlet that Squadron One faced earlier. The pilots all knew their chances were slim but if they opened a path for Instigator. They knew it would improve the chances for CSS Alabama to survive.

One thing now certain, CSS Alabama had proved to the Jupitorians they could hold their own.

This gnat (CSS Alabama) was getting under Admiral Moritar's skin. By the time the Jupitorians ended their temporary morass at watching the demise of their own great Planetary Assault Ship, the ragtag force of TR-3Bs was nearly upon the secondary group now traveling 90 degrees course from the Alabama and starting to swing their helms to match the course change and position for attack.

EXT. CGI. SPACE GROUP OF JUPITORIAN SHIPS ATTACKING. 20 SECONDS.

The Jupitorians attempted to keep the escorts in front of the Planetary Assault ship, the loss of which would be detrimental to the fleet and seriously erode their ability to withstand the growing war of attrition ongoing back in their neck of the woods where the Imperialists were being confronted by survivalists hell bent on saving their worlds from the relentless plunder the most horrible beings in the galaxy inflicted upon them.

Because of the course change and relative motion of the TR-3Bs that were slowly falling behind in bearings as they transited perpendicular to Alabama's track were now on the flank of another Planetary Assault Ship.

EXT. CGI. SPACE. TR-3B'S APPROACHING JUPITORIAN FORMATION OF SHIPS.

This maneuver created a monumental screw-up on the part of the Jupitorian escorts. They never should have allowed the Earth fighters to be this close to the Planetary Assault Ship. If they changed course now to go after the TR-3Bs that would give the CSS Alabama a chance to change course again and possibly hit them with propulsion thrusters.

There was also risk the CSS Alabama would wipe out many TR-3Bs in the process, but that was a calculation Tom would have to quickly do in his head to decide if he really wanted to squander those brave men on a 50/50 shot at the escorts. He would keep his powder dry as long as possible.

EXT. SPACE. JUPITORIAN COMMAND SHIP.

Admiral Moritar was suddenly in a fit of rage as he watched all this unfold. Just like before lasers were not effective until the TR-3Bs got close and Instigator knew not to group with the others and present an inviting target.

The instigator had his nuclear detonation switch armed and ready to hit the trigger detonating the weapon if his ship suddenly got lit up. He probably had one second to respond. Instigator hoped he would get in close before he hit the switch. His buddies in Squadron One were flying incredibly acrobatic to keep the Jupitorian gunners focus off Instigator in the greatest display of heroic support ever displayed.

EXT. CGI. SPACE. TR-3B CRASHING INTO THE SIDE OF THE JUPITORIAN PLANETARY ASSAULT SHIP AND HYDROGEN BOMB DETONATING.

As Brad Howard saw the huge two-mile-long ship come really close he knew it was now or never. He felt sorry he would wipe out some of Squadron Two in the process. He calculated his TR-3B would crash into the side of the ship in about three seconds, so he put his finger on the trigger and counted down 3, 2, 1, and screamed a few expletives of surreal profanity then hit the switch. His consciousness then ended as his timing calculations were perfect.

A few milliseconds after the TR-3B crushed open a weak spot in the hull, in the most perfect attack that could possibly occur, the blast from the special weapon melted the side of two-mile-long planetary assault ship immediately cooking off munitions that blew in half and killing the entire Jupitorian assault division fighters currently in suspended animation.

With the front half of the Jupitorian Planetary Assault Ship suddenly dark because all electrical power was severed, the multitudes of beings onboard quickly succumbed. This time a Proton Distributer Weapon was not needed as the shockwave from Instigator's weapon placed the power plant in maximum output and an uncontrolled energy spike created a horrific explosion that shot the front half of the Planetary

Assault Ship right at two escorts severely damaging one and forcing the other to do such a radical maneuver it was immediately out of position to continue the battle any time soon.

<u>INT. SPACE. JUPITORIAN COMMAND SHIP.</u>

Admiral Moritar now must have felt like Napoleon at Waterloo as the battle unfolded.

The once proud Jupitorian Fleet, even if it did eventually take out the Earth ship had just sustained its most agonizing defeat in their history.

Admiral Moritar feared that should word get out to the Jupitorian enemies that a low-class planet in the Scullion Sector just wiped out two Jupitorian Planetary Assault Ships and several Escorts rated as Heavy Cruisers, they might become bolder and actually consider attacking Acropolis. These thoughts were going through Admiral Moritar when he was suddenly snapped back to reality by Commander Zorgiev.

> COMMANDER ZORGIEV
> Admiral, we are getting distress calls from the Cruiser Orizon.

> BATTLE FLEET COMMANDER
> ADMIRAL MORITAR
> What happened to it?

> COMMANDER ZORGIEV
> *Orizon* was severely damaged when *Interstellar* blew up.

> BATTLE FLEET COMMANDER
> ADMIRAL MORITAR
> This last attack effectively reduced the Jupitorian fleet by two more ships. This command ship and a few escorts with significant firepower are all that is left striking power. Perhaps it would be better if we turned around now and went home?

> BATTLE FLEET COMMANDER
> ADMIRAL MORITAR
> Commander Zorgiev, signal to the fleet we are reversing course and heading back to Acropolis.

> COMMANDER ZORGIEV
> Admiral Moritar, we can't leave now!

BATTLE FLEET COMMANDER
ADMIRAL MORITAR
Commander Zorgiev, you have your orders.

COMMANDER ZORGIEV
Are you a coward?

BATTLE FLEET COMMANDER
ADMIRAL MORITAR
We went into this battle halfcocked. We didn't do critical planning or assessment of the enemy. The enemy has maintained tactical control of the battle, strategic brilliance, and deployed weapons in ways we could never imagine from such a primitive civilization.

COMMANDER ZORGIEV
What's our next move?

We'll go back to Acropolis and regroup and rethink strategy, one of a winning one.

COMMANDER ZORGIEV
I hope you realize the Grand Constabulary will probably have you executed for treason if you abandon this battle?

BATTLE FLEET COMMANDER
ADMIRAL MORITAR
In doing so if I save all your lives and what's left of this fleet, then I'll be grateful, but I doubt I will let the Grand Constabulary have the satisfaction.

COMMANDER ZORGIEV
What about the Cruiser Orizon.

BATTLE FLEET COMMANDER
ADMIRAL MORITAR
Have one of the escorts pull out of line and go back and administer aid.

COMMANDER ZORGIEV
Right away Admiral.

<u>INT. SPACE. CSS ALABAMA CONTROL ROOM</u>

Captain Gilbert was thinking about his next move. The attitude on the bridge was somber and he could see fear in most of their eyes. It was moments like this why John Harris wanted Captain Gilbert for command. Most would buckle under pressure and not bring such ingenuity into resolving this situation.

CAPTAIN GILBERT

WE have been extremely lucky up until now. But our time might be running out.

XO REILEY

We have one special weapon left, but the 3rd and 4th squadrons are mostly rookies.

CAPTAIN GILBERT

I understand these are not the same quality of the pilots we lost in Squadrons One and Two. You need to select one of them to take our last pickle if necessary.

XO REILEY

Since we are down in pilot strength, we have a pilot I assigned to Squadron Three since he has gone through a lot already, I know I can count on. Clarance Williams call sign Blaze.

CAPTAIN GILBERT

Blaze proved we can count on him the way he had to leave the Jupitorian planet. You will have to give him special instructions.

XO REILEY

It's not every day a leader gets the chance in a single day to ask his men to make the supreme sacrifice.

CAPTAIN GILBERT

I'm sure Blaze understands what he must do to save this ship.

XO REILEY

Not a single pilot from squadrons one and two survived the fighting. Some of them got a few good licks in before they were killed, but the most important sacrifice they made was opening the pathway to allow Azzie and Instigator to deliver their game changing weapons.

CAPTAIN GILBERT

In future battles that strategy may not be possible because the enemy will be expecting it. Fighting at high-speed also gives a new realism to space warfare none of the planners ever envisioned.

XO REILEY

Alabama has remained unscathed, but I feel her time was running out. We might be one attack away from losing it.

The sensor operator unexpectedly diverted Captain Gilberts thoughts actions he was planning on doing, one might consider a hail marry pass.

SENSOR OPERATOR

Captain, the enemy is either decelerating or they are changing course!

Captain Gilbert started focusing on his screen and viewing the remnants of the enemy ships off his port side.

SENSOR OPERATOR

Captain, the enemy ships are lit up like they were maneuvering, and the interpolated bearing rate indicates they were drawing aft.

Everyone stayed focused on the Jupitorian formation and even though it would take a couple days to get their velocity heading in the direction of their desired course there appeared to be a noticeable growing separation between the two forces.

CAPTAIN GILBERT

I wonder what they are doing.

XO RILEY

Maybe they decided they had enough and are going home to regroup.

CAPTAIN GILBERT

Well, if that's the case we can count on them not being back for a couple more years. That should give us time to prepare. We obviously have a lot to learn.

NAVIGATOR

We should be able to watch them for a long time on this course.

CAPTAIN GILBERT
Yes, let's stay on this course until we feel confident,
they are opening.

WEPS
Photonics Spectro Metering Interpolators are showing
a red shift on the Jupitorian rocket engine burn
indicates they are moving away from us in relative
speed, even though they may still be going backwards
and deaccelerating.

CAPTAIN GILBERT
Any estimates on differential relative speed change?

WEPS
Scrolling back on time buffers, based on Cosmic
Interpolators forward CSS Alabama, forward motion
was approximately 3LS prior to the attack and the
Jupitorians were exceeding our speed upon approach
as much as ten percent.

Ranging tools that utilize Cosmic Interpolators to
establish base speed and differential shift created
by measurements with Photonics Spectro Metering
Interpolators show increased differential speed now
almost -2LS. That confirms they are opening the range
significantly.

Except for leaving the bridge to make a head call, Tom stayed there for twenty-four
hours straight closely observing the flare from the Jupitorians rocket exhausts. The
Jupitorians were either decelerating or accelerating in the opposite direction or both,
which would be the case if they reversed course.

If there were no aspect changes, then the Jupitorians would be on a specific course and
even though they would be flying backwards decelerating the actual inertial velocity.

The relative distance between the Jupitorians and Alabama would soon greatly increase
because Alabama was not slowing and going on a prescribed course that was more of
a curve that would slowly turn into a straight line. The range of the Jupitorians slowly
increased and the size of the contrails diminished and grew smaller which gave further
assurances they were moving away.

Tom didn't notice Shelly since she had been around so often, she was almost like a
crewmember. During this entire ordeal Shelly spent a lot of time on the bridge taking

abundant notes. If they were censored and confiscated, she might be able with legal help to force USSF to store her notes in the national archives for a later date when they were declassified. Shelly would have access to these notes in the event she wanted to write a book or do an exposé or for whatever reason.

One thing Shelly knew, the way Tom Gilbert handled himself on the bridge was legendary. John Harris had guessed correctly when he sponsored Tom and did his utmost to get him selected for the CSS Alabama's Commander's role. Shelly had reservations that Commodore Riley or Commodore Avery could have achieved any of this. In fact, she was quite sure they all would be dead had either of the other two been selected. One thing Shelly realized more than anything now: *Space Warfare* was no longer a theory but a fact.

Shelly Brown might be a Senator's Aide with little military experience, but she knew one thing vividly now. Earth was ill prepared and by the grace of God we just missed a pounding that most likely might have occurred if Tom Gilbert did not used his intuition and skill in handling this mission. *After finishing off CSS Alabama, would the Jupitorians have continued to Earth and wiped it out?*

Sadly, the *Project Jupiter* mission would all be wrapped in secrecy. The world would never know what happened. Shelly knew one thing coming for real. The pilot's families would grieve their loss and be told some BS story of how they died.

Shelly correctly assumed Tom would be greatly relieved when his change of command was over most likely within months of returning to Earth.

More SITREPs were sent and eventually it was clear the Jupitorians were heading back to their own planet. Admiral Moritar also sent Jupitorian SITREPS, but his ship would most likely beat the SITREPS home.

The crippled Jupitorian cruiser was beyond repair, the crew transferred to the cruiser sent out to assist and as they were leaving the scene, they sent a Proton Distributer Weapon into the side of the damaged escort from a safe distance and observed the fireball that was created as a result. There was not much comfort on that ship, but it made its way back to Acropolis where crew members from the damaged cruiser were permanently transferred to other ships.

Admiral Moritar assumed he would most likely be executed for failure to carry out his orders, but unfortunately by pulling half the fleet away from the war zone, it caused irreparable damage to their forces and he and the remnants of his fleet were sent bypassing Acropolis back to do more fighting.

As Jupitorian Fleet Admiral fighting inside a solar system Moritar was more into his game in this type of battle. He slowly rectified the situation and restored the stalemate.

He knew however his worst days were ahead when he was recalled to Acropolis to face the Grand Constabulary.

DEBRIEFING

By the time CSS Alabama was on its final course to the rendezvous with Vicksburg, the crew was getting *Channel Fever*. That's a nautical term used to describe restless sailors who knew they would soon be ashore on liberty enjoying the finest pleasures in life that typically included alcohol and fine-looking ladies with distinguished ability they could bestow upon them.

Months turned into weeks and weeks into days. Based on Admiral Gilbert's recommendation, CSS Vicksburg had done a course reversal that took about a week and was now heading back to Earth. Alabama traveling at a higher velocity would catch up to them coasting all the way.

Vicksburg sent out hourly position data which Alabama factored into their navigation formulas and by the time they came within radar range they had good track on them. Based on Tom's recommendation Vicksburg energized its rear dry-dock lighting intermittently which acted as a beacon they could detect on their infrared imaging system at long distance. As they drew closer, they coordinated their velocity and eventually were able to fly in formation side by side at a safe distance.

Vicksburg Commander didn't want to lose the opportunity and launched a TR-3B to position itself to photograph the two Space Carriers flying side by side. Had the CSS Alabama not lost so many TR-3B's in the battle they would have launched the squadrons to get pictures of them flying with the carriers for publicity.

<u>EXT. CGI. SPACE. TR-3B SQUADRON FLYING OUT IN FRONT OF THE TWO SPACE CARRIERS FLYING IN FORMATION. IMAGERY OF THE SPACE CARRIERS FLYING BY. 30 SECONDS.</u>

Having two ships simplified their defense plan as one ship concentrated in front of the formation and the other crew paid complete attention to the rear. The crew of the Alabama took control of the rear searches as they were still spooked from their recent experiences.

The crew of the Vicksburg had been briefed by their Commander of what the Alabama just went through from the SITREPS they had started receiving a week prior. A week later they were inside the Earth's solar system and decelerating.

Because communications were now more functional even though it took three hours to get an answer, orders were given that Alabama would go into Space Dock while the Vicksburg would patrol inside the solar system and was restricted to five hundred thousand miles away from Earth.

More SITREPs were sent and eventually it was clear the Jupitorians were heading back to their own planet. Admiral Moritar also sent Jupitorians SITREPS, but his ship would most likely beat the SITREPS home.

The crippled cruiser was beyond repair, the crew transferred to the cruiser sent out to assist and as they were leaving the scene, they sent a Proton Distributer Weapon into the side of the damaged escort from a safe distance and observed the fireball that was created as a result. There was not much comfort on that spaceship, but it made its way back to Acropolis where crewmembers from the damaged cruiser were permanently transferred to other ships.

Admiral Moritar would most likely have been executed for failure to carry out his orders, but unfortunately by pulling half the fleet away from the war zone, it caused irreparable damage to their forces and he and the remnants of his fleet were sent bypassing Acropolis back to do more fighting.

As Jupitorian Fleet Admiral fighting inside a solar system Moritar was more into his game in this type of battle. He slowly rectified the situation and restored the stalemate. He knew however his worst days were ahead when he was recalled to Acropolis to face the Grand Constabulary.

DEBRIEFING

Alabama was ordered to transfer the remaining special weapon to Vickburg in case it was needed. Even though Vicksburg's CO wanted to *Shanghai* these Alabama pilots, he unfortunately could not apply the two-million-mile rule and had to allow them to fly their TR-3B to the planet surface after the special weapon was unloaded and safely stored in a special magazine.

With all the TR-3Bs gone and the Space Dock opened for them it was now time to do the docking maneuver. Soon afterwards a lot of events would occur. There would be an intense number of debriefings. Tom was relieved to be docking in Space Dock #1 which he was familiar with. Space Dock #2 had a new construction ship in it well underway in its construction.

<u>EXT. CGI. SPACE CSS ALABAMA MOVING INTO THE SPACE DOCK 30 SECONDS.</u>

With autopilot the Alabama slipped slowly into the Space Dock into its cradle. Soon it was optically verified in its docking position and restraints were engaged by hydraulics as the huge opening slowly closed and the dock would be slowly pressurized.

Since Alabama had been in the near vicinity of several nuclear explosions the hull would be swiped for radiation to make sure it would be safe for workers. The tubular gangway went across and mated to the side of the ship. Since nobody had contact with aliens and Blaze was only possibly in contact with air particulates and he subsequently went through decontamination, the crew was suddenly given the best news ever. They would not be taken to Arizona for medical isolation quarantine.

Shelly Brown was relieved she would soon be on her way to the planet. A relief crew was there to take over all the functions of the ship over the next few days so the crew who was well overdue some R&R could be sequentially relieved and rotated to the planet for well-deserved R&R.

The captain if he chooses is always the first person off the ship out of Navy Tradition carried over to the United States Space Force. But today to celebrate the fact they were all alive minus the pilots who made the supreme sacrifice, Shelly Brown who was standing near the hatch was invited by the ship's Captain Gilbert to leave with him. Now that they were back from the mission Tom Gilbert would revert to his official rank of admiral.

ADMIRAL GILBERT
Ms. Brown, it would give me great pride if you would
please lead us off the ship.

SHELLY BROWN
Thank you, Admiral Gilbert, I feel honored.

No crew member or rider was allowed to remove anything from the ship. Security would come in and remove everything. Any personal notes would be confiscated to be censored. Any information deemed compartmentalized was restricted and not allowed to be removed and likely would go to ships shredders that would now be brought aboard since there was likely a number of documents created that would never be allowed to see the light of day.

As a junior officer Tom Gilbert observed submarines shredding a lot of logs they were required to obtain for 90 days and on some missions were directed to destroy for security reasons.

Waiting on the Space Dock were a group of people in suits including John Harris who was all smiles.

The homecoming was rather happy for Tom Gilbert since he had just established a milestone in *Space Warfare*. Surprisingly, the Former President was there beside John Harris. It would have been the perfect homecoming except one of John Harris' nemesis was also there, Kevin O'Toole.

Kevin O'Toole had been promoted within the CIA and was now the deputy in charge of the CIA's newly formed Space Division. When the NRO went to the USSF, the CIA lost a lot of influence. Likewise, when the Air Force was downsized and placed under the Army, all those strong Air Force-CIA ties were lost. The Air Force no longer had much to say about Area 51. The USSF was now calling all the shots.

The former USSF Secretary Margarette Mackworth had been relieved. Her fraternization with junior engineers finally caught up with her and she was forced to resign. John Harris was acting USSF Secretary until a permanent assignment could be made. He informed the President he did not desire the position and was planning on retiring real soon.

The former President said and smiled and held out his hand to shake Tom's.

FORMER PRESIDENT
Good to see you, Admiral Gilbert.

ADMIRAL GILBERT
Thank you, Mr. President.

FORMER PRESIDENT

You had quite a mission. I was given permission to read some of your sitreps. I'm very proud of you and am glad you were selected to lead this mission. I'm not sure another person could have got everyone back safely.

ADMIRAL GILBERT
It was touch and go for a while.

FORMER PRESIDENT

All I can say is what you accomplished is truly remarkable and welcome back.

ADMIRAL GILBERT

Thank you, Mr. President, that means a lot to me coming from you.

After all the greetings were made and the former President completed his welcome back to the Alabama, he was whisked away on a waiting TR-3B shuttle taking the VIPs back to Earth.

After a few minutes John Harris then informed Tom Gilbert what he already predicted would happen.

JOHN HARRIS

We are going to be shuttled down to Area 51. You are directed to go with us for a debriefing.

Tom Gilbert understood the acting secretary of the USSF would soon be giving him orders.

ADMIRAL GILBERT
As you wish, Mr. Harris.

Commodore Avery was there to welcome Tom Gilbert back and informed Tom of his promotion.

COMMODORE AVERY
I'm now an admiral selectee and will be turning over
to a new guy the following week.

Admiral Gilbert assumed Commodore Riley was no doubt due to be reassigned and most likely selected to Admiral Rank. Tom Gilbert also assumed he too would most likely be relieved and face an inquisition on the loss of two squadrons and the pilots.

Shelly Brown flew in the VIP craft that was taking the former President and his Secret Service detail, along with the two NASA scientists to the planet, was very happy her mother's health was holding up. As soon as they were close enough to receive radio waves and the emails were forwarded, she got a condensed version of what her mother had done while she was gone.

EXT. CGI/REAL TR-3B VTOL LANDING AT ANDREWS AFB NEXT TO HANGER. IT THEN PULLED INTO HANGER BY A LIMO.

Today the TR-3B shuttle landed at Andrews Air Force Base. Shelly Brown had a limo provided to her as the passengers climbed out of the TR-3B inside the hangar at Andrews Air Force Base.

Senator Bosworth, still holding his office, barely, was stuck on Capitol Hill in a critical vote in the Senate called as soon as he was informed Shelly was at Andrews, he requested *to meet Shelly later that day.*

SHELLY BROWN
I want to spend the rest of the day with my mother. I
can meet you in the morning.

SENATOR BOSWORTH
It will have to be late in the morning. Let's meet for
lunch.

SHELLY BROWN
Where at?

SENATOR BOSWORTH
If it's okay, the congressional cafeteria, I'm super busy tomorrow.

SHELLY BROWN
That will be fine.

In twenty minutes, she was ringing her mother's doorbell. She had no keys with her.

EXT./INT. DAY SHELLY BROWN MOTHER'S HOME

SHELLY'S MOTHER
Look who's here!

Shelly's mother grabbed her, and they stood there hugging as if there was no tomorrow.

SHELLY BROWN.
It's so wonderful to be back. The first thing I want to do is take a long hot shower then relax a bit and try to forget the past four years.

SHELLY'S MOTHER
When you left, a government man came about a week later and said you would be gone for an extended period and that you had volunteered for an assignment.

SHELLY BROWN.
Actually, I was Shanghaied.

SHELLY'S MOTHER
Taken without your permission?

SHELLY BROWN.
It's a long story, I'd rather not get into it now.

SHELLY'S MOTHER
Okay, dear, take your shower, you'll feel better then. I'll make you some chicken soup and maybe you'll feel better.

SHELLY BROWN.
Thanks, that sounds good.

Tom and the other group boarded another TR-3B set up as a shuttle and were soon on their way to Area 51. They were soon down in the SCIF that General Harris knew all too well, though modernized quite a bit in the past 4 years._

INT. DAY AREA 51 UNDERGROUND SCIF

ADMIRAL GILBERT
Why did we have to come here?

JOHN HARRIS.
We needed some place ultra-secure to make sure none of this information leaks out.

ADMIRAL GILBERT
All right.

JOHN HARRIS.
In a moment we will start replaying slices of the video you sent us.

ADMIRAL GILBERT
This should be interesting.

The video viewer could fast forward, reverse, stop, etc.

John Harris fast forwarded to one of the sections that had good video of the Invincible Class Jupitorian Planetary Assault Ship.

JOHN HARRIS.
You are sure this ship is two miles long?

ADMIRAL GILBERT
Certainly. We had radar verifications.

JOHN HARRIS.
Some of USSF Scientist say it appeared longer due to modal distortion giving a false indication.

ADMIRAL GILBERT
Mr. Harris, my radar operators used all their ranging tools we know the exact distance and based on the length of the Jupitorian ship image we recorded broadside at that distance with zero Doppler for a couple minutes, we know it is two miles long.

JOHN HARRIS.
Why do you think the Jupitorians have such large ships?

ADMIRAL GILBERT
They are most likely Gator Freighters; they haul forces used to invade planets.

JOHN HARRIS.
If they were going to invade Earth, why didn't they just come directly here if that's the case?

ADMIRAL GILBERT
In my time with the Ponarian before we dropped him off at the Jupitorian planet, we had lengthy discussions. I recorded audio clips of those conversations which are inserted in my BMMR (Basic Mission Milestones Report).

JOHN HARRIS.
Why would they send an invasion fleet just to destroy your ship?

ADMIRAL GILBERT
The Jupitorians are arrogant imperialists and have been for several million years. They were not sent to invade this planet; they were sent to destroy my ship because I embarrassed them during our escape from their planet.

JOHN HARRIS.
What made them turn around? They still had a superior force.

ADMIRAL GILBERT
That's a mystery, I think because we got so lucky, they got spooked and decided to withdraw to figure out what went wrong.

JOHN HARRIS.
Do you think they will come back?

ADMIRAL GILBERT
It will not be for a couple years as the distance is so great. But yes, I think they will come back to exact revenge. We blooded them really good.

JOHN HARRIS.
What led to your departure the way it unfolded?

ADMIRAL GILBERT
They first tried to grab the TR-3B, then they sent their planetary defense ships after us. They also sent them after the TR-3B when it escaped. This fleet was not present when we were there. They had to pull it from the War Zone.

JOHN HARRIS.
They're in a war?

ADMIRAL GILBERT
According to the Ponarian, they are in perpetual war with nearby solar systems standing up to the Jupitorian Imperialism.

JOHN HARRIS.
It took them more than a year to catch up with you, why is that?

ADMIRAL GILBERT
We obtained a significant velocity before our final turn to point this solar system. If I did any more acceleration prior to that turn, I would have burned up quite a lot of fuel stabilizing the new course. By delaying until the turn, I could put the extra fuel into the final stretch home when the crew would become far unrulier as the days were dragging on. This delay in the high-speed run gave them enough time to catch up to us.

JOHN HARRIS.
How did you detect their presence?

ADMIRAL GILBERT
We saw some strange shimmering probably due to modal distortion our surveillance photonics, and I devised a way to use our propulsion to light up the space and get a view of approaching Jupitorian ships that was setting up for a sucker punch.

JOHN HARRIS.
How did you deal with it?

ADMIRAL GILBERT
The Jupitorians sent a single ship in to get us, figuring they would come up our blind spot at 6:00 o'clock and

nail us in the engineering spaces is my guess. I used our rocket exhaust to slice through the Jupitorian ship rendering it useless.

JOHN HARRIS.
Then what happened?

Tom Gilbert then gave a rundown of all the action and the recording of all the gun camera video simulcast the Alabama recorded.

JOHN HARRIS.
It looks like all those laser attacks did a good job of lighting up the space around you which enabled some good gun camera video.

ADMIRAL GILBERT
It sure does, and the reason why those laser beams are so short is due to the velocity the ships were traveling, they could only extend out a limited distance before the light beam diffused into harmless globs of light.

JOHN HARRIS.
No doubt had you been going slower; those lasers would have sliced you open like a can opener.

ADMIRAL GILBERT
Yes, the lesson learned when facing the Jupitorians is to make them chase you at high-speed which evens the playing field.

The two episodes where the hydrogen bombs were delivered were somewhat difficult to watch knowing these men were flying to their deaths.

ADMIRAL GILBERT
That video shows incredible bravery and sacrifice.

JOHN HARRIS
It certainly does, just like pilots in some of our wars.

ADMIRAL GILBERT
Every pilot who flew the gauntlet deserves at least a Distinguished Flying Cross.

JOHN HARRIS
I will make that recommendation to the President.

John Harris was copying several notes. Those notes would have to be carried by special courier to the Pentagon where they would be serialized and stored in a SCIF until the president read them. After that reading, the notes would likely get shredded.

<u>EXT. CGI. SPACE AZZIE'S TR-3B GUN CAMERA VIDEO</u>

ADMIRAL GILBERT
This is the gun camera video piped from Azzie's TR-3B and recorded live by the Alabama over our multi-channel combat receiver system.

The men in the room watched Azzie's TR-3B's gun camera video show it getting closer to the two-mile-long Jupitorian ship including the voice over of Azzie, aka Rudy Wilcox say out loud,

AZZIE (a.k.a. RUDY WILCOX)
DURING MISSION REPLAY
They are lighting my ship up with a laser, I'll be dead shortly so goodbye.

The video then turned into a noise display.

JOHN HARRIS
I take it that's when the bomb went off.

ADMIRAL GILBERT
Yes, about five seconds after the attack and the fireball distinguished in micro gravity, we could see much of the front of the ship had been blown off. Later we observed a very large explosion. Not sure what caused it, perhaps the power plant failure mode caused a catastrophic end to whatever was left of the ship.

Soon they were watching Instigator's (aka Brad Howard's) gun camera video.

ADMIRAL GILBERT
This pilot, Brad Howard, managed to get all the way to that two-mile long Jupitorian ship without being destroyed. The video went out exactly at the time we calculated the TR-3B hit the side of the ship and the detonation trigger was hit simultaneously.

<u>EXT. CGI. SPACE REPLAY OF INSTIGATOR CRASHING INTO THE JUPITORIAN PLANETARY ASSAULT SHIP</u>

Looking at all the laser light going off in all directions shooting at the few remaining TR-3Bs, the Alabama's photonics recorded the massive explosion. After about eight seconds they could see the ship had been blown in half and strange-looking fires were shooting out that could not be explained.

JOHN HARRIS
That's an amazing sight.

ADMIRAL GILBERT
Yes, it wasn't long afterwards that Jupitorian ships began a course reversal. We didn't know what to expect and all we had left was one more special weapon loaded with a good pilot and two more squadrons of newly trained pilots that I felt would simply get destroyed if we sent them after the enemy.

EXT. CGI. SPACE REPLAY VIDEO OF JUPITORIAN REVERSING COURSE IN TIME LAPSED PHOTOGRAPHY.

JOHN HARRIS
How long did it take them to reverse course?

ADMIRAL GILBERT
This video we compressed in time lapsed photography so you could see the maneuver in a few minutes. Their ships were able to turn 180 degrees very efficiently, but the momentum did not change to the other direction for almost a week, though we could see the Jupitorian fleet slow down measurably after a day or so.

JOHN HARRIS
Your target range rate indicated opening even though their inertia was still in the same direction?

ADMIRAL GILBERT
That's correct, we were above light speed when the combat commenced and when it ended because we were accelerating in attempt to get away from them.

JOHN HARRIS
Do you have any idea how fast their ships can go?

ADMIRAL GILBERT
We were not capable of determining their speed capability, but I think their speeds as well as our own

can be a lot higher than we realize. The problem comes down to: Will there be enough fuel left to slow down?

JOHN HARRIS
I can see where that could be a problem.

ADMIRAL GILBERT
Even worse, had we not had the Ponarian with us, we never could have found them and his insights in guiding us to constantly create new maps enabled us to find the way home. Based on this trip, I believe a ship can get lost in space easily.

JOHN HARRIS
How much food and water did you have left and how much longer could you have remained in space?

ADMIRAL GILBERT
The water recyclers helped of course, but in terms of food, I doubt we could have lasted another six months.

JOHN HARRIS
What do you suppose would have happened if you ran out of food?

ADMIRAL GILBERT
My speculation is members of the ship may have resulted in reverting to cannibalism as a last means of survival.

John Harris then dropped the anti-morale bomb on Tom.

JOHN HARRIS
I'm sorry to inform you, Admiral, but you are not going to be relieved of command for a while. If there is any possibility the Jupitorians would come into our galaxy, we need to have a seasoned commander on board.

ADMIRAL GILBERT
What about Commodore Riley, he was with me the entire time and as executive officer, gained vast knowledge of space carrier operations.

JOHN HARRIS

Admiral, that was the next thing I was going to inform you of. Commodore Riley is going to be transferred to CSS Vicksburg and take over as their Commander. Vicksburg's CO, who is a great new construction oversight officer, is going to be transferred to the new construction hull currently in Space Dock #2.

ADMIRAL GILBERT

Mr. Harris, I really need some time off. I'm exhausted. This four-year trip took a lot out of me.

JOHN HARRIS

Admiral, I understand that that's why we are going to let you go on leave now. Commodore Riley, who will soon be pinning on his stars as Rear Admiral, will remain onboard Alabama overseeing the refit for the next thirty days, while you are taking a break. When you get back to the ship thirty days from now, he will be given some time off and then transferred to CSS Vicksburg.

ADMIRAL GILBERT

I wish I could take more than thirty days off away from the ship.

JOHN HARRIS

We are going to need some heavy patrolling for a while in case the Jupitorians turned that fleet around and started heading this way. We have set up two patrol zones and you will deploy the TR-3Bs as long-distance scouts.

ADMIRAL GILBERT

The TR-3Bs can't really travel that far in space, how will they patrol?

JOHN HARRIS

That's where your carrier comes in. You will sew an area with all four squadrons, fully armed and ready, and you will fly around their patrol zones, dropping them off and picking them back up in a systematic manner. It's really going to be just like you were on a carrier at sea, but instead will be in space deploying space capable air wings doing a Combat air patrol (CAP).

ADMIRAL GILBERT
How much area do you think we can cover using this method?

JOHN HARRIS
It's funny you asked. We have a couple PhDs from MIT who will be flown up to Alabama and the Vicksburg when you push out to your patrol zones and show you the math, and help you design your search plans for maximum rate of coverage. We realize it will be very porous at times, but it will be a lot better than no eyes and ears out there.

ADMIRAL GILBERT
What about the KH-14, Hubble, Roentgensatellit (ROSAT), and some of the other surveillance capabilities?

JOHN HARRIS
Not enough resolution and density to cover all the areas, that's where you come in. You will be vectored into all the blind spots.

ADMIRAL GILBERT
What blind spots are you referring to?

JOHN HARRIS
On the other side of the sun or Jupiter, or Saturn.

ADMIRAL GILBERT
Anything else?

JOHN HARRIS
Yes, this is the sticky part. You will be given a couple extra days on top of your thirty days of requested leave to carry out another special mission for me.

ADMIRAL GILBERT
And what is that?

JOHN HARRIS

We are going to have a memorial for all the pilots who died on this mission at Arlington tomorrow. I'm going to send you there to represent yourself, the Alabama, and the United States Space Force.

ADMIRAL GILBERT

Sure, I wouldn't mind meeting with the families of the deceased pilots. What am I authorized to tell them?

JOHN HARRIS

None of their relatives are Q level cleared, nor will they ever be. I've been instructed all space combat is Q-level classified and NO-FORN until further notice.

ADMIRAL GILBERT

What about Shelly Brown and the two NASA scientists, they're already off the ship.

JOHN HARRIS

They have all received a special briefing and know the consequences if they reveal any of it.

ADMIRAL GILBERT

Shelly Brown wrote copious notes during the mission, I'm sure she expects to be given her notes or good reason why she can't access them.

JOHN HARRIS

Her notes are now in the national archives in Q-clearance section. Since such files are only downgraded on twelve-year intervals, she will most likely be deceased by the time they are downgraded as unclassified.

ADMIRAL GILBERT
She works for a powerful Senator.

JOHN HARRIS
Yes, she does, but he's on our team now.

ADMIRAL GILBERT
What does that mean?

JOHN HARRIS
It means he couldn't get elected city dog catcher without our help.

ADM ADMIRAL GILBERT IRAL GILBERT
How do you help him?

JOHN HARRIS
We electronically alter the votes and send people around pollsters to convey they strongly support him.

ADMIRAL GILBERT
That's highly illegal.

JOHN HARRIS
The alternative could be mass panic if the public was led to believe there are aliens, and they might be on their way to this planet to wipe us out.

ADMIRAL GILBERT
Understand all.

Tom Gilbert was soon on his way to building 27 where a jet was waiting for him to take him to Reagan National Airport.

There currently was a news blackout on the CSS Alabama and the public had long ago given it up for good. The plane he was flying on was a supped-up Gulfstream 850. By the year 2026, Aerospace had transcended to a new degree in commercial travel.

To maintain some aerospace manufacturing in the United States in view of unfair trade competition around the world and ventures by Chinese, British, French, and others, the USSF secretly funneled alien technology into the principal companies which allowed them to build air frames that were 50 percent lighter but 200 percent stronger.

These super pressurized aircraft with special propulsion systems produced a service ceiling of more than one hundred thousand feet. However, the FAA would never give permission for a civilian aircraft to go above fifty thousand feet. Tom's plane was descending into Reagan International in just two and a half hours.

The unmarked plane pulled up to a gate that was used only a couple times a day by a small airline that operated much the way *Air America* did in the 1960s. Their profit margin was low, but they managed to stay in business. Providing gate access to these unmarked jets netted them some hefty fees and they knew which side their toast was buttered and never revealed to anyone the nature of that business.

Most of the people departing on those jets walked through security with a special escort and avoided all lines. If there was any luggage, it was delivered directly to the plane by the airline company as another task their customer paid generous fees to provide.

The Gulfstream 850 engines were shut down at the gate, the door opened and just outside the craft was a couple airline employees and a limo. Tom was escorted fifteen feet to the waiting Limo which then took him out of the airport to Jefferson Davis Highway, U.S. 1 to his hotel in Crystal City, the Hilton.

ARLINGTON

Nobody knew Tom Gilbert was back, and nobody was expecting him. His chore for the rest of the day was to get a dress uniform in shape for the festivities the next day, as grim as they would be.

Nothing prepares a commanding officer to meet the families of fallen heroes. In fact, in the normal course of warfare, they seldom or almost never meet the family though many try to write heartfelt letters to their loved ones. Tom's problem is, he had over two squadrons of pilots who were killed in mortal combat.

Even though the government offered to pay for the transportation and accommodations to any family member who wanted to attend the memorial, less than 25 percent indicated they wanted to attend. In most cases the relatives had given them up for good long ago. Four years is a long time to wait to hear of the status of their loved ones. Angry allegations and accusations plagued the government because family members didn't buy their loved ones would be gone for four years.

Some wives who reached points of desperation, and found alternative spouses pressed the point where the government gave them death certificates allowing them to remarry and move on with their lives. It was a complicated mess to say the least.

During the last month on the CSS Alabama's return to Earth, ship started receiving radio transmissions from USSF who advised crew members of special circumstances with their families. All communications were censored by Tom Gilbert and his communicator to determine if it was appropriate to inform a crew member before they arrived.

No news was better than bad news.

Many of those who had lost their wives or husbands as part of the cover-up to hide the real nature of the mission, were not informed about their spouses until the ship was docked in Space Dock #1.

Even though they had the ability to sedate a crew member, they didn't want to be able to medicate and control a couple dozen zombies during long periods of the mission.

Deaths and other tragic events were also obscured from crew members so as to not affect their personal psyche.

Those people with bad news were the first to leave and taken to USSF Headquarters to receive special briefing with counselors to assist their transition due to unforeseen circumstances such as car wrecks, cancer, crime, and a variety of reasons.

In Washington, D.C., because of unexpected events such as a military officer suddenly arriving without his luggage due to transportation issues, one can rent anything including uniforms for any rank. Tom had a relationship with one such rental, where he rented suits and uniforms and all he had to do is contact them, tell them what he needed, including shoes and sox, and they would deliver it to the hotel within three hours ready to try on, with a tailor in the event some last-minute alterations were needed.

By the time it was around dinner, Tom had tried on his rental uniform and the company employees had already left. He was all set for the morning at Arlington.

Pentagon speech writers had already been busy and texted him a document to use the following day. That was good for Tom because it saved him several hours and with the tremendous psychological drain he exhibited the last few days, he just wanted to rest and relax.

But Tom Gilbert felt wound up psychologically. The first thing that popped in his head was he could go to a bar and get a bite to eat and a stiff drink and come back and pass out with a wakeup call he would initiate before he stepped out of the hotel.

Tom walked around the corner crossed Jefferson Davis Highway, and remembered there was a Howard Johnson's hotel up the street with a pub in it. He didn't feel like going to the sports bar, or other noisy places. He had not been in D.C. in a while and the Howard Johnson's was no more. What stood in its place was a Holiday Inn.

<u>EXT./INT. EVENGING CRYSTAL CITY IRISH PUB ON JEFFERSON DAVIS HIWAY.</u>

Tom Gilbert approached the Holiday Inn, anyway, feeling the walk made him feel a lot better exercising in real gravity. As he got up to the hotel, he was happy to see there was an Irish pub by the main entrance. He went inside and quickly found a seat at the bar that was half empty.

The place was cozy, and no doubt was jammed on Friday and Saturday evenings. *It was probably pure chaos on St. Patrick's Day.*

<u>INT. EVENING WASHINGTON DC SHELLY BROWNS HOME (WITH MOTHER)</u>

Shelly Brown had been enjoying her mother all day long. After taking a Hollywood shower and applying copious amounts of perfume and cosmetics, she suddenly felt much better. *She would never leave Earth again for the rest of her life for any reason!*

Shelly had mentioned to her mother the conversation she had with Admiral Tom Gilbert just as they were going into combat.

SHELLY BROWN

I somehow thought he felt we were all going to die so he revealed his soul to me and disclosed he had always liked me. I know what he really meant. He had an emotional attachment to me he never revealed and couldn't because he was the ship's captain.

SHELLY'S MOTHER
Why do you think he did that?

SHELLY BROWN

I think Tom Gilbert had reason to believe we all would probably die. So, there was no reason to hide his feelings, that normally a Ship's Captain must do.

SHELLY BROWN'S MOTHER

In life when we stumble into certain situations, we often tend to bear our souls to someone important to us. I think that's what happened.

SHELLY BROWN

Please do not repeat any of this to anyone, or you will put me in danger.

SHELLY BROWN'S MOTHER

Don't worry, dear, your secrets are safe with me. I understand what you have been through and it's best we do not reveal these things to others as it would complicate your life.

Shelly was so happy she had such a wonderful wise and sophisticated mother.

SHELLY BROWN'S MOTHER

When a man reveals something like Admiral Gilbert did in such circustances he did, is a very special event in your life.

SHELLY BROWN
What do you mean by that?

SHELLY BROWN'S MOTHER
You all thought you were going to die. He bared his soul to you. He was sincere and honest with you. The affection is genuine.

SHELLY BROWN
You think so?

SHELLY BROWN'S MOTHER
What he was saying to you in his own words, was he loved you.

SHELLY BROWN
But he never ever made a pass or any hints or suggestions in over four years.

SHELLY BROWN'S MOTHER
He's the ship's captain. Some things he can't say on his ship as much as he would like to have. He only took the moment when he did because he honestly didn't think you would all survive.

SHELLY BROWN
Why do you think he did that?

SHELLY BROWN'S MOTHER
I think he wanted you to know if you all died that day, that he had affection for you, and if there were any other circumstances, anything is possible.

SHELLY BROWN
So, you think he was emotionally attracted to me and if it were not for the fact we were trapped on his ship, he might have made the first move?

SHELLY BROWN'S MOTHER
Absolutely.

Shelly was taking it all in when suddenly, her phone rang. The caller I.D. indicated it was Senator Bosworth.

SHELLY BROWN
Hello.

SENATOR BOSWORTH
Shelly, this is Senator Bosworth.

SHELLY BROWN
Hello, Senator, what can I do for you?

SENATOR BOSWORTH
Shelly, I just got word they are having a memorial for crew members who died during the Alabama's mission tomorrow at Arlington.

SHELLY BROWN
Is that so?

SENATOR BOSWORTH
Yes. I would go myself, but we are expected to have that key vote tomorrow on the USSF appropriations around the same time. I would like you to go to represent me.

SHELLY BROWN
I would be delighted, Senator.

SENATOR BOSWORTH
Thank you, I appreciate that.

SHELLY BROWN
Who will be giving the eulogy?

SENATOR BOSWORTH
From my source, Admiral Gilbert will be the keynote speaker.

SHELLY BROWN
Is he in D.C. now?

SENATOR BOSWORTH
Must be if he's going to be in Arlington at 09:30 in the morning.

SHELLY BROWN
Interesting.

SENATOR BOSWORTH
Okay, I'll let you go now so you can spend some
time with your mother. Call me tomorrow when you
get a chance and fill me in on what all happens at the
memorial.

SHELLY BROWN
Will do.

SENATOR BOSWORTH
Goodnight.

SHELLY BROWN
Take care.

Shelly's mother overheard most of the conversation and knew Shelly had some things
to do tomorrow and was probably tired herself.

SHELLY BROWN'S MOTHER
Shelly, I'm going to go lay down now.

SHELLY BROWN
Okay, Mother.

A few moments after Shelly's mother went to her bedroom, Shelly was sitting there
thinking about their conversation and could not get Tom Gilbert off her mind. The
thought he was in D.C. also had an effect on her.

Shelly had her cell phone in her hand and even though it had not been used in four
years, she found that after she charged it up for a while, it was good as new and
working.

In a playful manner she scrolled through her contact information and dreaded the fact
she had about fourteen thousand text messages and emails she needed to delete.

Then it hit Shelly, she had Tom Gilbert's phone number.

I wonder if that number is still any good.

Shelly thought long and hard for a few moments. She knew that if Tom Gilbert blew
her off if she attempted to contact him, she would be crushed. But on the other hand,
if he was sincere during battle stations, she wanted to know.

Just like her mother articulated, this was a come to Jesus rare moment where real sincerity and feelings were exposed.

Shelly took that fateful step. She was a risk taker; otherwise, Shelly never would have ended up being the chief advisor to a U.S. Senator.

Shelly dialed Tom Gilbert's number.

Tom might not have answered his phone or even looked at it as he was temporally zoned out sipping his first drink when the bartender prompted him.

<u>EXT./INT. EVENGING CRYSTAL CITY IRISH PUB ON JEFFERSON DAVIS HIWAY.</u>

BARTENDER
You going to answer your phone, buddy? Is your wife
hunting you down?

Tom snapped out of it looked down at the caller I.D. and saw the name Shelly Brown.

Tom was quite surprised but was melancholy as he had just had thoughts running through his head of the dreadful day ahead of him. It would be a surreal moment facing all those families. These were special families because their loved one happened to be some of the bravest and greatest men and women that had ever lived, making the supreme sacrifice so that he and his ship would live and come back to fight another day.

Tom did not answer the phone quick enough because of his temporary mental paralysis. However, something told him to call her back immediately. He wanted to call her and hear her voice. His inward being was now coming alive and facilitating a transcendence which he needed now more than ever. He then touched the call back icon which started the phone ringing in the opposite direction.

Shelly was momentarily crushed that Tom didn't answer the phone. Then she started analyzing it could be inconvenient, he might be in the middle of something where he couldn't answer. And just as she was psychologically preconditioning herself for disappointment, her phone rang! And it was Tom Gilbert on the caller I.D.

SHELLY BROWN
Hello.

TOM GILBERT
Shelly?

SHELLY BROWN
Yes.

TOM GILBERT
This is Tom Gilbert.

SHELLY BROWN
Hi Tom, thanks for calling me back.

TOM GILBERT
How's everything, is your mother, okay?

SHELLY BROWN
Yes, everything is fine here.

TOM GILBERT
Good.

SHELLY BROWN
Say, Tom, Senator Bosworth asked me to go to Arlington tomorrow to attend the memorial for the crew members who did not make it back.

TOM GILBERT
I see.

SHELLY BROWN
That's not why I called but I just wanted you to know I would be there tomorrow representing the Senator at his request.

TOM GILBERT
You are more than welcome to attend, and your presence will make it a happier occasion for me. I'm looking forward to seeing you there.

SHELLY BROWN
Tom.

After a delay without any more words, Tom instinctively asked.

TOM GILBERT
Shelly?

SHELLY BROWN
Tom, you probably are wondering why I really called.

TOM GILBERT
What is it you wanted to discuss?

SHELLY BROWN
Are you in D.C. now?

TOM GILBERT
Yes, I'm in Crystal City, I walked a few blocks from my hotel to get some exercise in real gravity and sample some alcoholic beverages. I've not tasted in four years.

SHELLY BROWN
Sounds like an excellent way to unwind considering the circumstances.

TOM GILBERT
Hopefully after a few drinks I can crash and get my clock restarted back to normal Earth Time.

SHELLY BROWN
Would you like some company? I could be there in a few minutes?

Tom thought about it momentarily, at first wanting to avoid possible conflicts of interest, if there were any, then felt a strange emotional sensation he couldn't quite understand and automatically responded as if his temporal reasoning was almost like an out-of-body experience and responded.

TOM GILBERT
Yes, I would like that.

SHELLY BROWN
Where are you located now?

TOM GILBERT
I'll text you the locator map.

SHELLY BROWN
Okay, I'll see you in a few minutes.

Shelly knew her mother had just went to her bed but probably wasn't asleep, so she went to her bedroom.

<u>INT. EVENING WASHINGTON DC SHELLY BROWNS HOME (WITH MOTHER)</u>

SHELLY BROWN
Mom?

SHELLY BROWN'S MOTHER
Yes, Shelly, what's up, dear?

SHELLY BROWN
I'm going to go meet Tom Gilbert. I have a hunch I
want to figure out.

SHELLY BROWN'S MOTHER
Be careful, Shelly, I don't want you to be heartbroken.

SHELLY BROWN
I'm a big girl. I can handle myself. The real question
is, can Tom handle himself?

SHELLY BROWN'S MOTHER
Well, you are sort of a lioness, don't eat him alive!

SHELLY BROWN
I promise to be gentle with him and not break his heart.

SHELLY BROWN'S MOTHER
Okay, honey, tell me about it later.

Shelly hugged her mother strongly. Her world and her universe had changed. Just when she thought her life was complicated, it now transcended to a new level.

Since Shelly was a master makeup artist and had already put on her war paint, all she had to do was slip out of her casual clothes and put on something mildly seductive. She already knew from her experiences in space the real person Tom was, always a gentleman, clever, kind, and sensitive. In the bottom of her heart, when he was calculating they were all going to die because the aliens were just too powerful for them, he revealed himself.

In that one fragile moment, Tom Gilbert's armor cracked and some of his essence seeped out and now Shelly knew the truth. It was no longer a question of what the facts were, it was now a negotiation of how they should proceed. What's Tom's life going to be like and how is space going to be a part of it and for how long?

Shelly didn't want to bother with an Uber or a Lyft and didn't care. She continued receiving her salary even though she was absent for four years. Her wonderful mother guarded her financial assets, and they grew handsomely while she was gone. A Taxi fare to her was chump change. Shelly called the taxi using an APP on her phone she used in the past and thank God all that still worked.

Within seven minutes after hanging up with Tom, Shelly was dressed and out on her mother's porch waiting for the CAB which pulled up a minute or two later. From her mother's house it didn't take too long to get to Crystal City and to the address Tom had texted her.

<u>EXT./INT. EVENGING CRYSTAL CITY IRISH PUB ON JEFFERSON DAVIS HIWAY.</u>

Shelly was slightly apprehensive as she got out of the cab after paying the driver and casually walked into the half empty Irish Pub. Both seats on either side of Tom had been occupied and Tom had politely asked the bartender to make room for his friend who was arriving in a few minutes. Tom had ample cash with him and had already tipped the bartender extremely well who was more than accommodative. Tom looked kind of pale from lack of natural sunlight and was slightly weakened by reduced gravity over the past four years. People who had moved were anxious to see how this fella's friend appeared.

Shelly had worked out hard on Alabama for the past two months and her diet had worked miracles. Perhaps Tom's kind words had some motivating factor, she wasn't sure. Tonight, even though her clothes were four years old, they were still new, and she looked exquisite. People at the bar immediately thought she was a $10,000 call girl which did operate in Washington, D.C., and were usually provided to congressmen by foreign lobbyists, usually former congressmen ready to sell out their country for personal gain.

Shelly felt compelled to display her true feelings like someone wore their dignity on their sleeve. She walked up to Tom, gave him a hug and a kiss on the cheek, leaving behind a lipstick mark that other women in the club were suddenly jealous of.

Tom, feeling the effects of the alcohol drink he had half-finished as well as the psychophysical reaction to the splendid beauty this gorgeous creature radiated, suddenly felt light in the head. Few people ever had or ever will experience the radical events in their lives such as an intergalactic space battle and the grim reminder of how fragile life is such as Tom and Shelly did together.

Tom recalled Riley's comments right after the space battles.

XO RILEY
That Shelly is full of piss and vinegar.

TOM GILBERT
Another Unsinkable Molly Brown?"

After Shelly sat down next to Tom on the bar stool, there of course was very curious looks. Most of the customers were regulars who lived within a half-mile or less and knew each other. This couple was complete strangers, and there was something odd about them. It was clear to the casual observer there was some type of attraction for each other, and their behavior was dignified, but at the same time, something was going on.

TOM GILBERT
You look nice tonight.

SHELLY BROWN
Thank you.

TOM GILBERT
I'm glad you came by. I was just trying to calm myself
down thinking about tomorrow and what I'll be facing.

SHELLY BROWN
I know it's going to be tough on you. No man deserves
this much responsibility. It would crush mere mortals.
But you have an inner strength that many do not have.

TOM GILBERT
Thank you for your kind words.

SHELLY BROWN
I'll be there for you tomorrow. You did a lot for me,
more than you will ever realize.

TOM GILBERT
I thought I screwed up your life more than anything.

SHELLY BROWN
No, on the contrary, you advanced me far more than I
would ever allow myself. You changed me.

TOM GILBERT
Hopefully something good will come of it.

SHELLY BROWN
It already has.

As they sat there talking about trivial things, avoiding any further references to tomorrow and their future, that mutual attraction was supreme. The feelings were modulating, and the desires flourished. As they gazed into each other's eyes, expectancy and gratification signaled a tapestry of guidance that would redirect their energies towards subsequent actions.

After Tom finished his second drink, he knew he was reaching the dangerous limit, and so did Shelly who suggested they leave.

SHELLY BROWN
Tom let's go for a walk where we can talk in private.

TOM GILBERT
Okay.

Tom paid his bar bill and gave the bartender a tip that was rare and magnificent. The bartender suspected something was going on and these two struck him as rather an odd couple and the way they spoke to each other was uncommon and quite serious. Several days later, as he saw Tom's picture in the paper and discovered the media was hounding Shelly Brown, Senator Bosworth's aide, he realized that was the couple he had served. And now it made perfect sense to him why they were acting kind of strange.

alone,elly and Tom walked down the sidewalk adjacent to Jefferson Davis Highway towards the Hilton Hotel the conversation began and was now much more fluid and open since they were alone affording them the privacy to speak what was on their minds.

Shelly had wrapped her arms around Tom's left arm giving a sense of gratification and admiration.

SHELLY BROWN
When you said those things to me on the ship when
we encountered the Jupitorians, why did you pick that
time of all to say those things to me?

TOM GILBERT
I wanted you to know in case something happened to
us as I expected it would.

SHELLY BROWN
So, you really thought we were all going to die?

TOM GILBERT
Yes, I didn't think we stood a chance. Our survival is
a miracle all in itself.

SHELLY BROWN
I took what you said to me in all sincerity. I figured it would not be the time or place you would say something you didn't believe was true.

TOM GILBERT
Well, now you know how I was feeling at the time.

SHELLY BROWN
Tom, tell me, how do you feel now. Has anything changed?

TOM GILBERT
I feel the same.

SHELLY BROWN
I kind of thought you did.

TOM GILBERT
Okay.

SHELLY BROWN
Tom, may I ask you a question?

TOM GILBERT
Sure.

SHELLY BROWN
Why is it you never asked me how I felt?

TOM GILBERT
To be honest, I didn't feel like I had the right to know how you felt.

SHELLY BROWN
Tom, it's okay, I give you the right.

The two stopped. They were under a streetlight where they could clearly see each other's face, and peer into the other's soul. The transcendence was immediate and evocative.

A few hours later, Tom was snoring. It was obvious to Shelly Tom needed some rest for his big day tomorrow. She slipped into her clothes and out the door. In five minutes, she was at the front entrance and the hotel security had called her a taxi. Shelly was in her bed sleeping like a lamb by one-thirty A.M. after setting her alarm for 7:30 in the morning so she could get up and properly dress for the memorial.

Shelly's mother was recently retired and available to help her daughter all day long if necessary. After informing her mother she had to go to Arlington for the memorial, her mother offered to drive her there and back, which Shelly gratefully accepted.

There was ample parking set aside for the families and those invited to attend. Shelly informed the parking valet who she was, and the kind gentleman told her and her mother they could get out of the car here and when the service was ended to come back here and they would bring her car, after giving her a small piece of paper with a claim number on it.

Shelly and her mother, both dressed in black, found seats near the rear of rows of folding chairs put out. The Marine Corp band was there playing some somber music. Shelly thought *some of it sounded like Mozart's Requiem.*

Around 9:30 A.M. a string of limos pulled up. This was a low-key event that was not telegraphed to anyone except the immediate family members. No news outlets were invited. It was a private affair.

In the first limo the President and the former President got out and were immediately surrounded by a dozen Secret Service men. The family members were taken back. It wasn't all that it seemed to be at first. In the second car, John Harris and Admiral Gilbert got out and quickly walked up to the President and the former President. In the following cars Commodore Riley and Admiral Selectee Avery along with Kevin O'Toole and a few other USSF officials emerged.

The dignitaries were escorted to a couple rows of seats perpendicular to the audience as well as the speaker's podium.

After the dignitaries were all seated, a man in Marine Corp uniform approached the podium and stated he was a chaplain and would now request a moment of silence.

Soon Tom was at the podium and introduced himself and quickly drawing great stairs from the deceased relatives. He then introduced the former President who was the principal in starting the United States Space Force. The Former President approached the podium then gave his few minutes of kind words to the family reminding everyone their relatives were instrumental in starting the space force and as principal "plank owners" of the Alabama had done more to further its capability than any prior space program in American History.

The former President then introduced the current President who then gave an excellent speech and praise for the great courage and sacrifice these USSF personal displayed in uncompromised fashion.

John Harris was then introduced and gave a brief history of the USSF and the contribution all the pilots had made to the success of the mission.

Finally, Tom Gilbert was back at the podium giving the final words and compelling statements that left no dry eye in the audience. The marine band started playing and the crowd approached Tom and the others and mingled with them and took a lot of pictures.

This is what got Tom and Shelly in all the newspapers.

The news media had forgotten all about the CSS Alabama and certainly Tom Gilbert. As Tom worked his way through the crowd, shaking hands and simply giving his aura to the families who appreciated his eulogy, which was uncommon, yet insightful, he eventually found himself with Shelly and her mother.

Shelly introduced her mother and Tom, being somewhat emotional at the time, gave Shelly's mother a big hug that transferred warmth and affection as if he were her own son. Shelly's mother could feel the sincerity in Tom. Tom Gilbert then also took the occasion to hug Shelly and forgetting where he was at the moment during a mental transcendence completed the hug and an affectionate quick kiss that got caught on camera. Shelly was all smiles. Later one of the news reports stated that if Tom had a beard, the couple could easily pass for the lovely couple Prince Harry and his bride Meghan Markel several years before.

Up through noon that day, there was no reporting or public knowledge of these proceedings until one of the relatives put on face book the picture of the *CSS Alabama's Captain Kissing His New Love.*

Because of the way social media works, certain face book postings get multiplied, especially as embellishments are added along the way and it fans out. It did not take long before a major newspaper reporter got the face book pictures and story and went to the editor and received blessings to do an investigative report on this news topic that they felt would go viral. And indeed, it did.

Even worse, a disgruntled hotel employee identified the woman to the newspaper as seeing her leaving Admiral Gilbert's hotel early in the morning after a *lovers' tryst.*

Senator Bosworth's office was called for details, then the investigative reporter discovered *Shelly Brown had disappeared for four years!*

The following morning, Tom was called on his cell phone by John Harris.

JOHN HARRIS
Look out the window of your hotel.

TOM GILBERT.
What's going on? It looks like a lot of cars and people down there.

JOHN HARRIS
Yeah, that's all for you. Those are TV and radio station trucks.

TOM GILBERT.
How did this happen?

JOHN HARRIS
The newspapers have found out about you and Shelly Brown. Someone took a picture of you kissing her yesterday. Your picture is on the newspaper's front page.

TOM GILBERT.
What do we do now? My vacation probably isn't going to happen.

JOHN HARRIS
This is what I suggest, why don't you go back up to CSS Alabama and relieve Riley, then in thirty days he can come back and relieve you and we'll figure out a way to give you a vacation with some privacy.

TOM GILBERT.
I suppose I did this to myself.

JOHN HARRIS
You know you did. Kissing Shelly Brown at that memorial was out of place for such an event. You opened yourself up for exploitation.

TOM GILBERT.
Okay, I'll get ready, but I would like to meet with Shelly before I go back up to CSS Alabama.

JOHN HARRIS
We can probably sneak you out of there like we did the last time. Do you have somewhere that you would like to go?

TOM GILBERT.
Yes, somewhere they would not expect us.

JOHN HARRIS
I think I know just the place. Get ready, someone will
be over in an hour to pick you up.

Tom wanted Shelly to know what he was doing so she wouldn't feel like this was simply a one-night stand, so he called her cell phone.

Shelly looked at the caller I.D. then answered the phone.

SHELLY BROWN
Hello, Tom.

TOM GILBERT.
Hello Shelly, how are you doing today?

TOM GILBERT.
I'm sort of doing okay, but I've been having to explain
a few things to my mother.

SHELLY BROWN
I see.

TOM GILBERT.
What's up, Tom, it's kind of early, I didn't expect to
hear from you until later today. I figured you must be
super busy, especially with all the newspaper people
hounding you.

TOM GILBERT.
That's why I'm calling.

SHELLY BROWN
Which means.

TOM GILBERT.
I was sincere in everything I said to you and still feel
that way nothing has changed, but I need to tell you
what is happening to me.

SHELLY BROWN
Alright.

TOM GILBERT.

John Harris called earlier and decided to send me back to Alabama for a month. Riley will be brought to the planet and given leave. By sending me away for a month they hope the press coverage will die down since I'll be out of reach.

SHELLY BROWN

Shelly was silent taking it all in trying to figure out what all this meant. She trusted Tom to have good judgement and do the right thing and hesitated to say anything at the moment.

TOM GILBERT.

Shelly, in one month I will be brought back to the planet and given thirty days leave. John Harris says he knows a secluded place I can go to that will be free from the press and I'll have some privacy.

SHELLY BROWN
Okay.

TOM GILBERT.

Shelly, if you can somehow work it in your schedule, I would like you to meet me wherever John Harris arranges for me to go.

Shelly threw Tom a curve ball.

SHELLY BROWN
Hopefully that's not Area 51.

TOM GILBERT.

Area 51 is the absolute last place I would want to be. He hasn't revealed where this Camelot is, but knowing how smooth John is, I would anticipate it's a very nice place.

SHELLY BROWN
What about after your thirty days' leave period?

TOM GILBERT.

The ship will be wrapping up its refit about that time,

I'm sure the USSF would expect to send me out on the Alabama for some REFTRA.

SHELLY BROWN
What does that mean?

TOM GILBERT.
Refresher Training. More than likely, we'll lose possibly half the crew and have a bunch of new green guys who need some space time to learn their operational skills.

SHELLY BROWN
When will you have some long-term quality time away from Alabama?

TOM GILBERT
I've already been in command for almost six years. The only reason why they haven't relieved me and put a new guy in my position is the fear we could be forced to deploy immediately.

SHELLY BROWN
What's your long-term plan?

TOM GILBERT
Eventually they will send a prospective Commanding Officer – PCO to CSS Alabama and after a break in period he would relieve me. After that because of my age and I could retire sometime afterwards, it's unlikely they would send me out in space again.

SHELLY BROWN
I'll let Senator Bosworth know I need some time off a month from now. He's going to want to know why I need thirty days, it's highly unusual.

TOM GILBERT.
Tell the good senator to allow you the time off or I'll Shanghai you and keep you in my space cabin during the next underway.

SHELLY BROWN
You probably would, wouldn't you?

TOM GILBERT.
I did it once, I could do it again.

SHELLY BROWN
Did you do that on purpose?

TOM GILBERT.
I wanted to get to know you really well.

SHELLY BROWN
After four years in space together I think you know me well now.

TOM GILBERT.
Yes, those four years allowed me to grow very fond of you.

SHELLY BROWN
Tom, can I ask you a question?

TOM GILBERT.
Sure.

SHELLY BROWN
When did you first decide you liked me?

TOM GILBERT.
Don't laugh. The first time I saw you on the Metro.

SHELLY BROWN
You got to be kidding me?

TOM GILBERT.
I really liked what I saw, and I said to myself, it's a terrible shame I probably would never have a chance to meet such a fine lady as you. And now here we are four years later. It was an extraordinary coincidence."

SHELLY BROWN
Will I be able to communicate with you while you are on the Alabama in the Space Dock?

TOM GILBERT.
Actually, yes, you will. When I get up there, I will make arrangements with my security officer to make a

channel available for you to call in, which only I will be able to access.

SHELLY BROWN
How does that work?

TOM GILBERT.
It's identical to a phone in a meeting, but instead of having a group of people in a corporate setting, we'll have privacy, including live streaming video if that's what you would like.

SHELLY BROWN
That sounds good.

TOM GILBERT.
Listen, Shelly, a car will be picking me up in less than an hour. I'll be back aboard Alabama in two hours. You will receive a text message sometime later today, a call-in number and the passcode to allow you to get in. Video will also be set up so you can see me on your cell phone and if you click 'okay' when you get the page, then I'll be able to see you and hear each other's voices at the same time.

SHELLY BROWN
Okay, that sounds good.

TOM GILBERT.
I must hang up now and get ready. We'll talk again later today.

SHELLY BROWN
Okay, Tom, stay safe.

TOM GILBERT.
I will, Shelly. I'm sorry I have to leave like this, but others are calling the shots.

SHELLY BROWN
I understand, don't worry. We'll make up for it a month from now.

TOM GILBERT.
Will do. Goodbye until then.

SHELLY BROWN
Bye, Tom.

As promised, on the hour, a limo pulled up to the Hilton and Tom was called,

LIMO DRIVER
Your ride is downstairs.

Tom left with what he arrived with, not much. As soon as he stepped out of the elevator, there was mayhem and chaos in the hotel lobby. In about five seconds he heard someone yell,

NEWS REPORTER
There he is. There's Admiral Gilbert.

Halfway to the front door Tom experienced camera men shoving their cameras in his face. His subtle thoughts were, *I really would love to shove that camera up your ass.*

There was a little pushing and shoving and the news media people were being complete assholes as far as Tom was concerned. As he hit the entrance a couple men in suits approached him and one of them, a bruiser shoved a couple camera men real hard backwards who then collided with other camera men and within three to four seconds, these *facility* guys had Tom in the limo which was screeching tires and moving out before some idiot got in front of them and blocked their exit.

Within two minutes they were heading down Jefferson Davis Highway towards the beltway that would take them eventually to the Interstate and then off to Andrews Air Force base, where a TR-3B was waiting for Tom, along with a few others needed up on the Space Dock.

The following day when Shelly got off the Metro at Capitol Hill and was walking towards the Capitol, she suddenly discovered she was a person of interest, as a dozen media types descended upon her chasing her all the way into the security check point inside the Capitol, where the security personnel quickly came to her rescue and moved the media people out of the building with threats of arrest and confiscation of their expensive camera equipment.

The public was now fascinated about the commander of the very first Space Carrier and apparently a woman who was reported to be Admiral Tom Gilbert's girlfriend or secret lover.

Another series of information that was circulating is *this woman apparently disappeared four years exactly at the time the Alabama made its maiden voyage* including providing some of the best photographs ever taken of Uranus.

As soon as the press discovered the woman was none other than Shelly Brown, chief aide to Senator Bosworth, overnight an almost cottage industry developed seeking out any and all information on Shelly Brown. The fact Shelly Brown was an exotically beautiful African American woman helped create some of the most salacious material ever produced in what was now apparently forming yellow journalism that surpassed anything "fake news" ever attempted.

Shelly's impeccable dress and uncharacteristic beauty that stood out gave the photogenic opportunity some of the yellow journalists used to sell their stories and increase circulation. A lot of people like to look at beautiful women, and when one is suddenly revealed *wrapped up with a Space Force Commander and an aide to one of the most outspoken U.S. Senate*, the yellow journalists had an extraordinary run of exhibits the public seemed to never outgrow.

Senator Bosworth didn't mind all the free publicity. Every time the media spun stories about Shelly Brown, the Senator went to her defense publicly. Some political science experts later stated, Senator Bosworth would not had been reelected without all that free publicity, to the point his opponent was begging the media to let up on Shelly Brown, since he knew the damage it was doing to his own campaign.

The real crescendo happened when certain media outlets were trying to get comment from the Senator and later because of leaks, from the USSF, why Shelly Brown had been absent for four years and was not back in the public eye until the discovery was made, she was probably Admiral Tom Gilbert's secret lover.

The media discovered the address of Shelly Brown's mother and the next thing apparent was the block was full of TV station vans with satellite antennas on the roof tops. Shelly's privacy was now fully violated.

Senator Bosworth knew the answer. Shelly's mother was retired so she didn't need to stay home, and he then made arrangements to fly them both on a private jet to a rich supporter in Minnesota. Senator Bosworth's friend Alex had once owned Casino's up and down the Mississippi river and had his own private jet and runway on his four-hundred-acre estate with a twenty-four-acre lake in the middle of it.

In the middle of the night, a private security firm had two SUVs that pulled up in front of the Brown residence. The police who were now patrolling the street and forcing the crowds and the TV trucks to disperse had been notified this transportation would arrive around 2:00 A.M. and were ready for them.

Several police officers were stationed in front of the Brown home and suddenly the porch light went on and Shelly's mother left the house carrying a suitcase, which one of the police officers who was a gentleman quickly requested permission to carry it for Mrs. Brown. Shelly a short distance behind was also carrying a suitcase and a laptop bag and another police officer grabbed her bag and promptly carried it to the second SUV parked directly in front of the home. Security men simultaneously got out of the SUV, opened the rear passenger door and Shelly and her mother got in the car which drove off following the lead car within ten seconds.

The news media was slightly out of position and the purpose of the second SUV was now made clear. The second SUV pulled out around the first which then started driving in a zigzag pattern thus putting a halt on traffic that would want to chase the SUVs.

It didn't take long for the SUV to go to Reagan International Airport where a security detachment escorted the SUV into the secure area of the airport right up to the same gate that Tom Gilbert had used and it was more than coincidence a Gulfstream 850 was parked there, fueled up with a crew aboard ready for immediate takeoff.

Twenty minutes later the jet was airborne and traveling a lot higher and faster than Mrs. Brown ever experienced. Shelly could also feel the enormous thrust and movement and when the jet leveled off, they were in darkness and could easily see the curvature of the planet. The stars were now just as bright as Shelly remembered while she was aboard the Alabama.

Two and a half hours later, the jet started descending and soon it landed where Alex lived in Minnesota about seventy-five miles distance to Fargo, North Dakota. He was a gentleman, Senator Bosworth's top campaign contributor, and fully supported the idea of the United States Space Force. The least he could do would be to help the Senator hide his top aide and her mother for a while until the heat died down.

Within a couple days, the news media finally figured out Shelly had skipped town with her mother and since there was nobody who saw how she departed, the media had no way of tracking down where she went. The joy of having a private plane to get in and out of airports without a lot of publicity is why the super-rich bought such jets.

Alex lived somewhat in fear. He was an extremely wealthy man, and there had already been one attempt on his life, which by a miracle and the grace of God, he survived. He already had six former Navy Seals on his security detachment and retained them for private security after he sold his business to a private investment group.

Therefore, between the dogs, the former SEALS, and a few other bad asses that protected the estate, if a dumb newspaper reporter attempted to break in, it would be a coin toss to whether the former SEALS would work them over before they handed them over to the police. In one case where a rather female reporter was caught with her cameraman, she was warned,

SECURITY DETACHEMENT REP

The next time we catch you here, you will be working for the Mexican Drug Cartel, and you may not like the job they would have you do.

Alex, being a kind gentleman, made Shelly and her mother quite comfortable for the next thirty days.

Shelly had a wireless connection thanks to Alex and his system was a lot more secure than what she normally used.

Shelly at first was a little hesitant to inform Tom Gilbert of her situation because she didn't want him to have any issues or become upset about the circumstances, since it was already bad enough. But she knew she had to give him the details of her predicament, otherwise his trust could erode.

Alex likes good-looking women and probably could have easily had his way with Shelly, and in fact was looking for a mate to have children with. However, he had respect for men in uniform, and knew the huge sacrifice Tom was making and learned of some of his activity from the Senator who told him more than he legally should have. But Senator Bosworth knew Alex was not the type of person to repeat confidential information.

Thanks to the fact Shelly and her mother were traveling incognito and it was easy to disguise the mother with hair die and Shelly with a different hair style, they were soon enjoying freedom again and several times a week Alex took them to Fargo, North Dakota, for shopping, movies, and other activities.

Alex was somewhat conspicuous person, driving around in a Rolls Royce, but the locals who had some exposure to him, simply thought the women were another couple of fashion models he had brought in for personal enjoyment, though one of these two models seemed to have lost some of her luster with age.

Nobody had ever seen Shelly with the type of hair doo she sported, and her makeup was completely different, almost the plain Jane look she had on the spaceship for four years because up there nobody gives a damn how you look!

Those thirty days gave Shelly some breathing room and helped her slowly get over *Space Lag.*

Alex actually took a liking to Mrs. Brown, though she was old enough to be his mother, but nothing would ever come of that because he was still trying to figure out how to meet and seduce the future mother of his children without them discovering he was a super wealthy guy. He didn't want a gold digger marrying him for his money, then sued for a divorce soon after a child was born to get a long-term meal ticket. He didn't want a woman too young or too old because she needed to be healthy for childbirth.

Eventually the thirty days were up. Commodore Riley completed his leave period and reported back for a temporary assignment overseeing the remainder of Alabama's refit. A new XO was also sent to Alabama to take over from Riley when Tom returned in approximately thirty days. Riley would then report to Vicksburg where he would relieve the commander who would then take command of hull #3 in Space Dock #2.

Tom flew by TR-3B shuttle down to Andrews where he was put in a limo and driven to Reagan International to catch his ride to the secret destination.

The fact John Harris was in the limo did not surprise Tom, as he had not revealed the secret vacation, he had lined up for him due to security precautions to help keep the media away from them.

JOHN HARRIS
Hello, Admiral.

Tom Gilbert acknowledged John Harris in a respectful manner.

TOM GILBERT
Good morning Secretary Harris.

JOHN HARRIS
Please call me John, we are in private settings.

TOM GILBERT
Sure thing, John.

JOHN HARRIS
Your ride to your vacation site should be pulling into
Reagan about now. They will be taking on fuel to
make an Atlantic Ocean crossing.

TOM GILBERT
Are we going to Europe?

JOHN HARRIS
No. Near Casablanca.

TOM GILBERT
Why there?

JOHN HARRIS
I have a friend who is the major investor in Ouarzazate
in the Atlas Mountains.

TOM GILBERT
That's probably kind of expensive. How much is that
going to set me back?

JOHN HARRIS
Don't worry about it, your rooms and accommodations
have already been paid for.

TOM GILBERT
How so?

JOHN HARRIS
You have a secret admirer who insisted on paying for it.

TOM GILBERT
Who might that be?

JOHN HARRIS
Well, if I told you, it would no longer be a secret, right?

TOM GILBERT
I suppose so.

MOROCCO

The trip to Reagan International was rather quick. Just like before, they went to that
obscure carrier gate, and as expected, there was a Gulfstream 850 sitting there looking
ultra-modern and with radically slick aerodynamics. Carbon nano tubes and graphene
had produced fuselage materials that cut the weight of the plane in half allowing more
fuel and more powerful engines requiring much stronger engine mounts.

There was a portable ladder leading up to the cabin door. The Gulfstream 850 could
deploy its own ladder, but the crews preferred not to use it because it would result in
the requirement to clean all the foot traffic on it. Using the airport's portable ladder and
the small Persian rug at the entrance way helped to keep the plane a lot cleaner. Tom
had virtually little to no luggage or personal items. He wasn't aware his vacation was
starting immediately.

TOM GILBERT
I really didn't come prepared with much.

JOHN HARRIS
Not to worry, anything you need will be at the resort
you are staying in.

TOM GILBERT
All right.

JOHN HARRIS
If something comes up, me or someone you know will fly out and make a personal visit. Recommend no phone calls while you are there because people will be able to locate you.

TOM GILBERT
Understand all.

JOHN HARRIS
By the way, there is another group traveling with you. They have their own accommodations to help hide who you are.

TOM GILBERT
This ought to be interesting.

JOHN HARRIS
Why don't you go up on the plane and see who is waiting for you?

Tom suddenly had a strange feeling and knew that John Harris probably had a few surprises lined up for him.

The car door was suddenly opened from outside. John Harris reached out to shake Tom's hand and as they shook, John had one last word.

JOHN HARRIS
Tom, you have done a lot for your country. There are some people who really appreciate what you have done.

TOM GILBERT
Well, I'm grateful that I'm still alive. Some brave men gave it all fur us such as Azzie and Instigator. I'm alive today thanks to them. I owe them and quite a few others more than gratitude.

JOHN HARRIS
Tom, enjoy your time. See you in a month.

TOM GILBERT
Okay, goodbye.

Tom, with a small grip that contained toothbrush, toothpaste, razor, deodorant, and a few other items, got out of the car and walked to the aircraft ladder. He had been directed to wear civilian clothes, preferably tourist clothes when he left the Alabama earlier, which is contrary to normal protocol, but the direction came down from above and he didn't mind the fact he wasn't wearing a uniform, hopping on to this private jet.

Shelly and her mother had been asked to keep the window shades down while the plane was parked on the tarmac, and not to get near the door because they didn't want someone outside the plane to get a lucky photograph of them and tip off the press they had left in this private jet. As soon as Tom stepped inside the plane, the door was shut and Shelly was prompted,

AIR HOSTESS
Ma'am, you may move around the cabin until we get
ready for takeoff.

Shelly had been sitting beside her mother who felt Shelly was like a kid who just found her long lost puppy. The physical reaction to seeing Tom was clearly obvious to Mrs. Brown who knew her daughter had strong affection for this wonderful man who was straight as an arrow, kind, and deliberate.

Shelly approached Tom and within seconds they were in each other's arms showing gratification and appreciation on many levels.

Mrs. Brown looked on with utter tenderness knowing what her daughter and this man had been through. She also knew as an astute observer how this transcendence evolved into what now had become a public spectacle because as the public discovered more and more, the media had a surreal appetite to dig deeper into their private lives which resulted in a sense living hell. The fact her daughter had been embroiled in Washington politics added an entire layer to the fabric of the ongoing discovery and feeding frenzy just like a pool of *piraña* fish.

Piraña fish

SHELLY
Tom, I hope you do not mind, my mother is traveling
with us. Under the circumstances she also needed to
get away from Washington, D.C.

TOM
Understand, and I'm sorry if in some way I added to
her misery.

SHELLY
No Tom, it's not your fault. The public's appetite for
the media to reveal our stories is just too great.

TOM
The perfect storm when someone in politics is involved
with a big new entity such as the United States Space
Force.

SHELLY
Yea, and the public barely knows the half of it.

AIR HOSTESS
Admiral Gilbert and Ms. Brown, would you please
take your seats, we are going to shove off now and
get going.

SHELLY
All right.

Soon the plane was heading for the end of the runway and given a higher priority than the seven commercial passenger jets in line waiting for their turn on the runway.

Shelly sat next to her mother right across the aisle from Tom. The plane rolled onto the runway, the pilot gunned the engines and the plane had enough thrust where they all were pushed hard against their seats.

Thanks to the stronger air frame, lighter weight and stronger engines, the jet had a steep angle as it was ascending into the heavens. Tom looking out the window in the sunny bright day saw the Washington landscape shrink in size and the area seemed to gradually get darker as the plane climbed heading up to one hundred thousand feet which allowed them to see the curvature of the planet. Heading east as fast as they were going quickly turned the day into evening and in four hours, they were descending into the Casablanca area down below forty thousand feet before they made landfall because civilian jets were restricted in Morocco.

Ouarzazate Morocco had a modern airport and four different airlines serving it, thanks to the movie industry growing there.

Gulfstream 850 only needed five thousand feet of runway, but the airport's 9800-foot-long runway would accommodate 747s and Emirates Airlines was Airbus 380 there and to Casablanca for the growing tourism.

The dozen major movies filmed there and as recently as 2023, had created a lot of external interest. Lying 3800 feet above sea level in the Atlas Mountains gave it a unique weather system. Even though there were five months out of the year where the local temperature could reach 110 degrees, it was more like San Diego California, most of the time in the 70s and 80s, with the desert directly to the south which manifested much of the movie industry.

Movie company employees could be on the set during the daytime out in the desert area, and by evening back in balmy 75-degree weather, dry and comfortable with low humidity. Yet in nearby Atlas Mountains, where it snowed in the wintertime, there were plush green valleys from the snow runoff. During the recent few years, due to the unexpected Cooling phenomena, temperatures were dipping lower and the snow pack was much higher. Mountain streams were flowing far more often and deeper.

Tom would normally had thought John Harris was nuts for taking him to Ouarzazate Morocco, but after they checked into their lovely hotel and spa, Le Berbere Palace and doing a little soul searching, realizing it would take an effort like this to afford them some privacy, he suddenly realized the brilliance of John's plan. The amenities were fabulous at this five-star hotel that catered to the wealthy, and operated like Vegas, *what happens in Ouarzazate, stays in Ouarzazate.*

Wealthy Arabs who wanted to spend some quality time with their mistresses out of public view came to places like this. In most Muslim countries where alcohol and drugs are greatly frowned upon, Ouarzazate Morocco, provided anything you wanted, but also with the ambience fitting a king.

There were five other hotel spas in this community that were ever as nice. This was one of North Africa's best kept secrets, though after filming "Game of Thrones" in Ouarzazate Morocco, Hollywood elites suddenly were spending as much time there as they end up in Switzerland.

There were a few interesting places to visit on organized tours during the day such as Kasbah of Taourirt, Kasbah Ait Benhaddou, Kasbah Aksar, and Ouarzazate old town. On one day they took an excursion through the valley of the Draa River into the Sahara.

Also, simply enjoying the pool and a swim was what the doctor ordered. Unlike Shelly, Tom still needed to get over his space lag. The three of them ended up under a canvas shaded area next to the pool where the moderate temperatures were just about perfect and the service of drinks and snacks was superb.

Several days after settling in to such a pleasant daily routine, Tom suddenly explained.

TOM GILBERT
You know I've always wanted to visit Casa Blanca.
We are a short distance away; we should take a trip
over there.

SHELLY BROWN
Sounds good to me.

Mrs. Brown was along for the ride and enjoyed the wonderful company Shelly and Tom provided and was more than willing to try anything they had to offer. They were fantastic traveling companions.

SHELLY
How are we going to get there?

TOM
Let me check the airlines.

Tom searched on his cell phone and found a nonstop flight, one hour and twenty minutes.

Not like flying in the Gulf Stream 850, but at least it gets there. Maybe we should plan on spending the night there. We'll keep our rooms here and let the hotel know we are leaving for a day and will be back and watch our rooms for us.

Soon, the trip was planned, and they went packing a few things for an overnight stay. The weather in Casablanca was almost identical to Los Angeles and both Cities were on the West Coast of major continents.

Casablanca was the first city in Africa to build a high-rise building. It also had Hassan 2nd Mosque which has the tallest minaret in the world at 689 feet, completed in 1993. The associated mosque can hold twenty-five thousand people inside and another eighty thousand outside.

Approximately five million people live in Casablanca, but each day seven million people work there.

Port De Peche in Casablanca was definitely on the bucket list to visit and on a text message John Harris sent advising Tom of some good places to eat. Until you've had fresh fish prepared by fabulous Berber chefs, you have no idea what you are missing. The same thing could be said for eating fresh fish in Shizuoka, Japan.

If it had not been for the typical misbehavior of the American news media, Tom and Shelly probably would never have gone to Ouarzazate and Casablanca Morocco. Shelly's mother was impressed at how much Tom was a gentleman and always considerate of her needs. *He's the type of military person who would never leave anyone behind, Mrs. Brown thought.*

Sadly, a good number of highly trained people had died for Tom fighting off the Jupitorians, which he couldn't avoid. Trading two squadrons of pilots and TR-3Bs was probably a good outcome considering over three hundred crew member lives were saved and more importantly, forced the enemy turned back when they might have continued on to Earth and laid waste to the planet with huge Hydrogen Bombs like they did Mars nine hundred thousand years ago.

Tom having taken Taxi tours in Japan checked with the Airline and their prospective Casablanca hotel to determine if either one of them *had connections with a cab company that did those.*

RECEPTIONIST
Yes, Mr. Gilbert, we do have cab tours. All day or half
a day. How many in your party?

TOM GILBERT
Three Adults.

RECEPTIONIST
For half a day, with a party of three that will be
$250.00."

TOM GILBERT
That sounds reasonable.

RECEPTIONIST
Do you want me to book that tour for you?

TOM GILBERT
Most definitely, how about after lunch, that will give
us an opportunity to check into our hotel and drop off
the small luggage we have.

RECEPTIONIST
If you don't have too much luggage, you can just put
your items in the trunk of the taxi.

TOM GILBERT

We'd still like to get into our rooms to make sure we are checked in.

RECEPTIONIST

Mr. Gilbert, we can check you into the hotel room remotely, you don't need to waste your time going directly to the hotel. Also, you get four hours for half-day tour, and if you want to take a lunch break in the middle, that's not a problem, but I would highly recommend you offer the cab driver lunch.

TOM GILBERT
Does the cab driver speak English?

RECEPTIONIST

Yes, all our cab tour drivers speak English unless you request a Spanish- or French-speaking person, we have drivers we can assign who speak those other languages.

TOM GILBERT
Does the $250.00 fee include the tip?

RECEPTIONIST

Yes, it does, however if you take a break for lunch, recommend you offer the driver lunch which will make him happier to have a break in the middle of it. Also, if you start your taxi tour from the airport, you can avoid the taxi fare to your hotel.

TOM GILBERT

Okay, book us the taxi tour to begin after we get our luggage at the airport.

RECEPTIONIST

Your driver will have to sign up at your baggage claim, that's where you will meet him.

TOM GILBERT
Okay, sounds great.

The three travelers made their way to Casablanca. Just like the airline company employee stated, at the baggage claim area a man silently stood with a sign: "Tom Gilbert."

Some of the most innocent events are spawned by coincidences and accidental exposures. One of the other passengers was filming the baggage claim area putting together a video record of their exciting trip to Casablanca. The person didn't know who Tom Gilbert was, and as the tourist was filming, Tom Gilbert walked over to the cab driver and notified him who he was, and they shook hands. Tom turned around and faced Shelly and her mother.

Shelly was such a beautiful woman and Tom increased her propensity to make herself look even more glamorous. The photographer, just another person out of the Beltway saw the beautiful woman and was adorned by her beauty and could not resist to get some of her on film and eventually all three. Anyone with the least amount of sophistication would realize this was a special woman with a special man. In fact, all day long during their taxi tour, every time they were exposed to the Moroccans, there was a distinct reaction of appreciation and mystique. Later that day, the photographer posted the video on his Facebook page.

The photographer had a friend who worked for The Washington Post and had the beat on the city and Capitol Hill. Normally she would not have paid much attention to the Facebook video except for the content, Casablanca which to a journalist raises some interest, especially if they have never been before.

The world was looking for Tom and Shelly. They had simply disappeared. The fascination was growing daily especially when all the details slowly started coming out who they were along with the rumors, Shelly had been cast away four years on *Tom Gilbert's Love Boat,* as the Yellow Journalists had reported.

Journalists are kind of crazy how words and names pop out of nowhere. They have instant reactions, and an uncanny ability to connect the dots. One could say a journalist is in the dot connecting business, whereas Tom was in the dot stacking business (leftover term from a previous generation fire control systems on submarines using computer algorithms to target enemy ships). During those past years before new technology made it all obsolete the Fire Control Technicians (FT's) were called Dot Stackers or Female Torpedomen.

In viewing the video, the journalist suddenly saw the name Tom Gilbert. There had been plenty of TV coverage. His face was now recognized by half of the planet. She had seen Tom Gilbert on TV probably fifty times over the past couple days in uniform and in civilian clothes and in some of the tender moments with Shelly Brown. When Tom turned around to call out to Shelly Brown, his face was fully exposed. The journalist's heart just about jumped out. She knew that was filmed TODAY!

Moments later when Shelly Brown's face was suddenly shown and shortly her mother who had also been seen on TV, there was the story of the century. The journalist knew where Tom Gilbert and Shelly Brown were hiding!

Within five seconds, Amy called the editor.

EDITOR

Hello, Amy, you are the last person in the world I would expect calling this time of day.

AMY

I'm sorry for interrupting your evening, sir, but I have a gigantic lead on a story.

EDITOR

Oh yeah, what's that about?

AMY

Sir, I know where that Space Commander Admiral Tom Gilbert is hiding with Shelly Brown.

EDITOR

Well, if you know, then probably so does the rest of the world by now.

AMY

No, sir, they did a fantastic job of escaping and I know exactly where they are tonight.

EDITOR

Just where is that?

AMY

Casablanca, Morocco.

EDITOR

How do you know this?

AMY

I just got the video from a friend; would you like me to forward you the link so you can watch it yourself? It's on a Facebook account.

EDITOR

Sure, I'll pull it up on my Super-pad.

The Super-pad was the cat's meow in 2026. Supercomputer capability on a wafer-thin notepad like device with video and pixel capability that was only in experimental labs just a couple years before.

AMY
The segment where Tom Gilbert is shown starts around
the one-minute mark if you want to fast forward to it.

The editor was watching the video and fast forwarded it to the one-minute mark, and suddenly there was Tom Gilbert. Being the editor of an exclusive newspaper in Washington, D.C., all the top Senator aide and lobbyists were always on their radar screens. Shelly Brown even more so after the revelations over the past couple days and the United States Space Force was doing a very bad job of damage control and someone was leaking information.

John Harris had a gut feeling it was Kevin O'Toole doing the leaking because he was in the process of a power play to grab more power and wanted one more step up the ladder to DCI.

And there Shelly Brown was. Just as beautiful as ever. Shelly Brown's time with Tom Gilbert was already affecting her imagery. Women falling hopelessly in love tend to bloom like a flower, and Shelly was now in full bloom. The fact the three were traveling together underscored the closeness of the relationship.

Amy hit pay dirt. Even if they could not track them down in Casablanca, they would beat every other news media outlet exposing the love nest of one of the most interesting military people that lived since General Patton. In fact, General Patton had never done anything that came close to what Tom Gilbert had just pulled off.

Amy suddenly was given the trip of her lifetime. To reward her for breaking the story, the editor was sending her to Casablanca with a hasty glued together news team including a couple professional photographers, and a spot editor who would take Amy's reports and smooth them over before emailing them to the paper where they would hit the digital media immediately upon receipt.

The shrewd editor was not going to wait for Amy's next transmission. He already had enough to insert in the following day's paper, they would make the deadline by a mere twenty-seven minutes!

By the time the story came out in the next paper, Amy and her group were halfway across the Atlantic on the next flight out of Dulles on their way to Ireland. From there they had connecting flights on Ryan Air down to Casablanca. It wasn't the best, but it was the fastest way to get there.

Tom's day had gone well. They had driven around the city, looking over World War II landmarks, the few that remained, the fabulous mosque, and when he suggested they stop at *Port De Peche* for lunch the driver appeared most happy.

As they all exited the cab, Tom informed the driver.

TOM GILBERT
Sir, if you would please allow me, I would like to buy your lunch.

TAXI DRIVER
I would really appreciate that, Tom.

The reaction was very friendly and appreciative. For the rest of the day, Tom, Shelly, and her mother received a world class tour second to none. Tom hit the mark with the driver, who admired Tom being with such an exquisite looking woman, and guessed the other female was her mother.

Casablanca was transcending from poor to rich. The metamorphism was quite astonishing to someone who visited every five years or so. Arab and African oil money was pouring in. Rich Nigerian oil men traveled to Casablanca that had seedier parts of town, mainly due to the flow of the migrant population.

During the workday, Casablanca had almost as many workers as in New York City. The big difference is New York City has a lot of financial district workers, Wall Street, and world trade.

Besides the nearby movie filming Ouarzazate Morocco nearby deserts and in the Atlas Mountains the quickly expanding Arabic singing stars and recording predominately now came out of this region. Even though Lebanon and Egypt produced a number of great Arabic singers, the gems came out of Morocco. Their singing voices were superb and their exotic appearances made them appear as the most beautiful women in the world. Their sophisticated cinematographers that had a lot of training with Hollywood were putting out increasingly successful singing videos.

Hollywood had their fingers into some of that since the gross income of some of these female Arabic singing stars was up there with Western and Asian singers, the whole Arabic singing genre was expanding at a dizzying pace with Casablanca at the epicenter of change.

Casablanca is everything under the kitchen sink from North African trade, some of which was still by caravans of camels, trucks, railroads, ships, and numerous manufacturing and numerous arts and crafts.

The Phoenicians, Spaniards, and Portuguese had left their mark on Casablanca which eventually had French influence. During WW2 it was the main staging base for all of the North African fighting including preparations for landing on North Africa and later Sicily. From an outside observer, Casablanca is improving quickly as American cities decayed.

Tom was smart at only scheduling an overnight trip. He didn't know what to expect and didn't want to be stuck in Casablanca in case he didn't like it. Their accommodations in Ouarzazate were very comfortable, and the facility had lots of security to protect rich clientele who went there for that very reason.

They informed the hotel they would be checking out around noon and had flights to catch in the afternoon.

The newspaper had free-lanced journalists in places like Casablanca, they hired for support roles.

As soon as the mission was underway, one of very few persons they had in North Africa they trusted was currently in Casablanca working on some personal projects. Stan Baker was contacted and faxed a contract for services the paper wanted from him, including hiring some private detectives to help track down Tom Gilbert and Shelly Brown.

The paper had a problem. Stan Baker was corrupt and was always willing to take a big bribe. He knew paparazzi in Paris who would pay big bucks for a tip like this. The paper would never know how the paparazzi discovered the subject of their escapade that was now descending upon Casablanca like sharks approaching their quarry in the water.

Amy and her team were due to land in Casablanca shortly after noon. They wanted to be in position to approach the love birds and force them to admit or deny, they were on vacation together, which would confirm they were a couple and the rumors of the Tom Gilbert Love Boat, would suddenly become reality and the hottest story of the century.

What did they do for four years on the love boat was another question everyone wanted to know which now was the closest guarded secret in the USSF. The memorial service at Arlington with the President and former President was still sending political shockwaves through the capital and congress was pissed they were not receiving information except from the ass kisser Kevin O'Toole who was leaking like a sieve.

The morning headlines were now showing up on newsstands as Amy's plane was on its final approach to Casablanca.

Even though Casablanca media had not detected nor knew Tom Gilbert was in town or understand the sensationalism currently in the news cycle back in America, it caught on quickly because they always like to reach out to American tourists and give them some news coverage.

No sooner that Tom and Shelly and her mother were in the boarding area to head back to Ouarzazate, Tom's cell phone rang and it was John Harris.

JOHN HARRIS
Hey, bud, hate to be the bearer of bad news, but the
local newspapers somehow discovered you are in

Casablanca. You should be expected to be sought out
by media types really quickly.

TOM GILBERT
Damn, just when we were unwinding and starting to
have fun!

JOHN HARRIS
My advice is you to leave and go back to Ouarzazate
for now, and you may have to leave there as well if you
want some privacy.

TOM GILBERT
Okay, thanks for the heads-up, we'll figure something
out.

Tom's plane was then boarding, so he ended the conversation and walked aboard the
Moroccan Airline 737 and was soon seated and happy they only did the short trip.

No sooner than he got on the plane, the Ryan Air passengers came walking through the
terminal on their way to baggage claim. Amy missed running directly into Tom Gilbert
by less than five minutes. She almost had her interview at the airport!

Everyone was happy to get back to Ouarzazate. Casablanca was an interesting place to
visit, but Ouarzazate just felt better to be at.

It took a couple days and a lot of money paid to private investigators to learn Tom
Gilbert escaped their trap.

Tom and Shelly soon decided to take a trip to Marrakesh. This time instead of flying,
they hired a driver with a nice car. Even though they traveled mainly on two-lane
roads, and restroom accommodations were sometimes primitive where they had to
stop, the scenic drive through the Atlas Mountains was awe inspiring.

No sooner than Tom and the Browns checked out of their Ouarzazate resort, Amy and
her army descended upon it. The paparazzi were thick as thieves and the hotel was
actually grateful the party had left so as not make it awkward for their other clients.
This time the private detectives were not able to track down Tom because they no
longer had airline employees to bribe to discover where they were heading.

Marrakesh is not a good place to go if you want to avoid the paparazzi. The French
love Marrakesh and travel there in large numbers. Numerous wealthy French own
properties in Marrakesh always leaving open windows of opportunity for creative
operators to figure out a way to get access to their intended subjects.

Marrakesh was quite a bit different than Casablanca. Only about one-seventh the size, the pace is certainly a lot slower, and the automobile congestion is considerably lower. Marrakesh is also a lot more in tune with pedestrian traffic. Casablanca has very poor pedestrian crossings all over the city, almost as an afterthought. Marrakesh on the other hand has so many attractions in the center city area and many markets, they have no choice but to be very accommodative towards pedestrians.

Food and entertainment and crowds are far more extensive in Marrakesh. Shelly and her mother were immediately interested in visiting the "souks" to go shopping and then to a full body message and skin scrub.

Traveling by hired car is what got the group to Marrakesh here undetected, and they managed to not be found during the entire stay in Marrakesh.

Amy and her team eventually had to leave. They were exasperated because the paper had shelled out big bucks and came up with one thousand leads and not one time laid their hands-on Tom Gilbert and Shelly Brown. As a small victory, they did eventually find the driver of the taxi tour and after extensive interview and lots of bribes, they did hit a small treasure in the driver had zapped quite a few pictures of Shelly and Tom with his cell phone camera when they were not paying attention, not that he felt they were someone important, he just liked them a lot by the way they treated him and took the pictures mainly for fond memories.

The cab driver's memories grew even fonder when he discovered how much the paper was willing to pay for all his pictures and his story. So, Amy didn't leave Casablanca empty handed, but she never got the personal interview either. She did however have the satisfaction her paper printed the story and had Admiral Tom Gilbert on the front page after paying out some funds to Amy's friend to outright buy the video she posted on Facebook and exclusive rights to it.

The vacation didn't end in Morocco.

Shelly and her mother had become good friends with Alex the month before, and he also happened to own a chateau in Switzerland. One day when he and the Senator were talking, and the senator relayed the newspaper story and how they were being relentlessly bird dogged in Morocco, Alex made a suggestion.

ALEX

I have a nice Chateau in Switzerland with lots of
security. Ask them if they would like to stay there for a
while. I have a maid, chef, and butler there at the estate
that can take care of them.

John Harris was soon called by the Senator and the offer was made. John Harris knew a little of Alex's shady past because he was a gambling casino tycoon, but also knew he was a clean cut in general and Senator Bosworth's leading contributor. Tom Gilbert was duly informed and readily agreed to go there knowing his location in Morocco was tenable at best.

During their last night in Switzerland, the staff at Alex's mansion who had connections to the best couture designers that had offices nearby fitted the three out handsomely so they would appear lovely at the symphony that evening.

The symphony is where Shelly Brown and John Harris finally got discovered by the paparazzi and as they were leaving the venue after a marvelous time hearing a lovely Prokofiev piano concerto performed by Yuja Wang and Brahms Symphony Number Four, the paparazzi took hundreds of pictures and videos. Amy soon observed all this on social media especially when it went viral on Tiktok. Since Shelly was with her mother and Tom, it was good enough proof for Amy to write another story about the couple that had managed to evade the media with the greatest of expertise. Since Tom and Shelly always traveled with her mother, photographed together in America, Casa Blanca and now Switzerland, it conveyed they were not only a couple but FAMILY.

Amy would make it her personal goal to be the first person to get a picture of Shelly's growing belly in pregnancy when that day happened.

Switzerland rounded out the vacation and soon it was time for Tom to report back to the United States Space Force where he expected to be busy for a while in REFTRA work. He was sad however that Riley would be leaving him now. He had a new XO and Wing Commander.

Shelly Brown slowly got her balance back firmly and after it was made clear, her mother's home would be protected around the clock by a prestigious security firm thanks to a private donor (whom she suspected was Alex). The Browns went home. Since they had been gone for quite a while, the news media more or less gave up on them. They were no longer the leading story in the news cycle as election year was unfolding.

Shelly reported back to Senator Bosworth's office feistier than ever. She had an entirely different outlook on life. Her resentment to the man who Shanghaied her because he could thanks to the two-million-mile rule was now the emotional foundation to her.

Shelly of course secretly hoped Tom Gilbert would be relieved as Alabama's CO and given a desk job in Washington, so their lives could be much simpler. As long as he remained the CO of Alabama, he would be in the crosshairs of every media organization on the planet.

Nevertheless, Vicksburg was now out "steaming" and taking away some of the interest that had been levied exclusively on Alabama.

Some of the questions that were not answered is "Where did you go for four years?" and "What did you do while you were away for such a long period of time?"

Then the rumors kept flying that Shelly was gone four years on the "Love Boat." Nothing could be substantiated, and even though other countries were demanding disclosure, the United States Space Force kept its classified lid on everything.

Long before undocking was scheduled, a new snag suddenly appeared. The government always knew we had traitors among us. To weed them all out was impossible, because most were so well-hidden becoming moles in some cases thirty years prior and only activated under certain conditions.

One such USSF mole informed his FSB (KGB) handler.

USSF FSB MOLE
The Ponarian is missing.

FSB (KGB) HANDLER
How long has he been missing?

One gem produced was disclosed by the USSF-FSB mole.

USSF FSB MOLE
He left with the CSS Alabama four years ago and never returned.

Vladimir Putin wasn't done with the Ponarian, he wanted another meeting and wanted to bring in one of his top Russian Scientists to meet and discuss the overall galactic situation with the Ponarian to get a sense of how backwards and ill prepared Earth was.

Putin made it clear to the President.

PUTIN
I want another meeting with the Ponarian.

PRESIDENT
I'm sorry, he's currently not available.

When the excuses kept rolling out Putin finally decided to call a spade a spade and frankly confronted the President.

PUTIN
We know you took the Ponarian on the CSS Alabama
when it left here four years ago on a secret mission.
Where did you take him?

The President was now caught in a scenario. Obviously, the Russians were controlling some American traitor, and knew a lot of what was going on. It was going to get increasingly difficult to ignore Putin's demands to see the Ponarian.

With the third hull in Space Dock #2 being built, it stands to reason the Russians could outright declare USA was weaponizing space.

To Putin's surprise the President was increasingly thinking of disclosing some of the alien business in light of the fear we might be on the verge of being sucked into a galactic war with a much more powerful enemy.

Even though the President suspected the Russians knew quite a bit about the TR-3B aspect of the Space Carrier, we had never officially admitted it carried four squadrons of TR-3Bs stored in conformal slots in the hull, which avoid a real hangar bay, that would be impossible to design for routine space operations.

The President then decided to invite Putin to Area 51 to meet to discuss a way of disclosure and work in a cooperative manner, especially if the big showdown was going to happen within a couple years as expected.

<u>EXT. CGI. DAY PUTIN'S ARMADA ARRIVING AT AREA 51.</u>

An unmarked Russian Jet escorted by several fighters with temporary markings to hide the fact they were Russian Air Force Jets, all descended upon Area 51 landing on 17L and 17R. The base was in lockdown mode as if it was up postured for a TR-6 test flight or dealings with the KH-15.

The President and Vladimir Putin met in the Ponarian's former residence. It was cleaned out. All the artifacts were gone. During the two-hour meeting between the two with two translators, they both concluded an element of disclosure between their governments was necessary. It was clear to the President after an hour that Putin had a good source inside the USSF, a mole he would have the FBI find. When the enemy knows what cards, you are holding and you know he knows what's in your hand, there can be no bluffs.

RUSSIAN PRESIDENT VLADIMIR PUTIN
Ладно, господин президент, хватит всякой ерунды,
где Понарян? Вы его куда-то высадили, и что
заставляет меня не верить в то, что вы превратили
космос в оружие вопреки всем нашим договорам?

RUSSIAN TRANSLATOR
BORIS BAKATIN
Alright Mister President, us cut out the bullshit
now, where is the Ponarian? Did you drop him off

somewhere and what makes me want to not believe
you have weaponized space against all our treaties?

It came down to the President applying common sense in how he stated to Vladimir
Putin.

PRSIDENT

I'll let you send an observer to one of my Space
Carriers. At a future date we should meet and explore
ways we can build some cooperation and design
systems to defend this planet.

The President wasn't going to allow a Russian on
the Alabama. He did not want to risk crew members
inadvertently disclosing mission information. The
decision was a Russian General would be put on the
Vicksburg which was operational The President lied.

PRESIDENT

CSS Vicksburg is getting ready to go on a Patrol where
we are concerned, we may come across Aliens. I'm
going to invite you to put one of your Space Force
Generals onboard that cruise. I'll be open to ideas
he may come back with so that in the future we can
coordinate Earth's defenses against Aliens, which I
think is now necessary.

AMERICAN TRANSLATOR
KEVIN ALVEY

CSS Vicksburg готовится отправиться в патруль,
где мы обеспокоены тем, что можем встретить
пришельцев. Я собираюсь предложить вам
посадить на борт этого круиза одного из ваших
генералов космических сил. Я буду открыт для
идей, с которыми он может вернуться, чтобы в
будущем мы могли координировать защиту Земли
от инопланетян, что, я думаю, сейчас необходимо.

A week after Tom Gilbert returned to CSS Alabama, Gary Prien relieved Commodore
Riley as XO and Wing Commander.

Riley then went aboard Vicksburg as PCO and sadly had considerably more space time
than the CO he was relieving. The major part of the turnover was establishing material
condition of the ship and evaluating the crew to determine weak areas that needed

more OJT and time in the simulators which were both back on planet Earth or built into ship's system software.

There were several individuals including John Harris and Kevin O'Toole who did not want a Russian General aboard the Vicksburg. Unfortunately, the President and Putin made an agreement and there was no turning back.

Aleksandr Bondarev was the first Russian to get a ride on a TR-3B as he made that fateful journey to the Vicksburg. Aleksandr Bondarev was allowed in most of the spaces, but was restricted going into the communications room, special weapons area, and Maneuvering and Engineering spaces when plant condition Alpha was set. Plant condition Alpha was set and green lights indicated it which occurred during acceleration or deceleration.

VOICE OVER

> The stage was set, Russia would now have a ring side seat for the next confrontation with Aliens. This mission would change world politics forever. Alien issues were now far more compelling than the petty squabbles nations on Earth had throughout time. None of this would have happened without the *Unites States Space Force*.